Endangered Fae

SEMPER FAE

ANGEL MARTINEZ

Semper Fae
ISBN # 978-1-78686-374-4
©Copyright Angel Martinez 2018
Cover Art by Emmy@studioenp ©Copyright October 2018
Interior text design by Claire Siemaszkiewicz
Pride Publishing

Published in 2018 by Pride Publishing, United Kingdom.

Pride Publishing is an imprint of Totally Entwined Group Limited.

SEMPER FAE

Dedication

To all the misunderstood monsters — once there was a little girl who loved you better than the heroes and made up alternate endings so you would live.

Chapter One

Unforeseen Circumstances

While fae and humans cannot, as far as we know, transmit diseases across species, magical diseases come with their own hazards...

— D. Sandoval, *Basic Fae Relations*, State Department Publication, F-201-01-12A

"Thank you, Mr. Patterson, it's a generous offer." Diego fought against a weary sigh. "But the fae don't have any interest in mass production. Even if such a thing were physically possible, the final result wouldn't meet their standards."

"But think of the revenue, Mr. Sandoval!" the voice on the phone enthused. "Even if we're talking about a small quality dip, the merchandising alone —"

The cell phone rang from Diego's desk drawer, the strains of Mendelssohn's *Midsummer Night's Dream* floating across Patterson's oily business-speak.

"I'll present the proposal to their majesties, Mr. Patterson, but I can almost guarantee the outcome of —"

"If I could present it myself," Patterson broke in. "I'm certain we'd have a positive result."

Diego Sandoval, the Human Consul for the Fae Collective, ran out of his legendary patience.

"*Thank you*, Mr. Patterson, but that won't be possible. Now, I need to cut this short. I have other things to see to today. It's been a pleasure talking to you." It had not, of course. "Goodbye."

Normally his admin, Carol, would have handled the likes of Mr. Patterson, but she had been away from her desk when the call came through. He could hear her scold him, *Why didn't you let it go to voicemail, Mr. S.?*

"Why weren't you where you're supposed to be?" Diego muttered as he fished in his drawer. He stared at the display, which showed Carol's desk phone. "And why are you calling my cell?" He put the phone to his ear. "Hello?"

"I did it!" Finn's voice yelled over the line. "Hello, my handsome husband! I called you!"

Diego laughed. Finn in the office explained a lot, distraction-wise. "Yes, you did." Then realization dawned. "You did? You dialed the numbers? Carol didn't help you?"

A pooka's brain could hold any number of complex magical structures. Shapeshifters and workers of water magic, they were capable of astounding things. Math was *not* one of them, and Finn had struggled simply to learn numeric symbols.

"No, I did it." Finn's smile lit up his voice. "Just me. I have it!"

"*Mi vida*, that's wonderful. I'm so proud of you."

"I think I'll call Zack next." Finn's voice faded — apparently he'd turned away from the phone. "I can do that from here, can't I, Car—"

A violent sneeze interrupted his question. Diego heard a clunk as if the phone had been dropped. In the background, Carol screamed.

Before his brain had time to register shock, Diego hurled himself from his chair and dashed down the hall to the front office.

The sneezes continued unabated and Diego turned the corner in time to see a rhinoceros knock the computer mouse off Carol's desk as it turned, sneezed and vanished, replaced by a black tortoise. The tortoise sneezed and became a rooster. Sneeze. Ferret. Sneeze. Panther. Sneeze. Cricket.

The rapid succession of shifts finally ended with Finn sprawled naked and moaning on the hardwood floor, the three office staffers huddled behind the farthest desk.

"Everyone all right?"

"Yes, sir," Carol answered for them all.

"The scream was because...?"

"He was a rat for a second. Sorry."

"Deep breaths," Diego told his startled office staff. "Just stay out of his way for the moment. Carol, run downstairs and see if any of the healers are in house. If not, see if someone's willing to go through the doorway and find Eithne. Brad, grab a blanket for him, please."

He crouched down to address Finn. "*Caro*, are you all right?"

"No," Finn said on a whimper. His nose wrinkled. "Best move back, my heart. It's—"

Diego only had time to scramble back three feet before the explosive sneezes returned. Feeling helpless and confounded, he could only watch as Finn sneezed through elk, goose, spider, blackbird, bull and salmon in rapid-fire shifts.

"Bloody hells," Finn moaned as he returned to his own form, his long, black hair a tangled mass hiding half his face.

"You're sick, aren't you?" Diego risked a hand on Finn's shoulder, his normally cool skin furnace-hot.

"No!" Finn snapped, then he sneezed again. Badger. Sneeze. Vole. "Perhaps."

"I'd take you to bed, *mi amor*—"

"Best not, my hero. I might shift to dragon and crush you." Another sneeze. Cormorant. Sneeze. Back to Finn who clutched his head in both hands, whimpering.

Heels clicked back down the hall toward them double-time, accompanied by Carol's voice, "He's in here, Princess Eithne."

"*Gracias a Dios*," Diego breathed in relief.

Eithne rushed in to kneel beside him, her black-furred ears swiveling atop her head. As a healer, she often spent her days at the Fae Embassy. Because she was the daughter of the Fomorian king, Diego relied on her advice and her good sense. She smoothed her short kilt over furred thighs, the only clothing concession she made for human sensibilities, and placed a hand on Finn's forehead.

"Poor Fionnachd," she murmured. "Are you cold?"

"Yes. Like a frozen lake." Finn curled into a tight ball.

"And your head hurts?"

"It will split in two any moment."

She turned to Diego. "You may move him now, if you wish. This will go in cycles."

"So you know what this is?" Diego prompted as he slid his arms under Finn to lift him.

"Oh, yes."

That was all she would say, though, and Diego assumed she didn't wish to discuss it in front of the staff. He followed her upstairs to his living quarters. To the right, Zack's bedroom door stood open, as it always did when he was away, everything neat and military polished, the bed made with precise hospital corners. Eithne shoved open the left-hand door that led to the suite Diego shared with Finn, the exuberant mess quite a contrast to Zack's need for everything-in-its-place.

As gently as possible, Diego settled Finn on the king-sized four-poster bed and dragged the covers up over him. "Will he be all right?" he asked, fighting to keep the trembling from his voice.

"He will tell you otherwise, no doubt," Eithne said as she took Finn's face between her hands. "But he will live. Fionnachd, look at me."

Finn did as he was told, black eyes swimming with pain as he gazed into hers. His panting slowed, his trembling ceased abruptly, then his eyes slid shut.

"There. Let him sleep," Eithne whispered.

"I will." Diego took her arm. "But could you please tell me what this is?"

She twined clawed fingers carefully with his and led him out into the hall. "I have not seen this in over a hundred years, but it was once common. It is shifter's fever."

Diego swallowed hard. "Is it...bad?"

"By that do you mean is it deadly? Then no." She patted his chest. "Do not look so distressed. Your mate will be well again. There will be these bouts of uncontrolled shifting, followed by blinding headaches and a period of exhaustion. The time between will become longer and longer as he recovers. I have no doubt that he will whine and complain and try your patience before long, but he will not die from it."

"So it's something like a shifter version of a human cold?"

"Something like, yes."

11

"Wonderful," Diego snorted. "The uncommon cold. What do I do for him?"

"Comfort him, coddle him, and when the pain is bad, you know how to put him to sleep as I did. Stand clear when the sneezing begins. And keep other shifters from him."

"So it's contagious? Are you taking it back with you? Shouldn't you wash your hands or something?"

Eithne's feline eyes crinkled in amusement. "I do not shift, my dear druid-bard. I cannot carry this illness."

"Oh." Diego scrubbed his hands back through his hair. "So I can't carry it either?"

She laughed softly. "You do everything else that is not possible. But no, humans have never caught fae afflictions."

Another thought occurred to Diego as she turned to go. "Eithne? You said you haven't seen this in over a century. Why did Finn catch it now?"

"For attention, perhaps?" She smiled still but shook her head, obviously puzzled. "I have no answer for that."

Later, with the workday over and Finn through his second bout of sneezing and headaches, Diego sat beside him on the bed, trying to coax him into swallowing some peppermint tea.

"My throat is lined with sand," Finn moaned.

"I know, *mi vida*. The tea will help." Diego slid an arm under Finn's shoulders to lift him and help him drink.

True to Eithne's predictions, Finn had no qualms about complaining. Some of it was for attention — Diego knew his spouse well enough for that — but it concerned him that Finn was so weak and his complaints so listless. Diego turned on the TV to distract him and let Finn snuggle close, his head resting on Diego's stomach. Two pundits argued over some point of economic policy, deadly boring, but he hoped Finn might doze off. A wave of guilt washed over Diego as he stroked Finn's back, his cock stirring at the simple feel of his husband's naked skin.

"You need not feel so ashamed, my heart," Finn murmured and slid his hand down to cup Diego's burgeoning erection. "I'm flattered that I still please you in such a sorry state."

"Stop that." Diego pulled his hand back up. "I'm not going to take you while you're sick."

Finn huffed out an irritated sigh. "At least change the channel to something less dreadful."

"You'd rather watch one of your entertainment news shows?"

"Yes."

Diego snorted but changed the channel. "You're going to rot your brain with those."

"I like knowing who is screwing whom and so on." Finn nestled closer and kissed Diego's stomach. "It's rather fun."

"If you say so."

The normal parade of overrated pop stars and Barbie-cloned actresses flitted across the screen. Finn devoured it all, staying stubbornly awake, while Diego began to doze off. He jerked awake when one of the hosts uttered a name he knew.

"Fae Collective Ambassador Prince Lugh mac Ethnenn was in New York a few nights ago and, ladies, your hearts are going to break when you see the tape we received from outside a popular Manhattan nightclub. So stay tuned!"

"Damn it," Diego growled, now very much awake.

He had cornered Lugh the last time he was on the island and had engaged in a long and frank discussion with the *sidhe* prince about cameras and paparazzi and being discreet in his affairs. The world's human governments needed to take the fae's ambassador seriously, not regard him as a playboy. Lugh had protested that his encounters with humans had been brief and had not progressed beyond a kiss or two, but he had promised to be more careful. Now this.

The show returned to the host with a flattering still of Lugh in the background. Handsome even for one of the fae, but larger and more powerful than most of his more slender *sidhe* cousins, Lugh rarely took a bad picture. He wore his thick, black hair loose these days instead of in his warrior braids, since he said humans liked it better that way. His blinding white smile in this picture was nothing short of devastating.

"Ever since the fae decided to go public," the host began, "Prince Lugh has been in every girl's someday-my-prince-will-come fantasies. There's been a lot of speculation about possible royal matches all over the world. But, ladies, we hate to disappoint you. A picture says a thousand words."

The screen switched to the promised clip, a grainy security camera shot at the back door of a club. Lugh had someone up against the wall, his broad back hiding the person he kissed so thoroughly for a moment, but then he turned…

"*Ay, Dios,* no," Diego murmured.

"Yes, folks," the TV host went on. "It's obvious which way the prince swings now and where he's given his heart. We've confirmed that the man in this clip is his bodyguard and personal aide Zachary Morrison, who retired from the U.S. Marine Corps to assist the fae in…"

Diego turned the sound down, his stomach sinking to his feet.

"What is it, my love?" Finn turned on his back to look up at him. "This is not a surprise. We knew they would someday."

"I know." Diego heaved a breath. "It's not that. It's that they plastered it all over the news, over the whole continent. This isn't going to be good for Zack."

Finn's brow creased as he puzzled it through. "Ah. You mean Zack is still in the basement?"

"The closet, *mi amor*. Still in the closet. Yes. His family doesn't know, and this is a hell of a way to find out."

Chapter Two

Too Much Courage, Not Enough Sense

Censure because of sexuality is unheard of among the fae. Same-sex relationships are treated in the same way as bi-gendered pairings and casual sex among the unattached is the norm. Multiple long-term partners are not uncommon, though all parties must be aware and equally consenting. Most fae, whether they openly admit to it or not, are fiercely territorial.

—D. Sandoval, in an interview with *Human Relations Magazine*

"He's a *queer*, Marion! You're son's a fag!"

"Watch your language, Jim. I won't have it in the house." Zack's mother turned to him, her face lined with worry. "Sweetie, it wasn't you, I know. That fairy prince probably just grabbed you and kissed you. They're strange folks. It's not your fault. I know you don't want to say anything bad about your boss and all, but you can tell me what really happened."

Zack rubbed a hand over the back of his neck. When had his mother gotten so small? And his father so old? "Look, Mom, Dad, it's not like I didn't want to tell you someday. But it just hasn't come up—"

"Now you know why he never brought girlfriends home!" his retired-sergeant father bellowed. "He wasn't married to his career, he was boning—"

"Jim, please! This is hard enough!"

"I didn't have boyfriends, either, Dad." Zack felt the flush rise up to his hairline but he kept his voice calm. "I haven't had anyone. But it's true. You need to know and I should have told you before…all this. I'm gay. No way around it."

"And this is what you bring home to us? All this shit on the TV that the neighbors have to point out to your poor mother? You're a disgrace! A discredit to the Corps and your family!"

"Yeah, well, don't ask, don't tell, Dad. Even after that, it wasn't easy. Why do you think I've been alone so long?" Zack held up a hand to cut off his father's next tirade. "I'm sorry. I'm sorry you had to find out this way and I'm sorry it's made you unhappy. I'm not sorry about who I am." He turned to grab his coat from the wall hook. "I'm going out for a walk. I need to cool down. You need to cool down. Maybe we can talk like grown-up people later."

"You little shit! How dare you take that tone with me? I oughta take—"

Zack sighed and walked out of the door. He had too many years and too many horrific experiences under his belt to be cowed by his father now. *Still hurts, though.*

He'd played the scene out in his mind again and again over the years, how he would make sure his father was sober and everyone was calm, how he would come out to them, serenely and matter-of-factly. Except he never had, and now, instead of being able to work through it in the privacy of the family, the whole state knew. Hell, the whole country knew — his conservative, Midwestern parents exposed to the malicious whispers of neighbors and congregation members. At least, that's how they would see it. Did see it.

Damn.

He should have been really pissed at the big guy for putting him through this, but he couldn't muster any anger toward Lugh. *Not the first time he's kissed me. Not like I didn't like it.*

Zack's hand stole up to his lips, still able to feel the tingling from that passionate, desperate lip-lock in the alley.

'Tonight, Zachary, please," Lugh had whispered in his ear. "Don't torture me any longer. I need your strong arms around me, your skin next to mine...'

Right. The thought of fumbling through his first night of sex with someone who had centuries of experience had stopped him cold, made him back off in embarrassment and, once again, gently refuse. As always, Lugh had respected his wishes. Even though he was powerful enough to have shoved Zack against the wall and taken him right then and there, he never pushed further than Zack let him, never forced the issue. It had been with clenched teeth and a tormented groan that time, but still the prince had backed off.

He loved Lugh for that. *Stupid jerk. You've loved him from the first time you saw him.* That first heart-stopping meeting in the middle of a skirmish, Lugh shining like moonlight and ripped like a god in his skin-tight silver armor. Damn, damn and damn. He had to stop thinking like this. Lugh was a prince and his grandmother's Champion, *and* the ambassador to the whole human world. He could never love a human, an ex-soldier, a nobody without any rank or importance.

Not the way Finn loved Diego. It was in his eyes every time he looked at Diego. Every time anyone mentioned Diego, there it was, that contented I'm-his-for-all-eternity look. Lugh was fond of him, sure, but his eyes wandered everywhere. He wasn't a one-man kind of fae, and never claimed he could be.

Unfortunately, Zack needed someone who was his and only his, so, of course, he had the bad sense to fall for someone he couldn't ever have that way.

"Dumb jarhead," he muttered as his feet hit the path that led to the park. "Sabotaged yourself again."

When he reached the lake, he stopped, shoved his hands in his pockets and pulled in a deep breath of cold air. The full moon perched huge and white on the tops of the pines, her twin shining up in rippling splendor from the surface of the lake. It was a beautiful scene and being out in the still of a late autumn night with no machine noises did calm him. If he hadn't gone into the service, he probably would have been a forest ranger or something. *Peaceful…*

The first scream ripped the night in half. Zack dropped to a crouch. His hand shot to his hip where no weapon rode as he tried to pinpoint a direction. The second scream spun him to his left. Down the path toward the trees, a girl stood with her back to a lamppost, frozen in an attitude of sheer horror, while a male figure grappled with…

"Holy shit," Zack whispered as he ran to help.

A huge muzzle rose and fell. Sharp teeth flashed in the moonlight. One of those gigantic hybrid dogs? A hyena? What the hell was that thing? The figure on the ground received a moment's reprieve as the beast turned toward the pounding of Zack's boots. A boy, probably the girl's date, staggered up and ran like hell.

Coward. Zack couldn't help the thought even though he knew the boy had done the right thing as the beast turned on him, snarling. He put himself between it and the girl, and only had time to shout over his shoulder, "Run, damn it!"

The thing leaped at him, spittle flying from canines as long as Zack's hand. Instinct and adrenaline kicked in. Zack seized it by the throat, pressing his thumbs hard into its windpipe. Its breath reeked. Its ice-blue eyes held madness.

Momentum on its side, it hurled Zack to the ground, the air forced from his lungs as he slammed into the concrete path. He kept his grip, heart pounding against his breastbone. Any slip would be the end of him.

"Oh my God! Oh fuck! Hurry! It's gonna eat him!" The girl hadn't run. She was screaming into her cell phone.

Not just for himself then—he had to hang on for the kid. The monster snapped at his face and lunged again. Something was wrong about the shape of its back. Its limbs were jointed in a way no canine's should be. Its *hands* closed over his biceps, claws biting through his coat into his skin.

Holy fucking hells. This thing has thumbs.

Back claws scrabbled, ripped into his legs. The beast shifted position and lunged again. Zack's arms trembled with the strain. Its front claws tore at his chest, agony in the wake of those talons. His left hand lost purchase. The thing's teeth sank into his shoulder.

Someone was screaming. It might have been the girl. Might have been him. Hard to tell when the world had collapsed to nothing but searing points of pain. Sirens. Shouting. Gunshots. Everything faded into the nightmare hum inside his head. *I'm never seeing my Prince again…*

* * * *

"Zachary? Do you hear me, braveheart?"

A strong hand held his, dragging Zack from the dark. "Lugh?" his voice creaked out in a spare whisper. "How…?"

"Shh. Lie still. You called me."

"I did?"

"Yes. The…" Lugh hesitated as he did when he searched for a human word. "Medics are coming. You are gravely wounded. Stay still and quiet."

"You—" Zack gasped after breath. Why was it so hard to breathe? Or see, for that matter? The world was so dark, Lugh nothing more than an indistinct lump against the sky. "You zapped…yourself here. No car. No escort."

"Please don't be annoyed with me, Zachary. I could not ignore such an urgent summons. Not from you."

Now what's that supposed to mean? "Call…Diego…"

"I shall. Never fear. Shh. All will be well."

Lugh's hand on his forehead felt so good there, a calm spot in all the dizzying agony.

"Lugh…"

"You are so very courageous. But I wish you had more sense." Lugh's voice might have cracked or it might have been Zack's imagination. "Please, my brave Zack, please don't die."

Chapter Three

Fairy Prince

There are more things in heaven and earth, one of your bards once wrote, referring to those realms outside of normal human awareness. We are some, though assuredly not all, of those things…

—Prince Lugh mac Ethnenn, initial address to the U.N. General Assembly

Lugh blinked back the sting invading his eyes. It would not do to weep here, among strangers, in the cold, forbidding world of sharp chemicals and steel that was a human hospital. He drew a deep breath, fighting for calm, trying to banish the image of Zack bleeding on the ground.

"You're that fairy prince, aren't you?"

He lifted his head out of his hands. A human woman sat across from him in the waiting room. Her voice had been wary but her eyes held curiosity.

"Yes." He forced a little smile for her. "Are you waiting for news, too?"

She shrugged. "My brother. Car accident. He was drunk again. Probably won't pull through this time."

Lugh blinked at her. "You don't seem...upset by this."

"After it happens enough times, you kinda get numb, right?"

"I am sorry."

"Yeah. Me too." She stared into the middle distance for a long moment, then turned weary eyes to him. "What about you, Your Highness? What're you doing hanging out by the ICU all by your lonesome? Don't you usually have, like, an entourage? Security or something?"

"I am here with my security." Lugh nodded to the swinging doors which led to the treatment rooms. "He's in there. He saved two young humans from being attacked by...an animal. A mad dog, perhaps. I was not with him."

"Oh, man. That's rough. He gonna make it?"

Lugh stared at his hands. Zack's blood still stained his fingers. *My brave Zachary...* "I am not certain."

They sat in silence, the distant sounds of machines pinging and soft shoes hurrying down corridors accompanying their thoughts.

"Pastor says you're a demon."

The pastor is a puddinghead. Lugh fought against a sigh. "Does he?"

"Yeah. 'Cause you've got cloven hooves."

"There must be many demons in the world, then."

"Why?"

"Every goat and pig and cow has cloven hooves."

She laughed, a choking, unhappy sound, but still a laugh. Then her curiosity won out over her bitterness again. "Why do you have hooves?"

Hearts and minds, Zack always said. If he had to win over the human race one at a time, he would. "My father was *sidhe*, a particular kind of fairy. *Sidhe* always have two shapes, one fae and one animal."

Her forehead wrinkled. "So you're a cow?"

"Bull," he corrected gently.

Another short laugh erupted from her. "Oh, duh. Right. You'd look pretty silly with cow titties, huh?"

"I would think so."

She regarded him steadily, her eyes still sharp despite her weariness, her human soul still shining in a warm glow despite what must have been a hard life. "They wouldn't let you back to see him, huh?"

"No. Only family. His parents are with him." Lugh rubbed at his temples, fighting a growing headache. "They are… They blame themselves. They argued. He left the house, and was wounded then."

"Yeah, well, that's what good parents do," she said softly. "They blame themselves. Those kids, they'd probably be dead, though, if your man hadn't come along, right?"

My man… He turned that over a moment and decided she only meant it in the employer sense. "True enough. I hope they will see it. Perhaps it will help them if…" He trailed off, shaking his head against the thickening of his voice.

"He won't die, Your Highness," she said with a crooked smile. "He's the hero here. Not supposed to work that way, right?"

Comfort came in the strangest forms sometimes. He managed to return her smile. "Right." He startled as a bumblebee hum tickled his thigh. Cell phone. Damnable thing, but Diego did insist he have one. He wrestled it from the tight front pocket of his jeans and flipped it open. "Yes?"

"Don't 'yes' me, damn it! I got your message, where the hell are you?"

"It warms my heart that you are worried for me, little man. I am in...the city where Zachary's parents live."

"I know you're in St. Louis." On the other end of the line, Diego took a deep breath. "Where in St. Louis? Specifically? It's a good-sized city."

He held the phone away and asked his waiting room companion the name of the hospital. "Thank you," he mouthed to her before he relayed it to Diego.

"You had no idea where you were." Diego sounded weary and aggrieved. "You had to ask someone. *Dios*, how did you even get there?"

"One of the handsome police officers brought me."

"Okay...all right." Lugh could picture Diego's hand running back through his black curls in frustration. "How's our Zack?"

"I have no more news yet." Lugh cleared his throat to steady his voice. "Diego, I wish to bring him home. We could —"

"Let's get him stable first." Diego's tone dropped to a gentle murmur, a caress over Lugh's frayed nerves. "Probably not a good idea to move him yet. Listen, I'll put two of the boys on a plane. They'll be on their way out to you soon so you're not alone. Please stay put, okay?"

"Why not you?"

"Finn's very sick. He needs me here." Diego hesitated. "I wish I could just make a door and come to you, but we've talked about unexpected magical doors in human places. And I can't translocate like you do.

Don't cry, big guy. Oh, damn. It'll be all right. Shh, hush. *Carajo*. I'm sorry…"

Hardly aware he was until Diego said not to, Lugh bit on his knuckle to stifle the sobs. "He's dying, Diego." He barely felt the hand on his shoulder, had missed the moment when the woman moved across the room to him. "I can feel it. Feel him slipping away moment by moment."

He hoped the long pause was Diego thinking. *Please, please, I will beg if I must.*

"Stay on the phone." Diego's voice was still gentle but bolstered now by hard-forged resolve. "I'm going to get your mother. And Faolchú for backup. Don't hang up. Clear your mind. You're going to need to help me with this. Oh, and warn anyone around you what's going to happen."

Lugh accepted the tissue the woman handed him. He dried his face while he explained to her, "There will be several people coming through a hole in the air in a few moments. Please don't be frightened. One of them may have a wolf's head if he doesn't think to cast a glamour. That would be my cousin. He thinks himself fierce but it's all bravado."

"All bark and no bite, huh?" Her hand trembled as she gave him a second tissue.

"You needn't stay if you're frightened."

"I'm not scared of nothin'. Just a little nervous. But if they're your relatives, they're probably okay."

He heard the magic gather before the doorway manifested, a dense wind shrieking through his heart. The power, the raw, white gold glory that was Diego, announced itself to any who were not enchantment blind. He reached for it, guiding Diego's hand so he would find the right place to punch through.

"Here they come." He put an arm around the woman to shield her since Diego's haste might make him careless.

Through all his past lives, Diego's potential had been at his fingertips. In some of his earlier forms, he had realized it in spectacular ways, calling uniquely human magic to him, though Diego didn't recall. In his current life, Diego was far more powerful than ever before. If not for his tender, compassionate heart, he could have been a dangerous and frightening man.

Wind sang through the waiting room, eddies swirling magazines from the tables and sliding the unoccupied chairs across the floor. A shriek and a loud crack split the air. The doorway blossomed in the middle of the waiting room with Diego at its center.

"Step through, please." His soft voice held more authority than most men did with a shout. "I'm not leaving this open while we do search and retrieval."

Eithne came through in her favorite human glamour of a lovely, graceful woman with raven-black hair, her healer's satchel slung over her shoulder. She rushed over to Lugh as a huge man in the official green and gold dress uniform of the fae stepped through after her. Lugh let go a sigh of relief. Faolchú had remembered to alter his appearance to one of a handsome man with thick black and silver hair rather than wearing his normal lupine visage.

"My Lugh." Eithne took his face between her hands. "You are so pale."

"I will be well enough, Mother. Once we take Zack home."

His human companion gaped. "That's your mom? She's so…"

"Beautiful? Yes, she is." Lugh gave the woman's hand a squeeze. "Not every royal mother looks like Queen Elizabeth."

Diego stepped through the magical doorway and the momentary view of his office at the embassy vanished as the hole in reality snapped shut behind him.

"Got it." She gave him a little shove. "Go get your boy, Your Highness. All this magic, you've gotta be able to come up with the happy ending thing."

"Will you be all right alone?"

"It's okay. I'm used to being alone." She touched his arm when he stood, drawing his attention. "And, Prince Lugh? Don't let nobody tell you you're a demon. Just 'cause you have cow feet."

"Thank you, I won't." He smiled for her as he let himself be led away. Hearts and minds. Zack would be proud.

Diego took his arm, speaking softly. "If it's possible, I'd like to do this without causing too much disturbance and without upsetting Zack's parents."

Faolchú broke in. "What are you afraid we'll do? Draw steel and begin making threats?"

"Yes. Exactly. Which is why I made you leave the sword in my office." Diego shook his head. "This isn't the same as rescuing prisoners from some secret government base. We have diplomatic clout on our side, but it's best if we're patient and charming."

"I can be charming," Faolchú said with a hand on his chest.

"Yes, I know." Diego pointed at the swinging doors. "And I want you to turn the charm on full blast. There'll be a desk with nurses right through that door. I want you to distract the staff while we slip by. I can cover our passing to some extent, but anyone paying attention will still question a sliding spot of darkness."

Faolchú gave him a very human military salute. "As you wish, Consul. Any sacrifice for the cause."

Lugh let him clear the doors before he let out an angry snort. "Buffoon. He jests at Zachary's expense."

"No, he's not. He was frantic when we heard what happened." Diego tilted his head to look up into Lugh's face. "It's just his way of dealing with things. Would you rather have him sobbing and ranting?"

"No, I suppose that wouldn't be helpful."

The little window in the right-hand door afforded them a view of the desk. Faolchú's voice drifted back to them. "Good evening, ladies! Captain Faolchú of the Fae Collective. I wonder if you might lend me some assistance?" He leaned against the high counter of the desk, his uniform jacket straining across his broad chest. Three sets of eyes fastened on him and remained firmly glued as the wolf-Champion smiled and chatted amiably.

Diego raised a hand and bent the light around them. Lugh's view of the world broke into strangely angled planes, indistinct and distorted as if he suddenly gazed through a smoky, many-faceted crystal. The women at the desk didn't seem to notice when the doors swung open a second time and didn't react at all to the spot of darkness as it slid past them.

When they turned a corner, Diego let the spell go and the world rushed back in, too bright and sharp-edged.

"If we're intending on using diplomatic clout to retrieve him, why are we pad-footing like egg thieves?" Lugh whispered.

"There's no way to avoid a scene over getting Zack out of here," Diego told him. "But I'd rather one later, when we already have him and have spoken to his parents, than sooner, before we even find him." He stopped, apparently uncertain. "Which way?"

"Come." Lugh took Diego by the elbow and pulled him down the hall with his mother trailing them. No one had told him which room was Zack's, but he knew the way. He could feel that brave heart struggling to beat, the pull so strong on his own he felt like a hooked salmon.

Zachary... His heart faltered in his chest. Zack lay so still, a gray pallor creeping over his skin as if death had already drawn her shroud over him. The gasp and hiss of the machine breathing for him sounded too much like a dying warrior's last breaths.

"What the hell is he doing here?" A broad-shouldered man, tall for a human, blocked his path to the bed.

Battlefields and years of sorrow rode behind the man's eyes, the evidence of too much hard drinking on his face. *Zack's father.* Lugh blinked away a sense of dislocation. This would be Zack someday, if he allowed bitterness a home in his heart and wore the weight of his years like an ever-growing burden of stones.

Diego stepped between them. "Mr. Morrison? Mr. James Morrison? We spoke on the phone." He extended a hand. "I'm Diego Sandoval."

The man shook his hand, bemused and off-balance. The red-eyed woman in the chair by the bed rose. "Oh, Mr. Sandoval, it was good of you to come all this way."

"Please, call me Diego." He stepped over to Zack's mother with the father in tow. "Zack's very important to us. Personally, and to the embassy."

"Was," growled Mr. Morrison. His jaw jutted as if his defiance could beat back his grief. "Doctors say he won't make it through the night."

31

Eithne had slipped around Diego and was already at Zack's side, her hand pressed against his faltering ribcage. With the parents distracted, Lugh took the opportunity to go to the bedside as well. He closed his hand around Zack's unbandaged forearm.

"Stay a few moments more, braveheart. Help is here."

"Lugh?"

"I'm right beside you. Don't leave me."

There it was again, that fleeting internal communication. He had achieved mind-to-mind contact with so few humans over the centuries. Even bespeaking Diego was unreliable and intermittent. But Zack's desperate call had ripped him from sleep, sent him hurtling across a continent before he'd had time to draw three breaths. There had been no fear in the sending, only a desolate sorrow.

He drew his first full breath in several minutes when the soft green glow of his mother's magic enveloped Zack's chest.

"That's why we're here to help," Diego explained to the Morrisons in the background. "We have...abilities human doctors lack."

"You mean that unholy fairy magic." Mr. Morrison spoke the last word as if it were poison. He pointed an accusing finger at Eithne. "You get away from my son! It's that...that fairy prince's fault all this happened in the first place!"

"It's not tricks or the Hollywood version you see in movies," Diego soothed. "It's not evil or unnatural. It's simply learning to use the universe's energy in different ways than we're used to."

"Please, Diego," Mrs. Morrison sobbed. "If it saves our boy, I don't care what it is."

"Marion!"

"It's not the prince's fault," she went on, heedless of the tears dripping from her chin. "You said so yourself, Jim. Now stand back and let them work."

Lugh could feel Mr. Morrison trying to cling to his anger, but anguish soon crept in to smother it. He folded his distraught wife in his arms and sat back down.

"There." Eithne withdrew her hands. "I cannot heal so many wounds at once. He's too depleted. But I have closed the hole in his lung." She glanced across Zack's chest at her son. "Pull the thing from his throat. Slowly. Gently."

With a vise tightening around his heart, Lugh complied, willing Zack to keep breathing with every fiber of his being. His chest heaved, his handsome face contorted with pain, then he coughed twice and was still.

"No," Lugh whispered. "Great Mother, no…"

"Hush, my darling," Eithne said as she bent close to Zack's ear, her hand on his chest. "Zachary. Sweet boy, you cannot tell me you have forgotten how to breathe so quickly."

A shudder passed through Zack's body, hard enough to shake the bed. Then Eithne's hand rose as his chest expanded, first in a halting, stuttering gasp as if he emerged from icy waters, and finally in a deep, even rhythm.

"He's breathing," Mrs. Morrison whispered. "He's breathing on his own."

Diego put a hand on her shoulder. "Yes. But he probably has a long road to recovery still. We'd like to take him with us. Back to the embassy where he can be comfortable in his own room, where healers can be with him around the clock."

"This is a good hospital," she protested.

"I'm sure, but I think Zack needs more right now," Diego said gently.

"You'll take him to that damn fairy island, and we'll never see him again," Mr. Morrison said, his jaw set.

Lugh leaned in to kiss Zack's forehead and rose to face the parents. He was the ambassador, wasn't he? Time to start behaving like one instead of hiding behind Diego. "We don't want to separate you from your son, sir. I will arrange special visitation visas for you. We'll have the staff make travel arrangements. You are most welcome to see him and I'm certain it would be a comfort to him to have you there." *At least I hope, if you haven't pushed your son too far away.*

For a moment, Mr. Morrison sat with his head bowed, his thick neck red with some emotion Lugh hoped wasn't fury. Finally, he looked up, though he spoke to Diego. "All right. You got his lungs working again. You sure as hell can do the rest better than these clowns here."

Diego thanked them both, shaking hands and offering reassurances as Eithne unhooked Zack from all the wires and tubes attached to him. Alarms pinged and footsteps hurried down the hall. Lugh gathered Zack up to his chest, cradling him as gently as a newborn sparrow chick while Diego intercepted the medical staff, arguing with them even as he stepped into the corridor to call the magic for a doorway.

"Faolchú! We're going!" Lugh bellowed as he followed Diego into the hall where the nurses were making dire threats about security and police.

The heavy thud of Faolchú's boots grew louder as he pelted down the corridor, skidding around the corner in his haste to reach them. Diego had the door open, the magic winds whipping the nurses' hair into birds' nests. His office was once again visible through the doorway.

"Ladies, I am sorry, but we have to go. I'll call the hospital administrator in the morning to straighten this all out. Thank you for taking care of him." Lugh strode past the stunned nurses, through the doorway, and heaved a sigh of relief to have Zack home.

Chapter Four

Fever Dreams

The fae have no taboos regarding nudity and most live clothing-optional lives. With that in mind, we advise any guests who may be distressed or offended by naked fae to remain in the human-staffed office area of the complex.
—Orientation Guide for Visitors to Tearmann Island

Light pressed against him, heavy and unwelcome. Zack moaned and tried to roll away. A warm body curled beside him prevented the movement. His hand brushed against skin. *A warm, naked body.*

He forced his eyes open, the lids so heavy he wondered if he might need a winch. A spill of fox-red hair lay on the pillow. A graceful slender curve of shoulder peeked out from under the sheet.

"Sionnach?" *That's not my voice...*

The body rolled to face him and Zack found himself staring into jewel-bright green eyes. "Good morning!" The Fomorian herald propped himself up on one elbow. "How do you fare?"

Zack tried to sit up and found he couldn't even lift his head. His chest hurt, his legs ached, and his head felt like someone had pumped toxic sludge into it. "I feel terrible."

"Of course you do." Sionnach leaned forward to kiss his forehead. "I'll fetch one of the healers for you."

"Um…Sionnach?" No, that raspy, broken whisper really was him. "Why are you in my bed? Did we…?"

"Did we what, hero of the iron caverns?"

Zack felt himself flush.

"Oh!" Sionnach's silvery laugh filled the room. "No, no, my dear. We have not mated. While you are deliciously handsome, you were far too gravely wounded. Even Faolchú would not think of it at such a time. And Angus would most likely box my ears, in any case."

Sionnach rose from the bed, his white-tipped, russet tail waving behind him. At least with Sionnach, one could pretend he was half-dressed, since he had fur from the waist down.

"So, um, what's the deal?"

"The deal, as you say, is that you have been terribly chilled." Sionnach patted his hand. "The healers asked us to take it in turns lying beside you to keep you warm."

"Us?"

"Myself and Angus. And yes, Faolchú, the big oaf. He's been so worried for you. Nathair—"

Zack smiled despite the pain, picturing this strange parade of bed companions. "Was Finn here, too?"

"No. Finn has been ill and is not permitted to leave his room for fear of infecting other shifters." Sionnach tilted his head to the side, his smile just short of wicked. "But Lugh was here when he could be."

"Oh." Zack cursed his fair complexion as he felt his blush deepen. *Not that it means anything. Everyone else was here, too.* But he remembered bits and pieces of dreams with Lugh holding his hand, begging him not to die. Another thought occurred to him. Hadn't he been in Missouri? "How'd I get here, bud?"

"The Consul broke his self-imposed rules for you," Sionnach said softly. "He made a doorway into human territory and retrieved you."

Zack wished he could think straight. The whole nightmare mess wasn't making sense. "Wait. I thought you could only make those magic doorway thingies between this world and the Otherworld."

Sionnach gave him an odd little smile. "No one taught our Diego that magic has limits, and so he does as he wishes." His tail waved behind him as he left the room.

Of course. Diego had done the retrieval. That fact shouldn't have hurt so much.

"God, Morrison, you're an idiot," he whispered. "You survived. Whatever else happened, you're alive."

He hoped someone would tell him what really had happened, and soon. The bits and pieces he thought he remembered just didn't seem possible. *You live with fairies, you guard a fairy prince, one of your best friends is a shapeshifter who can turn into a dragon, and you're having problems with a mean dog with thumbs?*

Yes, he was. The thing that had attacked those kids wasn't just a mean dog. He had felt the malevolence from it, looked right into its crazed eyes, and the beast had stared back at him, not like an animal would, but with malicious intent. That thing had wanted to cause pain. At least that's what he remembered. He wanted someone to tell him he was wrong.

"Zachary, you're awake!"

"Hey, your furriness. How's everything?" He smiled, never so glad to see black furred ears.

Eithne slid up onto the bed beside him and took his face between her hands. They had pads and retractable claws like a cat, but they were still hands. "You are still too pale."

"I'm sorry," he said as a reflex.

"None of that. I'm so pleased to see your beautiful eyes open." She ran a hand over his hair, down his throat and over his chest, purring all the while.

"What's the prognosis, Doc?"

She smiled and rubbed her furred cheek against his. "You will live, healer-warrior. Regaining your strength may take some time, but you are mending well."

Her kitty facial expressions were tough to read sometimes, but he thought he caught concern in her eyes. "What is it? What's the part you're not telling me?"

"It's...naught to be anxious over." Her smile never faltered.

"What? I'll never walk again? I'm gonna lose the arm? C'mon, Eithne, I'm a big boy. You can tell me."

One pointed ear twitched atop her head as if flicking off a fly. She watched him for several long moments, searching his face. "What do you recall?" she asked. "Of the attack?"

"Most of it. But it's hard to tell how much was real. I mean, it couldn't have been, right? Upright monster that looked like some demon dog with thumbs. Right out of some bad B movie." He swallowed hard since her face still didn't register anything. "The police found it, right?"

"The police..." The Fomorian princess frowned. "They shot at your attacker, though they claim they could not see it clearly. It ran. They followed its trail with dogs and stick lights."

"Flashlights," Zack corrected absently.

"Yes. What they found was a naked man lying dead in the woods."

"So the thing attacked him, too?"

She looked away, though her claws still combed through his hair. "The man died of a gunshot wound."

Zack's heart lurched. His brain skittered away from the only possible answer. "What does all this mean?"

"Perhaps nothing. It is dangerous to draw conclusions before we know more." She turned back to him and smiled. "Danu and Balor wish to hold a feast in honor of your bravery. As soon as you are able to sit unassisted."

He let out a snort. "I'm not a kid, Eithne. You can't make me forget everything by promising me a party."

"I meant to do no such thing," she said with a laugh and leaned in to kiss his forehead. "Have you had terrible dreams? Does your heart race without reason? Is there a burning under your skin?"

"Um…no. I mean, I had some bad dreams about that monster, but who wouldn't?"

"Then we should not be concerned. And it has been far too long since the fae courts met in celebration. If —"

A series of gunshot-sharp sneezes from across the hall interrupted her. After the tenth sneeze, a tortured crack followed by a crash further disturbed the peace. A soft voice drifted out from behind the door, then Nathair emerged. He closed the door behind him and leaned back against it with a weary sigh. The scales along his arms and atop his head, normally bright green, had a dull cast to them. At least Nathair wore jeans on his perfect, compact body when he roamed the embassy.

"Everything all right, bud?" Zack called out, his voice a little less hoarse now that he'd been using it.

Nathair caught sight of him and managed a smile. "Zack, you're awake! You look much improved."

"Never mind me, what happened in there?"

"Ah. Finn's sneezing fits…perhaps they've told you? No? They cause uncontrolled shifting. This last fit was all sea creatures. The orca broke the bed."

"He okay?"

"Well enough. Oh, he's come to no harm." Nathair rubbed a hand over the side of his face. "But he asks endlessly when Diego will be finished with work. Demands stories and tea and to have his back rubbed. He is restless and weak, bored and petulant."

Zack raised an eyebrow at that. Years of dealing with difficult patients had given Nathair the tolerance of a saint. It wasn't like him to sound like he was close to strangling someone in his care. "Sounds like you need a break, bud."

"I need Faolchú at the moment. Finn insists that the only reason he shifted to orca is that he has been on land for so long. He wants to be placed in the tub."

Eithne rose and glided from the room. "I will fetch him." She caressed Nathair's cheek on her way down the hall, making good her escape so she didn't have to answer Zack's questions. Something had her worried, no doubts there, but she clearly wasn't sharing until she was ready.

After Faolchú had carried Finn to the sunken garden tub down the hall, the upstairs quieted again. Occasional splashes drifted to Zack and the soft rumble of Faolchú's voice, but these were peaceful sounds. He found his eyes sliding shut and wondered if Eithne had done something to make him sleep. Probably. Unconscious was one thing, but the body needed real sleep to heal.

Maybe Diego would have less evasive answers when he came upstairs after work, or maybe Lugh was due in soon. Lugh. He'd clop up the stairs, his hooves ringing on every step. He'd be wearing the royal dress uniform he put on for state occasions, the one with the waist-length jacket with all the gold buttons, so tight across his huge, ripped chest. He'd have that heart-melting smile turned on full power. He'd unbutton the jacket slowly, then the white dress shirt underneath, leaving them both on and hanging open to frame his gorgeous pecs and that bounce-a-racquetball-off-it abdomen.

Zack chuckled at himself when he realized his little fantasy had gotten him hard as hell. With thoughts of Lugh climbing into bed with him, wrapping those powerful arms around him, he drifted off to sleep.

At first, the fantasy carried over into his dreams. *Lugh seized his mouth in a ravenous kiss, his tongue plunging hard into Zack's mouth. Huge hands slid down to cup his butt. Zack moaned into the erotic assault, grinding his painfully hard erection against Lugh's stomach.*

Fear stiffened Zack's spine when the dream shifted suddenly. Lugh's tender murmurs deteriorated into snarls. The face trying to kiss him no longer belonged to the prince, its features distorted by rage or madness. Zack tried to shove the stranger away but now claws dug into his back. His heart raced and he cried out as the thing holding him snapped at him with jagged, dagger-long teeth.

Heat surged through him. His skin burned and itched as if a thousand electrified spiders raced over his body. He roared and slammed his fist into the thing's chest. His knuckles tore through skin. Bone cracked as its sternum splintered. Zack reached inside and an unholy triumph gripped him as he ripped its heart from its chest. It beat against his hand, the heat searing his palm. He stared at it, watching each chamber pulse in succession, the scent of blood filling his head. A sudden hunger raced through him. He would have his enemy's strength if he ate his heart. His jaws ached as he opened his mouth to sink his teeth into the pulsating muscle.

"Zack?"

The soft voice jerked his gaze up to the face across from him. It wasn't the stranger and it wasn't the beast. It was the girl from the park. He had ripped her heart out.

He dropped the heart and screamed.

"Zack? Zack!"

Something had him in its grip, shaking him. The clinging tendrils of the nightmare finally fell away to reveal Diego hovering over him.

"Zack, bud, it's all right." Diego perched beside him on the bed. "Just a bad dream. You're safe."

He ran a hand over his eyes, trying to get his heaving breaths under control. "Sorry, Mr. S. Did I wake you up?"

"No, no. It's just after six. I finished up in the office and was coming to check on Finn and heard you, ah, in distress."

"Oh. Was I screaming like a little girl?"

Diego chuckled. "More like whimpering like a puppy."

Something about that comment disturbed him, something just out of reach that he couldn't remember. He shifted uncomfortably, tugging at his T-shirt. "Could you open the window? I'm so hot."

"I'm not going to say anything about you being conceited," Diego teased softly, his expression concerned. He put his hands to either side of Zack's face. "You're fevered, hon. Hold on a sec."

Those hands felt wonderfully cool. Zack relaxed back against the pillow as Diego's eyes unfocused, soothing coolness flowing from his hands in lapping waves.

"Better?"

"Yeah." A year ago, Zack would have given anything to have Diego's hands on him like that. Now, it simply felt good and the magic he shared so unstintingly was amazing, but the terrible longing for the man himself had faded.

"I'll get you some aspirin and hopefully it won't come back. But you yell if it does, you hear me?"

"That's my line," Zack said with a little smile. He'd been a medic and a nurse for long enough that it felt strange to have someone else saying those things to him. "Diego? Eithne wouldn't tell me much. What happened out there? Do we know?"

Diego shook his head. "Not really. I know I have conflicting information in the police report, but given the time of day and the panic of those involved, I'd say that's expected. I know… Well, maybe know is a strong word."

"What?"

"When you're better, I have a set of files I want to go through with you that the staff have been compiling for me. It's probably because my brain wants connections and maybe neither your incident nor any of these other things are actually related. But I have a nagging feeling that it's all part of the same whole."

"You know my head hurts, right?" Zack said on a heavy sigh. "So why's everybody talking in circles?"

"Let's call it the File of Strange Happenings for now." Diego patted his leg. "If I knew anything concrete, I'd tell you. You know that."

"'K. FOSH it is, then."

Diego laughed. "Get better, Sergeant. We need you back at work."

A fit of sneezes came from across the hall, followed by a low, pitiful moan.

"And I need to go before someone thinks I've abandoned him."

"*Tu esposo es enfermo*," Zack got out, concentrating on one word at a time.

"*Está enfermo*," Diego corrected, beaming. "But that was good. Your Spanish is—"

Whatever else he said was lost when a vision appeared in the doorway. Lugh stood there in his royal best, so like Zack's earlier fantasy that his breath caught. His coal-black hair fell loose down his back in a midnight cataract. His smile went straight to Zack's core.

"Hi." *Oh, yeah, good one, Morrison. You sound like a breathless teenybopper.*

"My sergeant is awake at last," Lugh said as he strode into the room. "How long do you propose to continue this malingering? I expect you back by my side soon."

Zack couldn't help a grin at his mock-imperial tone. "Sorry, Highness. Not up to me. Gotta ask the docs."

Lugh rolled his eyes and took the spot on the bed Diego had ceded to him. "Wonderful. My mother will keep you on bedrest for the remainder of the year just to annoy me."

Diego bent to kiss his cheek and Lugh's on his way out. "Glad you're home, big guy. Zack, I'll be right across the hall if you need anything."

Long fingers twined with Zack's. Lugh's need for physical contact was familiar by now, but the simple act of holding hands still made giant moths flutter in his stomach.

"Everything go okay, Highness? You have one of the boys with you out there?"

"Kevin and Marcus accompanied me to the ball at the Austrian Embassy." Lugh stroked the back of his hand with his thumb. "It was an elaborate affair. One of the Foreign Service officers taught me to waltz. I wish you had been there, though."

"I know. I'll feel better when I can watch your back myself, too."

Lugh's smile slipped a hair. "Yes, yes, of course. I always feel more secure when it's you by my side."

"What's wrong, Highness? Did I say something stupid again?"

"No, no." Lugh stared at their joined hands. "I've been...worried for you, Zachary. When you were dying, I thought... It's simply been an anxious time."

Lugh's eyes glittered, his thick lashes sticking together suspiciously. Fae males cried so much more openly than human males, but the prince knew it made Zack uncomfortable, so he generally tried hard not to.

"It's okay, Highness." Zack reached over to pat his hand. "I'm not as big as you Otherworld warriors, but I'm still pretty damn tough. You didn't think I was giving up that easy, did you?"

"Of course not." Lugh wiped his eyes on his jacket sleeve. "Not my brave sergeant." He managed a soft smile. "Are you warm enough? Do you want me to stay with you tonight?"

The thought of Lugh lying down next to him made his heart stutter. Hell, he could even keep the uniform on, all those buttons pressing up against him…

"Yes… I mean, no! No. That is, it's not necessary," Zack fumbled on, his face growing hotter and hotter. "I mean, I'm warm now and I…I don't need it anymore. Having someone in the bed with me. Not that it's an awful thought or anything… Damn it."

He turned his face away, feeling like a complete fool. A gentle hand cupped his cheek and turned his face back.

"Zachary, when you are well and we can converse on equal footing again, you and I need to discuss some things."

"Okay. I guess… Yeah, probably."

Lugh patted his shoulder and went to the door, Zack's eyes wandering down to where the pants clung to his prince's rounded, muscular ass. God, if he blushed any more, his head would explode.

"Lugh?" He waited until the *sidhe* prince turned to him. "I'm glad I got to see you again."

Lugh's only answer was a wink and a grin before he eased the door shut.

Chapter Five

Strange Happenings

It is neither nature nor the reaction of magic within the fertile soil of the human field, but the very act of being human that causes such aberrations.

—Hssetassk, from *Conversations with the Wild Fae* by D. Sandoval

Zack put his feet up on the ottoman Diego shoved his way. Two weeks after the attack, his legs still ached and stairs were a challenge. But damn it, he'd been going stir crazy stuck in bed. Eithne had finally said he could go down to the offices if someone walked with him.

The file Diego had set in his lap got stranger with every page he turned. Snippets of police reports, local newspaper articles and blog entries from reputable sites all told tales better suited to the tabloids. Stories of spontaneous human combustion, of people floating or fading from sight. One article even discussed a teacher who could read her students' thoughts.

"Now that's a scary idea," Zack muttered. He frowned when he turned the page. The designation on this next paper was a familiar one. "Mr. S.? How'd you get hold of classified documents?"

Diego cleared his throat, one hand running back through his black curls. "Ah, well. That's something I don't want leaving this room. Agent Pulaski sent them to me."

"*Gerry* Pulaski?" Zack gaped at him. "Same guy who almost got us killed? Angus is gonna have a stroke."

"That's why Angus can't find out. He's finally dropped the extradition suit, but I know if Gerry's name comes up, for any reason, he'll be right back to screaming for blood."

"He won't hear it from me," Zack said. Guilt still ate at him. Angus' tortured sobs as he'd held Sionnach's shaved, unconscious body still haunted him. He'd been doing his job, just as Agent Pulaski had, but he'd had a part in that fiasco of an operation which had nearly cost four fae their lives. A year later, Finn still had dismemberment nightmares.

Never mind that it was all a huge misunderstanding. Never mind that he had ultimately made the right decision, the moral decision, instead of just following orders. Whenever he found Nathair in the garden staring out at nothing, when Finn woke up screaming, when Angus flinched from a spark or Sionnach's beautiful eyes filled with tears for no apparent reason, the guilt gnawed at him.

He fought to concentrate on the page in front of him, his forehead crinkling in disbelief. The documents from the bureau described attacks on East L.A. gang members. The bodies were exsanguinated, but without any arterial wound to explain the complete absence of blood. The only marks on the bodies, besides a few bruises, were two precise punctures at the throats, identical in each case.

"Vampires?" Zack glanced up. "This is getting just a little too *X-Files*, even for me."

"I know. And you haven't even gotten to the emails."

Zack cocked an eyebrow at him and turned the page. The next few pages were emails either addressed to Diego directly or sent through the embassy website. They came from individuals and from groups with names such as 'Rhiannon's Heirs' and the 'White Council', most of them badly written. Grammar and typing skills aside, they all asked questions in the same vein, questions about magic. How was this or that done? How did Diego learn? What was the source of his power? Would he come and teach, please?

"We have a leak?"

Diego gave a dismissive wave. "We have rumors from the IER and the more recent incident at the hospital. After that, the internet takes care of the rest."

"I don't like the tone of some of these, Mr. S. I don't want you leaving the island without an escort, all right?"

"But they're probably mostly just kids," Diego protested with a little smile. "You make it sound as if someone might kidnap me."

"Someone might, if they're desperate. Sounds like some of these people are messing with things they can't control. They might kidnap you anyway. You need to start understanding that you're an important man."

"No, I'm not," Diego murmured.

Zack snapped the folder shut. "These people don't agree with you." *And neither do I.* "Just don't go off alone. Please. And Finn, when he's better, doesn't count as an escort. He's more ADD than most five-year-olds." He eased over to place the file back on Diego's desk. "But that's not why you wanted me to look at all this stuff."

"Right. It's not."

"You said something before about connections."

Diego leaned back in his chair, staring up at the ceiling. He did that a lot when he puzzled through something, so Finn had painted ethereal, filigree designs in blue and green overhead to help him think. "It's just hard to say. Have these things always gone on and we're just hearing about them now because we're involved in the, ah, unusual? Or are we hearing about them now because of a sharp increase in such things? And if that's the case, why now?"

"Uh-huh. Don't expect me to believe you haven't already come up with your own answers." Zack watched the shadows gathering in Diego's eyes and didn't have to think hard to guess. "You think this all has to do with the door between the worlds, with the Earth magic and the Otherworld magic being able to flow back and forth again."

"The timing seems awfully coincidental, don't you think? I open a permanent way through the Veil, and now all this."

"Maybe. Or maybe the fae coming out in the open makes it easier for other things to come out in the open." Zack drummed his fingers on the chair arm. "And blaming yourself won't do anything but cost you sleep."

Diego let out a snort. "Not blaming myself would make me someone else."

"True. But I don't know anything about this stuff. Not much, anyway. Ask me about stuff I know, medical questions, weapons questions, I can answer those."

"I just want someone else besides me thinking about it. Another set of eyes, another brain." Diego tapped the folder. "I think your attacker is part of all this, too."

"You think maybe he was fae?"

"No, hon. I'm pretty sure he was human. I think he's... I'm not sure."

Zack exhaled a long breath. "Werewolf. Nobody wants to say it. You all think he was."

"Maybe. It's one possibility."

"But I haven't gone all furry or anything. Isn't that what's supposed to happen? It bites you, you get infected?"

Diego patted his hand. "I don't know. We just have old stories and movie versions. I do know Eithne's concerned that the bite on your shoulder isn't healing, and that you're still so..."

"Say it. Weak."

"Lethargic."

"Dog tired."

"Was that a joke?" Diego choked on a snicker.

Zack spread his hands in front of him. "A guy can't joke at his own expense?"

"I suppose it's better than howling."

"Oh, that was bad, Mr. S. I'm gonna call the authors' guild and have your license revoked."

* * * *

"Are you ready?" Lugh tapped politely on Zack's door. The man was happy to swim naked in

Otherworld pools, but he nearly expired from shame if one caught him half-dressed in the human world.

While Lugh had trouble understanding, he still worked hard to respect those sensitive points. A muffled curse and a thump from inside Zack's bedroom made him fling etiquette aside. The door slammed open with his hasty entrance and his heart gave a painful thud. Zack knelt on the floor clutching his shoulder, only one arm in his shirt.

Lugh crouched beside him. "Zachary…"

"S'okay, Highness. Don't look at me like I'm dying." Zack pulled in a shuddering breath and eased his left arm into its sleeve. "Tried to move too fast. Pulled on the shoulder. Not as bad as it looks."

The pain was so fierce it took you out at the knees and it's not as bad as it looks? "If you don't feel well enough for this, I will go and tell them so."

"God, no. They've been planning this for weeks now. I can't do that to everybody."

Though his arms ached to gather Zack close, Lugh limited himself to lifting the unbuttoned shirt from Zack's shoulder and running gentle fingertips over the still-angry wound. "It's hot, my dear."

Eyes the color of mourning dove pinions gazed up at him. Zack licked his lips. "Yeah. Hot." Then he ducked his head, his cheeks a lovely shade of pink. "I mean, yes. A little. It's not so bad."

"I think my sergeant would say so even if someone had lopped his head off." Lugh shook his head. He pressed his hand over the bite marks, concentrating a bit of his magic there to pull the heat into his own body. He was no healer, but this much he could do. "Better?"

Zack nodded and went so far as to lean his head on Lugh's shoulder. Oh, how he wanted this. He wanted so much more, wanted his beloved sergeant's hard-muscled body stretched beneath him. On top of him. Beside him. Wanted to feel his powerful thighs around his waist, his strong arms holding tight around his back. But this tender moment of trust made all the denial worthwhile. Yes, he wanted to pound into Zack, to make him writhe in ecstasy, shout and come like a geyser, but for spots of time like this, when Zack came to him and touched him unbidden, he was willing to wait for the rest.

"Lugh?" Zack's trembling hand rested on his bare chest.

The ache grew to encompass Lugh's entire being. He put a finger under Zack's chin to lift his face. "Tonight. We will talk tonight. But first we have a feast to attend, do we not?"

Zack nodded and sat back on his heels to button his shirt. The withdrawal was a dagger in Lugh's heart, the terrible stab of an opportunity forever lost as Zack pulled back physically and emotionally from him again. He made a tactical retreat to lean against the wall, waiting patiently as Zack fumbled with his buttons and climbed his way back to his feet. Human pride could be a prickly thing.

The clothes suited him. The charcoal pants hugged the perfect globes of his backside, the blue shirt clung to the muscles of his chest just enough to tease. The clothing was unnecessary, though, and Zack certainly had nothing to hide. Lugh wondered if he might be self-conscious about the scars. Possibly. Though they were warrior's marks he should have worn proudly. Suddenly feeling underdressed in only a kilt, Lugh forced a smile and held out a hand.

"I don't need—"

"Let me act as escort for you today." Lugh caught Zack's hand and tucked it into the crook of his arm. "You are the hero of the hour and should arrive borne on a litter of rose petals. But since you would refuse such things, perhaps you might accept arriving on the arm of a fairy prince?"

"Oh, well, since you put it that way." Zack shot him that charming, crooked grin that always melted Lugh's heart and fell into step beside him.

Tall for a human, he was still half a head shorter than Lugh. The difference in stature often sent fierce waves of protectiveness through him, though he knew quite well how little Zack needed his protection.

The door across the hall opened. Zack shoved Lugh behind him as Finn stepped out.

"Where're you headed, bud?" Zack asked.

Finn's bright grin looked a bit guilty. "I'm coming with you."

"Doesn't sound like your best idea." Zack took a step forward to block his path. "Contagious, remember?"

"It's been weeks!" Finn actually stamped his foot. "I am bloody sick of being shut up in that cursed room all alone! I haven't even sneezed since last night."

Lugh leaned against the wall, waiting for the inevitable. Finn's eyes still held a glint of fever. Sure enough, the pooka's nose wrinkled and he turned his head back toward his room to let out an explosive sneeze. Finn vanished, replaced by a handsome black hare sitting in the sudden heap of his clothes.

"Bloody hells." The hare sneezed and shifted to eagle. Another sneeze and he changed to hedgehog. The hedgehog sighed and trundled back to the bed where it used its thick claws to climb up the sheets. It sneezed once more to become a dejected Finn, curled naked and sulking atop the covers.

"How about I bring you some ice cream later?" Zack asked gently.

Finn sniffed and hid his head in the blankets. "No. Thank you. I simply wanted to see everyone."

"You'll be better soon, hon."

"Hmph."

Zack chuckled. "Though you're really cute when you pout. Anyone tell you that?"

An irritated snort came from the blanket nest. Then Finn lifted his head, his expression serious. "Zack, go. Their majesties adore you, but I would not take the notion of being fashionably late too far."

"Personal experience?"

"Oh, yes." Finn waved a hand at them. "Go. Heroes should be feted and the feast for you is long overdue." One last sneeze turned Finn into a shaggy Icelandic pony reclining on the bed. "Tell my husband not to stay overlong."

Zack promised and closed the door, though he hissed at Finn to shut up when he began to hum something.

"What song was it that offended you?" Lugh asked, gratified when Zack took his arm again without prompting.

"Nothing. Never mind."

The first set of stairs posed little difficulty, but by the time they had reached the level belowground where the fae had their caves and tunnels, Zack was gasping.

"Shall I carry you?"

"Um, no." Zack leaned a shoulder against the wall, rubbing at his chest. "Gimme a sec. My heart's...galloping."

Concerned, Lugh slid an arm around him and pulled him close. When Zack accepted the support and leaned into him, his alarm grew. Zack's heartbeat thundered in Lugh's ears, drumming a desperate staccato against his chest. Panting breaths deteriorated into tortured gasps. Just as Lugh was about to reach with his mind to call for help, Zack sagged in his arms, his heart returning to a normal rhythm.

"Sorry," Zack murmured. "Guess I'm still a little woozy. Know how Finn feels. Just want to be well again."

"You will be," Lugh said atop his close-cropped, golden hair. *You will, you must. Gods, please, my Zachary, you must be well again.*

He kept an arm around Zack's shoulders — to steady him, he told himself — and ambled slowly through the corridors with him until they reached the room with the gleaming door. Two feet thick, of bespelled battle silver that Lugh had forged himself, the door was wise enough to prevent the entrance of those with evil intent and strong enough to withstand modern human explosives and blowtorches.

Diego had wanted the passage through the Veil as secure as possible. Zack had insisted on installing the retinal scanner as an added security measure since fae retinal patterns differed wildly from human ones. Anyone could leave the secure room to make the passage from the Otherworld to this one, but only one of the fae and certain select humans could enter from the outside.

A tilt of his head toward the scanner gained them access and Zack's eyes lit up, as they always did, when the green world across the Veil came into view. Outside the embassy, a thunderstorm lashed the walls, but through the glowing doorway, high white streaks of cloud painted a brilliant cerulean sky. A field of lush grass and yellow flowers stretched before them, with the edge of the *sidhe* forest visible in the distance. Not far from the doorway, fae crowded the field in all their multihued, multi-skinned glory, lounging, dancing, flying, eating, wrestling and conversing.

A familiar russet-haired figure turned and gave them a flirtatious wave. Lugh chuckled. "My cousin is incorrigible."

"Sionnach knows how gorgeous he is," Zack countered with a fond smile. "He just likes other people to notice, too."

They stepped through and Sionnach bounded to them and stood on tiptoe to wrap his arms around Zack's neck. "Our hero has arrived!" he exclaimed, pressing his lithe body close.

Altogether too close for Lugh's liking—he had a terrible urge to shove his cousin away. Now from whence had that sprung? He had never acted in a jealous fashion toward his lovers. Not that Zachary was his lover. Great Mother, but the sergeant confused him.

Others gathered close to greet Zack, wheat-haired Angus nearly knocking him over in his enthusiasm, Faolchú sweeping him up in his arms to swing him around, the *féileacán* in their small forms dancing about his head in a firefly rainbow. A deep, rumbling growl scattered them all.

"So, boy." King Balor towered above Zack, eight feet of massive muscle, boar bristles and tusks. "Finally done lying about all day? Not content to be waited on hand and foot in your own bed, you have to come here for it as well?"

Lugh flinched. His grandfather was most likely joking, but his thunderous expression made it difficult to be sure.

"Thought I'd better come check up on things, Your Majesty," Zack said, tilting his head back to look up into Balor's face. "You know I can't leave you all alone without you getting into trouble. And I thought you might want to sit by me and feed me grapes."

Silence fell over the gathering. Even the birds seemed to hold their breaths as Balor scowled down at Zack. But Zack obviously knew the Fomorian king well enough by now and met the baleful glare of that one visible eye without flinching. Balor threw back his head and laughed as he pulled Zack into a surprisingly gentle embrace.

Lugh felt suddenly bereft as his grandfather led Zack away to the abundance of food. That should have been his arm around Zack's shoulders, him beside his brave sergeant as the fae competed to bring him tempting bits of this and that.

"Sulking does not become you, Shining One."

Startled out of his reverie, he turned to find Morrigan at his shoulder, her sharp teeth glinting in the sunlight. "Staying out of the way does not constitute sulking."

She shrugged, her long claws clicking as she watched the scene before them. "Perhaps not. But that pitiable, lost look on your face does."

"I'm certain I don't know what you mean."

"Males are hopeless." She shook her head on a snort. "Why must you make everything so complicated?"

He arched a brow at his shield companion. "Because sometimes it is."

At least Zack enjoyed the attention. He smiled and laughed, conversing easily with the fae who would have left him thunderstruck and speechless a year earlier. But now he knew their names and their histories, had helped many of them with questions about the human world and had even taught some of them — the ones better able to concentrate on rules — to play baseball.

Lugh smiled. Perhaps it was not so blasted complicated after all. Perhaps —

With a soft cry, Zack suddenly doubled over his knees, his face a mask of pain. His previous thoughts scattering, Lugh raced to him, unceremoniously shoving everyone else out of the way.

"Zachary?" He tried to hold him still, but Zack twisted and writhed in obvious agony. "What is it, my dear?"

"God...oh, God," Zack gasped out. "On fire...something's eating...my insides...fuck!" He clawed at his shirt, ripping the buttons off in his haste to be rid of it. For a moment, Lugh thought the shirt itself might be the culprit but Zack continued to moan and writhe after he had torn it from his body.

"Lugh! Help me!"

The cry tore at his heart. He had never felt so helpless and useless. "Mother! Where is she? Someone go and fetch her!"

It was not his mother who came, but Danu, the gathered fae parting before her regal passage. Her green hair whipped about her head from the wind she generated in her anger. The queen of the *sidhe* pointed a long finger at Zack and spoke in a frigid, commanding voice, "He cannot be here. Not now. He endangers us all."

"Grandmother, what are you saying?" Lugh cried out in anguish. "We must help him!"

"The sergeant knows why he must go." She stepped closer, menace in her eyes. "Go, Zachary Morrison. Run far from here. As far from the embassy as you can. Away from other living things before it is too late."

Zack staggered to his feet, his eyes filled with horror. He let out an agonized cry and fell to his knees again. Danu came toward him with relentless purpose as he backpedaled, one arm clutched around his stomach.

"Grandmother, leave him be!"

"No. It is death and terror if I do and this field will run red with the blood of slaughtered fae as it did in ancient times." She raised her arms above her head, the white glow of her magic surrounding her. Before the eye could blink, she had vanished and a huge she-bear reared up in her place.

"Go!" The bear roared and lunged at Zack, her claws raking red trails on his bare shoulder.

Zack backed a step and another, his eyes glistening with unshed tears. Then he turned and fled back through the doorway, back to the human world, stumbling as he ran, his terrible pain radiating to every being within shouting distance.

"No!" Lugh bellowed, his shift to bull as unconscious as his rush after Zack. *"Zack! Zack, don't go! Please, wait!"* He shouted in his mind, hoping for that connection between them. No reply. Only Zack's footsteps dashing through the halls ahead of him. By the time he reached the door to the garden, snorting and blowing, Zack was gone.

Chapter Six

Beast

There is a tide in the affairs of men… I like the sound of the words but what does it mean? Are there visible human tides? If I stand overlooking Times Square, will I see them? And do they crest and ebb with the cycles of the moon?
—Finn Shannon, from *Conversations with the Wild Fae* by D. Sandoval

Zack ran, the chill autumn rain unable to penetrate the fire racing over his skin. The conflagration had spread to every part of his body, every cell an individual island of agony. He expected smoke to rise from his skin. He stumbled drunkenly from the pain. Still, he ran on. He had to get away.

He leaped the low wall at the end of the garden and raced out into the gathering dusk, where jagged lightning spears lit the dunes and rocks. Out into the hinterlands of Tearmann Island, where no one but the sea birds lived—he knew why Danu had banished him.

The thing no one would talk about was happening and soon he would be a crazed, homicidal beast.

I should throw myself from the cliffs…

The thought tugged at him. Everyone would be safe if he did and the pain would end. He stopped atop one of the sheer cliff walls, on the promontory where the terns made their nests, shuddering, gasping, staring down into dark waves that pummeled the white fingers of rock below. Something held him back.

Fists clenched, he threw back his head and howled in his frustration and anguish. The sound echoed endlessly off the cliff faces as if he had suddenly multiplied a hundredfold. He flung himself away from the edge and staggered back to the interior, until he collapsed, hidden among the dunes.

He stared at his hands. On such a black night, he shouldn't have been able to see them. Colors were muted to shades of gray, but he saw everything around him as clearly as if it were a sunny afternoon.

The pain ratcheted up another notch and Zack cried out in horror as the bones of his hands shifted, elongating and changing shape with terrible snaps and creaks. He thrashed on the sand as the long bones of his arms and legs followed suit. *Someone help me… God, make it stop!*

He screamed when his facial bones slid forward and his teeth grew too long for his mouth.

* * * *

Lugh jumped the garden wall, tossing his horned head as he hunted for Zack's scent. *Cursed, bloody rain. This couldn't happen on a clear night?*

He didn't care what his grandmother thought. Zack was alone out there, in pain and truly afraid for perhaps the first time in his life. Whatever else might or might not lie between them, Zack was one of *his* warriors, and a prince of the *sidhe* did not abandon one of his war band.

When the howl ripped through the night, slicing through the lashing winds and rain, the hair along Lugh's back stood on end. He retained his four-hoofed form for surer footing and dashed off after the anguished sound.

* * * *

A heartbeat reached his ears. Hunger gnawed at his insides. Blood. Flesh. The burning need overrode everything. There. By the clump of dune grass. Movement.

He crouched, lips pulled back from his muzzle in a snarl. A flash of shadow, quick, scurrying. He pounced, the rat squeaking and twisting in his claws. For a moment, he stared, fascinated by the heat, by the speed of its heartbeat. He bent his head and bit it in half, shivering with pleasure at the rush of blood over his tongue, the feel of flesh giving under the strength of his sharp teeth.

Fur, tail, skull, he devoured it all, then licked his hands, whimpering in confusion. More. He needed more. The rat had been too small, finished too soon. His insides ached with need. So empty. So hungry.

He roared his frustration and rose, scenting the rain-soaked air. Lights in the distance. Larger prey. He would go there, where so many hearts beat. There he would rend and tear. He would feed until he had silenced the emptiness.

* * * *

The second howl took Lugh deeper into the dunes. His heart had nearly failed when he had followed Zack's scent to the cliff's edge, but no body lay broken on the rocks below. When he found a footprint leading away again, his relief made him dizzy.

Thunder cracked, the storm directly overhead. In the sporadic flickers of lightning, Lugh spotted the running figure, not running away from the embassy as Zack had been, but back toward it.

Something was wrong about the shape of the figure and the way it ran. Lugh pushed himself to greater speed, racing to get ahead, to put himself between that wrongness and all those lives at the embassy. Finn was upstairs alone. The office staff would be finishing up for the day. Security would be changing shifts.

As he topped the rise of a tall dune, he shifted back to his *sidhe* form. The figure below came to an abrupt halt halfway up the dune. Roughly man-shaped, the thing before him could only be described as monstrous. The arms were too long for a human's, indicating that the thing could run on all fours if it chose to. Shaggy, rain-matted fur covered its body. Canine ears perched atop its head and its face was a nightmare mix of human and beast, its nose and mouth elongated into a snout full of jagged, too-large teeth. But the eyes, oh, those eyes. Zack's eyes stared out of that misshapen face, clouded with madness, but still his beautiful gray eyes.

"Zachary?" Lugh spoke softly, taking slow steps toward him. "It's just me. It's all right, my dear. I won't let anyone hurt you. We'll find a way through this."

The thing that had been Zack watched him with animal suspicion, lips pulled back in a snarl of fury. The eyes flicked down. Lugh had only enough time to plant his feet and bend his knees to take the brunt of the assault when the beast lunged at him. It leaped up the dune in three bounds and struck him with bone-jarring force.

Its momentum threw Lugh onto his back. Winded, he still managed to keep his grip on the beast's arms. It snapped and roared, trying to gain the leverage it needed to tear at his throat. Far stronger than Zack in his human form, it might have succeeded if Lugh had not been the veteran of centuries of combat.

He hooked a leg around its waist and flipped them. With his weight on top, it was easier to keep those teeth from him. He pulled at the flows of magic, using the charge already in the air from the thunderstorm, and sent a small lightning jolt through the beast's body. It jerked and went limp.

Lugh released his hold on the furred wrists. Sorrow washed over him even as his mind raced to come up with a solution, even a temporary one. He had to keep Zack safe. He stroked the damp muzzle. "I'm so sorry. I didn't want—"

The beast's eyes flew open. It lunged at him, fingers closing around his throat. As its claws bit down on his windpipe, Lugh's temper snapped. He took the beast by the throat and crotch and hurled it to the ground. It shook its head and attempted to rise but Lugh flipped it on its stomach and forced its arms behind its back.

"Enough!" he roared. "I am here to help you! To protect you! And I will truss you like a war hostage if I must!"

With his knees holding the struggling beast down, Lugh tugged the belt from his kilt. He looped the belt around its throat and tied its arms behind its back. If it struggled too hard, the beast would cut off its own air and lose consciousness. So he hoped, at least.

Still it did struggle, trying to get its knees drawn up to rise. Fighting with himself to remember Zack was probably somewhere in there still, Lugh grabbed it by its neck and crotch again, preparing to lift and slam it back to the sand. The beast stilled. It whimpered and pushed back against the hand on its crotch.

"You like that, do you?" Lugh tried an experimental caress of furred balls and was rewarded with a needy canine whine. *Zack, this is Zack. Dagda's spear, I shouldn't be doing this...*

It felt like some odd sort of violation, touching Zack like this when he had no ability to consent. But the beast, Zack, pushed up on his knees, head and shoulders pressed into the sand, more than giving consent. He pleaded for it in little pants and whimpers, pushing his ass against Lugh's palm.

He wished he knew more about werewolves, for that was assuredly what Zack had become. The fae had killed them in centuries past if they wandered into the Otherworld during the change. In the mortal world, the fae simply avoided them. Their ravenous nature made them dire threats to all life, forever devouring any life in their paths. Forever hungry.

With another little whine, Zack pushed back harder. He uttered a low-throated moan when Lugh's fingers skimmed up his crease. Who would have thought the hunger was sexual as well?

Zack writhed desperately, choking as he pulled too hard on his impromptu collar.

"Shh, easy." Lugh spread his knees to cover him from behind, both to keep him still and to assert his dominance. It seemed to be what Zack wanted. "I'll take care of you."

Though his cock was hard and aching, he resolved to use only his hands. He had nothing to ease the way and, beast or not, he would not hurt his Zachary. He reached underneath to take Zack's furred erection in a firm grip. All wriggling and struggling abruptly ceased. Zack's only movement was the rhythmic pumping of his hips as if his whole awareness now centered on his cock. Perhaps it did.

Lugh tore his kilt from him so there would be nothing between their bodies. He kept one palm flat between Zack's shoulder blades to keep him down while the other kept a tight hold on his thick cock. By no means cruel, he wasn't particularly gentle in his strokes. The harder he gripped, the more Zack seemed to relax into his touch.

Those mad gray eyes drifted shut. When Lugh settled his erection against the cleft of Zack's furry ass, a purring moan of pleasure rumbled in Zack's chest. Lugh pumped his hips, letting his cock slide teasingly over Zack's puckered entrance, keeping time with his hand. He felt guilty for taking any pleasure in the strange situation, and so held himself tightly in check, denying himself the release he wanted so desperately.

But not like this. Gods, not like this...

He wrapped an arm around Zack's chest to hold him tight. Zack's breaths grew short. Lugh felt furred balls draw up tight against his own. Zack froze, the muscles in his back and legs trembling. His eyes snapped open. He howled, bucking and jerking under Lugh as his seed splashed hot across his hand.

"Hush, gently now." While Lugh didn't make the mistake of untying his hands, he did hold Zack tenderly as his body calmed. The scent of his arousal and his climax nearly drove Lugh mad but this was about getting Zack safely through the night, not about his pleasure.

A mere five minutes later, Zack was grinding back against him. Lugh stole a hand to what should have been his spent cock, only to find it rock hard again. He lost count of how many times he made Zack come after the sixth or seventh, but fulfilling his endless hunger through the slaking of his lust was far preferable to the alternative.

Finally, Zack collapsed on his side from exhaustion. Lugh curled up behind him, both arms wrapped around his waist to ensure he wouldn't run. He rested his head against a heaving shoulder and let the tears fall. Sorrow and frustration warred in equal measure. His Zack would be forever changed. He had heard that many werewolves, the ones who had good hearts, did not live long. They took their own lives or put themselves in situations where others would.

He hated the Were who had done this, but that one was dead. The only other place to direct his anger was at himself. If he hadn't kissed Zack that night, none of this would have happened.

* * * *

Lugh woke with the sun shining on his face before he realized he had dozed off. When he found his arms empty, he panicked and sat up with an anguished cry. Beside him lay his still knotted belt, his torn kilt and the most beautiful wolf he had ever seen. As large as some cart ponies, the golden wolf gazed at him with patient, gray eyes, plumed tail thumping on the ground.

"Zack?"

The wolf wriggled to him and placed his head on Lugh's thigh with a contented sigh. The transition was done for the moment and as Lugh had hoped, the madness had disappeared with the raving beast. Perhaps Zack would spend the next three days as a wolf but at least as a sane wolf. It gave him three days to decide how to keep Zack alive when he returned to human form.

He buried his fingers in the thick ruff of neck fur, so wonderfully soft compared to the coarse fur the beast had. "Well, we had an interesting night, eh? Let's go and see if Faolchú has some venison he doesn't mind sharing."

Chapter Seven

Wolf in the Fold

It's not so much having a kinship with wolves. I am a wolf. The wolf was born with me and will always remain. To try to separate the Fomorian from the wolf would be to take a saber and slice me rather messily in half.

—Faolchú Earthshaker, during a televised interview, CBC

Diego finally persuaded Danu to let them search at first light. She had spelled the doors to the embassy shut, adamant that she would allow no one out to hunt for Zack and, as she put it, her 'thickheaded, arrogant Champion'.

He knew she worried for them. Her anger said as much. But she would not have anyone else endangered to help someone for whom it was already too late.

"It's never too late, Zack," Diego muttered as he trudged behind the hunters. "Don't you let anyone tell you so."

"Did you say something, light-wielder?" Angus straightened from peering at the ground, his eyes red-rimmed from tears and lack of sleep.

"Nothing. Just worried."

Angus nodded and raised his face to the sun. His body melted, feathers blossoming on his skin until a golden eagle stood before Diego in place of the *sidhe* herald. "We are all anxious," the eagle said with a clack of his beak. "I will fly ahead and perhaps spot something from the air."

"Fly well, Farseer," Sionnach whispered to the speck of raptor disappearing over the dunes. He buried his face in his hands and began to cry.

"Hey." Diego pulled him close, letting him sob into his jacket. "He'll be all right. Angus is well out of reach up there."

"I...know..." Sionnach sobbed. "But Zack... He's... It's not..."

Ever since his time as a government-held experiment, Sionnach had become fragile. He buried it most of the time, showing the world his cheerful, cheeky face, but when emotions ran high, he would fall apart again.

"I know." Diego stroked his hair. "Zack's a good man and he didn't deserve this. It's not right. And we're all worried. But we're going to help him through this." He pushed Sionnach back far enough to see his face. "Aren't we?"

Sionnach nodded, breaths shuddering as he tried to compose himself. A few steps ahead of them, Faolchú lifted his head from the trail, his gray-furred ears twitching. "I smell wolf."

Golden feathers glinting in the sun, Angus returned on powerful sweeps of his wings. "They're coming! I see them!"

"Both of them?" Diego called up.

"Yes! Together!"

Despite the obvious joy in Angus' voice, Faolchú thrust the smaller fae and Diego behind him. His jaw tight, he watched with narrowed eyes as two figures crested the nearest dune.

Lugh waved to them with a bright smile as he strode toward them, his other hand buried in the neck fur of a huge wolf. The animal's shoulder was at Lugh's waist, its tongue lolled out in a lupine grin. It had fur the color of a certain sergeant's honey-blond hair and expressive gray eyes that were altogether too familiar.

"Zack."

The wolf broke from Lugh's side, loping toward them. At Faolchú's growl, he skidded to a stop, ears flat, front feet splayed, lips pulling back from his teeth.

"Wolves." Nathair sighed and stepped between them. He swatted Faolchú on the nose. "Be nice. This is no time for threat displays." Then their little garden snake turned to Zack. "Put your teeth away, golden one. You know this wolf. You've slept together. Played together."

Zack cocked his head to the side, listening to Nathair with his ears pricked forward. He trotted forward, tail wagging hesitantly and proceeded to sniff at Faolchú's crotch. In turn, Faolchú crouched down to sniff at Zack's fur until both wolf heads, gold and black-and-silver, were nuzzling at each other, licking and nudging in greeting.

"Welcome back, Sergeant," Faolchú murmured with a suspicious hitch in his deep voice.

Diego turned away with a lump in his throat, the truth hard to face and harder to bear. He looked up at

Lugh instead and reached out a hand in concern. "You're hurt."

"Scratches, little man. A few bruises, perhaps." Lugh rubbed gingerly at the gashes on his neck. "We had a bit of a tussle before we came to an understanding."

"Did you hurt him?"

Lugh's dark brows drew together and Diego knew he had offended his friend. He waved a hand to where Wolf-Zack jumped up to put his paws on Nathair's shoulders and lick his face. "Does he appear mortally injured, Consul? Do you think me such a brute that I would harm someone so dear to me?"

"No. Of course not." Diego put a gentle hand on Lugh's arm. "I'm sorry. We were scared to death for both of you."

Lugh drew in a slow breath. "Forgive me. I am… It was a long night."

"So he's not like the thing that attacked him? He gets to be this pretty wolf instead of a monster?"

"Not precisely."

Lugh sank down to sit on the sand, knees bent so he could rest his arms on them. It was a perfectly natural posture except he was stark naked and exposing just about every asset nature had given him. Diego fought against the need to blush and sat beside him.

"So what then?"

Angus had returned to the ground and to his *sidhe* form. He threw his arms around Zack's furred neck and soon the lot of them were rolling in the sand, mock wrestling.

"I know, or have known, precious little about Weres." Lugh managed a smile as Zack pinned Sionnach, who squeaked as his ear was quite thoroughly licked.

"When we did see them, it was in their monstrous form. I didn't realize the raving beast was transitional."

"Transitional?"

"Yes. Between the human and the wolf. I'm not certain if it had to do with time, if the change to wolf was inevitable, or if it was the satisfying of certain conditions that allowed it."

"You're not speaking too clearly."

Lugh rested his forehead on his arm. "I'm not feeling terribly clear, either. Werewolves are so dangerous because hunger consumes them. Until last night, I thought that hunger was only for flesh and blood."

Diego pondered that a moment. Lugh's apparent weariness, his unclothed state… "*Dios*, you didn't. You and him? While he was…"

"Yes." Lugh's head jerked up. "I mean, no! I did not. That is I did, but not for me. His needs had to be seen to. I did not take him."

"Ah." He had never seen Lugh so rattled. "So he's safe now? For another moon cycle?"

"I don't know. I truly wish I did. It is my hope that he will be wolf until the moon wanes again. But what if he becomes the beast again at moonrise?"

Diego chewed at his bottom lip, considering. "I suppose we need to be prepared, then. From what we saw last evening, we should have plenty of warning. We'll check to see when moonrise is tonight—"

"Seven-twenty-six," Nathair called over.

"Ah. Thank you. We'll get him to a locked room no later than seven and make sure we have restraints ready. I don't want him running off into the wild again where we have no idea what's happened to him."

"I will stay with him. If he does shift again, he will be dangerous," Lugh said as he drew spirals in the sand.

"You look like you need to rest, big guy," Diego said.

"I am fae. You do recall that? I am able to go months without sleep."

Diego shook his head. "Doesn't mean you should. Go take a nap. Leave him with his friends today. They'll watch over him."

As if to illustrate the point, Faolchú left the little group lolling in the sand. "Diego, would you mind if we raided the kitchen? Zack is hungry and there is precious little game on the island."

"And do we have a brush for fur?" Sionnach added. "His pelt is simply full of sand."

"Yes, to the kitchen raid, and the brush is in the drawer under the microwave." Diego stood and held out a hand to Lugh to pull him up. "Try to keep him away from Danu and don't let him wander around the offices, please."

He left the quartet of fae in the kitchen debating whether to give Zack a steak whole or cut it up for him, and led Lugh by the hand into the little common room at the back of the embassy.

Though he knew Lugh would heal quickly, he still brought a clean washcloth and dabbed the blood and sand from his cuts before urging him to lie down. "Look, I know you're the toughest badass out there, but we might need your strength later. Just rest a while. I'll make sure you're up before dinnertime."

Lugh's huge hand closed over his forearm. "Diego..."

He leaned in to kiss Lugh's forehead. "I wish I could say everything was going to be okay."

"Why not?" Lugh asked plaintively. "Tell me you have all the answers, as you always do. The little man who brought me back from the brink of death, who opened the way through the impenetrable Veil. Who holds the wild heart of a pooka in his hands. Surely you will have answers."

"The little man is at a loss and respects you too much to lie to you," Diego said gently. "We'll all put our heads together on this. We'll find a solution that works as best we can. But I can't promise to cure him."

"I know." Lugh lay back, closed his eyes on a weary sigh and let Diego cover him with the blanket from the back of the sofa.

Except for the boisterous chatter from the kitchen, silence pervaded the embassy. The human staff, prevented from leaving the previous evening, had slept in the fae caverns downstairs — far preferable to trying to sleep in office chairs. Diego went to his office and sank down in his chair, running a hand over his stubbled cheek. Carol had printed out his schedule for the day and had set neatly on the corner of his desk. There would be order, apparently, in the face of any chaos, if she had anything to do with it.

"*My love?*" Finn's thoughts reached him, warm and worried. "*Is all well?*"

"*He is home,* mi vida." Diego sent in return. "*Safe and unharmed. He is quite a handsome wolf.*"

"*Oh.*" Finn was silent a long moment, then his thoughts took on a wistful note. "*I wish I could see him.*"

"*He's having breakfast right now, but I'm sure he'll be happy to come upstairs later.*"

"*Do you think so? And should he, since he is a shifter now as well?*"

"*That's very sensible and considerate of you. But he's still human, so he can't catch fae diseases. I'll ask him to come see you, or have Faolchú ask him if he doesn't understand me.*"

Finn seemed cheered by this and settled back into a quiet, warm presence snuggled against Diego's mind.

While they rarely intruded on each other's thoughts unless one of them was in obvious distress, it had become a comfort to have Finn always within easy reach, even when miles separated them.

He eased back in his chair as his monitor powered up, his eyes burning from lack of sleep. If he had any sense, he'd take his own advice and snatch a nap while the peace lasted. First, he needed to check if anything urgent had come in overnight. The usual bulletins and inquiries populated his inbox. Carol would take care of most of them. He sent a vague promise to the Russian Embassy regarding a visit to the island and made a note to speak to their majesties about the request. A quick note went to the Secretary of State, reassurance that, yes, all was well and Prince Lugh did not at all blame the U.S. for the attack on his aide.

Yet another email from someone named 'Minky' who wrote on behalf of The Silver Adepts made him sigh. They were one of the more persistent groups of magic enthusiasts, obviously young from the tone and construction of the emails.

Hi Mr. Sandoval —
Wasn't sure if you got the last msg. Didn't hear back. If you don't want to help, please tell us, we'll find someone else.

He recalled the previous emails and felt a bit guilty for ignoring them. Whether this group had any real connection to the flows or not, he had no idea, but he did know what it was like to feel frustrated and frightened by a gift he had no idea how to tap into or control. What could it hurt to give them a little advice?

Dear Minky —

My apologies for not answering sooner. We have been a whirlwind of activity here and I have fallen behind shamefully with correspondence.

Please understand that I am still learning to ride the flows of magic myself. My first experiences were during seizures — not conducive to learning. The actual learning began one day playing in the water with a féileacán pair...

* * * *

"Well? What's he say?"

Minky wrinkled her nose. "He's telling us to play with water."

A mug sailed across the room to shatter against the far wall. She flinched, wishing she really could disappear.

"Fuck! I knew it! He doesn't even take us seriously!"

"O.M.G. Chill, Bran." Kara crossed the room with a wastebasket to pick up the shards of ceramic. "Such a drama queen. Read it to us, Mink."

She took a deep breath and read the Consul's reply. It was a nice reply, polite and friendly—he seemed like such a nice man—but she couldn't help the disappointment in her voice.

"He won't teach us." Will's voice cracked and broke. "He just thinks we're a bunch of stupid kids."

"We are a bunch of stupid kids," Kara said in a dry tone.

Brandon paced, the tendons in his neck standing out like bridge cables. "He's safe on his island, surrounded by the fae. He's not out here, feeling what we feel. He has to know. He has to—"

"Why do we need him, anyway?" Nate balanced a ruler on his hand, his eyes glazing over in concentration as it lifted from his palm and floated to the center of the room. "We're learning."

Brandon snatched the ruler from the air and broke it in half. "Not fast enough! Making office supplies fly isn't going to do a damn thing!"

Will buried his face in his hands, his shoulders shaking in silent misery. Brandon rolled his eyes but went to gather Will in his arms. "Hey, c'mon, babe. We'll think of something. I'll think of something."

* * * *

"Highness...Prince Lugh..."

Someone touched his shoulder. His eyes snapped open. Carol stood over him, her face crimson. He ran a hand over his eyes and took a belated look down at his body as he sat up. Blankets covered him but by Carol's complexion, he was certain they had slipped off while he slept and she had just replaced them.

"Your pardon, Carol. I didn't wish to offend you."

"You didn't. Big difference between embarrassed and offended, Highness." She handed him a cup of tea. "Mr. S. thought we should probably wake you up."

He glanced out of the window at the late-afternoon sun sparkling on the fountain in the garden. "Yes, thank you. Most likely best." He sipped, grateful for the slide of hot tea along his parched throat. "Would you know where Diego is now?"

"Oh, sure." She pointed with her chin. "He's out walking in the garden with Sergeant Morrison. Well, the wolf that's Sergeant Morrison, anyway." She fussed about the room for a moment, straightening magazines and picking up cushions. "I'm leaving for the night, Highness. The rest of the human staff, too. Captain

Faolchú said he and some of the Fomorian warriors would take security detail at the front door and the docks."

Lugh nodded. When exactly Faolchú had acquired the title, he couldn't recall, but the humans had given it to him since he commanded the Fomorian war bands. "That's wise, I think."

She gave him a long look and said softly, "You be careful tonight, Highness."

"Perhaps nothing will occur."

"Maybe not," she said in a voice that made it clear she didn't entertain any such optimistic notion.

She left him with a pot of tea, a cucumber sandwich and one of his kilts discreetly draped over the arm of the sofa. Amazing woman. Not a drop of ability to tap into the flows and still she always seemed to know exactly what was needed. Anyone would have been lucky to have her at their side.

A flush of shame interrupted his musings when he realized he had no idea if Carol had a spouse or a lover. He knew nothing about her outside of the embassy walls, nothing about any of the staff once they left for the day. Zack most likely knew and he was certain Diego made it a point to know. He had to start paying better attention to the humans in his life, stop relying on Diego and the staff for everything.

He stretched to crack his back in several places and rose to put on the blood-red kilt Carol had left.

"I do wish she had chosen a different color," he murmured as he made his way out of the back door to the garden.

He found Diego on a stone bench in the wisteria arbor, Zack stretched out at his feet, dozing on the flagstones. One back leg twitched as Zack dreamed.

Lugh hoped they were good dreams, full of rabbits to chase and pack mates with whom to run.

Diego glanced up at him, then at the sun dropping lower against the trees. "Look well, O Wolves," he said softly.

"Pardon?"

"Sorry. From Rudyard Kipling. It's a story about a boy raised by wolves. I'm not sure why the scene keeps playing over in my mind. Not as if Zack will ever belong to a pack."

"We are his pack, then." Lugh crouched down when Zack raised his head from his paws, tail thumping. "Which rather turns the story on its head."

"I guess it does."

The tone pulled Lugh's head around. Diego sat staring into the distance, pale and drawn.

"Diego, are you ill?"

"No." Diego bent and stroked Zack's thick ruff. "Not physically. I can't help thinking that I've done all this, though. Finn's illness. The vampire in L.A. The uncontrolled incidents of magic in humans." He swallowed hard. "Zack."

"What do you mean? How could you have done all of these things?"

"There haven't been werewolves in the world in the last century. Or magical illnesses. Or magic at all."

"Ah." Lugh thought long and hard how to answer this, afraid that he would drive Diego further into his self-recriminations. He covered Diego's knee with his hand. "For good or ill, light-wielder, this is the way the world was meant to be. If these things occur again, it is only because they have before. The world was slowly dying, yours and mine. You have restored it. The restoration has consequences, surely, but they are no more than the natural order of things. Sunlight and storm."

"Please don't lecture me about balance and order," Diego said as he jerked his knee away. "My beloved spouse has been sick for a month and Zack's a freaking werewolf!" He buried his face in his hands. "*Dios, ay Dios*...where will it end?"

Lugh rose, a sudden irritation prickling his spine. "There is no end. Only new threads knotted to the old. Until the stars cease to wheel above and the sun goes out, the ocean silenced, there is no end." He gestured sharply. "Come, Zachary. We must be prepared for what might come with moonrise."

The wolf heaved himself to his feet, licked Diego's hand and trotted after. While part of Lugh ached to leave Diego sitting alone and bereft, the greater part was irritated at the hand wringing when there were things to see to.

Footsteps echoed behind him on the path. "Please." Diego touched his arm. "Forgive me. I'm running on no sleep and too much worry. What can I do to help?"

Lugh leaned down to kiss the top of his head to accept his apology. "Barricade us in. No matter what you hear, no one opens the door until morning."

"But I could –"

"I know you could." Lugh held up a hand. "You could do any number of things. Better than I. But I think it's safest to leave it with just two. If he turns again, he may even know me still since I was with him during his last beast phase."

Diego clamped his lips together in a thin line, obviously considering further protest. "All right. But if you call for help, I'm coming to help."

"Fair enough. Does the room have what I requested?"

"Everything you asked for. And a few things you didn't."

"Thank you."

After much discussion, the room they had settled on was Zack's bedroom. As far as possible from the fae caverns, it also had the added virtues of storm shutters on the windows and heavy, masculine furniture. Lugh nodded his satisfaction as Diego closed and barricaded the door behind them. Everything breakable had been removed, including Zack's pictures and the mirror from the dresser. Lugh fully intended to have the beast well in hand before anything might be broken, but he didn't want to risk damaging Zack's few possessions.

The leather restraints lay on the floor. Zack nosed at them and took a strap between his teeth to shake it back and forth.

"That is not a plaything, Zachary. Please put it down."

Zack complied and sat watching him, tongue lolling out. He obviously understood far more as a wolf than he did as the were-beast. Lugh sat with him. They still had half an hour before moonrise.

"I will not hurt you." He took the golden muzzle between his hands, gazing into attentive gray eyes. "But I may need to do things I would not if circumstances were otherwise. I hope you will understand and that you can forgive me. What I do, I do to keep you safe and to keep you from harming all those dear to you."

With a little whine-yawn, Zack jerked forward to lick Lugh's face and butt at his chest. It seemed a gesture of comprehension.

Besides the restraints and the bottles of water Lugh had requested, Diego had piled clean towels and bed linens on the dresser and set a bottle of oil on the nightstand. The care inherent in these little gestures touched Lugh, regret stealing up on him over his earlier impatience.

Evening crowded out the light as the last fingers of sun vanished in the trees. He sat on the floor with Zack, unhappy anticipation making the minutes crawl. Softly, he sang of old deeds and battles to pass the time, with Zack curled up against his thigh. Soon enough, though, he felt the tug of the moon.

Zack whimpered and curled into a tight ball, muscles shivering under his fur.

"I hear you, my braveheart," Lugh said as he took a firm hold of his scruff. "Let it begin. We are ready."

He moved back, kneeling on the floor to keep his limbs out of reach of snapping teeth. A growl rumbled from Zack's chest, like distant thunder at first, growing in volume and threat as the storm of his change neared. Suddenly he twisted violently. With a snarl, he snapped at Lugh's exposed knee. The teeth only scraped, though, and Lugh seized the thick ruff in both hands, fighting to keep the struggling wolf down.

No more time for regret or reflection, Lugh's muscles strained as Zack lunged and jerked against his hold. The frightened, angry snarls soon alternated with whimpers. Sickening crackles and creaks of tortured muscle and bone echoed off the walls as the body under him began to change. Zack flung out a desperate howl as his paws grew fingers and his limbs elongated.

Sweat trickled down Lugh's back. He gritted his teeth as he struggled not to lose his grip. If he made a mistake here, lost his hold for even an instant, the chances of his survival would be a wager he didn't wish to take. He waited until Zack had fur-covered arms and legs before he moved.

"Forgive me," he murmured as he let go with one hand long enough to strike two hard blows behind Zack's ear. The change continued even though Zack lay momentarily dazed. Lugh snatched up two of the restraints and buckled them around Zack's wrists, then heaved him up onto the bed and lashed them to the bedposts.

Already recovered, Zack renewed his struggles, but now all Lugh had to do was deal with one leg at a time. Within moments, he had Zack fastened spread-eagle, face down on the mattress. Panting, Lugh took a moment to calm his pounding heart. The arrangement would keep them both safe through the night, but not if Lugh simply left him to howl and struggle against his bonds. Either the leather would snap or the bed would break, and neither would take long.

He eased onto the mattress, kneeling between Zack's widely spread thighs. Perhaps there should have been revulsion in touching what he had always seen as an abomination. But the body before him was still Zack, and though the madness had him in its grip and his body was a contorted parody of itself, there was still a strange and terrible beauty in its primal ferocity. Lugh's body responded to the animal need and he fought down his own urges, angry at his lack of control.

He palmed one of the furred balls and the were-beast stilled with a soft, needy whine. A simple stroke up and down the crease had the beast pushing up into his hand, hips pumping to drive his erection against the blankets.

"Good, that's it, my dear." Lugh spoke softly, murmuring encouragement. The first orgasm shook the bed with shocking speed. Lugh hoped that meant it might be easier to satisfy the hunger this time since the beast was less intent on fighting him and more desperate for his attentions.

He waited until the shuddering howls quieted, then spent a few minutes stroking the were-beast's back. The calm lasted only until he caught his breath. Lips pulled back from razor teeth, he turned his head and snapped at Lugh's hand, snarling and twisting against the leather. His teeth closed on empty air, which seemed to frustrate him more. After another moment, Lugh abandoned trying to soothe him as he thrashed more and more violently.

"Blood and thunder, Zachary," he muttered and reached underneath to grab hold of Zack's cock. "Calm yourself."

The musk of Zack's arousal, wild and heavy, made Lugh's head spin. It was all he could do to keep himself from plunging into that body. He uncapped the oil bottle, clumsy with one hand, and poured a small stream down the cleft between furred cheeks. Another whine of need told him the were-beast approved of the unexpected sensation.

He stroked with one hand, letting the oiled hand tease at Zack's hole and slowly stroke his balls. Careful never to let his fingers enter, Lugh concentrated instead on the hard, coarse-furred erection. It might frustrate the were-beast to be denied penetration but there was a line he would not cross. Necessity was one thing, violation another. Even if the beast wanted it, Zack most assuredly did not, and had made himself quite clear on more than one occasion.

Depending on who lay beneath him, Lugh was not always the gentlest lover. Many of his lovers had wanted harder, rougher, and had begged for it. But that was the distinction. They had given him leave.

Zack's body froze in a rictus of pleasure, teeth bared, before he jerked hard against Lugh's hand and let loose the howls of his second climax. Lugh fought his own needs down and brought him to completion repeatedly. At the seventh or eighth orgasm, Zack's furred hip rubbed against Lugh's achingly hard cock and he lost his battle. His seed spilled in heated white ropes across Zack's fur.

It almost seemed to be what the were-beast needed. After a few more wriggles and guttural moans, Zack drifted off into an exhausted sleep.

Lugh sat for a time on the edge of the bed, face buried in his hands, fighting back his tears.

Chapter Eight

Gathering Storm

The second principle of magic: things which have once been in contact with each other continue to act on each other at a distance after the physical contact has been severed.
—James G. Frazer, *The Golden Bough*, 1922

The second morning went much as the first, though this time Lugh fought off his weariness to watch the were-beast change to wolf in the early morning hours. Though no less disturbing in its sounds, the violence of the evening change was missing. With more slender limbs, the wolf slipped his restraints during the change and happily curled up beside Lugh to nap.

The last evening of the full moon, again, proceeded much as the second had. At the moment of change, though, the were-beast hesitated before he began snapping and struggling. He scented the air with a puzzled whine as if he searched for something. Lugh held out hope that perhaps the beast was trainable and might come to recognize him as a source of reward rather than threat over time.

The moment of peace was too short, though, and he had to stun Zack again before he could fasten him down. Holding Zack, touching him, even in this form, was torture, almost as if someone with malicious intent had granted a wish for him. *Yes, you may touch your love, hold him, bring him pleasure, but he will not know you, will only use you to slake his lust, and in the end will not recall your hands upon him or your tender words in his ear.*

He allowed himself to lose control more quickly this time, to see if the beast truly did crave his climax. Perhaps it was the waning moon or perhaps it was the scent of his seed that calmed him, but Zack settled into sleep soon after.

Lugh lay beside him, tormented and exhausted. At least his Zack would return in the morning. They would be able to talk then and Lugh would beg his pardon for all he had done.

Toward dawn, a low moan pulled him out of a dazed torpor. The were-beast pulled hard against the straps, teeth bared. His eyes rolled and he shifted restlessly before a howl leaped from him. Thrashing and snapping, the beast began his final change. Limbs shortened, shoulders broadened, the snout retreated to human features.

Lugh hurried to unbuckle the restraints as they pulled on Zack's arms and legs. The difference in length would be enough to yank his arms from their sockets.

Finally, Zack lay on his stomach on the mattress, wholly Zack and nothing else. His eyes glazed, he moaned in pain, seemingly unable to move.

"It's over, my braveheart." Lugh stroked his back softly. "All will be well."

"Lugh?" Zack shifted to gather his arms under him.

"Shh, lie still, my dear. You are most likely sore and exhausted."

"I don't..." Zack's voice was raw, as if his vocal cords had been scraped with a file. "What the hell...happened?"

"The change. You have been shifting from were-beast to wolf for three days."

Zack levered himself up on one elbow, blinking. "I...God...did I hurt anyone?"

"No one. You must rest."

"Bed...you're..." Zack sat up with a groan, clutching his head. His eyes roamed over the stained sheets, the restraints at the bed's four corners, the semen drying on his chest and belly. "What the...fuck? Lugh?"

"There were..." Lugh's explanation faded in the face of Zack's growing horror. He swallowed hard. "Zachary, please, let me explain."

"Explain?" Zack lurched from the bed and fell when his legs wouldn't hold him. "What in God's name did you do?"

Lugh rose, realizing too late that he was still stark naked. Dear gods, could it get worse? "The were-beast needed certain things. Hungered for things. It was either slake this need or fight it as it lusted after flesh."

Zack ran a hand over his back where the product of Lugh's own climax still lay drying. His expression flew swiftly from confusion to suspicion to horror. "You... Oh, holy shit."

"Zachary, I was only —"

"You were only what? Taking advantage?" Zack scuttled back when Lugh reached for him.

"It was to keep you safe," Lugh said miserably, letting his hand fall back to his side. "To keep everyone safe."

"You couldn't just chain me up until it was over?" Zack curled up by the wall. "God...oh, my God..."

Lugh knelt out of reach so he wouldn't be looming. "I hoped to keep you from harm. There was such violence in the beast, such —"

He saw the fist coming before it struck and braced himself so he would not pull away. Zack connected with his jaw with war-hammer force, rocking his head back.

"You bastard! You selfish, fucking bastard!" Zack's hoarse voice broke and wavered even as he bellowed. "Couldn't get what you wanted by asking, so you had to take it?"

"I did not think —"

"No, of course you didn't! There's no fucking way you could understand! A two-thousand-year-old being with hundreds, maybe thousands of lovers under his belt, how could you?" Zack curled around his knees. "Fuck, oh fuck. Please, leave me alone. I don't want to see you. I don't want to hear your voice. Please. If you ever felt anything for me, just go."

"I cannot," Lugh said as he stared at the carpet. "Diego must let us out. Unless I break the door apart."

Zack crawled to the door and began pounding on it. "Diego! Diego, open the damn door! Now! Please, please, open the goddamned door!"

The door across the hall slammed open. Bare feet slapped against the hardwood in the hall. "Zack?"

"Diego!" A sob cracked Zack's shout. "Open it! Now!"

Heavy scrapes sounded on the other side of the door. The edges of the wood glowed white where Diego removed his barrier spell. The door flung wide even as Zack pounded on it.

Diego crouched to catch Zack before he could fall into the hallway. "Easy, easy, there. What's happened?" He glanced between them, face pale with shock.

"I have done harm here," Lugh murmured as he rose. He wrapped a towel around his waist, shaking his head. "I did not intend it, but I have. Zachary, I am so sorry."

"Sorry. He's sorry," Zack got out in a choked whisper. "I guess that makes it better."

Lugh heaved a shuddering breath, the ache in his chest growing to a sharp, agonizing pain. His heart was breaking. He felt as if he might die from it. Further words stuck in his throat as Diego took Zack in his arms, rocking his shaking frame gently. He didn't quite understand it, but Zack's anguish permeated the air. Somehow he had done terrible harm and had lost something infinitely precious.

He stumbled from the room, barely keeping his feet. Down the stairs, through the halls, he finally collapsed in one of the kitchen chairs, staring at the knots and whorls of the table. The meaning of the patterns eluded him, though, as he sank into silent despair.

* * * *

"Let's get you cleaned up."

Zack allowed Diego's soft voice and gentle hands to propel him toward the bathroom. A few years before, his unit had been caught in a mountain blizzard. In howling winds and frigid cold, they'd had to leave the shelter of truck canvas to dig and push the vehicles out.

Every muscle had burned, his limbs so heavy he felt as if he might break through the frozen ground.

He felt something like that now, except nauseous and dizzy on top of it all, and with a terrible sense of a dark chasm opening up under his feet.

"So Finn says that in his experience," Diego was saying as he filled the tub, "and, frankly, I don't really want to know where he gets experience with werewolves, but he says he has known them to be depressed after the change. I hope that's all this is, hon, and that you'll feel better after some rest."

He slid his hands under Zack's arms to help him up. While Zack wanted to protest that he could get into a damn bathtub on his own, his legs barely held him. Would this happen every month? Did it get better or worse?

"I'm sorry," he whispered as Diego lowered him into the water. The heat eased the ache in his muscles and joints but not the heavy pain in his chest.

"For what?" Diego sat on the tiles that surrounded the sunken tub, one hand still on his arm as if he feared that Zack might decide to slip under the water and drown. "So you planned to have a werewolf attack you and nearly kill you?"

Normally he would have laughed. He wasn't certain he recalled how. "For…I don't know. All the trouble. Worry. Strain."

"We care about you, hon. Can't help that."

"Yeah." Zack turned his head away, afraid he might see pity in Diego's eyes.

"*Mira*, you don't have to tell me what happened. But I'm here if you need to tell someone."

"Was it bad? The change?"

Diego laced their fingers together. "I don't know. I didn't see it."

"No one but him?"

"Right, no one but Lugh saw the actual changes."

"So that stuff he was saying about terrible hungers...he could've made it all up?"

"Well, no. I didn't see it, but I felt it. The were-beast, the madness, that is. And Finn did, too. It felt like..." Diego stopped, chewing on his bottom lip. "That black, hollow emptiness, the ravenous hunger. The wendigo felt something like that."

"Oh." Zack clung to his hand as the room tilted. "I don't feel so good."

He realized he had grayed out when a cold cloth pressed over his forehead, Diego calling to him from a few hundred miles away.

"Still with me?"

He glanced up at Diego, relieved when he only saw concern in those dark eyes. "I hit him."

"I figured that much. Your knuckles are split from hitting that hard head." Diego handed him the soap. "Wash up so we can get you back in bed. You want to tell me why you punched him?"

Zack ran the soap over his arms and torso mechanically, pulling on sore muscles. His eyes followed the ripples from his movements. "He tied me down to the bed and used me like a sex toy."

The long silence made him wonder if he'd embarrassed the hell out of Diego. Finally, Diego spoke gently, though a hard edge ringed his words. "Was there penetration? Did he actually use you that way?"

"How do I know?" Zack bit his lip as his shout echoed in the bathroom. He struggled to lower his voice. "I don't remember anything. Would I know that?"

"You'd probably be sore."

"Everything's sore." He heaved a shaky breath, hesitating over his next sentence. "I don't know. I really don't. Diego…that was my first time. With anyone. Doing anything."

"*Dios*. Oh, Zack, I'm so sorry." He laid a hand on Zack's shoulder. "I don't think he knew, either. He really was just trying to keep you safe."

A bitter laugh jumped from Zack. "Oh, yeah. Which is why I woke up with his spunk all over my back. Dammit. It's just as bad as getting someone drunk and raping them. I didn't have any say in it, couldn't tell him no or stop." His breath hitched and he ran a hand irritably over his stinging eyes. "Why did I bother saying no all this time if it was gonna end up like this?"

"My love?" Finn stuck his head around the door. "I've changed Zack's sheets."

Diego looked at him in obvious surprise. "Did you? That was very thoughtful, *mi vida*."

Finn shrugged. "One learns, living with humans."

With Diego on one side and Finn on the other, Zack managed to towel off and to make the walk back to bed. The hallway had never stretched out so long. His legs had never felt so much like rubber bands.

He settled back against the pillows after a long drink of water. "I don't want to hear that I have to talk to him, okay? I don't think I can ever look him in the eye again."

"No one will force the issue," Diego reassured him. "You want Finn to stay with you? I have to go downstairs for a few minutes."

"Yeah. All right." He might have fallen into an emotional pit, but he was smart enough to know he shouldn't be alone.

Finn curled up beside him. Weird how that felt completely natural and comfortable. Maybe not so weird since he trusted Finn completely. He had joked once that it was because he'd walked around with Finn's hand in his pocket and the hand had been a perfect gentleman. It had been a severed hand in a jar, but Finn still thought it was funny.

"Zack?" Finn watched him, black eyes unreadable. "The *sidhe* Champion has made me angry, too, at times. But is it truly such a terrible thought? To have lain with him?"

"You hear everything, don't you?"

"You were not terribly quiet."

"Yeah, well." He heaved a shuddering breath. *Shit, I am not going to cry.* "It wasn't the being with him, bud. It was how."

Finn propped his head on one elbow. "Shall I call challenge for you? Go and beat him senseless for causing you grief?"

"Um, thanks for the thought. You're still under the weather, though, and I don't want you getting hurt."

"Just as well, I suppose." Finn stretched out on his back. "Diego most likely wouldn't take it well."

* * * *

"Did you know he was a virgin?"

Lugh startled and his head jerked up. Diego leaned in the doorway, arms crossed over his chest. "Pardon?"

"Zack. Did you know?"

"Virginal?" Lugh grasped after a hundred thoughts at once, all of them skittering away. "But surely…a human male at his age… How could this be?"

"So you never talked about it. All the times you kissed him and groped at him, you never thought to talk to him."

"I wished to. The chance eluded us. I had made suggestions, certainly, proposed joinings. He always refused."

Diego's voice softened a hair. "Even knowing that, you still don't really know why, do you?"

"Why he refused me? I thought...no."

"You're right. Most males his age would have had lovers. Especially someone as hot and sweet as Zack. But certain things are important to him. Monogamy. Fidelity. Waiting for the right person to have that first experience with. He knows your history, your reputation, and I guess he figured you couldn't give him those things. He wouldn't have asked you to change for him."

Shame flooded through Lugh. He had acted on assumptions, on things he thought he knew about humans, and had stolen something precious from Zack, something he could not, even with all his power, return. "How do I make amends? How can I atone for this?"

"I don't think you can, big guy. Zack needs to work things through himself. You need to give him time. And space."

"Yes. Yes, by all means. Whatever he needs." Lugh yanked a hand back through his hair. "I am a great fool, Diego. I fear I have damaged things beyond repair."

"You do have feelings for him."

It was not a question. A shudder raced through Lugh. He felt as if he might shatter on the next hard breath. "Yes. He is...very dear to me."

Diego snorted but was kind enough not to press the question.

"I will go, then, so my presence here does not distress him. To the apartment in New York, I think. I will have appointments to keep in the city this coming week at any rate."

He rose but Diego caught him by the wrist. "Don't you dare translocate there. You take a security detail. Maybe a friend, too. You shouldn't be alone right now."

"But I am," he answered miserably. He pulled Diego into a hard embrace. He needed something to fill the void in his arms or the emptiness would devour him. "Don't fret so, little man. I may feel as if I will die of grief, but I know I most likely won't." *Perhaps.* "I'll...speak to Carol. Make proper arrangements."

"Good."

"Take care of him, please."

"We'll do everything we can."

* * * *

A scream jerked Mink awake. She looked across the room where Kara had sat up.

"Was that Will?" she whispered.

"Yeah, dammit. I wish Bran would muzzle him so we could sleep for once."

"That's not nice, Kara. Those dreams scare Will out of his mind. They hurt him."

Kara's eyes glittered in the moonlight. "Bran could wrap his lips around Will's dick. That'd shut him up."

"Ew! That's just... Bran would do that?"

"Well, duh. He is Will's boyfriend, you dork."

"No, I mean..." Minky flapped her hands in embarrassment. "Bran's, like, top, right?"

"Also duh. Bran likes the control. Likes to make Will squirm and beg and make those little seagull sounds when he comes." Kara did an imitation that was a little too close to the mark.

"Oh, God! TMI, TMI!" Minky clapped her hands over her ears. She hurried out into the hall, tugging her penguin-print pajamas straight. What Brandon and Will, or anyone, did behind closed doors was their business. She didn't want to hear about it. Asexual, Kara called her, saying she was sex-averse, too. *Maybe. Sex is just gross.*

Her inhibitions were a little odd to some people, she knew, but they weren't even the half of the weird situation. At first, it had just been her and Kara—the only person in Minky's physics lab who would sit next to her. From lab partners, they'd become friends and later roommates when they'd both wanted to move off campus. Kara was caustic, sarcastic and prickly, but she was a protective social shield for Minky.

Then Will had appeared one afternoon, coming to sit with them without invitation in one of the student lounges. He was quiet and sweet and seemed terribly lonely, so even Kara didn't have the heart to shoo him away. Will's elfin beauty drew plenty of eyes and eventually pulled Brandon in like a magnet. Brandon arrived in their lives like a hurricane, arrogant and sure of himself, full of ideas and energy. No one quite recalled agreeing to it, but he soon had them playing Dungeons & Dragons every weekend, old school, with paper and pencil, with calculations and adventuring done in their heads instead of, in Brandon's words, "some lame-ass program."

Others drifted in and out of this core group for several months, but no one else ever seemed to fit. It always came back to the four of them. Kara and Brandon bickered. Minky had conniptions over the increasing PDAs between Bran and Will. But they had fun together. They felt like they belonged together.

Then Nate sat at their table one day. With his sleepy smile and his tousled brown curls, no one questioned his presence, and suddenly, though no one said it, they felt complete. Nate fit, as no one else had, as if they had all known him for years.

The magic, the real magic stuff, came out of the woodwork soon after. An accusation of cheating one day left Nate wide-eyed and shaking. He had been rolling all sixes for two hours and Brandon insisted the dice were loaded.

'I'm not cheating," Nate had said in a small voice. "I'm just thinking about sixes.'

Brandon narrowed his eyes and handed him a different set of dice. "So think about threes instead."

Nate rolled, his eyes unfocused, and only threes showed topside for a full ten minutes.

After that day, they'd all begun to discover what Brandon jokingly called their superpowers. Kara could find lost things. Nate could move things with his mind. Brandon had a Voice he could use to influence people to do what he wanted. Minky could fade into the background, distracting people's minds from her so she went unnoticed. Poor Will had the most powerful and terrible gift. He had premonitions and vision dreams and they usually weren't nice. Lately, his dreams had gone from ominous to freaking scary.

Now, Minky raised a hand and gave a hesitant knock on Will and Bran's door. "You guys okay?"

Another scream answered her. Nate joined her in the hall, yawning and scratching his stomach. He completely bypassed her inhibitions and opened the door. One quick glance and Minky retreated into the hall. Brandon was naked, straddling Will. Never mind the fact that he was trying to pin Will's flailing arms, she still wasn't certain they hadn't interrupted something.

"Christ, Bran," Nate said on another yawn. "Quit fucking around and wake him up. He's gonna have a coronary."

Minky covered her eyes as a soft orange glow filtered from the bedroom. The others claimed they could never see it, but she could. Whenever anyone gathered power, she saw it. It scared the hell out of her. She willed herself to blend with the wallpaper. *You don't notice me. You don't see me.*

A roar like a dozen hurricanes gathered in the bedroom. Then Brandon let the power loose, using the Voice, his words huge and terrible as if they were written in twelve-foot scarlet letters in the air, impossible to disobey. "William! Wake Up!"

Scary, scary, scary…

"Where's Mink?" Kara had joined them and stood staring straight past her.

"Practicing how not to be seen." Nate waved a hand more or less in her direction. "She's here somewhere-ish. Being a fraidy cat."

"Not," Minky muttered and consciously let go the veil of magic that distracted people from her. If they were determined and stubborn, they might still see her, but her apartment mates usually didn't try too hard.

The sounds from the bedroom had shifted from screams to broken, gasping sobs. Brandon had passed out. Will wept on his chest.

"He overdid it again. No control." Nate shook his head as he walked over to the bed, checked Brandon's pulse then sat beside Will to stroke his back. "C'mon, man. You gotta tell it. Tough it out and let it go. Bran knocked himself out to call you back, don't let him down."

Will's breaths shuddered and heaved. He stroked Brandon's cheek. "I'm sorry, love. I'm sorry."

"Save it for when he's awake, idiot," Kara snapped. "Give."

Nate shot her a quelling look, kneading the knotted muscles at the back of Will's neck. Minky slid into the room and settled on the chair by the door. Tangled in the sheets, his face pale under his shock of white-blond hair, Will looked so vulnerable, so young. Hell, they were all young, Bran the oldest at twenty-one. This was way too much to put on a bunch of college kids. Failed college kid, in her case.

"Cyclones. Black cyclones," Will finally whispered. "Wherever they touch down, they leave everything twisted and charred. Ruin and horror. There were small ones at first. They came out of…out of unsettled clouds. But these…these were made. A powerful being made them. So much power. He'll kill us all."

"Was the being human or fae?" Nate asked.

"I don't…don't know." Will clutched Brandon's hand to his chest as if he needed one steady point in the universe. "He's so dark. So terrible. He shines with blinding light but devours all the light around him."

"You're not making any damn sense," Kara snapped.

Will swiped an arm over his eyes. "You wanted me to tell it. I'm doing the best I can."

Brandon woke with an irritated grunt. "Holy fucking hells." Will snuggled back into his arms while Brandon stroked his hair, staring up at the ceiling. "Somebody get me the aspirin. We can't just let it all happen. People are gonna die. I have an idea but I've gotta be able to think it straight through."

* * * *

Diego lay on his stomach in the meadow grass of the Otherworld, Danu stretched out beside him. The *sidhe* queen could be regal and terrifying when she chose, but this was the side of her Diego cherished, this half-wild mix of age and innocence that allowed her to sprawl in the grass with him watching crickets.

"What does one do with a werewolf?" he asked as he chewed on a violet stem.

"Kill it," she answered softly. "It is necessary for the evil ones and a mercy for the good ones."

"You know I can't, *majestad*. It's Zack. He gave up everything for us, and we love him dearly, Finn and I."

"We love him, too, Taliesin." She sighed and rolled to her side. "This is a human matter. So long as you keep this matter in the human world, I will not interfere. But I cannot help you. I know nothing of human maladies."

The way she said it implied that there was more. "Is there someone who might help?"

She stroked a curl back from his forehead. "Perhaps it is time to seek the advice of dragons."

Chapter Nine

Bane Sidhe

Interview, Sunday Edition, Sionnach Silvertongue and Angus Farseer, excerpt of transcript:

Interviewer: Do you agree with the strict restrictions on human travel to the Otherworld?

S: Honestly? I think it's simply too dangerous for humans. Too many unknown perils and possibilities that we take for granted. Very much like dropping a fae who has been out of touch with humanity for some time into the heart of Manhattan.

A: I suppose that's a joke at my expense.

S: Sorry, love, but I'm not the one who was mugged on Fifth Avenue.

A flash of red zipped past Zack's window. He surged up to press his hands against the glass even before his eyes focused properly. Heart hammering, he watched with avid interest as the cardinal flitted from branch to branch in the apple tree outside his window.

What the hell? He was practically panting, muscles quivering at being denied a chase.

"Acting like a damn dog. That's what it is," he muttered. "Gonna have to watch that."

He stretched to pop his back. Oh, that felt good. He felt good all over, surprisingly so, strong and better rested than he had in years. His shoulder didn't even twinge anymore. A glance down revealed the wound finally closed, a pink scar where the angry, seeping red had been. The werewolf's teeth marks had gone from refusing to heal to month-old wound status in a matter of three days. Maybe there were small benefits to being one of the shaggy set.

Lugh's scent still permeated the room. It should have made him angry, but the spicy male musk filled him with longing, the ache around his heart matching the one spreading through his groin. He wanted to go back, wanted to say things that should have been said, wanted —

"Wait. Why the hell do I smell him at all?" He drew in a slow, careful breath. Lugh. His own sweat. The wood. Different kinds of wood smells from the furniture and the floor. Fabric softener from the towels on the other side of the room. "This'll take some getting used to."

He slipped into his bathrobe, grabbed hold of the doorknob and yanked it right off. Shocked, he stared at the metal ovoid in his hand. A clank from the hallway told him the other half of the knob had fallen off. At least he didn't have to call for help to get out of his own bedroom again. Easy enough to reach inside the door and pull the latch open.

His eyes met feline ones when he opened the door.

"It seems your door has broken," Eithne said, glancing between the knob in her hand and its mate in his. "Shoddy craftsmanship."

"Um, right." With exaggerated care, he took her half of the assembly and put the whole mess on his dresser. "Are there things I should know, your furriness? About this whole lycanthropy thing?"

"You are the first werewolf I have known. What sorts of things?"

"I can smell stuff. I mean, of course I could smell before, but now it's new stuff. Like maybe you would. Or maybe a dog would." He wrapped his hand around a bedpost and lifted. The head of the solid oak bed rose three feet without much effort. "And I seem to be stronger. I don't know how much yet."

"Ah." She took his arm and led him down the hall. "Perhaps these are things that will pass as you grow further away from the full moon. Or perhaps there have been true changes to your human body. For now, I think I should turn on the shower for you so Diego need not replace those knobs as well."

"I can replace a doorknob," he said as his face heated. He let Eithne turn the water on for him, though, and promised to be more careful.

Breakfast smelled heavenly. Bacon, eggs, toast, hash browns, coffee — each individual scent competed for his attention, making his stomach growl and his head spin. He managed to make it to the table, showered, shaved and dressed, without any more breakage.

Diego turned from the stove to grace him with a smile. "How do you feel?"

"Honestly? A little too good."

When he had explained about the bird, the doorknob and his new super-nose, Diego only nodded. "I guess we have to expect side effects."

"Is that what we're calling this? It's not some pharmaceutical thing."

"No. That would come with a long-winded, legal-vetted pamphlet ending with 'in rare cases, patients have suffered stroke and even death'."

"Funny guy." Zack closed his eyes and sighed in satisfaction when Diego set a plate in front of him. "But I think I can forgive you."

Diego settled across from him. "And Lugh?"

"I'd like to be able to eat, Mr. S. Can we not talk about him?"

"Sorry. He's gone to New York, just so you know."

Zack tried to steel his heart against the roil of emotions churning there. The prince had run. First sign of trouble and he ran away. It confirmed what Zack had suspected about Lugh and relationships, but it also left a gaping hole in the center of his chest that he was gone. Why the hell did he still care?

"He took staff with him?" There, he could be professional about all this.

"Marcus and Kevin for security detail."

"That's it?"

"That's all he would take."

"No one to keep him on schedule? No extra hands for the dinner with the Secretary General?"

"I had a hard enough time getting him to take two. He wasn't quite himself when he left."

Zack shoved the rest of his bacon in his mouth to gain a moment. *I don't feel bad for him. I'm not the bad guy here. I don't care if I hurt his feelings.* Except he did, and no matter how furious he was, he still worried. "Maybe I should go out there."

Diego raised an eyebrow at him. "Probably not your best idea this week. Besides, I have a different mission for you. After breakfast, I'd appreciate it if you get dressed appropriately for the Otherworld."

"Danu want to see me or something?"

"No, we're going on the journey you've always wanted." Diego took a sip of his coffee, regarding him closely. "You and I, we're going into dragon territory."

Fork halfway to his mouth, Zack stared at him. "Seriously? You're not doing this to...I don't know...distract me?"

"If I could take all the pain away so easily, I would. Eat your breakfast, hon, or at least close your mouth. I don't know what's really happened to you, in terms of what's happened to your body, or what to do about it. Neither do the fae healers or Danu or Balor. The internet is hopeless on the subject. There aren't any reliable books. Danu suggested we talk to the dragons."

"Dragons. Wow. It's just...wow." Embarrassed all over again, Zack ducked his head and plowed through the rest of his breakfast. Apparently, the sooner he was ready, the sooner they would leave.

* * * *

The hardest part had been deciding what to bring. Oh, the little bit provision-wise was easy, and the canoe Diego had requested. But dragon visiting required a gift. He'd been told that enough times to have it sink in. He discarded anything with steel parts, thought about bringing duct tape, but decided that might be too dull, and finally settled on a Rubik's cube. Geeky? Hell, yeah. But it was plastic, colorful and a visual riddle, all things dragons were supposed to appreciate. At least Finn said they liked plastic.

The poor lonely pooka wasn't happy about his husband going off without him, but the tears and arguments had all been spent by the time he came to say goodbye. He pulled Diego into his arms and gave him a kiss hot enough to curl an iceberg's toes. Zack had to turn away. Their open affection didn't embarrass him, but it was a knife through his heart to watch such unquestioned faith and understanding. Finn hated being left behind, but he knew Diego had to do this, knew that he would return.

Semper fi.

At Cian's Ford in the Otherworld, fae from both courts stood on the bank of bright green grass to see them off. Colors had always seemed so much brighter to him here than in the human world, jewel-tones of heartbreaking clarity. Now the colors were so vibrant, so alive, he thought they might speak. Maybe it was his excitement, but maybe the change had affected his sight as well.

"You should have a guide." Sionnach tugged on his arm, his voice trembling. "You should not go alone."

"I'm not alone, beautiful. Diego's with me." Zack turned to him, concerned.

Sionnach flung his arms around Zack's ribs, bare since he wore nothing but the cornflower blue petal-cloth kilt King Balor had given him.

"You're shaking. What's wrong?" Zack held him tight, uncertain what else he could do.

"There has never been..." Sionnach started and shook his head when his breath hitched. "You are the first. The first were-being to be granted safe passage. Balor and Danu have both decreed it. But there are those outside the courts' influence. I am frightened for you."

I'm kinda frightened for me, too. "It'll be fine. You know I'm tough, and I've got the most powerful human sorcerer on the planet with me, right?"

Sionnach stroked delicate claws through his hair. "Stay to the river, Sergeant, for as long as you can. It will be safest. Even so, you must cross through *bane sidhe* lands. They may only watch and let you pass. They may try to delay your progress. If they show themselves, be still. If they bind you, do not struggle."

"Um...okay." Zack filed the information away, knowing enough about fae at this point to listen to any warning, no matter how odd or veiled. "I got it. Now, dry those pretty green eyes. You're beautiful when you cry but you're kick-ass gorgeous when you smile."

Laden with well wishes and bits of advice, they were finally able to disentangle themselves from the worried fae and begin their journey downriver. Zack, the more experienced boatman, took the rudder position. Since they headed downstream, he could have kept them to a good pace on his own, but with Diego to help paddle, they sped along.

Profusions of flowered vines overhung the banks amid dark cypresses. In many spots, the vegetation stretched over the river in astounding cathedral arches of emerald, pendulous, melon-shaped flowers in scarlet and gold, swinging like strange, alien bells in the breeze. The spice and tamarind scent overwhelmed Zack at first, making him dizzy and a little queasy. Eventually his new senses grew accustomed, though, and he started to pick up other scents underneath the flowers. The sharp smell of river mud competed with the earthier tones of wood and dozens of smaller scents that teased at him but he couldn't identify them.

Enough to make a guy nuts. "Diego? What's the river called?"

"This is the Alainn. I'm told it means 'beautiful'."

"Not the most original name."

Diego laughed. "No, but the fae aren't always complicated. They enjoy the obvious, too."

Zack wasn't sure if he meant more than what he said but he let it go in favor of guiding them around fingers of rock in the middle of the current. They spent most of the day in companionable silence, each lost in his thoughts. It still amazed Zack how comfortable and comforting it was to be with Diego. A short, whirlwind year ago, he'd been all fanboy nerves when they'd told him who his patient was. His colleagues had been clueless, but Diego Sandoval had been, and still was, one of Zack's favorite writers. Too bad he didn't have as much time for writing anymore.

And a lot of that's my fault. Damn it.

When they started to lose the light, Zack searched the banks for a likely place to beach the canoe for the night. He steered them to a sand spit where stones had forced the riotous vegetation to leave an empty space. At first glance, the flint-gray rocks seemed just another random tumble, left behind by some natural builder — flood, earthquake, the unstoppable creep of glaciers. On closer inspection, he realized the surfaces were too smooth, the shapes too regular.

"I thought the fae didn't build," he said, his voice soft out of respect for the ancient stones.

Diego gave him an odd look. "The *sidhe* don't, but you know the Fomorians do."

"Yeah, but never aboveground." He shook himself, trying to get rid of the uneasiness creeping up his spine. "And they're all immortal. Why let something fall apart like this?"

"I suppose there might be some of the same reasons humans do." Diego lifted their packs out of the canoe while Zack pulled it onto the sand. He took a deep breath, eyes closed. "I don't feel old violence here. More a feeling of...haven." He ran his hand over the closest stone. "I don't think this is a ruin. I think these were placed here just the way they are."

"Why?"

"There are no breaks, no cracks. It looks like a jumble to us, but I think it's purposeful."

"Maybe we shouldn't be here." A whiff of something caught at the edge of his senses, a hint of exotic spice but with a chill undertone.

Diego shook his head with an exasperated chuckle. "It's getting dark. I don't think we should be paddling at night, no matter how good your night vision's gotten." He turned away from examining the stones. "Whatever you're picking up from this place, is it threatening? Territorial?"

"No, just..." Zack hesitated, casting about for something concrete. "Just strange. Sorry. Guess the whole heightened senses thing has me edgy."

He settled next to Diego and fished a protein bar out of his pack. They would build no fires here, so food would be either foraged or cold. It would have been difficult to starve in the Otherworld, at any rate. Abundance took on new meaning here, with berries and nuts in hundreds of edible varieties everywhere one turned.

"So what'd you bring?" he asked between bites.

"Hmm?" Diego gazed into the little crystal sphere he always wore around his neck. What he saw in it, Zack couldn't imagine and he never asked.

"For the dragon lord, what did you bring?"

Diego cleared his throat and shot him a crooked smile. "Silly Putty."

Zack choked on a laugh before he thought about it. "Bet it's something they've never seen before."

"I'm counting on it. And I've done my research so I can explain the chemical structure if he asks."

"Surprised if he di—" Zack cut off abruptly. The strange, frigid spice scent hit him hard. "We got company."

Diego put a hand on his arm. "Don't get up. Stay still."

A tremor of adrenaline raced through him, but Zack stayed put, peering into the dark woods. He knew they were there but he still couldn't stifle a gasp when they materialized from the trees. His improved night vision picked them up quite clearly. Impossibly tall, at least ten feet, the willowy figures moved without a single snapped twig or leaf rustle. Their pale skin shone with a milky blue iridescence, their features so delicate and fine he thought at first they were all female. Subtle differences in body structure hinted at both sexes, though.

Male or female, seven of them surrounded the little camp and leveled spears at the human intruders. Zack swallowed hard, fighting against his instinct to shove Diego behind him. Those weren't primitive weapons pointed at them. They glowed and hummed in a way that made the inside of his head itch.

"*Bane sidhe,*" Diego whispered. "Don't move."

"Hadn't planned on it," Zack forced out against his dry throat.

One of the strange fae crouched in front of Diego. Silver eyes stared down at him like twin moons, without the distinction of pupil or iris. They lent an illusion of blindness but Zack was damn sure they saw everything.

"Light-wielder." The fae's voice sounded like half a dozen flutes played softly, trilling notes more than words. "Darkness follows."

Diego folded his hands in his lap and took his time answering. "There's always darkness. Do you mean my companion?"

"Your wake," came the non-answer. Then the silver eyes turned on Zack, the *bane sidhe's* lips pulling back to reveal sharp teeth. "Devourer."

Zack thought he probably meant the whole werewolf thing. "It's not something I wanted. I'd change it if I could."

"You will be sifted." The *bane sidhe* rose and gestured sharply.

Three more came forward, each holding a silver rope. Zack tried to keep Sionnach's advice in mind and stayed as still as possible as they fastened the first rope around his throat. His muscles trembled with the effort of inaction and his blood sang in his ears as the rope settled against his skin, so cold it burned. They bound his arms behind his back, each wrist lashed to the opposite elbow, then lifted him to his feet as if he were a child's toy.

Diego, he realized in a mix of irritation and relief, they left unbound. One of them simply reached down to take Diego's hand and began to lead him into the trees.

Afraid they were about to be separated, Zack called out, "Wait!" He lurched forward, trying instinctively to tug free. The rope around his throat tightened. His knees met the ground hard as he struggled for air.

He heard Diego pleading somewhere nearby, "Please don't hurt him. He's a friend."

"To whom?"

"To me. To the fae," Diego went on desperately. "To life."

The pressure eased and Zack pulled in a whole breath, dark spots flitting over his vision. They lifted him back to his feet and yanked off his kilt.

"He may yet live," the first *bane sidhe* said.

Zack stood stone still when he realized where the third silver rope was going. "Oh, you have got to be kidding."

One of the females tied the last rope around his cock and balls. She took the free end of this rope and used it as a leash. Even a small tug was enough to get him moving and Zack followed awkwardly behind her. He doubted it was meant as humiliation, simply a practical way to keep a captive's attention, but he still flushed hot at such intimate handling. *And God help me if I stumble...*

The trees soon gave way to meadow, the soft grass soothing against his skin. He tried to keep his mind off the rope around his genitals but the biting cold made it impossible. Damn it, it hurt, and forced him to an odd, splay-legged gait that did nothing to restore his dignity.

"Zack? You okay?" Diego called back as the ground rose in a gentle incline.

"I'm good. Mostly."

A hill rose before them so suddenly, Zack missed a step. Thankfully, one of the tall fae caught his elbow before he could fall. He could have sworn nothing had been there a moment before. Maybe they'd turned to the right or left and he hadn't realized it. *Hard to concentrate with cold silver fire acting as a cock ring.*

An arched opening appeared in the side of the hill, and he was damned sure that hadn't been there before either. The entire party trooped inside and Zack twitched in reaction when the arch snapped shut behind them. *Liking this less and less all the time.*

A narrow corridor took them through bare earth, forcing them to walk single file. One of the *bane sidhe* kept a hand on his shoulder, which gave him some hope. At least they were being careful captors.

The passageway opened into a huge space, the vaulted ceiling lost in the shadows. Luminescent fungi provided enough light so that even Diego didn't stumble on the uneven ground. He was up ahead, pleading with the apparent leader for Zack's release, explaining about the safe passage given by the courts. The male fae regarded him with what seemed to be a patient expression. Then he patted Diego on the head and motioned for him to take a seat on one of the moss-covered rocks.

"Diego?" Zack called to him as they led him to the center of the chamber. "You get a chance to go, you take it. Don't stay for me."

"I really wish people would stop saying things like that to me," Diego grumbled. "You don't seriously think I'd leave you."

"Serious as a heart attack. You're too important. They cut you loose without me, you beat feet."

"Going to pretend I didn't hear that." Diego reached up to touch the arm of the *bane sidhe* leader. "What will you do?"

"Sift him," he answered.

These fae spoke understandable words but in a completely different language. Finn had always said they were strange. He'd never really explained *how* strange.

The female with his cock-leash stopped, so Zack halted a step behind her. She threw back her head and uttered a piercing, ululating cry that jarred Zack's bones and made his heart stutter. *There's where the whole banshee shriek legend comes from...*

From the gloom, maybe from other chambers and hallways, maybe from the earth itself, dozens more *bane sidhe* appeared to join the original seven. They surrounded Zack, humming and trilling. None of them touched him, but his feet suddenly left the floor. He fought to stay calm and relaxed as his body levitated to horizontal, eight feet off the ground. They weren't going to let him fall. Why go through all this trouble just to drop him on his head?

Leash-holder coiled her rope and set it on his stomach. No more need to keep hold of him. He couldn't move anything but his eyes. Some sort of test or inspection was about to begin. All right with him as long as he wasn't going to be dissected.

He struggled to unclench his jaw. Helplessness wasn't a feeling he tolerated well. The *bane sidhe* gathered close, their chill scent making his head swim. Suddenly they moved as if they had one mind. Hands touched him, fingertips caressing his arms, his stomach, his thighs, his face. They touched everywhere—even the crack of his ass and the tender spot behind his balls weren't left out. He tried to think of it as a medical procedure, nothing more, and squeezed his eyes shut to help endure it. Their hands remained gentle but the uninvited contact felt like a violation.

The leader, who stood by Zack's head, made a chirping sound and all movement ceased. He pointed to a spot above Zack's heart, which meant, of course, that they all had to touch him there.

"The light..."

"Without him, hope dies..."

"Scudding clouds..."

"He mustn't..."

"It is the way..."

"To preserve it..."

"His heart is strong..."

He couldn't make a damn bit of sense out of what sounded like a debate. But after a long string of what seemed to him non-sequitur half-sentences from the group, leash-holder undid the ropes and took Zack in her arms to lower him gently to the ground.

They offered no explanation. Simply took him and Diego by the hand and led them back to their canoe. At the campsite, leash-holder crouched down to cup Diego's face between her hands.

"If only you could keep him near," she told Diego softly. "The dark comes."

With those incredibly unhelpful words, she and the others were gone.

Zack's muscles still shook from the strange ordeal, but at least they were both alive. He looked over at Diego, who was still staring into the curtain of cypresses and vines. "I'm kinda hoping that dragons are at least a little easier to understand," Zack said with a violent shiver.

Chapter Ten

Dragon Logic

For most humans, visiting dragons is not recommended. Their moods are difficult to gauge and a loss of temper, on your part or theirs, can be life threatening. If for some reason it becomes necessary to seek out a dragon, approach his territory slowly, unless you wish to be seen as a threat, and bring a gift, unless you wish to offend your host.
—D. Sandoval, *Basic Fae Relations*, State Department Publication, F-201-01-136C

"You're either with me or against me!" Brandon bellowed.

Kara advanced on him until they were nose to nose. Figuratively, since Kara's nose was at collarbone level on Brandon.

"That's gotta rate as the most epically stupid thing you've ever said!" she shouted back. "If one of your ideas is stupid, somebody needs to tell you! So I'm telling you!"

"It does sound kinda hard to pull off," Nate broke in more reasonably. "I mean, aren't the fae sort of ridiculous when it comes to alcohol? I read he's guzzled five pitchers, got up and walked away."

Minky sat curled in her corner chair, leafing through her copy of *A Pooka's Life* for the millionth time. It was one of her favorite books, but right now she was looking for a specific passage and she wished the rest of them would shut up.

The initial excitement after they found out Prince Lugh was in the city had worn off. The prince only came when he had appointments with U.N. officials and the core of Brandon's idea was a good one. Incapacitate the prince so that his human colleague, Consul Sandoval, would need to leave the island to keep these appointments. The bad part was, no one could figure out how to do it.

She found the passage she was looking for and smiled. She loved the way the pooka said things. In the book, Mr. Sandoval had called him Thistle, but everyone knew by now that he was really Finn Shannon, the Consul's lover and, more recently, husband.

"Catnip," she said into a break in the argument.

Brandon's head whipped around, his eyes blazing. "What the hell is that supposed to mean?"

Minky cringed, fading into the fabric of the chair.

"Please don't yell at her, Bran," Will said. "She can't explain if you scare her half to death."

"God." Brandon huffed out a breath, ruffling both hands back through his ebony hair. "Bunch of neurotics." He pushed past Kara and crouched in front of Minky's chair. "Okay, little bit. What are you trying to tell me?"

She wasn't trying to tell just him, but she wasn't brave like Kara to say so. "Catnip. It's, like, an intoxicant for them, like fae crack. Maybe we could smuggle some in to him."

Brandon's forehead creased and he had that condescending smile on his face. Minky wanted to slap him. It wasn't his idea, so he wasn't listening.

"And how in the world would you convince the prince to eat too much catnip?" he asked her in that too-gentle voice.

"Wait, hold up." Nate rose to pace. "According to *Fae Watcher*, he's only got two security men with him, and neither one's Morrison."

"Isn't that kinda weird? That he doesn't have his aide with him?" Kara asked, her voice still sharp.

"Not really. Poor sergeant's probably gonna be bedridden for a long time after getting mauled." Nate waved a hand impatiently. "Anyway, we're getting off track. So, three big guys in a condo, no staff to cook for them…what would you do, Bran?"

"Order out," Brandon said in a puzzled tone. Then he laughed. "Of course! They'll call for pizzas or something."

"Oh, please." Kara snorted. "You think the prince wouldn't smell freaking *catnip*?"

"See, I'm thinking we want him to," Nate continued, patting the air to stall further arguments. "He's without Morrison, and it doesn't sound like he's been out clubbing like he normally does, so he's already feeling kinda…"

"Depressed!" Will supplied, his eyes shining with excitement. "Yes! Everyone says they're lovers. So he has to leave his love behind on the island and the catnip would be like offering a bummed-out human a drink."

"And once he starts, he'll feel the happy buzz and keep going," Brandon said on a wicked grin.

"You got it."

"Nate, you're a genius!"

Minky rolled her eyes. It wasn't worth the argument.

* * * *

"Better this morning?" Diego asked as he rolled up their blankets.

"Much, thanks."

Zack was sure he'd scared the hell out of his traveling companion when he hadn't been able to stop shivering the night before. Diego had wrapped him in blankets, made him lie down and finally had lain down with him, curled up to his back.

"I'm a little freaked out still," Zack went on when Diego gave him a look. "But the weird, shaky feeling's gone."

"I think it was a physical reaction, not just being freaked out. They were reaching *inside* you. Not inside your body but inside your…" Diego trailed off. "Your aura, maybe? I don't know what else to call it."

"Do me a favor, Diego. Don't, please, don't tell me any more."

Diego nodded and shot him a little smile. "You do realize you've started calling me 'Diego' instead of 'Mister,' don't you?"

"Well, yeah," Zack grumbled. "I guess after someone holds you naked and wailing in his arms, it's kinda hard to be formal."

The rest of their journey downriver proved uneventful. When Zack asked why Diego didn't just make a door into dragon lands as he had to the hospital, Diego shook his head.

"The dragons need to feel us coming. And they will. It gives them a chance to gauge our intentions."

On the third day, they beached the canoe and continued on foot, over ground that became stonier and more sharply graded with every yard. Soon they climbed a steep path where Zack had to stop and wait every few minutes for Diego to catch up on his shorter legs. After one of these stops, Zack turned back to the path and halted, his way suddenly blocked by a golden-skinned young man.

Lithe and lean muscled, he wore nothing but a black torque at his throat, and as he approached, Zack had to revise his original impression. Not a young man, this was a fae of some sort, with the tapered ears of many Otherworld inhabitants. He had to blink, certain his eyes were picking up illusions in the bright sun. For a moment, he thought he had seen golden wings.

"There is nothing here for you." The golden fae stopped, arms folded over his chest. "Why do you hold your lives so cheap?"

Diego came forward, easing carefully around Zack. "My name is Diego Sandoval. I've come to seek council with Lord Hssetassk."

The fae threw back his head and laughed. "*You*, little man? You cannot be the Light-wielder, the great mage who flung open the Veil! And you bring this abomination with you?" He waved a hand at Zack. "I should end its miserable life and yours for your impudence."

Diego put a hand on Zack's arm. Not that he was going to rush the jackass and deck him, but he had to admit he felt like it. While he seethed, Diego smiled. He lifted his free hand and Zack felt all the hair on the back of his neck stand on end. The wind kicked up around them in miniature tornados. The air sizzled and popped. A softball's worth of plasma lightning hovered over Diego's palm.

"Shit. Diego, don't hurt him."

The fae backed up a step, suddenly far less sure of himself. Diego bounced the ball as if testing its weight, then hurled it into the clouds. A moment later, a clap of thunder deafened Zack.

A booming voice followed the thunder, echoing off the hillsides. "Are you daft, Gssetik? Bring the Light-wielder ere he leaves nothing of you but a pile of ash!"

"Yes, *skatath*," the fae, presumably Gssetik, replied in a small voice. Chastised, their antagonist became their guide and led them to the mouth of a cave set high on the hill. Cool air bathed Zack's bare skin, soothing after the sun's heat, and he took a moment once inside to let his eyes adjust.

He had to blink a few times, uncertain what he really saw. First, the cave seemed a comfortable size, with a ten-foot ceiling. Beautiful, golden-skinned young men lounged on stone sofas around the periphery. When Zack turned his head, the cave suddenly appeared massive, large enough to park a destroyer inside, with equally huge figures curled up around the edges — long, sinuous shapes with wedge-shaped heads, gleaming scales and wings. The young men were...

Dragons.

"The Were is not as blind as some." A deep, gravelly voice interrupted Zack's thoughts and the double-vision cave resolved into the smaller one. The voice belonged to another golden fae, this one larger, obviously older, power washing from him in almost visible waves. Arms crossed over his massive chest, his only clothing the mass of golden hair tumbling down his back, he stood in the center of the cave beside a stone table. "Our Knight of the Pen comes to us with a curse in tow. This is an odd way to begin a polite visit."

"My Lord Hssetassk," Diego offered, as he pulled Zack along to approach the older dragon. "I wish the visit could have been under different circumstances. But first, I've brought a strange substance which I thought might interest you."

He rummaged in his pack and handed the red plastic egg to the dragon.

With exaggerated care, Hssetassk opened the egg with one claw and tipped the putty out onto his palm. "Ah. Wonders from the human world." He prodded at it, pulling at it gently. "It is between one thing and another. How is it made?"

"It's a silicone oil, my lord, mixed with boric acid." Diego took out paper and pen so he could sketch the molecular structure for their host.

Zack found his attention wandering away from the technical analysis, especially since the naked young dragons decorating the room's perimeter were more interesting. Some slept curled on their sides, some read, and some preened and stretched. He had to look twice at a pair in the far corner. One with a red tinge to his golden hair crawled off his couch and onto his neighbor's where he began, without any conversation or apparent permission, to lick and suck the larger one's thick cock.

He turned away quickly, his face heating in spite of the cool cave, but the new direction wasn't any better. Another pair was going at it directly behind Hssetassk, growling and hissing while one flipped the other onto his stomach and impaled him.

The dragon lord looked up from Diego's papers. "Your Were is distressed."

"My lord, this is Zachary Morrison. He's only recently been cursed. Fionnachd might have mentioned him—the human warrior who helped rescue injured fae from the iron caverns."

"Ah. There are layers upon layers here. All the better. Might one ask the nature of your discomfort, warrior?"

"It's, ah…" Zack nodded toward the younger dragons, most of them now tangled in heaps of writhing limbs.

Diego glanced behind him, spots of color on his cheeks when he turned back. "Humans aren't normally accustomed to sex as a communal activity, my lord. Embarrassment, a fear of intruding, rather than actual distress."

Hssetassk shrugged. "They are young. Nothing but stomachs and cocks for the first few centuries. They begin to use their brains at some point." He pointed to several boulders, which rolled sedately up to the stone table. "Sit with me. Tell me of the human world and what has happened since I last laid eyes upon you."

"My lord. I don't recall ever meeting you," Diego said with a little frown.

"I did not say we met. I attended your nuptials, and saw you there."

"So you do come to the human world?"

"Infrequently. I prefer not." Hssetassk gestured impatiently at Zack. "Come, cub, settle. I believe we might both be civilized enough to keep our teeth to ourselves."

Zack slid onto the boulder seat across from him. Hssetassk was beautiful in his fae form, hard-muscled and imposing, but the dragon form still appeared as an overlay when Zack turned his head, and the dragon was spectacular. Gleaming gold with a pearlescent underbelly and throat, he would have been blinding in full sunlight.

"Gssetik." The elder dragon gestured to the youngster sulking by the wall. He approached warily and Hssetassk hooked a claw in his torque to pull his head down for a ravenous kiss. "We have guests, beloved. Bring the bowls."

It hit Zack suddenly that all the dragons were male. "Gssetik... He's your mate?"

Hssetassk stared at him with narrowed eyes, his strange vertical pupils contracted to slits. Then he made a strangled sound and burst into laughter. "Oh, poor cub! I glean that you meant no offense. You are without malice or guile. Though the thought of my Gssetik trying to lay is amusing."

"I think we have a semantics issue, my lord," Diego said with a little smile. "Zack meant a life companion, not someone with whom to make offspring. Does your mate live here, too?"

"Great Mother forbid," Hssetassk said as he leaned back to regard Diego in obvious horror. "My poor *laptas* would be slaughtered in days."

"*Laptas*?"

"My...fosterlings." He waved a hand to the orgy going on around them. "The younglings who belong to me."

"I'm sorry I'm so ignorant, my lord." Zack spoke softly, biting down on his injured pride. "So the females live somewhere else?"

"Yes. As is proper and sensible. They do not allow males in the nesting ground. For good reason. The younglings have no sense and the females prefer their own company. My mates call across the valley to me when they are in season and I visit briefly. You are not ignorant, cub. What human has seen aught of dragons these past centuries?"

"Yessir, that's true." Zack reached in his pack and brought out the Rubik's cube. "Though I know enough to bring something to give you."

"Ah! It is lovely!" Hssetassk's eyes devoured the cube. "A handsome gift, indeed. It is of that material made from the black water? Plas-stick, I believe the pooka named it?"

"Plastic, yes, and you can turn a layer at a time." Zack demonstrated before he handed over the cube. "To move the colored squares until each side is one color."

"I see. Clever indeed." Hssetassk's fingers twisted and spun the cube with delicate precision. He had the puzzle solved in thirty seconds, but didn't seem at all disappointed. "Marvelous."

Gssetik returned with bowls and a pitcher, and settled primly at the older dragon's feet.

"Try your hand, beloved." Hssetassk re-scrambled the cube's sides and handed it over. "It is a soothing puzzle."

With a little cry of delight, Gssetik seized on the cube and was soon engrossed in its movement. He had the original puzzle solved quickly as well, but then set about creating other patterns. A distracted smile played over his beautiful face as he leaned against Hssetassk's thigh.

"Beloved, manners," the dragon lord growled even as he stroked Gssetik's hair.

"Thank you, Were." Gssetik glanced up at Zack from beneath lowered lashes. "It is a wondrous gift."

The seductive look shot heat right to Zack's groin, ratcheting up the discomfort factor, but it was a hell of a lot better than the open hostility from before. "You're very welcome." Zack leaned his forearms on the table to address Hssetassk again. "Sir, is it rude at this point to tell you why we're here?"

A golden brow arched at him. "Abrupt, at the very least. I have many questions before I ask your purpose."

Shit. I was supposed to let him ask. Zack swallowed hard and plowed ahead, since the damage was already done. "Yessir. It's just...I'm getting the weird feeling time isn't our friend right now."

Hssetassk leaned toward him, flicking a disturbingly reptilian, forked tongue. "You have the scent of the hill people. They have told you aught."

"They told us precious little, my lord," Diego offered. "But what we could understand was disturbing."

"That they had a werewolf in their hands and let him go is disturbing enough," Hssetassk replied softly. "It is more common for those who go into the hill never to be seen again than otherwise."

"They seem to think I have something important to do, sir," Zack said.

The dragon lord nodded. "Yes, that would follow." He leaned back to scoop Gssetik off the floor and settle him in his lap. "But I do not engage in prophecy, at least not in such specifics. This is not why you came. Why have you sought me?"

"We had hoped, my lord, that you might know of something," Diego began, paused on a sigh, then rushed forward again. "A cure for lycanthropy, maybe, or some way to separate Zack from the were-beast, keep it from happening."

"Ha. You may as well request a cure for being human." Hssetassk held out his hand to Diego. "The only cure is death. To release him and allow him to continue to his next life. The Mother has gifted humans with this possibility."

Diego settled his hand in the dragon's grasp, a stubborn set to his jaw. "But if it's magic, the curse, then there has to be a way to undo it. They've told me before that I couldn't do things that I did."

"Hmm, yes. Those who told you did not take all the variables into account." Hssetassk turned Diego's hand palm up and held a claw over his index finger. "May I? Merely a drop?"

"Of course."

Diego winced when the claw punctured his finger and Zack with him. The medically trained part of him wanted to protest that the claw wasn't sterile and might not even be clean. But he figured the dragon didn't need further reasons to be offended. He only hesitated a hair when Hssetassk requested his blood as well. The finger prick was as neat and precise as any lancet. Zack couldn't complain about his technique.

"So." Hssetassk gestured at the blood drops on his palm. They expanded until Zack could make out individual cells and even further, to what he suspected was a subcellular level. The blood drops now formed twisting spires on the table, Diego's on the right, Zack's on the left. The center structures bristled with numerous protrusion, knobs and spikes in unfathomable patterns while motes of light whirled and settled, illuminating and casting fleeting shadows.

They reminded Zack of pictures of space stations from science fiction books and fairytale towers and…

"DNA. Dear God. Diego, do you see it?"

"What is this word?" Gssetik asked, tilting his head to look at the expanded blood.

"Genetic structures," Zack told him. "The blueprints, the design for a person."

"Yes. Good." Hssetassk nodded. "The central structures contain the inheritance, all that has been before. The smaller structures are the architects, which tell the structure how it will manifest. And the little ones, the *kelan*." He indicated the light motes. "That is how the world's magic reacts to the structure."

Zack felt an odd twinge of disappointment. Diego's *kelan* glittered on nearly every spike and prominence of his tower. The lights danced and swirled in eddies and currents, competing for space. Zack's looked like a half-abandoned ghetto housing project. A few sad lights shone here and there on the structure. Isolated colonies of sickly yellow-green huddled in crevices but the remaining motes seemed repelled and refused to settle anywhere on the blighted surface.

"I'm all…dark," he said, unable to keep the quaver out of his voice.

Hssetassk regarded him with a frown. "This causes you pain. Though it is not so unusual for a human." He gestured to Diego's tower. "That is unusual. But humans and magic are a difficult study. *Kelan* distribution in any fae is a product of bloodline. One young dragon will look much like another. A young *sidhe* like his cousin. We gather power as we age in our own distinctive racial patterns."

"And humans?" Diego asked.

"Humans are subject to the variable patterns of their kind. It is part of the wonder of being human. No two humans react in the same way to magic, even under identical circumstances. While some part of a *kelan* pattern might be inherited, there are myriad factors that influence how it will grow. Past lives. Encounters with magic beings and places of magic confluence. Terrible tragedy. Overwhelming joy. Contact with warped *kelan*."

"That's those, sir? The sick-looking batches?" Zack stared at them, a lead ball in his stomach.

"There are most likely some among those clusters, yes."

Diego got up for a closer look. "So if we removed them, Zack would be cured?"

"I suppose if you wished to kill him in the most painful way possible that you might try." Hssetassk shook his head. "Those are his *kelan*. You cannot remove them any more than you could remove his head and expect him to live."

"Oh." Diego settled back on his rock, obviously disappointed.

Zack patted his arm. "Guess I have to learn to live with it. Maybe it won't be so bad. Modify one of the rooms in the caverns. Lock me in. It's only three days a month, right?"

"Zack..."

"The rest of your *kelan* pattern does intrigue me, though." Hssetassk rested his chin in his palm. "Werewolves have so often lived in isolation, when they have been allowed to live at all. For human magic, isolation rarely allows new patterns to develop. Hence the practices of apprentices and covens among human mages. While you cannot excise the curse, I wonder if it will…evolve over time."

"Christ. You mean I might be more of a monster later on?"

"Who can say?" Hssetassk shrugged. "More likely, given your temperament and your circumstances, is that you may find a way to pattern the unsettled *kelan* in your blood. To acquire more conscious use of your potential."

Zack weighed the words carefully. "You mean work magic, sir? Like Diego does?"

The dragon's deep laugh vibrated through the floor. "Never as he does, cub. He is without peer. And, as I have said, every human is unique." He turned his head to nuzzle at his lover's jaw. "So like snowflakes. Equally singular and equally brief."

They talked for several hours more since the dragon lord had questions about the human world. His *laptas* moaned and growled through their multiple bouts of sex, but no one paid any attention. Toward evening, Hssetassk finally rose from the stone table to bid them farewell.

He put a hand on Zack's shoulder as he led them to the mouth of the cave. "Perhaps you will be a true shifter someday. Like the *sidhe*."

"I guess miracles can happen, sir." Zack glanced up at him and realized with a pang that he was the same height as Lugh. "Sir? Aren't dragons shifters?"

"No, cub." The fae shimmered and became a lion, then shimmered again and suddenly the true dragon, in all his shining glory, stood beside Zack. "A shifter becomes the form he takes. Dragons may take on different skins. But a dragon is always a dragon."

Zack walked down the path with Diego, deep in thought. Maybe they hadn't found a cure but he sure as hell had seen a lot on their short journey. He knew about the lack of sexual inhibitions among the fae, but experiencing it in such varied forms had driven it home. Lugh wasn't human, no matter how well he interacted with them. He'd been raised fae.

It had never occurred to Zack that something so basic, so ingrained for him, might be a struggle for the prince. Lugh had handled it badly, but maybe, just maybe, he had overreacted. Another thought suddenly occurred to him.

"What's the smile for?" Diego bumped shoulders with him.

"I was just thinking," Zack said on a helpless chuckle. "It's normal for dragons to be gay."

"It's normal for us, too, hon."

"Um, right, but lots of people wouldn't agree with you."

Diego's brows furrowed. "It's certainly interesting, though. I wonder if a truly hetero dragon would be considered an outcast."

"Maybe there just aren't any."

* * * *

Lugh sank into the overstuffed chair in the condo's living room. The gallery opening had exhausted him more than any battle ever had. Smiling and making polite conversation with a shattered heart was more difficult than he had imagined. He felt like such a fraud, pretending he understood humans when he had misunderstood so badly the one human more important to him than breathing.

"Highness? You didn't eat much at that shindig. Are you hungry?" Kevin leaned his head in from the kitchen.

"No, I…" Lugh waved a hand in negation, unable to speak past the lump in this throat.

"Well, we're gonna order pizzas, sir. Maybe you'll change your mind once they get here."

"Perhaps." He couldn't even find the energy to remove his jacket. How could he summon any to eat? Zack's face haunted him, horror-stricken and repulsed. If only he had found another way. If only his Zachary didn't hate him now.

Chapter Eleven

Bedroom Diplomacy

The very essence of romance is uncertainty.
—Oscar Wilde, *The Importance of Being Earnest*

"I could get in trouble for this." The delivery boy eyed Brandon's wad of cash hungrily.

"Who'll know? I'll pay you for the pizzas, you get an extra thirty bucks, and the girls get a peek at the prince." Brandon turned on his most charming smile and Minky fought not to roll her eyes. "C'mon, dude. Help a guy out here."

"Well. Okay. Since it's like that." The cash disappeared into the boy's jacket pocket and he handed the pizzas over before he sauntered away.

With a little judicious snooping and help from all the fae-obsessed blogs, it had been easy to find out which takeout places the prince's security trusted while they were in town. A few hours watching the door to the building until a delivery guy showed up was all it took after that.

Brandon set the stack of pizza boxes on the floor and opened them one at a time. "Hmm. Sausage. No. Pepperoni. No. Ah, here's a mushroom one. That's for the prince. And a spinach one. Think spinach and catnip go together?"

"Not the time to go all Iron Chef," Kara snapped. "How the hell should we know? Just do it."

"He has to eat it, right? If it tastes nasty, he won't eat it," Brandon said but he took the economy size bag of catnip out of his trench coat and sprinkled it over both non-meat pizzas. After a moment's consideration, he left a generous pile under the mushroom pizza as well.

"You think he'll eat it plain?" Minky peered over his shoulder.

"I think if he's snockered enough, he'll inhale it." Brandon closed the boxes and stood. "Okay. You two stay here. If this goes bad, run."

"As you wish, oh, king of melodrama," Kara said with a snort.

All the same, both Minky and Kara snuck to the bend in the hallway where they could hear the conversation at the prince's door.

"You're not the regular guy."

"Yeah, yeah, he called out sick. Somebody's gotta run the damn deliveries."

"Well, you be careful out there, kid. Lots of delivery guys getting jumped these days."

"Yessir. I'll stay sharp. Thank you, sir!"

Brandon swaggered back around the corner, a shit-eating grin on his face.

"What?" Kara whispered.

"Security dude gave me a freaking huge tip."

* * * *

"Highness? You wanna at least come and pretend you're hungry?"

Lugh heaved himself out of the chair with a sigh. His boys were concerned. It didn't do to worry them. When he entered the kitchen, a heavenly scent wrapped around him.

"Ah, catnip. That was very thoughtful, Kevin." He opened one of the boxes and inhaled the promise of oblivion.

Kevin leaned in to look in the box. "I didn't order catnip, sir. Didn't know it was an option."

"The kind ladies at Mario's must have been thinking of me, then. Would you like to share it with me?"

"Ah, no, Highness." Marcus shoved the two catnip-laden pizzas at him. "That's all you. A little oregano's nice but that's taking it too far."

"Very well. Would you be offended if I took these to my room?"

"So long as you eat something, sir, we're good."

Lugh nodded absently as he took the offered boxes. He had to be careful, of course, with a charity concert to attend the next afternoon and dinner with the Secretary General afterward. But a slice or two would do no harm. It would smooth the sharp edges from his misery and let him sleep. He needed sleep.

After two slices, he found the energy to undress. Good. Nothing worse than sleeping in one's clothes. It was excellent pizza, though, and he found he had an appetite. Three more slices vanished in short order.

A comfortable lassitude settled over him. His head felt as if it floated above his body. His lips had grown numb. A little more would be fine. He could handle catnip better than most. Just a little more to erase the image of Zack's anguish. He knew what he had done might not be well received. Anger, irritation over the loss of control, those things he expected, but he had been unprepared for the revulsion, the complete rejection. Zack had felt some attraction to him, he had been so certain. Somehow, he had misunderstood.

One pizza box sat empty. Such a sad sight. So he opened the second box. Delicious. *Damn Zack, anyway.* Lugh could have anyone he wanted, any of the hundreds of young men and women who panted after him at the clubs, begged and pleaded to be used for his pleasure. Why should he care what one prudish human thought?

A tear rolled down his cheek. Of course, he cared. Zack was everything he wanted, everything he needed. Warrior, healer, a soul both gentle and fierce, his advisor, his protector, his heart, his friend. Former friend.

Lugh began to sob as he devoured the remaining slices and every last scrap of catnip at the bottom of the box.

* * * *

Diego and Zack mounted the stairs to the embassy and opened the door to the sounds of shouting and running feet. For one heart-pounding moment, Zack was certain the building was under attack. Then Lori rushed into the reception room, breathless, but looking far more annoyed than terrified.

"Oh, thank God!" She seized Diego by the arm while he still struggled to get a shirt on. "You don't know how glad Carol's going to be to see you, sir!"

"What's happened?" Diego padded barefoot in the direction of the office.

"Everything's a mess. I'll let Carol tell you."

This wasn't immediately possible since they found Carol playing referee. Angus and Faolchú faced off, shouting at each other in the old language, words liberally peppered with angry gestures.

"Now, look, gentlemen." She stepped between them and eased them apart with a hand on either bare chest. "This won't help and you're scaring the staff. While I do agree that Captain Faolchú would do well in conversation, I don't feel comfortable sending him to a state dinner. Or have you finally learned to use a fork?"

Faolchú growled in a disgruntled way. "No. Ridiculous things."

"Right." Carol pushed on Angus' chest to ease him back another step. "And you, sir, can't have a conversation without turning it into an argument these days. Convince me that you can go out in the human world alone and not start a fight."

Angus turned away with a wordless, angry cry.

"Exactly." She turned and spotted Diego, relief draining the irritation from her face. "Mr. Sandoval! Thank goodness you're back!"

"Carol, what in the world's happened?" Diego asked softly, one hand on Angus' shoulder.

She shot a quick, uncomfortable glance at Zack and explained, "It's the prince, Mr. S. He went on a catnip bender last night and the boys can't wake him up. They even put him in a cold shower. He'll never make it to the concert this afternoon and he'll be in no shape for dinner tonight even if he does wake up."

"*Maravilloso*," Diego said in a dry tone. "Was he out somewhere? Is he at least in his own bed?"

"He stayed in last night," Carol said. "Apparently had the catnip on pizza."

"Of all the irresponsible…" Zack trailed off when Diego gave him a 'not in front of the staff' look.

"*Bien*. It's not so terrible." Diego raised his voice to be heard over the babbling din. "Please inform the appropriate contacts that I'll be attending in place of the prince. Just tell them he's ill and convey our apologies. I'll go change and make a doorway to the condo to get there in time. Does that sound like a reasonable solution?"

Several gusty sighs and "yes, sirs" answered him. Faolchú pulled Angus into a hard embrace, never one to hold onto his anger.

"I'm going with you," Zack said close to Diego's ear. "Just to the condo."

"You're sure?"

"I need to have a serious talk with him. This isn't like Lugh. He might fool around off duty but he's always been dead serious about his job."

Half an hour later, Diego had showered, shaved and looked fine in his best Armani suit. Zack had changed as well, for security detail, since Diego would need to take at least one of the boys with him. He felt better knowing they wouldn't be leaving Lugh short, and definitely felt more himself with a gun riding at his hip and sturdy boots on his feet.

He followed Diego through his doorway, careful to stand clear when Diego dropped his hand to let the way through snap shut behind them. Kevin and Marcus were waiting for them in the living room.

"Anybody want to own up on this one?" Zack asked his shamefaced subordinates. "How the hell did you let him get so shitfaced?"

"No excuses, Sarge." Kevin barked out. A retired Marine like himself, it was the expected response.

"Not accepting any. But I need to know what happened."

"He said he wasn't real hungry, Sarge," Marcus explained. "Not that we'd have known how much was too much, anyway. I mean, who gets high on catnip besides cats?"

"And when he locked himself in and started crying, we didn't think we should barge in. Just didn't seem right," Kevin finished for them.

"Okay, I can see that. So you found him this morning?"

"Passed out on the floor next to his bed. Breathing all right but unresponsive. Tried a cold shower. Tried ice on his back. Tried to get some tea in him…"

"Nothing."

Zack rubbed a hand over the back of his neck. "All right. We know better next time. Kevin, you're with Mr. Sandoval. Usual protocols."

"You're sure you're all right with this?" Diego asked.

"Go on. Get. We all have jobs to do here," Zack said with a little smile he hoped was convincing. Once the diplomatic party had gone, Zack went back into security mode. "Where'd the catnip come from?"

"Mario's."

"They've added it to their toppings?"

"Well, no…"

"So no one ordered it?"

"No." He could see Marcus' wheels starting to turn. "The prince thought the ladies put it on for him special."

"But no confirmation on that?"

Marcus flushed a dark red. "No, Sarge."

144

"You get on that. I'll go deal with His Highness."

Zack pushed open the door to the master bedroom and wrinkled his nose, discovering just how acrid catnip-drunk *sidhe* scent could be. "Damn it, Highness. You need a shower."

Not that the thought of bathing Lugh made him want to run away screaming. He lay sprawled on his back, covered only to the waist with a sheet, his hard body stretched out on full display. The thick outline of his erection bulged against the cotton. *Must be having one hell of a dream. God, I'm so stupid.*

He had no business thinking of Lugh that way. There could be no lasting commitment, so he wasn't starting down that road. The best he could hope was that they could come to an understanding and go back to a good working relationship. Yes, damn it, he was still pissed as hell and hurting, but he could put it aside and be professional.

Throwing open the curtains got no reaction. Neither did shaking Lugh and shouting in his ear. Worry crept in on spider feet. Was it possible to OD on catnip? He got a belt from the closet, folded it in half and twitched the sheet back from Lugh's hooves.

"Sorry, Highness," he apologized in advance. "But if this doesn't work, we need to get you medical help."

He hauled back and smacked the bottoms of Lugh's hooves as hard as he could, right over the sensitive parts in the center. A twitch and a soft moan gave him some encouragement, so he did it again.

Lugh rolled to his side with a pained groan. The sheet slipped to reveal his perfect, muscular ass. Zack had to fight to rip his eyes away.

"Highness? Can you hear me?"

"Zachary?" A scratchy parody of Lugh's voice drifted out from where he had hidden his head in his arms.

"It's me. Should I even ask how you feel?"

"Dreadful."

"Yeah, well. Serves you right." Zack turned, intending to get the aspirin from the bathroom, but he didn't get two steps.

Lugh jerked upright and rolled from the bed where his knees met the floor with a thud. He half scrambled, half crawled across the carpet, and flung his arms around Zack's knees. "Don't go, Zachary, please, don't go..."

What the hell? "Just want to get you something for your headache."

"Give me but a moment. Please." Lugh's grip transferred from his knees to his hand. "I have hurt you. And wronged you. I did not wish to but it makes no difference. I know the sight of me sickens you now. But I beg you to allow me to make amends. Set me a task, a quest, a series of labors as Herakles had set for him. Anything to mend what lies between us now."

"Whoa, there, Highness. Getting a little ahead of yourself there. You shouldn't be out of bed, let alone slaying hydras or whatever."

"Please, there must be something."

Zack swallowed against a dry throat, a quagmire of warring thoughts pummeling him. The hottest male on the planet knelt at his feet, begging for a chance to make things right. Said hottest male was close to tears, which Zack hated since it always turned him into a pile of nurturing mush. Not that Lugh ever used his tears to manipulate. He was just an emotional guy.

Aforesaid need to nurture would probably lead to other things, which Zack couldn't allow. The affair would only last until Lugh's need to fuck the next mammal with a pulse that caught his eye grabbed hold of him. *Shit. I'm such a mess.*

Against his better judgment, he reached out with his free hand and stroked Lugh's tangled hair back from his face. "Come on, bud. Let's get you back in bed. Let me help you. Then we'll talk like sensible people."

"As you wish," Lugh choked out.

Good a time as any to try out the super-werewolf strength. Zack bent down, slid his arms under Lugh and lifted him like a little kid. The prince was heavy as hell, he could feel it, but he didn't struggle or strain as he carried Lugh to the bed.

"Now, sit tight. Promise I'll be right back."

Lugh stared at him, speechless.

"Side effects," Zack said as he spread the sheet out over his patient.

He came back a few moments later with water, aspirin and a washcloth, which he handed over in order. "Wash your face off, Highness. You should probably have a real shower with soap and all but we'll wait on that."

"Zachary, please sit with me."

At least Lugh was calmer. Zack drew in a deep breath as if he was about to plunge into icy water, and eased down onto the edge of the bed. They sat in uncomfortable silence, each staring at his own lap.

"Grandmother would have slain you if you had harmed anyone."

"I know," Zack said softly, willing to let him get out whatever explanation he needed.

"I could not bear the thought. I only wished to keep you safe when I followed you out into the dunes."

"Not too bright. I could've killed you."

Angel Martinez

Lugh took a sip of water. "Yes. I had to take the chance. For you. If you had bitten me, there would have been no lasting harm. I simply hoped to keep you away from the others, to wrestle with you until the sun rose if need be."

"Yeah, well, you did a hell of a lot more than wrestle." Zack cringed at the bitter edge in his voice. The hitched, ragged breath from Lugh made him feel like a heel. So much for being professional. "Sorry, go on."

"It was by chance, in tussling with you, that I discovered the were-beast's need. No one would be in danger except me and I could keep you from injuring yourself rather than watching you thrash in your bonds until you broke bones or strangled yourself."

"So you fucked me?"

Lugh buried his face in his hands. "No. I would have hurt you."

"What then? Come on. Big, tough *sidhe* warrior should be able to get through this without falling apart."

"I simply touched you. I…used my hands to please you. Held you tight. Let you have what you seemed to need." Despite what Zack had said, tears crept out from behind Lugh's fingers. "It was terrible. To see you that way. To finally hold you in my arms and know…"

"Know what?"

"That you would have no memory of it. That you might hate me for it. Touch without warmth or joy. It was a torment."

Zack worried at his bottom lip with his teeth. He hadn't thought of that. Here he'd had some bizarre idea that Lugh had enjoyed sex with the were-beast.

"So…wait. You did climax, right? You did take some kind of pleasure from the whole thing?"

148

Lugh wiped the tears from his face, though his voice was still heavy and thick. "On a knife's edge, in fear and even in anger sometimes, the body can commit such betrayals. Sexual excitement can be tied to blood and violence. It does not make it pleasurable. I felt so hollow and empty."

"And you did this for three nights? For God's sake, why?"

"It matters not." Lugh shook his head miserably. "You have no faith in me."

"Damn it." Zack took Lugh's face between his hands and forced his head around. "Of course it matters. Especially when you're so miserable that you do stupid shit like eat ten tons of catnip. Why?"

Lugh tried to pull away but in his hung-over state, Zack was too strong for him. He sighed and closed his eyes. "Because...because you are the dearest thing in the world to me, my braveheart. I have loved you from the moment I set eyes on you, standing alone, fierce and defiant, against two fae Champions and an eagle-*sidhe* with madness in his eyes. You had no fear. You burned so bright. So sure in your convictions. So steady in the face of things you could not have known before."

"Oh. Guess that explains a lot." Zack shoved the dizzy warmth from those words down hard. "Look...I... It doesn't matter so much how I feel. Fact is, it wouldn't work. Great, you love me. That's great. But you need variety. They tell me you always have. I can't live like that. Start up with you, then wonder who you're screwing when you're not with me."

A terrible, choked sound caught in Lugh's chest. Zack eased him back against the pillows, worried he was having respiratory issues. Lugh's eyes held such anguish when they gazed up at Zack, he was sure his heart would break all over again.

"I have needed 'variety' because I have never found what I truly needed before."

"What's that, big guy?" Zack asked gently. "What do you need?"

"You. Only you."

The admission socked Zack right in the gut and sliced clean through all his carefully constructed defenses and his reasonable arguments. *Only you. Oh, God.* "Lugh…"

He leaned in, meaning to place a chaste, soft kiss on the prince's cheek. Lugh turned his head, though, and caressed his lips over Zack's. The tender, gentle touch was like a match to California brush in August. He seized Lugh's lips even as his own were captured, tongues competing to plunder each other's territory. Zack moaned as Lugh's tongue slid over the roof ridges of his mouth, all his years of lonely frustration coming to a high-pressure boil.

Lugh's hands slid up his chest, fingers shaking in his desperate haste to undo buttons.

"Wait." Zack caught his hands, kissing his fingertips. "Slow down a sec. This is gonna sound stupid, I know. But I've never done this."

"Never let someone undress you?"

"Um, no." Zack felt like his face might burst into flames. "Never made love to anyone. I mean, I understand the mechanics. Never had the hands-on training, is all."

Lugh's breath hitched as he jerked his head to the side and his hands fell away. "I know, my dear. I'm so sorry."

"No, no! Oh, damn, don't get all upset again." Zack rained kisses over Lugh's eyes and forehead, trying to distract him from tears. "Just...I've waited so long for this."

"Ah." Lugh pulled in a slow, shaky breath and his expression shifted to thoughtful. "There should be a sense of occasion then. And I'm not at my best. Perhaps I should clean up for you?"

Zack stifled a frustrated growl. *Right*. He wanted this to be special. No need to rush now, he had all afternoon and all night. *Only you...* The words sang in his head. Any minute now, he was going to wake up, alone and aching. "Good idea. You need help getting to the shower?"

"I'm feeling rather better," Lugh said as he levered himself up slowly. "I will manage."

While the prince hummed in the shower, Zack changed the sheets, cleaned up the empty pizza boxes and discarded, rumpled clothes and tried to calm his jangled nerves. It was too good to be true. He was an idiot three times over for giving in to this impulse. Thing was, after everything he'd been through, after everything he'd seen, he wasn't sure he cared anymore. He unhooked the gun from his belt and set it on the nightstand, considered a moment, then took off his boots as well.

Lugh emerged from the bathroom, toweling his hair dry. He'd put on the red silk bathrobe that always hung on the back of the door, the color glorious against his bronzed skin and ebony hair.

Zack's heart stuttered and gave a painful thud against his sternum. "God, you're gorgeous."

"I don't feel particularly handsome at the moment, but at least I'm clean," Lugh said with a little smile. He sat next to Zack on the bed and took his hand. "This is going about it all wrong, isn't it? I should be requesting the honor of your company for dinner. Asking you out on a date?"

A laugh slipped out before Zack could stop it. Lugh frowned at him, obviously hurt, so he hurried to explain. "If we'd just met, I'd say, yeah, dating would come first. You'd ask me out. We'd exchange phone numbers. We'd see each other a few times. Start hanging out on weekends. Maybe have sex and start talking about whose apartment we like better and who should bring a toothbrush over."

"Ah. Then you would be my...boyfriend?"

"Yeah." Zack couldn't help the lopsided grin. It gave him ridiculous warm fuzzies to hear Lugh say it. "But look, you and me, we've been through more than all that. You've carried me off the field when I was wounded. Slept with me to keep me warm. Saved my life at least twice now. We've had plenty of dinners together. Work together. Practically live in the same house. I appreciate the thought, but dating would be kinda going backward for us, don't you think?"

"It is too late to begin a relationship now?" Lugh's brow furrowed.

"No, I wouldn't say that. Not like there's only one way to do it." He lifted a hand to cup Lugh's cheek. "I thought you had a pretty good handle on how humans worked, bud. What's all this?"

"I had thought so as well." Lugh leaned into his touch, that simple gesture enough to make Zack's cock twitch. "Until I hurt you so badly. It has left me uncertain. Forced me to question assumptions."

"All right. Makes sense." Zack let his thumb trace over one high cheekbone. "I know I'm not like a lot of human males. I couldn't have boyfriends in the service.

You understand that, right? I mean, they've changed it now, but not when I first went in."

"It is a terrible, stupid thing to do to soldiers. Warriors fight all the more fiercely for a lover. But, yes, I understand why you could not."

"And I'm not a casual sex kind of guy."

"So I have come to understand."

Zack let his hand slide down to trace the strong jaw and the column of Lugh's neck. "Here's what I need. While we're together, I need to know you won't be sleeping around. Maybe it won't last. But as long as there's you and me, together" — Zack allowed himself a little grin — "and you want me as your boyfriend, you gotta promise there won't be anyone else."

Lugh caught both his hands, turned them and placed a tender kiss on each palm. "On the very earth that sustains me, I do so swear. You and no other."

"God, that's hot." Zack's voice trembled. His whole body shook with need. He slipped a hand free to undo the belt of Lugh's robe, practically drooling as the silk parted to reveal glimpses of the hard-muscled body beneath. "I want you. So damn bad."

"And I intend to give you all you desire," Lugh said, his voice a husky growl. "Though you must tell me if we hit upon something you do *not* want."

"I'll let you know," Zack murmured, watching Lugh's long fingers undoing his shirt buttons. "Nothing comes to mind."

"We will go slowly." Lugh tugged the shirt out of Zack's pants and pushed it off his shoulders. "I would rather take a spear through the heart than hurt you."

Lugh's robe fell open to reveal the huge erection lying ramrod straight and ready against his thigh. To Zack, it looked impossibly large. There was no way that gorgeous, monstrous cock would fit inside him. *Though it'll be fun to try.*

"Lie down, my dear." Lugh shoved gently at his chest, easing him onto his back. "Let me take care of you. This first time is just for you."

Zack didn't protest as Lugh undid his fly and pulled his pants and boxers down to his knees. He wasn't sure he remembered how to speak anyway. Lugh's breath teased at the heated underside of his cock. Zack's breath caught, fingers tangling in the silk still covering Lugh's shoulders. He cried out, his hips bucking off the bed when Lugh's tongue lapped over the slit.

"God...oh, God..."

"Shh, my braveheart. All will be well. You need only feel. Let the pleasure fill you. Let it take you."

Lugh's mouth descended over his balls. His tongue drew leisurely strokes over one then the other before he took one orb into his mouth, sucking gently. Zack moaned, his head rolling from side to side. It was too much. He was going to burst into flames. Lugh switched tactics, licking up the length of Zack's cock.

"Lugh..." Zack grabbed his head in both hands, not sure if he wanted to urge him on or to stop him. "I can't... I won't hold out like this."

"You aren't meant to," Lugh murmured against his skin. "You are meant to come, fast and hard, so I can taste you." He fastened his lips around the mushroom cap and plunged down Zack's shaft, taking the whole cock into the wet heat of his mouth.

Zack's eyes flew wide on a cry of ecstasy. His fingers tangled hard in the thick mass of Lugh's hair, still damp and cool. That cataract of hair trailed across his thighs and stomach, adding to the erotic torment. He hadn't done anything, not a damn thing to please Lugh, and there wasn't anything he could do about it. Lugh held him pinned, huge hands holding down his thighs, his wonderful mouth working his aching erection in hard-suctioned pulls.

He writhed and moaned, no longer able to find words. His balls drew up tight in a sudden, painful rush. Soft, panting whimpers climbed up his throat. Lugh pressed a finger against that sweet spot behind his balls. With a roar, he came, the rush and plunge of it making the bed pitch. His hips jerked up with each hard pulse. He expected Lugh to pull back, but he stayed latched on, swallowing every drop he offered, his moans of pleasure vibrating against Zack's oversensitive skin.

"Damn," Zack whispered, riding the dizzy aftershocks. "Oh, damn…I feel like an unraveled sweater." He forced his fingers to unclench so he could stroke Lugh's hair. "But you didn't get anything out of it."

Lugh nuzzled at his hip. "I'm far from finished with you." His head jerked up, sudden panic in his eyes. "Zachary, I have to leave you. I'm so sorry."

"What?"

"I have appointments. Flood and storm… What time is it…?" Lugh got halfway off the bed before Zack could grab him.

"Whoa, there, you gorgeous side of beef." He pulled Lugh back to his side. "Sorry, should have told you. Diego's gone for you."

"Ah." The news didn't seem to make Lugh feel better. He rolled onto his back, staring at the ceiling. "He should not have. It was my place to go, my duty. I have been remiss, indulging in self-pity."

That's more like my prince. "I'll see if he wants to beat you later."

Lugh gave him a sharp look. "This is not a matter for jest, Sergeant."

"No, you're right." Zack erased the smile from his face. "It was a stupid, selfish thing to do. You worried a lot of people and inconvenienced one of your best friends." He poked Lugh in the ribs. "But you're not made of stone, bud. Everybody has a crumbling point. Your friends'll forgive you and I'm sorry I was such a stubborn jerk and pushed you to it."

"You have forgiven me, then?"

"I let you suck on me like a lollipop, didn't I?" Zack tried to sound stern but a snicker still got away from him.

Lugh was on him before he could blink, hard body pressing him into the mattress, hands pinned above his head. "Still you make jokes at my expense."

"It's easy when you take yourself too seriously." Zack's voice dropped to a husky murmur. His spent cock reacted to Lugh's hard length rubbing against it, expanding as if it wanted to touch as much as possible. "You feel so good. Kiss me. Please."

"Ah, there's my well-mannered sergeant," Lugh whispered as he lowered his head to claim Zack's lips.

The tender exploration, full of heat and promise, soon escalated to ferocity. Zack lifted his head to meet Lugh's onslaught, their mouths devouring each other with bruising force. Their hips ground together, erections sliding, moans tangling with tortured breaths.

"I want you inside me," Zack panted out. "To hell with slow. I want all of you."

Lugh made a strange sound, a snorting, blowing of breath, and Zack realized the last time he'd heard it, the noise had come from a rodeo bull. His prince was barely staying in control and it was incredibly sexy.

"I don't wish to hurt you," Lugh repeated as he yanked off the rest of Zack's clothes.

"It's okay. I'm a big boy. Hurt me a little."

Lugh's dark brows rose. He gazed down at Zack for a long moment, hands sliding in firm strokes over his shoulders and chest. "My Zachary..."

He licked along Zack's throat, the wet slide of tongue decadent and wild. Zack shoved at the robe, desperate to be rid of anything other than skin. He let his hands wander over the broad expanse of back, over hard-muscled ribs and biceps a person could crack nuts on.

A hand slipped between Zack's thighs. He spread his legs wide, inviting the caress. A little gasp escaped when something slick touched his crease. At some point, Lugh had snagged a bottle of massage oil. He'd been too distracted to notice. Now the soft, woody scent of almonds reached him, a perfect counterpoint to Lugh's heady musk.

Slowly, gently, Lugh's finger teased at his entrance, sending sparks leaping up from his core. Zack bent his knees up, silently pleading for more. His breath caught on a stuttering moan when that single finger sank inside. It wasn't comfortable at first. It was a damn big finger, after all. But the friction against his tight ring as it slid back and forth was exquisite, and when Lugh penetrated far enough to stroke over the magic spot, Zack thought he might shatter from pleasure.

He grasped Lugh's head between his hands. "Don't tease too long. Oh...God... Please..."

"Steady, be easy," Lugh whispered. "You need a little more before you can take my girth."

"Arrogant, conceited bastard," Zack grated out, grinding his hips against the second finger Lugh allowed him. *So far, so good, oh, fuck, it feels good...*

"Merely realistic," Lugh said in a too-serious tone.

Zack reached between them and wrapped his fingers around Lugh's cock. He slid his hand up and down in firm, slow strokes, just the way he'd always liked it. His hand had been his only outlet, after all. *Okay, that and the occasional pillow.* "Give it to me. Don't make me wait another minute."

Lugh let Zack guide him, removing his fingers only when the head of his cock was in place. He drizzled more oil along his length, his thighs trembling as Zack worked the shining liquid along his shaft, making sure every inch was slick. Then he nudged gently, teasing at the tight ring, urging it to open for him.

The head breached Zack with an unexpected shove. His eyes watered, his stomach muscles taut against the sudden pain. Teeth gritted, he took careful sips of air, waiting for his body to adjust. Lugh stayed still, watching him intently.

"If it's too much—"

"Move a little. Just a little," Zack said between breaths.

Lugh rolled his hips, a gentle, circular motion that drove him farther in and back out by small degrees. The almost unbearable stretch melted into delicious pleasure-pain. He grabbed Lugh's ass and pulled hard, forcing him farther inside. It felt like a giant wedge was splitting him in two, as if Lugh would penetrate right through him. His prince wasn't arrogant. He was just huge.

"Zachary," Lugh said in a tender whisper. "Slowly, please. You are so tight. I feel as if you might snap me off at the base."

"Does it hurt?" Zack eased his grip.

"No, my dear, it's positively glorious." Lugh leaned his forehead against Zack's shoulder. "It has made me a wee bit dizzy, though."

"That's all the blood leaving your head."

"It's the delirious joy of finally having you in my arms."

"Enough with the poetry, Shakespeare. Are we doing this or not?"

Lugh chuckled and thrust in another inch, working his way in and out by slow degrees. The feeling of fullness was strange at first, then amazing when Lugh finally drove deep enough to stroke his prostate. Suns went into supernova behind his eyes.

"Yes...oh, yes," he gasped out. "Just like that. So good."

Lugh nuzzled at his throat, keeping his rhythm slow and steady. "Mmm, yes."

That huge cock split him in two and, yes, it hurt, but he wanted more. He wrapped his legs around Lugh's lower back, giving him a better angle. His arms twined around Lugh's neck, pulling him down. He wanted Lugh's weight, all of it, wanted to feel like he was being pounded through the mattress.

"Faster, a little faster. Please."

With another taurean snort, Lugh obliged, driving harder, shooting fireworks along Zack's nerves at the deepest point of each thrust.

"Babe, oh, God, tell me you're close," Zack got out between his teeth. He clamped down on every muscle he could to keep from coming too soon.

Lugh's only answer was a deep, throaty moan. He slid his arms around Zack, pulling him into a hard embrace as his rhythm sped. Zack gave up on trying to hold on, the storm of Lugh's passion sweeping him away in a tidal flood. Soft, escalating cries leaped from him as the pleasure climbed to a razor's edge, the pressure in his groin rose toward painful ecstasy. *Too much, too much...*

His fingers dug into Lugh's back. He threw back his head and howled as he came in rapid-fire pulses, his cries muffled when he latched his teeth hard onto Lugh's shoulder.

Some distant part of him was aware of Lugh's hips jerking into a desperate, uneven rhythm, of the *sidhe* prince's bass bellow as he came. He had become disconnected, floating in a sea of pleasure, happy to drown in it.

Lugh's panting breaths against his neck brought him back. Belatedly, he unfastened his teeth, the copper taste of blood on his tongue.

"Damn, I'm sorry." He kissed the bleeding bite marks.

"Hmm?" Lugh turned his head. "Ah. Please don't fret. Your passion unleashed was a wondrous thing."

"But I hurt you."

Lugh chuckled. "Only enough to add to the pleasure. And I will carry every bruise your fingers leave with pride. Take joy in every mark of tooth or nail."

"You've got a bit of kink in you." Zack smiled, reaching up to stroke his prince's face.

"Perhaps a bit." Lugh eased out carefully, sending leftover jolts through Zack with his withdrawal. He stretched out beside Zack, nuzzling at his shoulder. "Something has nagged at me."

"Oh, yeah?"

"What was the song Finn sang that made you so annoyed with him? The afternoon before your change?"

Zack put a finger under Lugh's chin to tip his face up for a tender kiss. "*Someday My Prince Will Come.*"

Lugh sputtered on a snicker. Zack raised an eyebrow at him and burst out laughing. It felt so damn good. Even better was having Lugh in his arms, laughing with him.

Chapter Twelve

Careless Words

Words were originally magic and to this day words have retained much of their ancient magical power. By words one person can make another blissfully happy or drive him to despair...

—Sigmund Freud, *Introductory Lectures on Psychoanalysis*

"We're heading over to the hotel for dinner." Diego tucked the cell between his ear and shoulder to free his hands for another autograph. The crowd outside the concert hall had made Kevin nervous, but Diego knew the value of interacting with the public. Hearts and minds, as Zack would say. "Everything all right there?"

"Yes sir, sure seems to be." Marcus' voice held a smile. "Least from the sounds in the bedroom, I'd say they're getting things worked out."

"*Gracias a Dios*. It was terrible to see them at odds."

"Mr. S., we gotta get moving here." Kevin's hand on Diego's elbow was just short of territorial.

"A few minutes won't hurt anything." Diego disengaged his grip as gently as possible.

"Can't you do like a personal force field or something, sir?"

"Relax, please. Fans and well-wishers. They don't mean any harm." Diego reached out to shake hands with a middle-aged mother, her two wide-eyed daughters in tow. While Kevin's instincts were sharp, he tended toward paranoia. Not a bad thing in one's security, but he needed to ease off sometimes.

"Mr. Sandoval, sir, would you...?"

The young man suddenly in front of him, clutching a copy of *Dragon Rites*, was arrestingly beautiful. Cerulean eyes regarded him earnestly, a hint of desperation in them.

Diego gave him a reassuring smile. "Of course. To whom should I make it out?"

"To William, sir. Thank you. You don't know how much this means to me."

"William? Kevin, isn't that your brother's name?" Diego turned to the man holding his elbow, his smile still firmly in place. "You're not Kevin."

The handsome young man who wasn't Kevin leaned in and spoke close to his ear, his voice deep, and his words impossibly huge despite being whispered. "You're Very Dizzy. Let Me Help You."

The words reverberated through Diego's bones, magic singing in the air in shivering arcs. He had only enough time to panic, to reach for the flows, before the words hit him like a wall falling on him.

He staggered as the ground fell out from under his feet. The hand on his elbow tightened, preventing his tumble into the abyss. A large body offered a shield and an anchor in the sickening lurches the sidewalk described.

"I...don't feel at all well," he whispered. He couldn't think, couldn't recall where he was or who walked beside him.

"It'll be all right, Mr. Sandoval." A strong arm slid around his waist, drawing him close in its protective circle. "Make a path! Get out of the way! Can't you see the man's sick?"

A few lurching steps took him forward. A black car waited, door open. He rallied enough to try to look back, but the movement only pitched him further into the heaving torrent of dizziness. "Where's Kevin?"

"He's okay, sir, don't worry." The voice was softer than the one with the gigantic, bone-shaking words. "Please don't be afraid."

Someone held him gently. The Voice returned, saying, "Sleep."

His eyes slid shut.

* * * *

"Bran? You okay?" Will reached across the seat to shake Brandon's shoulder.

"Don't feel so good right now," Bran muttered, his head leaned back. "It'll get better in a couple minutes."

"At least you didn't pass out this time," Nate said from the driver's seat.

Minky turned in the front seat to look behind her. "Yeah, well, now he has."

Will sighed and ran a gentle hand over Brandon's hair. It was a strange sight, Brandon passed out with his head lolling on the back of the seat, Mr. Sandoval unconscious with his head on Brandon's chest, and Will seeming worried and proud when he should have been jealous.

Maybe not so strange. Brandon had managed to incapacitate Mr. Sandoval's security, then Mr. Sandoval himself while Will distracted him, and finally put him to sleep, all without the loss of control that usually made him keel over right away. Will did have reason to be proud of him.

"You think he's okay?" Minky chewed on her thumbnail. "Bran didn't hurt him, did he?"

Will leaned over. "He just seems to be sleeping."

"Yeah, well, we're gonna have to hope *we're* all right when he wakes up. He'll probably be pissed," Nate said on a sigh.

"We'll explain things. He's a very nice man. He won't do anything to hurt any of us, even if he's angry."

Minky was certain Will was right. The face cradled against Brandon's chest was by no means delicate—a strong, handsome face with thick, dark lashes fanned out on olive skin. But she had watched him with the crowd, seen his patience with people, his natural empathy for each person to whom he spoke, no matter how simpering or tongue-tied. She just hoped all that kindness and patience translated into helping them.

* * * *

Diego woke from a strange dream of searching, frantically searching for something he couldn't name. He surged upright with a cry of dismay, disoriented and frightened.

Seizure? No. Nothing hurts. Everything feels too focused. But where the hell am I?

"Mr. Sandoval?" A gentle touch on his arm brought him face to face with the beautiful boy from outside the concert hall. William, that was his name. "It's all right, sir. You're safe."

"Did I faint?" He glanced around the shabby apartment. "Where's Kevin?"

A deeper voice answered, "He's fine, Mr. Sandoval."

Diego turned his head to find the much larger youngster who had spoken in his ear before. The young man had an ice pack pressed to the side of his head.

"Is he? Why isn't he here?"

A smile quirked at the young man's lips. "He's right where we left him. I told him not to move."

That voice — the Voice that had suddenly loomed over his mind — shut out all his own thoughts, and enveloped him in its brief commands. Diego pulled back out of reach, not at all reassured. "I'm not sure I want to talk to you. I believe I was speaking to William." Diego turned back to the blond. "I hope there's a good explanation, preferably one that doesn't involve bodily harm or ransom notes."

William dropped his gaze, a scarlet flush blooming on his cheeks. "We're sorry, sir, about all this. We just needed your undivided attention and couldn't seem to get it any other way." He pointed to the other occupants in the room. "This is Brandon. That's Nate over by the doorway. This is Kara. And if you squint and turn your head a bit, you should be able to see Minky by the wall—"

"Wait." Diego rubbed both hands over his face. "Minky? *Ay, Dios.* You're the Silver Adepts. Zack warned me this would happen."

"What would happen?" the more visible girl, Kara, asked.

"That one of the groups trying to contact me would try a kidnapping."

"This is *not* a kidnapping," Brandon growled. He flung away the ice pack and got up to pace. "You ignored our pleas for help, our emails, our phone calls. We have a serious situation developing. We need help. Your help."

The way Brandon assumed everyone should yield to him irritated Diego. He'd seen this type of young man far too often not to recognize the arrogance, the sense of entitlement. "Might just need something more specific than that," he said in a dry tone. "William, maybe someone could explain."

In halting, anxious tones, William began to tell him about the magic, how they had found their own abilities, and how they had been tracking a sudden outbreak of magical occurrences. Of particular interest to them were all the reports of magic used for harm and stories of what William described as 'creatures of darkness'. His voice shook as he went on to describe his dreams.

"I'll tell him, Will," Brandon interrupted. "It's too hard for you."

"Shut it, Bran!" the older girl, Kara, snapped. "They're his dreams, let him do it!"

Though his eyes looked like they held thunderstorms, Brandon snapped his mouth shut. Will made a placating gesture in his direction and went on in a trembling voice to describe the dreams. They had started as simple precognitive episodes, small incidents that had then happened the next day. A broken dish, the loss of a book, inconsequential things, until he began to dream of magical disasters. He had dreamed about the girl who had spontaneously combusted in the middle of a Chicago street. He had known her hair color, what she had been wearing and the nickname her friend had cried in horror as she went up in flames, all hours before the event appeared on the news.

The dreams grew worse, from isolated incidents to dreams of a malevolent, powerful being who directed chaos and destruction, who seemed bent on gathering dark magic to him.

"So we know he's out there, sir," Will finished in a hoarse whisper. "We know it can't be long before he starts his campaign. It'll be a war, Mr. Sandoval. Any good magic users will have to stand up to him. And we're not strong enough, sir. We need you. We need you to believe, and we need you to teach us. To train us."

Diego heaved a weary sigh, fingers buried in his hair. "*Bueno.* I understand why you're concerned. I even understand why this would drive you to such extreme measures. But the fact is that most of the magical accidents and incidents you're talking about are a result of the way being reopened between the worlds. The magic can flow again. It creates little storms and magical earthquakes as it comes into contact with isolated pockets of earth-bound magic. Nothing more."

"But the dark mage." Will's lower lip quivered. "He's real. I know it."

"Most likely he will be some day, *niño*. But if there was an evil being of such power running loose in the world, don't you think the fae would have felt him by now? Or perhaps I might have?"

"Maybe, sir. But what about the dark creatures? The vampires and werewolves?" Tears stood in Will's eyes now.

Diego's heart went out to him. Clearly terrified, this lovely youngster still felt obligated to save the world. He reached out to pat Will's hand. "It'll be all right, William. But what you need to understand is that I have so many obligations. I need to make certain that human relations with magical creatures are on a fair and just footing. I have obligations to fae royalty to look after their interests. Obligations to the inhabitants of the Otherworld to keep them safe. And obligations to *every* magical creature, no matter our human prejudices. There must be a compassionate response. Otherwise, we encourage pogroms and persecution. I have things to see to this evening, but I'll leave you my card. You call my admin in the morning, and we'll set something up. I—"

"Damn you!"

Diego suddenly found his upper arms in a vise grip as Brandon hauled him off the couch to face him. Wind whipped through the apartment as both of them pulled on the flows. Diego looked up into those angry, dark eyes. "I don't want to hurt you..."

"Why?" Brandon snarled. "Too goddamned posh to get your hands dirty? Fucking diplomat! Safe on your island while Will dies a slow death from these dreams!"

A sudden surge in power made Diego's breath lurch. He yanked at the flows, creating tidal pools of magic in the room, desperate to throw some sort of barrier between himself and this wild young mage.

The Voice slammed into him, ripping craters in his soul. "To HELL With Your Compassion! To Hell With Your Obligations! Your ONLY Obligation Is To Make THIS World Safe!"

Searing pain knifed through Diego's skull. A wrenching scream tore from him as pieces of him ripped away. The world shattered in a flash white as death.

Mr. Sandoval's terrible screams echoed through all of them. Minky stood paralyzed as Will struggled through the magic wind, shouting for Brandon to stop. Lightning slammed out from the consul and hurled Brandon across the room.

Blind. She was blind, would never see again. In spite of any melodramatic thoughts, though, her sight cleared little by little, the terrible afterimage of Brandon and Mr. Sandoval locked together still on her eyelids when she blinked.

Fire licked at the coffee table. Will crawled, coughing and sobbing, to where Brandon lay. Mr. Sandoval lay on the carpet, his body twitching and jerking.

"Oh, God, we've killed him," she whispered.

Nate yanked the coffee table into the middle of the room and smothered the fire with a blanket. He shook his head. "No, he's having a seizure. I read he has them sometimes. It shouldn't last too long." He moved furniture out of the way and loosened Mr. Sandoval's tie. "I hope he's okay, though. Bran shouldn't have said...those things."

Kara finished putting out the fire while Minky pulled over a chair to climb up and take the battery out of the smoke detector.

"If idiot Brandon's done any harm, he'll just have to fix it when he wakes up," Kara said. "I don't care how much his head hurts."

"I don't know if he's still alive," Will said in a choked whisper, his ear to Brandon's chest. "I can't hear his heart. His back might be broken. He —"

"Hey, hey, slow down, little dude." Nate moved Will out of the way with gentle hands and felt for a pulse. "He's alive, so ease down on the panic, okay?"

"Okay." Will drew in a shaky breath and swiped a hand over his eyes.

Mr. Sandoval's jerking movements quieted, his face pale and drawn.

"We should call nine-one-one," Minky said.

Nate let out a sharp laugh. "And tell them what? Oh, yeah, we were holding a diplomat hostage in our apartment when he had a lightning fit, body slammed our friend then had a seizure?"

"Shit." Kara stood in the center of the room, arms crossed tight over her chest. "Get blankets, Mink. We'll just have to apologize when he wakes up and if Bran doesn't wake up soon, we'll call the ambulance, and worry about how to explain later."

A soft moan came from Mr. Sandoval as Minky covered him with the afghan from the bedroom closet. He opened his eyes and blinked at her, his gaze unfocused.

"*Dios*. I feel so strange." He sat up slowly, rubbing his chest. "So…light."

Nate explained in swift, brief sentences what had happened, ending with, "We're so sorry, sir. Brandon didn't mean to hurt you…"

Mr. Sandoval's reaction was the opposite of what Minky expected. He turned his head toward where Brandon was sprawled against the wall. "Stupid child. Stupid, arrogant child. He should have his tongue cut out so he doesn't make any more *mistakes*."

"Are you, um, feeling okay?" Minky asked as she edged away from him again.

"That's a good question, *chiquita*." He used the couch to lever himself up to his feet. He shook his head and caught himself on Nate's shoulder when he swayed. "Am I okay?" He took two careful steps as if testing his balance. "You know, I think I am. I don't think I was before, but I think I finally am."

"What do you mean, sir?" Nate backed up a step as well. Something cold and hard in Mr. Sandoval's voice had them all easing away from him.

"I feel so free." He held out his hands. Sparks danced over his fingers, whirling into bright vortexes until tiny lightning storms hovered over his palms. He threw back his head and laughed. "*Dios*, I feel so damn *free*. So powerful. How could I have locked this away for so long? I could slaughter whole towns with a flick of my fingers."

"That doesn't exactly sound like a compassionate response, sir," Nate said as he backed up another step.

"Ah, now see, in that regard your stupid friend was right." Mr. Sandoval added rain to his palm-sized storms, his eyes glittering. "Compassion has its place, but it can cloud reason. Drown logic. It encourages sentiment over sense. And in this ever more dangerous world, we need more sense."

"I think...think you're not well, sir," Will said on a shuddering breath. "Who should we call for you? Someone at the embassy?"

"The embassy?" Mr. Sandoval's forehead creased. "No. No, they've kept me constrained for too long. Encouraged me to hide away from my true responsibilities. Hidden away while the world falls to pieces. It's my doing, the magical chaos. I need to face this."

He started to pace, running a hand back through his hair. "Yes…yes. There must be some order to things. Control." He stopped abruptly and whirled to face them. "Yes. There's only one way. I have to take control. No one else is powerful enough."

"What the hell, Mr. Sandoval? You sound like some comic book arch villain," Kara snapped. "Control of what?"

He blinked at her. "The world, of course. The magic in this world. The fae can take care of their world, but I'm human. Therefore, I'm responsible for this world. I need to seize control so that there will be order and, from there, security. Peace." He took a step toward Will and reached out to stroke his cheek. "Then beautiful William won't need to be frightened anymore. Wouldn't that be better, *dulce*?"

"Dictators have always said those things, sir," Will said on a hard swallow. "Nazis, fascists, they've all said the same."

"They all wanted power for the wrong reasons, William," he answered gently. "But I need to make the world safe. Come with me. You are a true oracle. I feel the power leashed in you. Stand by me and you'll have everything you desire. I'll teach you things you've only dreamed of. Such a beautiful creature deserves more than what a selfish boy could give him."

"But, sir…you're married," Will choked out.

"True. But Finn has had so many lovers. I think my husband would appreciate you." Mr. Sandoval's smile didn't reach his eyes. "He does get lonely when I'm working."

"No, sir. I'm not… That's…" Will shook his head frantically. "No."

Mr. Sandoval shrugged. "No matter. Now. Later. I'll leave the offer open. You'll get tired of that" — he waved a hand at Brandon, still sprawled unconscious by the wall — "sooner or later." Then he clapped his hands together, the sharp noise like a gunshot in the silent apartment. "So. I have things to set in motion. Tests to run. Evil to vanquish. If you'll excuse me."

Magic wind shrieked around them when he raised his hand. A ball of white lightning settled on his palm and shrank until it was no longer visible, the hum of it still singing along Minky's nerves. He hurled the tiny missile and a hole suddenly opened in the air beside the coffee table.

Not a hole…a gate, a door.

A hill of dry grass overlooked a sprawl of housing. Skyscrapers loomed in the distance.

"Goodbye, children," Mr. Sandoval said with that chill smile. "Stay safe. I'll come back for you someday. Find a place for you all in my new household. Except the big one." He nodded to Brandon. "He can crawl and beg before I'll take him in."

A little frown creased his forehead as he stared through the door in space, as if he tried to recall something. Then he shook his head and stepped through. With a whistling shriek, the doorway snapped shut behind him.

Will dropped to his knees with a desolate wail.

"Did he hurt you, Will?" Minky touched his shoulder with a shaking hand.

"No, no! Don't you see!" Will rocked, beating his fists on his knees. "The dark mage…he didn't exist before. We *made* him. Oh, fuck."

"To hell with your compassion," Nate said softly. "A man without compassion, with so much power…"

"Do not meddle in the affairs of wizards," Kara muttered on a huff of breath. "We have so fucked up."

* * * *

"Sarge?"

The knock on the bedroom door jerked Zack awake. He hadn't realized he'd dozed off, Lugh's head cradled on his chest, until Marcus called him.

"Yeah?"

"I hate to bug you right now, but Finn's on the line. He's freaking out and he's not making any sense."

Zack stroked a hand over the heavy silk of Lugh's hair. "Lemme up, gorgeous. I better check this out."

With a grunt, Lugh shifted his head over but made no move to get up. Zack couldn't help a smug grin. *Tired my poor prince out...*

"Sarge?"

"Just a sec." He pulled on his pants and opened the door enough for Marcus to hand the phone in to him. "Finn? What's up, bud?"

"He's gone!" Finn wailed in his ear.

"Who's gone?"

"Diego! Please, we have to do something!"

"Okay, bud, I hear you." Zack stepped out into the hall. "But I need you to take a deep breath. Diego's here in New York. Didn't he tell you before he left?"

A broken sob drifted through the phone. "I know he went to the city, I *know*! And I could feel him there, but now he's *gone*! Why won't anyone listen?"

A sliver of ice lodged in Zack's gut. "Marcus, get on the line to Kevin. When's the last time they checked in?"

"Not due to for another ten minutes, Sarge."

175

"Fine. We're doing a random check. See if you can raise him. His cell, Mr. S.'s, whoever answers." Zack returned to the receiver. "Finn? Did you feel anything strange? Like he was hurt or anything?"

Finn sniffed but he managed in a calmer tone, "He was there one moment, as he always is. I felt...I'm not certain. I think perhaps he was afraid. Or something took him by surprise. Then he was gone."

"You've called to him in your head? Tried to reach him? Nothing?"

"Not a whisper."

"Sarge?" Marcus called as he raced back from the kitchen. "I can't raise them. Kevin's goes to voicemail. Mr. Sandoval's doesn't even connect. The concierge at the dinner says they never got there."

"Shit." Zack moved even as he barked orders, striding back into the bedroom to get dressed. "We're taking the van, Marcus. Going down there. Highness, you'd better come with us. Rather have you in sight right now. Finn, bud, you stay put. Hear me?"

The voice on the phone no longer belonged to Finn, though. Carol answered him instead. "Zack? He's shifted to some sort of large bird and flown off. I'm sorry."

"Not your fault. I think we have to figure he's coming here. We'll keep an eye out for him." Zack yanked his boots on, hesitating only a moment to make sure Lugh was up and moving. The prince was already dressed in jeans and a T-shirt, his expression grim. "You heard?"

"Everything. If he has been harmed —"

Zack hooked the sidearm on his belt. "We do this by the book, big guy. No charging off into someone else's jurisdiction on vendettas. You stay with me."

"And if I do not?" Lugh growled.

"You really want me mad at you again?"

Lugh's shoulders slumped. "No."

"Let's go. I've got a bad feeling this is what the *bane sidhe* were trying to warn us about."

Chapter Thirteen

Harvest

*I hate the stars because I look at the same ones as you do,
without you.*
— Anonymous

"Kev?" Marcus shook Kevin by the arm.

Finding Kevin had posed no problem at all. He stood
like some paramilitary version of a fashion mannequin
in front of Lincoln Center, one hand raised to waist
height, fingers curled as if he tried to grasp something.
People looked him up and down as they passed but
they smiled and chatted as they walked on, obviously
convinced that he was engaging in some piece of
performance art.

"Is he paralyzed?" Marcus asked in a hushed tone.
"Neurotoxin or something?"

Lugh stepped close, sniffing the air around Kevin's
head. "Spell. It is a simple one. Perhaps I can…" He slid
an arm around Kevin's waist and whispered in his ear.

Kevin moaned and Lugh caught him before his knees could buckle.

"Goddamn, oh, goddamn," Kevin muttered as they helped him into the back of the security van and onto the stretcher Zack had insisted they install. At the time, he had been thinking about Diego's seizures and the ever-present possibility of iron poisoning for any fae on a diplomatic outing.

"Kevin, look at me." He shone a penlight in Kevin's eyes, watching for any uneven reaction in the pupils. "Anything hurt?"

Barrel chest heaving in ragged gasps, Kevin shook his head and croaked out, "BRW six two Z."

Puzzled, Zack repeated the disconnected words and it hit him. "License plate. Marcus, can you get me a plate check?" He patted Kevin's chest. "Good man. State?"

"Jersey," Kevin answered.

"On it, Sarge. Gimme a couple." Marcus settled in the front seat with the laptop, phone to his ear. Former NYPD, he had contacts in the department that helped cut through the red tape they might encounter as an international security agency.

"Can you tell us what happened?" Lugh asked gently.

"Kids. Damn kids. Took Mr. S." Kevin gulped a breath, the gray pallor beginning to fade from his face. "Whispered in my ear. Couldn't move."

"Took him? By force? Were they armed?" All sorts of terrible scenarios played out in Zack's whirling brain.

"No weapons. Whispered in his ear, too. Wasn't walking on his own. No violence. Seemed careful with him."

"They whispered in his ear," Zack repeated, mystified. "What kind of weird stuff are we dealing with?"

"Human magic," Lugh said. "The magic's scent is most assuredly human. I have heard of such things before, human mages who could speak compulsion spells."

"We got a match," Marcus called back. "Car's registered to a Nathan Cooper. Address isn't too far."

"Let's go, boys. They may have been kids, doesn't make them harmless."

At a red light, Marcus turned in the driver's seat. "You okay, you dumb jarhead?"

"I'm good, you brainless flatfoot," Kevin said with a wan smile. "Eyes on the road, babe."

They had come as a set. Kevin had left the Corps to be with the man he loved, working soul-draining customer service jobs rather than re-enlist and spend another three years apart. Marcus had been the one to spot the online call for qualified security officers for the Fae Collective and had pushed Kevin to apply. Both Diego and Lugh had been impressed with the former M.P., but when he'd learned accepting the job would mean relocating, he'd dug his heels in. If they wanted him, they would have to take them both.

After a brief interview with Marcus, there had been no question at all.

"Coming up on the building, Sarge."

"Good. No rushing in. Let me kinda...feel the vibe as we go." Zack unsnapped the top of his holster, just in case. "His Highness—"

"Goes with you," Lugh growled. "Magical backup."

"He's got a point, Sarge," Kevin said, testing his balance before he exited the van.

"And you should probably stay put." Zack wasn't sure who to turn his glare on first.

"There were at least four of them," Kevin pointed out.

Zack raised an eyebrow at that. Four kids against the four of them hardly seemed like fair odds. But then, this wasn't a football game. "Fine. But you start to feel less than a hundred percent, you fall back, got it? All right, boys, let's rock and roll."

Halfway up the second flight of stairs, Zack's head jerked up.

"What is it?" Lugh whispered.

"Smoke. Oh, shit." Body slamming caution against the wall, he leaped up the stairs, Lugh's hooves clattering in his wake. He realized belatedly just how fast he was moving when he reached the apartment door alone. He forced himself to wait for the rest of them to catch up.

Hand signals replaced words now. Zack motioned to Marcus to go in high while he went low. He raised a hand and counted down on his fingers from three...two...one...

Marcus kicked the door open and they spun to either side. Zack wasn't sure what he'd expected, but it sure as hell wasn't this. The little apartment looked like a cartoon Tasmanian Devil had ripped through it. Papers littered the floor. Books lay on their faces and spines, sad casualties of some cruel passing storm. Furniture lay overturned. The cheap, particleboard coffee table was still smoking.

Zack took quick stock of the horrified faces and holstered his gun. These kids looked shell-shocked, the ones who were still standing. One sprawled unconscious by the far wall. Another kid knelt by him, sobbing inconsolably.

"Who the fuck are you?" the brown-haired girl asked, trying for bravado while her voice shook in little earthquakes.

"Sergeant Zack Morrison, Fae Collective Security." Zack flashed his badge. People cooperated better when they saw one. "What happened here? And where's Mr. Sandoval?"

The one boy standing, a handsome youngster with a mop of thick brown curls, said, "We don't know what you—"

Kevin stepped forward. The young man paled. "The one on the floor. That's the one who spoke the spell. The little blond one distracted Mr. S. This one here…" He jerked his chin at the boy who had spoken. "Drove the car."

"Nathan Cooper, I'm guessing?" Zack said in a dry tone.

The boy dropped his gaze as he flushed bright red. "Yessir."

A tiny dark-haired girl, who seemed to be fading in and out of sight, said in a strangled voice, "He's gone. We didn't mean to. He's not himself and he made a door and left."

Lugh came into the apartment now and the youngsters all gasped. *Him*, they had no trouble recognizing. "Your friend is hurt. You are all badly frightened. I hear your hearts race. Let us help you. Tell us what has passed here."

The blond boy raised his tear-stained face. "Highness, can you help him?"

"We will do all we can." Lugh settled on the sofa so he wasn't looming, his deep, calm voice a natural balm to any frightened soul. "Zachary? Could you have a look, please?"

Zack crossed the room and crouched by the prone figure. Pulse was steady and strong. Respirations even. Normal reflex reactions. Lump on the back of the head... "Concussed, I think, Highness. He should be all right."

"Good. Come, my dears." Lugh patted the sofa. "Sit with me and tell me everything."

Once hesitantly begun, the explanations accelerated, four voices tumbling over one another in an avalanche of words. Zack wanted to swear and rant. This was exactly what he'd warned Diego about. But then they got to the part where Diego had changed. Icy spider feet scurried up his spine.

"My braveheart?" Lugh shot him a concerned look. "What is it? You've gone white as frost."

"Darkness follows...in your wake," Zack said softly. "They were trying to tell us."

Lugh shook his head. "Even those who know the *bane sidhe* do not always follow their meaning. Do not blame yourself. It is these youngsters here who must carry the burden of blame."

"We were trying to do something good," the brown-haired girl said with a scowl.

"Yes. But the way you went about it, did it feel right to you?"

They all shook their heads.

"Very well. Done is done, and your intent was not malicious. But you must come with us."

"Are we under arrest?"

"No, not in the usual sense. You are not safe here. The dark mage said he would return for you."

Zack stood with a sigh. He really didn't want to be saddled with a bunch of kids, and this was their own fault. Still, even if he could tell his conscience to shut up and abandon them, logically it was a bad idea. Diego, in his current state, might find them useful and it didn't sound like anyone needed to be handing him extra weapons. The sooner they found him, the better. *Damn it, we better find him quick.*

An ache lodged under his own heart to think of Diego, sweet, kind Diego, changed like that, as if his heart had been torn out. It reminded him of some story, something with snow in it...

And how the hell would they tell poor Finn? He rubbed his hands over his face, wishing he had followed his first instinct and insisted Diego cancel the appointments.

"The prince is right. Don't feel safe letting you all stay here." He managed a little smile for Lugh. "Think you can carry our new patient, Highness?"

Lugh simply rose and scooped the kid up off the floor. The boy probably weighed a good one-eighty, all hard-packed muscle, but Lugh cradled him gently as if he were a tiny pup. Any other scion of a royal house would have balked or argued about being used as a pack mule. Lugh had more sense, knowing his security needed their hands free, and Zack loved him even more for it.

"All right, kids. Five minutes to grab what you need. Then we're out." Zack looked from one to the other, all of them staring at him with some level of resentment or dismay. He sighed and moved from gentle persuasion to his best drill sergeant voice. "Now! Get your heads out of your asses! Move like you've got a purpose in life!"

They moved. The little fading girl actually ran. Only when they had all piled in the van did he take time for introductions. The blond was William Schoenberg. The name sounded vaguely familiar. The big kid was Brandon McLean and the more outspoken girl, Kara Watts. The little dark-haired one was Minky Jones, the Minky from Diego's email files.

"Sergeant? It's Sergeant Morrison, right?" Nate asked when they had Brandon strapped to the stretcher and had all crammed into the back of the van.

"Yes."

Nate jerked his head toward Lugh. "You're *his* Sergeant Morrison?"

"Yeah." Zack couldn't help the little smile. "I am."

"No offense, but weren't you almost dead recently?"

Zack fixed him with a bland look. "I got better."

"Um, right." Nate blinked, but didn't glance away. "Not being nosy. Just thought if there was some magic potion and stuff involved..." He nodded to where Brandon lay, his hand clutched between Will's.

"Got it. No, no magic potions. But if we need to snag a healer, we'll get one, don't worry."

Nate nodded and didn't ask anything further.

They seemed like good kids. A little messed up, a little lost, but they cared. Rare enough, in Zack's experience, and for them to take such risks showed even rarer courage. He wanted to be furious at them over what had happened to Diego, but in the face of their earnest desperation, it wasn't easy. Besides, Lugh was right. Done was done. Being mad about it wasn't going to get Diego back.

Zack overrode debate about returning to the island immediately. Security-wise, it would be better. He wasn't sure enough about Brandon's condition to subject him to the trip, though. Lugh could get back instantaneously, but it was strictly a solo proposition. He'd never been able to translocate with anyone in tow.

At the condo, Lugh placed his passenger on the sofa with exaggerated care while Zack directed the rest of the youngsters to get their various tech devices powered up. They'd had a glimpse of where Diego had gone. Now they just needed to ID the place.

"Diego can't build a door unless he knows where he's going or has someone on the other end to guide his mind." Zack penned a list of cities, trolling his memory. "I'll give you a list of all the cities he's ever visited that I know of. Of course he was born in —"

"Miami. Yes, we know." Kara cut him off. "And grew up here in New York. And lived in New Brunswick, we know all that."

"You know an awful lot. How long have you been stalking him?" Kevin rumbled.

"All of that's on his author bio at his publisher's website," Nate answered softly. "No big state secrets. We were fans, all of us, before the Veil opened."

"Great. So you have a start." Zack handed over his list. "Here's some more. And if you wait a couple, I'll have some pics for you. He always sends Carol phone pics from wherever he is. I'll have her email Minky."

"You need my email addy?" Minky said in a tiny voice.

"I think Carol already has it, hon. You emailed Mr. Sandoval enough."

"Oh. Yeah."

Zack left them to their task and pulled Lugh into the kitchen. "Unholy mess."

"Indeed." Lugh wrapped strong arms around him. "Should I look at the boy? I'm not my mother but I can accomplish small things."

"Yeah, if you don't mind. You're not pissed at them?" He rested his head on Lugh's broad shoulder, wishing he could take him back to bed.

"They are rash and foolish, but they are so young." Lugh's chest expanded in a sigh. "Yes, I am angry and I fear they may need to answer for their actions some day. But that time may never come. We may all perish first."

"Well, aren't you just a ray of sunshine."

Lugh put a hand under his chin and tilted his face up. "My Zachary, we should never be forced to face our beloved Diego in conflict. But if we do, know that a more powerful mage has never walked this earth. This is perilous."

"Yeah, well." Zack leaned up and caught Lugh's bottom lip between his teeth, tugging softly. "You think I waited this long for you just to lose you now? I don't think so."

A shuddering breath gusted from Lugh. "My fierce sergeant. Though if you insist on pressing up so close, I will feel compelled to take you right here on the kitchen counter."

Zack clicked his tongue in mock disapproval. "For shame, Highness. There are kids in the next room."

"I believe they are all of legal age." Lugh's brow furrowed.

"Kinky and an exhibitionist, too." Zack managed a grin despite the worry knotting his stomach. "All right, go see what you can do for Brandon while I call Carol."

Lugh's deep voice drifted from the living room as he spoke in soft, reassuring tones to Will. He was good with the kids, his quiet patience putting them at ease, and Zack's heart swelled with pride. That was his prince in there, back to himself, doing what he did best.

"Sergeant?" Carol's voice came over the line in her usual professional tones, though Zack knew her well enough to pick out the worry. "Are you finished keeping me in the dark today, or are things on a need-to-know basis?"

"Sorry about that." Zack slid onto one of the kitchen stools. "Things got a little hairy here. I'll tell you what I know, then I need to ask you a couple dozen favors."

"Zack, you're heading toward owing me the biggest box of chocolates any man has ever purchased, you know that, right?"

"Yes, ma'am. Godiva or Lindt?"

"Something Belgian, you cheapskate. Now give."

He caught Carol up on what he could, then asked for the photos, the Collective-owned helicopter for a pick up and a healer to stand by. Carol's fingers tapped away at her keyboard all through his requests.

"Sending the entire file with the photos, Max should be landing on the roof helipad in six hours, and Princess Eithne is right here with me. She'll be watching for your arrival." Carol hesitated a moment. "You may want to put the prince on the phone."

"Why?"

"I need official clearance for your guests."

Zack smacked his forehead. Forgetting his own security protocols. Only the royal family or the Consul could grant outsiders permission to step onto the island. "Right. Hold on a sec."

He switched places with Lugh, settling into the chair the prince had just vacated. Brandon's eyes were open but wandering.

"It's not on time," Brandon muttered.

"What's not, love?" Will stroked his face.

"Paving stones."

Will swallowed hard. "Please, Bran, you're not making sense."

"He might not for a bit." Zack patted his shoulder. "Just help him stay still and quiet. Don't think he's quite back with us yet." He looked around the room at the three other youngsters, eyes glued to their notepad and laptop screens. "Anything yet?"

Three heads shook, three sets of fingers flew over touchpads.

"Keep at it. Has to be somewhere he's been. Anybody have any objections to a little road trip?"

When Zack explained, they all looked at him as if he'd told them they were getting ponies for Christmas. The eager young excitement was almost suffocating. *Dear God, was I ever that young?* "We think you'll be safest on the island. But this doesn't mean you can wander back and forth to the Otherworld and bother busy fae. You be polite and you stay out of the way, got it?"

Three heads nodded mutely, eyes wide and shining.

"Good. Marcus, I'm catching a few Z's."

Marcus waved toward the bedroom. "We're good, Sarge. Maybe get His Highness to take a rest, too. Probably still not feeling too great."

There were a couple of snickers at the obvious ploy to give them some alone time. The kids were wide-eyed, but they weren't stupid.

"Catnip hangover's a bitch," Kevin rumbled from his place by the door.

All snickers abruptly ceased.

Back in the kitchen, Zack found his prince sitting at the counter, his head buried in his arms.

"Hey." He stroked his hand over Lugh's dark hair. "What's all this?"

Lugh heaved a long, shuddering breath. "All of this is my doing. If I had not been so selfish, so self-absorbed, none —"

"No, oh, no." Zack gave him a little smack on the shoulder. "We are so not going down that road."

He snagged three bottles of water from the fridge and one of the plastic bags from the cabinet. To the uninformed, the contents would have appeared to be trail mix, but this recipe had whole, uncracked kernels of wheat, rye and oats mixed in. Good for someone with a bull's constitution. Not so great for humans.

"Come on, big guy. Water, food, bed, in that order." He towed Lugh by the hand toward the bedroom. "I don't know if you boys have adrenaline crashes but you're going into some kind of crash, big time. We don't have time for you to wallow in it."

Lugh guzzled down all three water bottles in short order and plowed through half the bag. "But it is true," he finally said in a weary voice.

Zack shook his head as he lifted first one hoof, then the other to wipe them down with a damp cloth. "Lots of things've happened, babe. Lots of people had a hand in all this. I guess it's like what your mom told me once about prophecy. That the more you try to keep it from happening, the more you make for damn sure it'll happen."

"She said that?"

"Well, not in those words. I'm paraphrasing."

"Ah. It is true, beyond a doubt. But we knew of no prophecy."

"We didn't. William did. And tried to stop it." Zack eased the T-shirt off over Lugh's head and pushed him back against the pillows. "Damn it, that's not what I was trying to say, either. I'm not so good at this stuff.

You did a dumb thing. But the problem with Diego is not your fault. One thing led to another and to another."

He undid Lugh's fly and peeled him out of his tight jeans, trying to keep his eyes off the sizeable package at the front of his boxer briefs. "I need you strong. Need you focused. I don't think we can make it through this without you."

Lugh held out his arms and waited until Zack had settled against him, resting his head in the crook of one powerful shoulder. "You are better at this 'stuff' than you think," he said softly. "Stay with me?"

With a huge yawn, Zack nestled closer and slid his arm over Lugh's stomach. "You just try and get rid of me."

* * * *

He must have been more tired than he realized. When he woke again, the room was dark, the condo quiet. For a moment, he lay still, wondering what had jerked him from sleep. Lugh's scent surrounded him, a comfort and a balm. The prince slept, his chest rising and falling in deep, even breaths.

There. An odd scritch-scratch jarred his nerves, like a branch scraping the side of a window. No trees grew outside. They were twenty stories up. Zack slid from the bed, crouched low as he eased toward the window.

"My love?" Lugh whispered, his voice sleep-thickened and confused. "What is it? You seem to be growling."

Zack cut off the rumbling vibration, unaware that he had been. "Sorry. Think something's out there. Do you hear it?"

Lugh's dark eyes glittered in the gloom as he sat up slowly. "Yes. Zachary, please be careful."

"Just having a look." Zack lifted the edge of the curtain. He jerked back in shock when something slammed into the glass. "Shit."

He took a moment, heart pounding. What the hell had he seen? Feathers? As he listened, his newly sharp ears straining to pick out sounds through the thick glass, he became more certain. Wings rustled outside.

"Oh, damn." A sudden realization hit him. He flung back the curtains and threw open the window. A huge black bird fell through to land in a heap on the floor.

The bird, a hawk, he thought, breathed in shallow, frantic sips of air. Finally, it said, "You took your blasted time with that window."

"Finn?"

"It's certainly not the great Roc of Persia."

Oh, yeah. That's Finn. "Thought I asked you to stay put, bud."

Hawk-Finn settled his wings on his back, a tremor in his voice as he asked, "What has passed here, Zack? Where is my Diego?"

Zack rubbed a hand over the back of his neck. "A lot's happened. This isn't going to be easy for you to hear. Diego's—"

A soft knock on the door interrupted him. A timid voice called out, "Sarge?"

He opened the bedroom door to find Minky on the other side, her laptop clutched in both hands. "He's in L.A."

Chapter Fourteen

El Jefe

Power in the hands of the amoral man is unethical on a B-movie level. It is too obvious to be worthy of debate. Power in the hands of the self-appointed righteous man is more dangerous. The leader who seizes power by persuasion is far more dangerous than the one who shoots your grandmother to do it.

— Appoquinimink Jones, *Dangerous Paths*

Finn's anguished cry could have melted glaciers. "If he were in Los Angeles, I would still feel him! Where in all bloody hells is he?"

"I'm trying to explain, bud." Zack reached down to stroke Finn's feathers and received a hard nip for his efforts. "Ow, damn. That wasn't nice."

Lugh wrapped a blanket around his mostly naked body so he wouldn't offend the human youngster. He settled on the edge of the bed, trying his best to shield himself from Finn's anguish. It pounded at him in heavy waves, difficult to ignore. "Why do you believe he is there, my dear?"

Minky turned the device so they could all see the picture screen. She pointed to an image of a dry hillside overlooking a vast, sprawling city. "This is where he, um, stepped through. It looked just like this." She ducked her head, her voice shaking. "Nate said so, too."

"Why can't I find my husband?" Finn shrieked, his wings threatening the nightstand as they beat the air frantically.

The girl gasped and faded from sight, taking on the appearance of the wallpaper behind her.

"What is that?" Finn snapped. He walked awkwardly across the carpet toward her, his talons snagging on threads. "Why is she transparent?"

"Fionnachd, leave her be. You have frightened her." Lugh held out an arm and let Finn climb up to use him as a perch. "If you would give us room to speak, we will tell you the tale. But you must remain calm."

"Tell it, then," Finn snapped.

"Diego came to New York—" Lugh began.

"I know that!"

"Yes. And because I was not fit for a public appearance, he went to the concert for me. But there were human younglings there—"

"There were children in the concert?"

"No, waiting outside."

"What does this have to do with my Diego?"

"I will come to that, if you would listen."

Finn clacked his sharp raptor beak and ruffled his wings. "You are a dreadful storyteller, Lugh mac Ethnnen."

Lugh fought back a sigh and waved to Zack to continue. For reasons only fathomable to Finn, Zack received a more patient hearing, only punctuated by the occasional shifting of talons. At the end of the telling, Finn hopped back to the carpet, staring at the bedroom door, his mind completely shuttered.

"Finn, bud?" Zack took a hesitant step toward him. "Maybe tell me what you're thinking?"

Instead of answering, though, Finn began to give off the soft blue glow that heralded his shifting.

"Do we have any of his clothes here?" Lugh asked, certain Finn was reverting to his bipedal form.

"I don't think—" Zack cut off when the shifting form solidified, not as the handsome pooka, but as a snarling panther. "Finn, don't be stupid."

A low growl was all Finn gave in answer, thick, black tail lashing. Zack lunged for him, a hair too slow, and Panther-Finn shot out of the bedroom on an eerie, piercing roar.

From one heartbeat to the next, Zack hurtled after him, leaving Lugh blinking stupidly on the bed. His Zachary shouldn't have been able to move so swiftly.

"Dammit, Finn, no!"

Zack's bellow broke his shocked trance. Lugh lunged for the door and raced to the living room. He reached the others in time to see Finn, eyes glowing a murderous red, leap toward Brandon. With an inhuman snarl, Zack slammed into him, and bore the panther to the ground where they growled and snapped in a furious tangle of teeth and limbs.

"Enough! You will both cease!" Lugh roared, and found himself completely ignored. *Well and fine. No more words.* He waded into the fray, cuffed Zack hard on the side of his head and seized Finn by his scruff to pull him off. Marcus assisted, getting Zack in a good headlock and dragging him back, though the sergeant still made sounds that should never have issued from a human throat.

"Fionnachd." He gave the panther a little shake. "These are my guests. You are in danger of breaking a sacred trust."

The panther let out a soft, distressed mewl and began to glow. His hand was soon clamped around the back of Finn's neck, a naked, anguished Finn now kneeling at his feet.

"They've stolen my Diego from me," Finn whispered. "My love, my light…"

Lugh gathered him close as he began to sob. "Zachary, are you well?" he called over his shoulder.

"Yeah." Zack's voice held a gravelly edge, as if he might still growl. "Mostly. Sorry. Don't know what happened there."

The youngsters all stared, open-mouthed, eyes as wide as autumn moons. Nate recovered first. "So it's true."

"What's true?" Zack muttered as Marcus eased his hold.

"It was a werewolf that attacked you. And you are one. Or becoming one."

An uncomfortable shroud of silence settled, broken only by Finn's sobs.

"Perhaps such thoughts are better kept to yourself," Lugh said, his throat tight despite his calm words. "You do not know the sergeant well enough to ask such questions or make such presumptions."

"It's okay, Highness," Zack said on a weary huff of breath. "Not like Emily Post ever wrote anything about how to bring up the subject of lycanthropy." He crossed the room to put a gentle hand on Finn's shoulder. "Don't cry, hon, please. We'll find him. We'll get him back."

A low, steady beat as of giant locust wings reached Lugh's ears, growing louder by the second. "Max is here."

Zack hesitated. He seemed to be considering something. When he spoke, it was in that voice that expected obedience. "All right, kids. Gather up your stuff. You're going with His Highness in the Sikorsky."

"And you, my love?" Lugh spoke for his ears alone. "Where are you going?"

"To L.A."

"Not alone. I forbid it."

"Just to get there, all right?" Zack brought a blanket to wrap around Finn. "You take the kids and our guys, get everybody safe to the island. When I get there, I'll call you. You can zap yourself there in half a second and join me, but it'll take me hours to fly there first."

"I'm going with you," Finn said on a huge sniff.

Zack stroked Finn's tangled hair back from his eyes. "No, hon. You go back. Be safe. Who knows what we're walking into?"

Finn drew himself straight so he looked down at Zack. "Have you been inside Diego's mind? Would you know, by instinct, when he is near?"

"Well, no, but—"

"My mate, *my* husband. Do not think to shuffle me into a corner. This is my concern more than any other's."

It would have been a simple thing to knock Finn out and take him away. Easy to say he was distraught and not thinking clearly. But to see him so resolved, so deadly serious sent tendrils of sorrow through Lugh's heart. He had shared tender moments with Finn over the centuries, had more moments when he found him infuriating. This, though, this was a deadly determination so unlike the carefree Finn he had always known. So much had changed…

"My dear." He took Zack's face between his hands. "It would ease my heart to know you are not alone."

Zack opened his mouth as if to protest.

"Please."

For one anxious moment more, Zack hesitated. "All right…all right, then. Finn, bud, let's get you something to wear. Everyone else, get your asses in gear and up to the roof."

Relieved, Lugh pulled his Zachary close in a swift, fierce embrace. "Be careful, my sergeant."

"You, too." Zack poked a finger at his chest. "If there're any barriers you and your grandparents can set up around the island, do it. All his stuff is there. Chances are, he'll try and pop in at some point."

"It will be as you say, Sergeant." He sketched a little salute and turned to lift the still-groggy Brandon in his arms. "Pooka's luck go with you. Are you ready, my dears?"

The young people clustered around him, bags slung over shoulders, heartbeats a bit too fast. Kevin and Marcus led the way to the roof, where the helicopter still beat out its deafening, rhythmic song.

While he hoped they would find Diego and remedy the situation quickly, he had a terrible feeling it wouldn't be so easy.

* * * *

"Sit still, bud." Zack put a hand on Finn's bouncing knee. His fidgeting shook the whole row of chairs and garnered some dark looks from fellow travelers waiting at the gate.

"I'm sorry," Finn whispered miserably. "I hate airports. I despise all the *waiting*."

"I'm kinda surprised you're all right getting on a plane at all."

Finn rocked back and forth, chewing on his thumbnail. "I thought I could not for some time. Believed they must contain too much steel, like cars, and no one would line a plane with silk just for me. But Diego..."

His breath caught on the name, his eyes squeezed shut.

"Hey, it's okay, bud. We don't have to talk about it."

"No...no..." Finn shook his head, though what he disagreed with was unclear. "Diego said they weren't made of steel, but other things. Steel is too heavy. They need lighter materials. That made sense. The bones of birds are hollow, after all. I do not *like* flying in a canister, but it is faster than any wings I have."

Zack took Finn's hand to keep him from chewing his thumbnail off. "Hey. I went through a lot of trouble getting you that hand back. Don't gnaw it off again."

"Ha! Yes. Sorry." Finn gripped his fingers tight, his shivering telegraphing through his arm.

Should have brought catnip. Might've been stoned for most of the flight but at least he would've been calm. "We're gonna get him back. We will."

Soon enough, boarding began. Finn was an old hand at procedures by now, his ticket in hand as he approached the gate, but Zack found it worrisome that he barely thanked the pretty girl who checked him in and strode on without so much as a flirtatious smile.

Carol had booked them in first class, something the Collective could easily afford, to give Finn more room for his long legs. The flight attendants, male and female, fussed over him and normally Finn would have devoured the attention. Now he just clutched the pillow they'd brought him to his chest and stared out of the window, rocking. When the seatbelt light winked out, Zack put the middle armrest up, pulled Finn into his arms and glared once around the cabin to dare anyone to make nasty remarks. The couple across from them seemed uncomfortable, but no one said a word.

"Zack?" Finn finally whispered after the first hour of flight.

"What's up? Hungry?"

"No...I wondered...if he's gone, my Taliesin, my Diego..."

"He's not gone. We know where he is."

Finn shook his head. "I can't feel him any longer. What if that boy's careless spell has destroyed my Diego? Ripped his very essence asunder? What if all that remains is some heartless, hollow shell? Would you be able to destroy him, Zack? If it comes to that?"

"He's too strong. You know that. He might be lost right now but I can't believe someone could change who he is so easily. Not who he is at, you know, the center of himself."

"But what if it's so? Zack, I have a terrible feeling gnawing at me, a darkness that threatens to consume me. If innocents suffer..."

Zack hugged Finn tighter. He didn't want to think about it, but if he had to, he knew he would make a soldier's choice. If he had to take Diego down to save lives, if he ran out of options? Yeah, he would do it in the heat of the moment. He knew himself well enough. "It won't come to that. We're gonna find a way through this."

Finn shivered, clearly too upset to argue. He sniffled and muffled a little sneeze against his forearm. Zack twitched, ready to throw a blanket over Finn's next bizarre shift, but only Finn's hands changed into glossy black wingtips. He sneezed again and his hands returned.

At least he's getting better. I'll take something good today.

After they had finally arrived at LAX, Zack stood with Finn at the car rental counter. He had planned to wrap Finn up in the silk blanket he had in his bag, drive up into the Hollywood Hills where Diego had made his door and see if Finn could pick up a trace from there. The television was on in the little waiting area, the news airing some story about a riot in East L.A. He ignored it, until Finn tugged on his sleeve.

"He is there," Finn whispered, nodding to the screen.

Zack twisted around, trying to see whatever Finn had, but all he saw was a bunch of teenagers smashing the window of an electronics store. "Did you see him?"

"No. I saw his magic."

"You…Finn, what did you see?"

"His lance."

Zack whipped back around to the car rental employees, pointing at the TV screen with the scenes of rioting. "Where is that? What street?"

The girl squinted. "Can't be sure. I don't go down that way too much."

"It's on Cesar Chavez, sir," the young man beside her said with a jaundiced look her way. "You don't wanna go anywhere near there now, though."

"Right." He glanced down at the screen the girl was trying to get him to sign and barked out, "No insurance, no gas purchase, need a GPS, whatever vehicle you have first available. Can we get a rush on that?"

He'd rolled into sergeant mode without thinking, polite conversation be damned. The girl's eyes grew as big as dessert plates, but she *moved* all right. Within three minutes, they were in an Explorer, with a GPS, and a direction.

"All right, deep breath, bud." Zack patted Finn's knee as they took a sharp left. "Tell me exactly what you saw on the TV."

Finn shivered under the silk blanket that protected him from the iron content of the SUV. "The lightning lance. His weapon. I've never seen another summon one. It flashed by, into a narrow corridor between buildings, behind the humans smashing windows. I did not see *him* but he had to have been there."

"Did you see what he was aiming for?"

Finn shook his head, curling up under the blanket until only his shoes stuck out. Vague notions of somehow spotting Diego while they drove through the streets or maybe letting Finn get out and walk once they reached the neighborhood ping-ponged through Zack's overloaded brain. One of them should feel *something*.

Any search for recognizable magical flows became a moot point when they reached the corner of Cesar Chavez and Figueroa. A hulking monstrosity of an apartment building dominated the block, one of those mixed-use buildings that should have had stores on the street level and apartments above, though both retail and living space appeared largely vacant. On the roof nearest the corner stood a familiar figure, calmly surveying the police activity and now-fleeing rioters farther down the street.

"Finn..."

"I see him. Oh, I see him, Zachary, and my heart cracks."

Zack hauled the SUV over to the curb, never taking his eyes off their quarry. "He looks okay to me."

"It's him, my Diego," Finn whispered. "And not him."

"Well, we're here to start getting that fixed. Don't fall apart on me now."

Finn slid from the passenger side, pale and trembling but with a tight set to his jaw. "Shall I fly?"

"Rather you stay with me. Let's find a way up there." He flipped open his cell and made the call he'd promised. Lugh picked up halfway through the first ring as if he'd been holding the phone, staring at it, waiting for the call.

"Zachary?"

"We've found him. You got a fix on me?"

"I'll be with you in a matter of moments, never fear."

Zack had envisioned breaking a window or slipping in behind a resident but a broken security door served just as well. This time he purposefully matched strides with Finn as they raced up the stairs, unwilling to let the distraught pooka out of his sight for an instant. He wasn't sure why the growing feeling of dread was reaching suffocating, but his newer senses had been reliable so far. They reached a locked door with a sign indicating roof access. Zack pulled in a breath and kicked the door, trying to adjust for his new strength.

He failed miserably. The door exploded outward and ended up hanging on one broken, twisted hinge.

Finn regarded the door with an arched eyebrow. "Did it insult you out of my hearing?"

"Sorry," Zack muttered, though it was good to see Finn manage a bit of humor.

The amused glint in Finn's eyes lasted only until they stepped out onto the roof. He gripped Zack's arm hard, seemingly frozen in place.

Diego stood at the edge of the roof, his expression recovering from the shock of the door being kicked open. Diego's smile greeted them. His hands, so familiar, opened, reaching out to welcome them. The man before them was still their Diego…and he wasn't. Something chill and flat filmed his eyes. An odd twist had crept into his once warm smile.

"*Mi vida!* You've come! And Zack, too!" Diego beamed and motioned toward his feet where a young man lay sprawled. Tangled black hair tumbled over paper white skin, the arrangement of his limbs making it appear as if he had been dumped onto the roof from several feet up. "Do you see what I have here, Sergeant? It's our vampire!"

Zack put his hand over Finn's trying to calm him. "Is it? Did you kill him, Mr. S.?"

A puzzled frown creased Diego's forehead. "No, no. It wasn't necessary. Odd, really. I had thought a vampire would be more powerful. But he was easy to take down. Fast, strong, yes, but such unfocused power. More of a nutritionally challenged pitbull."

"Will you kill him, beloved?" Finn took a step forward, his voice trembling.

"We shall see, I suppose." Diego met Finn's gaze with a bright smile. "He will submit to me, agree to become something useful to me, or he will be destroyed. The same for any being of dark magic. They will obey me, call me *jefe,* or I take them out."

"Diego…love…" Finn stretched a hand out. "This doesn't sound like you. It's as —"

A shriek of wind interrupted him, followed by a thunderclap of misplaced air as Lugh appeared near the edge of the roof.

"Ah, the hero arrives," Diego said, his smile sliding toward frigid. "I see. My darling husband and my friend aren't here to help me. They're here to take custody of me."

Zack locked eyes with Lugh for a second, reassurance and silent signal. "Finn misses you, Mr. S. We all do. We're worried about you."

"You're not well, my friend." Lugh spoke softly, hands spread wide as he stepped toward Diego. "You must come home with us. We only wish to help you."

Diego heaved a sigh, shaking his head. "I know. I know you think something's wrong with me. God knows I'm different. I realize that. But I'm fine. I'm better than I've ever been. And I have important work to do. If you won't help me, you need to stay out of my way."

The hunter's instinct in all three of them had kicked in. Without communication, they had formed a half circle around Diego with Finn in the middle. "My heart, my own." The pooka's deep voice cracked and wavered. "We made a promise, you and I, never to shut each other out again. To answer when the other calls. To never again allow one of us to feel abandoned."

"I haven't abandoned you, *cariño.* You can't believe that." Something uncertain crept into Diego's eyes.

"What am I to think? You *have* shut me out." Finn heaved a shuddering breath. "I no longer hear you. I've called and called…"

"It's only until I have things in hand. I need to know you're safe."

With Diego's attention fixed on Finn, Zack only needed a spare hint of a nod to Lugh. Both of them moved faster than any human could, lunging for Diego in the same moment, one from either side.

Diego never took his eyes off Finn. He held up a hand toward Zack and suddenly, Zack's joints locked. He toppled to the rooftop, unable to rise. For Lugh, Diego simply lifted a hand and flicked his fingers. A sphere of ball lightning shot from his fingers, struck Lugh square in the chest and hurled him across the roof. He slammed into the access door with a clang, sliding slowly to the rooftop, out cold.

"Try to betray me again, *mi vida*, and I may rethink some of my promises." Diego's smile had twisted into something bitter and chill.

Finn dropped to his knees, arms out flung. "Don't leave me again! Diego, please! Take me with you!"

"Hush, shh. I can't trust you right now, my darling husband." Diego crouched and heaved the vampire's unconscious frame over his shoulders. "But soon you'll understand. I'm saving the world. You just don't see it yet. When you do, I'll send for you."

"Diego!" Finn wailed. He struggled to rise, apparently unable to get up off his knees.

"Don't fuss. It won't be long." Diego opened a portal as if it were as easy as drawing breath. The doorway showed dark woods. "Be safe, *cariño*. You'll hear from me."

Diego strode through, shouldering his vampire burden without a glance back. The portal closed behind him with a thunderous crack.

Zack's limbs unlocked as suddenly as they had frozen. He rolled onto his back. "Lugh?"

Muttered cursing came from a few feet away, so he decided his prince was all right. Their retrieval mission, however, was in tatters.

Well, hell. What now?

Chapter Fifteen

The Defense of Magical Beings Act

Any law restricting the rights of a minority group should have been met with vehement resistance. In any other political climate, it would have been.
— Dr. Nathan R. Cooper, *The Disastrous Year*

Minky sat on the edge of the fountain in the garden, swinging her feet. This place was, as Nate said, epically cool, but everyone was so damn touchy-feely. She twitched every time another pretty fae put an arm around her. Not that she wanted to hurt any of their feelings. She *liked* all the ones she'd met. But she needed a couple of minutes alone so she wouldn't run screaming.

Nate didn't have any problems with it. He hugged back. He cuddled. *Kara* managed all right, though she blushed when the pretty females stroked her hair. Even Will accepted the attention gracefully, though he'd been whisked down to the caverns with Brandon to have the big dork's head looked at, so she hadn't seen either of them for hours. She was pretty sure there weren't fairy dust CAT scans or MRIs down there, but apparently medical procedures took ridiculously long no matter what species.

"Astounding."

She squeaked at the bone-rattling deep voice and automatically faded into the stone of the fountain. When she looked up...and up...at the owner of the voice, she wanted to hide under the stones. The man, no not a man, fae, looming over her gleamed in the sunlight, massive in every respect and *naked*. She made sure not to let her eyes wander below his waist. The last thing she wanted to see was giant fae junk.

He smiled down at her, showing sharp teeth, and she gasped. He was one thing and another, the human-like shape more prominent but behind it, around it, through it, she clearly saw...

"Dragon," she whispered, then clapped her hands over her mouth when she realized the word had slipped out.

"Well done, little one. You do know I can still see you?"

"Yeah. Figured. I mean, you're a...a dragon." She didn't really know why that would make a difference, but some gut instinct told her it did.

"Hmm. Yes." The dragon settled on the fountain's edge beside her. He shouldn't have fit there, but somehow he did. "You are frightened of me."

Minky clamped her hands on the stones and forced herself not to flee, concentrating hard on being visible. "It's not just you. I'm pretty much scared of everything."

"Ah. You are part of the coven of children Lugh mac Ethnenn has brought to the island."

It was a statement, rather than a question, but still seemed to require an answer. Minky kept her eyes on her feet, letting them swing again. The dragon couldn't swing his feet. He was so huge that *his* feet were firmly planted on the ground. "Yeah. I mean, I guess. We're not really children, though."

"You are young humans coming into your power. To most inhabitants of the Otherworld, you are still children."

She nodded, not really offended. The dragon was probably umpteen thousand years old, anyway. "The others, they might be powerful and stuff. But not me."

The dragon laughed. It was an incredible sound, like one of those rain sticks playing alongside a bass drum, but the wonder of it didn't override Minky's embarrassment. *I sure don't think it's funny.*

"Oh, little one." The dragon's head tilted. "You have no idea what you are, have you?"

Before she could ask what he meant, his head shot up, his nostrils flared. He stared at a willow tree across the garden. Minky bit her bottom lip to keep from squeaking when a forked tongue shot out to test the air.

"The *sidhe* prince comes."

She knew enough about fae by now to keep her mouth shut. Prince Lugh had answered his cell about an hour before while they were all in the den inside the embassy. He'd been talking to the sergeant — she could tell by the worried warmth in his tone — then he'd just…vanished. She knew about the translocation stuff, sure. Knowing wasn't the same as seeing somebody pop out of existence, papers flying around as the air whooshed in to fill the vacuum.

Now the same whoosh and air-swirly thing happened again, except in reverse with the magic wind blowing out from the place the prince popped into – a prince who didn't appear pleased. In fact, he looked pissed.

The dragon cocked his head with a frown. His bass vibrated through the fountain when he shouted across the garden, "Shining One! What news?"

The prince's head jerked toward the fountain and Minky instinctively shrank behind the dragon's bulk.

"My lord?" Prince Lugh covered the distance between them in a ridiculously small number of steps and dropped to one knee in front of the dragon. "I had no word you were expected."

My lord? Oh, damn. Who am I really sitting with?

The dragon lifted one shoulder in a shrug. "Announcing my visits would cause too much commotion. I wished to see where things stood for myself."

The prince nodded, still on one knee. He looked so depressed, Minky had the weird urge to hug him. Not that she ever would.

"Events on the wind and skilled scrying most likely precede me." Lugh reached out a hand. The dragon took it and even the fae prince's fingers disappeared into that huge mitt. "You know of the dark mage, my lord?"

"We have had rumors of him long before this, yes. That he would be a human known and dear to us…distresses dragonkind."

Lugh bowed his head when he nodded again. "I went to retrieve him. To bring him back in hopes of a cure. I have failed."

The dragon snorted, steam curling from his nostrils. "You have failed in your first attempt. Surely Lugh the Shining does not cede the field?"

Anger sparked in dark fae eyes. Lugh's nostrils flared and Minky edged away, hoping a fight wasn't about to start. "No. I have never and will not now. Though perhaps if I were to approach alone, without warning—"

The dragon lord cut him off with a dismissive wave. "Perhaps. But remember, my *hssktet*, that this is human magic. And we do have human mages at hand."

Lugh reared back in shock. "They're children, my lord! I won't endanger them."

The forked tongue flicked the air again, heat radiating from the dragon's skin. "Power, *sidhe* prince. There is power here the likes of which humankind has not seen in centuries. Do not stand in my way."

After a shocked silence, Lugh pulled his hand free, shaking out his fingers. "No, my lord. Never that."

"Good." The dragon's enigmatic smile, neither cruel nor kind, certainly was less than comforting. "Perhaps you should seek out your grandmother. She will be anxious for news."

Minky tried to make herself as small as possible, though she already knew she couldn't hide from this being. *What does he mean? Don't stand in his way...what does he want from us?*

Lugh left them with a little bow, broad shoulders tense under his black T-shirt. The urge to run knotted in Minky's stomach. She was sitting next to someone who ordered royalty around like it was his god-given right.

"So. We should begin."

She was shocked into glancing up at him. "Begin what, sir?" she squeaked out, squirming under that steady alien gaze.

"Your education. I have not come out of mere curiosity."

"You want to *teach* us?" *Gah!* The things she was blurting out! The dragon was liable to eat her out of annoyance. "But human magic...isn't it different?"

The dragon lord stood and stretched, making her drop her gaze back to her feet. *He could at least put something on his big, buff dragon self. Seriously.* "Yes. Human magic is volatile and often difficult to untangle. But it is still magic, governed by the same universal laws as all magic. I will attempt a beginning. Help you reach for your birthright." He pointed to a wisteria-twined pergola. "Gather your coven mates. Meet me there. Time is in short supply."

Minky leaped to her feet and ran for the embassy before she realized she'd slid off the fountain stones. Maybe it was that voice, underworld deep and commanding. Maybe there was some magic compulsion in it that no one could resist. Though somehow she couldn't see Sergeant Morrison bowing to dragon demands. He probably would stand up to God if he needed to.

* * * *

"Lord Hssetassk is here doing *what*?" Finn's shriek echoed down the embassy hallways.

Zack had seen him upset before, even enraged, but this was approaching ballistic. It was freaking scary.

"He's teaching the kids about magic," Carol repeated, somehow remaining calm and sympathetic even faced with a pooka about to go postal, flames dancing in his eyes, hair whipped into a frenzy by a rising magical wind. "Finn, sweetie, if they'd had a teacher before, maybe none of this would've happened. It only makes sense, right? And I don't think you really want to start an argument with his lordship. How am I going to explain things to Nathair and Eithne when you wind up as pooka barbecue?"

She patted his chest and pulled Finn into a hug when he let out a strangled whimper. "There now. Come have some tea with me. You've had a terrible couple of days."

The wind collapsed, defeated by warm concern, and Finn let himself be led away, the beast tamed by their fearless admin. Not that Finn could ever truly be a beast, poor guy. His stress levels were just off the charts right now.

His and everyone else's.

By the time they'd landed at St. John's International, all the news agencies had been buzzing about riots in Houston and Detroit as well. Witchcraft Riots, the reporters were calling these disturbances, damn them. Nothing like fanning the hysteria. They all seemed to begin with magical attacks on someone of power in a public area, in a poorer section of town. 'Witch on witch violence' some idiot news pundit called it. The violence always escalated as more magic users were sucked into the crowd hysteria, either trying to defend themselves or attacking blindly out of fear. The police in every afflicted city seemed unable to find the ones who caused the most damage. Those individuals all mysteriously disappeared.

Though Zack was sure he knew what had happened to them, in part. Diego had whisked them away. At least he hoped so, and that Diego wasn't killing anyone. *Please, God, not that.*

A hand fell on his shoulder and turned him gently. He'd been so damn distracted he neither had heard nor smelled Lugh's approach. He had to stay alert, especially now, damn it, but it felt so good to rest his head on a broad shoulder and have strong arms wrap him up tight. They'd only been separated for a few hours, but it felt like centuries.

"Are you well, braveheart?"

"Yeah. I guess." When Lugh let out a sound of concern, he hurried to add, "I'm good. Not hurt or anything. Just…worried and frustrated all to hell."

"I presume you have watched the news, then."

"Yeah." Zack buried his face against Lugh's neck, drinking in his scent. "He's moving so damn fast. What the hell are we supposed to do?"

For a long moment, they simply held each other in the empty office, their breathing punctuated by soft computer noises. Finally, Lugh pulled back, his hands still on Zack's hips. "I have never been so unsure. He has not, as far as we know, killed. He leaves destruction in his wake but seems to have avoided causing irretrievable injury. Do we wait, to see his ultimate design? Do we try to divine a pattern in his strikes and hunt him with a greater force? And what is it we do here, exactly, if his goal is simply to capture those who would use magic for dark purposes?"

"It's wrong and you know it." Zack poked a finger at his shoulder. "Don't even try to tell yourself it isn't. Someone's gonna get seriously hurt. And even if they don't, what happens when he has 'control'? What's our doppelganger Diego planning then? This isn't going anywhere good."

Lugh stared at a point over his head. "He is still Diego. His thoughts have always been ordered…"

"Right. There has to be a pattern to what he's doing out there. We just need to figure it out." Zack grabbed his prince's hand and dragged him to the den. He switched on the news and grabbed a road atlas from the bookshelf, opening it up to the map of the continental United States.

Lugh sat on the edge of the sofa, arms resting on his powerful thighs. If he'd had canine ears, they would have been pricked forward. Zack pulled a red pen from the cup on the end table and circled Los Angeles.

"Okay, pretty sure I know why he went to L.A. first. That's where the vamp in his FOSH folder was."

Dark eyes blinked at him. "FOSH?"

"Sorry, the File of Strange Happenings he showed me before everything went all to hell."

"And is this file still in his office? Perhaps it would provide answers."

Zack flashed him a grin. "See, now my prince is thinking." He leaped up before Lugh had a chance to answer and dashed off to Diego's office. *Damn it, why didn't I think of it before?* A hard twinge in his chest stopped him at the door. Memories of Diego behind that big-ass desk, frowning in worry over some diplomatic problem or smiling in welcome—it hurt, to remember *their* Diego, who might be gone forever.

I don't want to hurt him but this new Diego scares the hell out of me.

The file still sat in Diego's unlocked top drawer, and that was so like his old friend, to be so trusting as to leave classified documents lying around, that the lump in his throat almost cut off his breathing. He swiped impatiently at his eyes and hurried back to the den. This sure as shit wasn't the time to start falling apart.

He divided the papers with Lugh and they spent half an hour searching through page after page. The whole thing would've taken seconds if these things had been compiled on the embassy's intranet, but no. Diego was old school and had to print it all out. Sionnach and Angus soon joined them, curiosity driving both heralds to find the source of rustling paper.

"For what do we search?" Sionnach plunked down cross-legged on the floor by Zack's feet, bushy tail curled across his lap.

"Here." Zack handed him a stack of pages and took a section of Lugh's to give to Angus. "Look for any mention of what Diego would have considered 'dark' magical critters and what cities they were spotted in."

Angus sprawled on the floor with his stack, his head in Sionnach's lap, almost identical frowns of concentration on their faces. Strange to see the two heralds so silent, so serious, but the past couple of months had been hard on everybody.

The list grew slowly. New York. Boston. Miami. Spokane. Poughkeepsie. But no mention, aside from Los Angeles, of the cities Diego had raided. Zack looked up sharply when the news channel began running stories about new riots.

Pittsburgh.

He added it to the list, staring hard at the names. "Houston... Detroit... Pittsburgh..."

His tired brain didn't make the connection but Sionnach, whose head retained every song he ever heard, began to hum *Life During Wartime.*

"Damn it!" Zack slammed his palm down on the coffee table, causing all three fae to jump. "He's playing games with us!"

"Zachary?" Lugh gripped his shoulder, and he realized he was shaking.

"Hold on…" With a muttered curse, he dug his phone from his pocket and did a quick search. "Talking Heads. He's pulling cities from Talking Heads songs. Was always one of his favorite groups. Probably end up in New York at some point, but I'd bet he saves that for later." His thumbs flew over the keys as he kept searching while he talked. A corner of his mind whispered to him that he shouldn't be able to text so fast. He told it to shut the hell up. "Memphis. He'll be going to Memphis next."

"Oh, yes?" Lugh leaned over his shoulder, forehead creased in confusion.

"Song lyrics. He's picking cities from Talking Heads' lyrics, wondering if I'd catch on. God. He'd do that sometimes. Recite bits of lyrics to see if I'd know the song. It's like his normal quirks all twisted up."

"Why would he focus on you?" Angus' head tilted to the side like the bird he was.

"He…" Zack shook his head. "We've been through a lot together. Maybe…maybe some part of him wants me to understand because he's sure Finn won't. Wants me to…I'm not sure. Either stop him or stand by him. Maybe some of both."

The fae in the room exchanged looks. "This is a human thing, I think," Sionnach said softly.

Lugh shook his head. "It is our Taliesin's heart crying out to us in anguish. He resides beneath the strange, cold façade still. It should give us hope."

"It should get our butts moving to Memphis if we're going to have any chance of stopping this." Zack stood. "I'll grab Carol. Lugh, I'd suggest gathering whatever battle group you think is appropriate."

"Finn?"

"Wouldn't leave without him."

* * * *

Minky cringed at the crack of the dragon lord's hand on Brandon's ass. Again. The first time had been kind of funny, but she had never enjoyed watching someone else being humiliated. Normally so confident and together, Brandon's repeated failure had left him frustrated, his face scarlet in shame, his jaw clenched tight. If he broke down, she might have to say something...

Whoa. Where did that come from?

"No and no!" The dragon didn't shout but the way his words snapped and popped in the air made his listeners wince. "Your impetus comes from your core but power comes from outside yourself!"

Brandon squeezed his eyes shut, obviously fighting his temper and tears. The dragon lord had already taught Nate and Kara how to reach for the magic all around them. They were getting it. The big guy couldn't.

"Sir?" Will asked softly.

"Yes, little seer?" Golden dragon eyes pinned Will where he sat on the swing under the wisteria.

"If that's true, and there's always the same amount of magic out there for everyone to use, why are some people more powerful than others?"

"Ah. Your *kelan* patterns..." The dragon lord settled cross-legged on the patio under the pergola, his golden skin a beautiful contrast to the gray paving stones. With a flick of his fingers over the stones where they had each donated a drop of blood, he displayed their individual *kelan* again as he had when they had first started the lesson an hour before. "Think of them as nodes onto which the world's magic may cling."

Kara's and Nate's were on the end, nearly identical as far as Minky could see, in the distribution and movement of the bright motes. Will's and Brandon's both shone brighter, though Will's had a quiet, waltz-like movement while Brandon's looked more like a rave. Her own...she didn't understand why hers were so different. The others had colonies of *kelan* clustered along their DNA strands. Minky's were more diffuse, like strings and webs of Christmas lights.

"The greater the number of *kelan*," the dragon went on, pointing to Brandon's sample. "The greater the potential. No matter how well trained, a magic user with fewer natural *kelan* will only be able to pull on the flows so far. One with a greater concentration, as with our stubborn one here, *should* be able to access far more power. To exercise far more control."

Brandon ducked his head, chewing on his bottom lip. He looked so miserable. *All this mess is his fault. I don't want to feel bad for him.*

Minky sighed and cleared her throat, forcing the question out when everyone turned to her. "But...sir? You said *kelans* are inherited. That most species have their own patterns."

The dragon nodded. "Human patterns are not as predictable as others. But there are certain traits shared by most humans, as we see here." Then he pointed to her strange, delicate-looking pattern. "You wish to know why yours is so unlike the others."

Minky nodded, trying to keep herself from fading into the wisteria vines under the alien weight of draconian eyes. She twitched, almost falling from her bench, when a loud sneeze erupted overhead. Another followed and a black tortoise fell from the pergola's roof to the stones.

What the...

The tortoise sneezed and vanished, replaced by a black swan, which sneezed and abruptly became a black butterfly.

"Thrice damned wisteria," the butterfly muttered. The butterfly opened and closed midnight-velvet wings, sneezed and vanished in favor of a fae male whose only covering was his long, blue-black hair.

"Fionnachd, you were welcome to join us in a less abrupt fashion," the dragon said in a desert-dry tone.

"Yes, well..." The pooka sat up, mirroring the dragon's position on the stones, his face a study in wounded dignity. "I had no wish to interrupt."

Will had shoved Brandon behind him, which would have been funny with their size difference if it hadn't been for the memory of their last meeting with Finn.

The dragon snorted and gestured for Will to sit down. "He means your beloved no harm."

"But, sir—"

"Calm. Fionnachd has come to see his child."

"My *what*?" Finn surged to his feet, spinning in a circle as if unsure who he should address.

"You were drawn here, pooka. You felt the pull."

"I was curious! It's my worst failing!"

"The centuries have thinned the blood but the magic breeds true."

Finn hid his face in his hands, whispering, "Oh, gods. I didn't think...did she even *have* children?"

"The answer sits before you. Did you not tell me once, Fionnachd, that you had tired of living in fear?"

"This isn't fear," Finn muttered, staring at Minky through his cascade of dark hair. "I'm just a mite, as they say, freaked out. The shocks follow too quickly these days."

Minky felt the blood drain from her face when she finally figured out they meant *her*. But she couldn't make any sense out of it. She knew her parents. She also knew the story about Finn's return to the world and that he hadn't been around when she was conceived. None of it made sense.

"She's transparent again." Finn shook his head on a sigh. He held out a hand to her. "Come away, human child. I expect we should...talk."

She flinched back, more rather than less uncomfortable.

"Why is she so frightened of me?" Finn's voice sounded plaintive and hurt, much different from the ferocious pooka she had first seen in Prince Lugh's condo.

"Besides the fact that the first time she saw you, you were a panther trying to rip Brandon's throat out?" Nate said with a wry smile.

"Well, yes. I've not even raised my voice today."

Nate cleared his throat. "Um, dude, you're naked. Minky doesn't do naked."

"Oh." Finn looked down at himself and even Minky had to choke back a snicker. "Oh, bother. Is that it? Easily remedied. Meet me in the kitchen. I'll be properly covered."

He stalked off and Minky breathed out in relief until she realized she was supposed to go after him. *Feet, you should move. Before I look really stupid.* But they decided they'd rather pretend to be stone and refused to budge.

"Mink? We're okay here without you for a little bit." Nate crouched down next to her bench. "I mean, I know you want to protect Bran and all—"

She ducked her head on a strangled snicker.

"—but His Lordship here said more than once that you're different. Maybe you need a different teacher."

Kara spoke up from where she stood apart from the rest, arms crossed. "Big girl panties. You can do this. Go talk to your great granddad, or whatever the hell he is."

Dread clutching her heart, she got up and dragged her feet inside. By the time she got to the kitchen, Finn was there, dressed in jeans and a Depeche Mode T-shirt, sprawled in one of the chairs, long, bare feet propped up on the table. At least they looked clean.

"I suppose I should offer you something." His fingers drummed restlessly on the chair arm. "Human young like soda, though, don't they? We don't have any of that."

"I...um..." Minky edged toward the fridge. "Water's good. You...do you want one?"

He leaned back, lacing his fingers over his stomach. "Thanks all the same, but no. Are you truly afraid of everything? Or only me?"

"Yeah. Pretty much." She took the chair farthest from him and put the bottle of water down since her hands shook too much. "Life, the universe and everything."

One corner of his mouth quirked up. "I like those books."

"What?"

"The Hitchhiker ones. Diego has read them to me." He faltered on his husband's name and Minky's heart cracked because of it.

"Oh. Yeah." She picked at the label on her water. "I, um...like them, too." She let her feet swing. Even the chairs in this place were too big. "Do you…do you have lots of kids?"

He blinked at her, apparently taken off guard. "Ah…no. I was never certain I had any. But there was one girl… I did suspect, perhaps…"

"Did she…you know, *know*?"

"That I was her sire?" He shrugged one shoulder, lips pressed in a tight line. "I never spoke to her, to my lasting regret. I will never know."

She opened her water and took a sip. "I'm sorry," she whispered, and she meant it.

"Not your doing." He finally looked at her again. "But here you are and here I am. That's a rather neat trick you've managed, this fading to transparency."

"It's just…something that happened. Can you do it?"

"Not the way you do. But I can become difficult to spot when I wish." He flashed her a hesitant smile and faded from sight. He didn't blend into the background. He really vanished until only his smile remained.

That disembodied smile reminded her so much of the Cheshire Cat, she let out a shocked laugh, then clapped both hands over her mouth.

"It's all right to laugh at my little jokes. You've nothing to fear from me," Finn said as he reappeared. He took his feet from the table, propped his elbow on the wood and his chin in his hand. "But then again, you've most likely inherited your fear. Cowardice is part of a pooka's nature."

She opened her water so she could roll the cap around on the table. "You're not."

"Of course I am. I would much rather crawl under a rock than become embroiled in confrontation. I'm frightened all the time."

"Yeah, but you still *do* stuff." She couldn't believe she was arguing with someone who could turn into a dragon and eat her. "You helped get the door opened again between the worlds. You're the one everybody listened to when the fae needed, you know, a place to stand."

His gaze was calm and steady, but difficult to read. "Perhaps I had a hand in things. Still scared spitless the whole time." He caught the cap she was rolling, tossed it in the air a few times and rolled it back to her. "Do you feel the flows? Or rather, are you aware that you do?"

She shook her head, more out of confusion than negation. "I feel…something. I mean, I know when other people are using power. Kara pulls in strings, just as much as she needs. Brandon pulls in huge, honking wads of it, like he'll never have enough."

Finn's eyes narrowed when she mentioned Brandon, but his voice stayed soft. "That one needs a leash. Or a muzzle. Perhaps both." He raised his free hand, palm up, and curled the fingers in one by one as if cutting off the topic. "Your pardon. Never mind that. Obviously you *do* feel it."

"Yeah, but…not when I look for it. Not when I want it, you know? Just when other people yank on the magic. That's what I feel."

"Sensitive…" He held a hand out toward her, fingers hovering over her arm. "But blocked. Your anxieties block your channels, I suppose."

"Great," she muttered, rolling the cap back to him.

He continued the game, putting a spin into the cap's trajectory as he sent it back. "Diego…was like that. When we first met."

So much sorrow, it's like he's drowning in it. "So what…what changed?" The cap went wide as she sent it back, nerves skewing her aim, and Finn had to snake out an arm to snatch it from the table edge.

"Sex," he answered with a wistful hint of a smile.

Of course. She sighed in frustration. "Not helping. I don't…" She waved a hand in a helpless gesture, then scrambled to catch the cap as it sailed back to her.

"*Kisk hesklss*, the dragons would say. Tree-like."

"Huh?"

"Most beings that have young…" Finn took the cap back, tossing it from hand to hand as he seemed to search for words. "They spend a bloody huge amount of energy on mating. Looking for mates. Courting them. Fighting for them. Mating with them. But most races seem to have some people who do not do this. Rather than running about in endless mating dances, they stand still. Do not engage. Observe. Tree-like."

"Yeah. That's about right."

"So." He spun the cap back to her. "You must have something that makes you…not afraid."

Not afraid. Was there anything? Reading was good, getting lost in someone else's problems. Sometimes, her friends, her *coven*…there were times when everything was going well and everyone was getting along, and the knots in her stomach went away.

"I guess—"

"Finn, bud." Sergeant Morrison stood at the kitchen door, pale, obviously worried. "You better come see this."

The pooka glanced between her and the sergeant, then jerked his head toward the door.

Me? Minky shrank back in confusion, but then wasn't given a choice when Finn grabbed her hand and dragged her along. Weird. She didn't cringe from his touch as she normally did other people's.

Their destination turned out to be the den where various fae and human staffers packed the room, perched on every piece of furniture and flat surface available. Several pixies fluttered around a table lamp. Those things made her nervous — too much like insects. Finn shocked her by tucking her under his arm and leading her over to where her friends stood in an anxious knot, the dragon lord looming behind them.

The television was on, showing a podium with all the trappings of a press conference about to start. Something big was up.

Sergeant Morrison came to stand with them. "They're going through the prelims. Which cities have been affected, injured counts, all that. The President's already said he's called in a 'widely respected expert' to help get a handle on the problem. Three guesses who."

Minky had already guessed who would be coming to the podium, but it didn't ease the shock one bit to see Mr. Sandoval again. Not the one everyone knew, of course. That Mr. Sandoval would have thanked the person presenting him and would have shuffled nervously for a bit before beginning. This man, this dark mage they had made out of Diego Sandoval, strode onstage with an air of command, his expression serious and full of the proper concern but overlain with enough arrogance to make Minky shudder.

"Ladies and gentlemen of the press," he began, both hands gripping the sides of the podium as if he needed to keep the world steady. "What we have on our hands today is a crisis of unprecedented proportions, a threat to our national security, our homes and our families.

This is not a crisis stemming from any external source, from terrorists bent on bringing this nation down or an outside economic threat, but rather from our own citizens. From our own children..."

He went on to describe what was happening as a plague of wild human magic, as a disease process that needed to be checked. His claim was that in previous centuries, humans taught their children how to deal with the magical world. Old wives' tales, old superstitions, all had their roots in magical training. But the modern world had neglected those teachings. Too much had been lost. The sudden re-manifestation of magic in the human population had resulted in wild talents and dark illnesses of a magical nature.

"...vampirism, lycanthropy, pyromancy — these are human conditions, caused by the distortions of untrained human mages. But I believe there is hope. I believe we can, if Congress is willing to act quickly and decisively, restore order and provide assistance to all those afflicted. We can hide our heads in the sand and wait for chaos to devour every city from coast to coast, or we can build a new model of government, lead the world in the training of magical youth and the treatment of magical maladies."

He held up a sheaf of paper. "I have here a proposal that, with the President's approval, I intend to set before the House this afternoon."

A clamor of voices rose from the room. Mr. Sandoval raised his voice above the noise. "The Defense of Magical Beings Act calls for the creation of a Department of Magical Education and Security. Through this agency, we will be able to register and monitor all magical beings within our borders. We will, in fact, be able to prevent violence before its inception..."

Minky stopped listening as her blood pounded in her ears. Registration was always the first step, wasn't it? Before they rounded up all the undesirables and made them disappear.

Chapter Sixteen

Bullheaded

To love a warrior is to resign oneself to waiting. Waiting for the battle to be over. Waiting to hear if your love is unscathed. But when shield companions find love with one another? Which one of the pair is consigned to waiting then?
— Nathair Greenhands, from *A Social History of the Fae Courts*, Appoquinimink Jones

Lugh listened as patiently as he could as the humans explained what the press conference had truly meant. Certainly, he understood the words but not the implications. Horror took hold when the young humans told him about Nazis and all the terrors they had visited upon the world. Surely Diego, even in his changed form, would never resort to such things?

But amidst all the reasonable sounding proposals about education and assistance, he had used words such as 'cleansing' the human race of dark magic and 'suppressing' the tide of magical disasters. These did not have the sound of innocuous, benign things.

"I need to go to Washington," he said softly, distracted by visions of witch-hunts.

"Don't you even think about popping down there alone, Highness." Zack stared at the television, his voice a dangerous growl. It sent an unexpected shiver down Lugh's back.

"But I must go. The news people include fae in all this talk of registration. I must speak for us."

Zack jerked his head around. "It's not safe, damn it! Not alone!"

"Zachary..." Lugh put a hand on his shoulder, squeezing gently. "I am the appointed ambassador for all fae. I cannot cower here when my obligations are clear. He speaks to the human government. I must be there as well."

"What if that's what he's looking for? Did you think of that? Get you off the island? Separate you from anyone who might protect you?"

"You're simply being overprotective. There would be people, large numbers of people, around us at all times. And truly, what could he possibly want with me?"

"Damn right I'm overprotective! Fuck! How hard is it to accept some help?" Zack tore himself away with a strangled cry and stalked out of the room. His boots rang through the halls, each anger-driven footstep threatening to crack floorboards as he stomped up the stairs.

"Good one, Highness," Kara said from his left. "Epic fail."

"Indeed." Finn nodded to the hall. "This might be one of those times to go after an angry lover, eh?"

Lugh glared from Finn to the young humans, all of them watching him expectantly. "The last time you went after an angry lover, Fionnachd, he nearly killed you."

"Ah, well." Finn gave an airy wave. "Zack has no lightning. The worst he would do is strike you. Rather hard, mind you, but still…"

"Your words are most inspiring," Lugh said in a dry tone. "Perhaps I will have you give speeches before battles."

"I live to please, Shining One." Finn swept an elaborate bow and more than one human child snickered. "He worries with good reason. As much as I wish to rush to where my beloved is, my feet are ice considering it. That man in Washington is still Diego, with his sharp mind. There will be turns within turns in his plans."

The prettiest human male, Will, touched Lugh's arm hesitantly. "The sergeant loves you, sir. Or he wouldn't be so mad."

Lugh cut short the angry words he had mustered, struck by that simple statement. If it was so obvious to human children… He patted the youngster's hand and hurried from the room, following the trail of Zack's passage, trying to shove his own temper down.

He found Zack in his bedroom, pacing, arms folded tight over his chest. The sergeant gave him one quick glare before he looked away again, eyes fastened on his boots as he strode from one corner of the room to the other.

"Zack…love…"

"You're just gonna do whatever the hell you please, anyway. I don't know why I waste my time. Goddamn royal egos."

The anger he'd tried to banish boiled to the surface again. "I cannot simply stand by and watch while decisions are made regarding *my* people. Perhaps humans can, but ego or not, I am a *sidhe* prince, my queen's Champion as well as the Ambassador—"

Zack suddenly turned and leaped at him with a bone-rattling growl. He slammed into Lugh, furniture and hanging pictures rattling as his back hit the wall hard. Forearm shoved against Lugh's throat, Zack held him pinned, fury-driven strength shocking the fight from him.

For a moment, they stared at each other, Zack's breaths coming through gritted teeth. Without easing the pressure on Lugh's windpipe, he grated out, "I can't lose you. Not now."

"You won't," Lugh managed in a strangled whisper.

He was about to take hold of Zack's arm to push him off when the pressure suddenly eased. Zack grabbed his head in both hands with bruising force, and yanked Lugh's head down, their lips colliding with ferocious desperation.

Lugh stumbled as Zack spun him away from the wall. His flailing hands latched on to hard biceps as they wrestled for control, a strange, jerking dance that brought them nearer to the bed with each hard-won step and turn. Zack's moan vibrated over his tongue. His hands seized the neck of Lugh's T-shirt and tore the fabric from his shoulders. He clawed the shirttails from Zack's jeans and yanked the shirt over his head, trapping Zack's wrists behind his back in the cuffs.

"Leggo," Zack snarled.

The bull inside Lugh pawed the floorboards and snorted. "Not until you calm down."

"Fuck that."

Zack yanked his arm up so violently, Lugh feared he would dislocate the shoulder. Luckily, the cuff button ripped off first, flying across the room to hit the mirror with a delicate ping. Lugh found himself seized again and flung down on the bed on his back with Zack sprawled on top.

The cold fury in Zack's eyes had given way to animal heat. He licked his lips as they halted again, skin scorching skin where their bare chests pressed together.

"Pants," he growled.

"Yours, too," Lugh shot back, shocked at the rasping growl of his own voice.

After a bit of clumsy groping, accompanied by snarls and a couple of kicked shins, jeans and briefs joined the ruined shirts on the floor. Zack fastened his lips to the side of Lugh's throat with bruising force. Already aroused to the point of discomfort, Lugh groaned and thrust his hips up, grinding his aching erection against Zack's.

Again, Zack surprised him, hooking an arm under his knee and shoving his leg up to his chest. Fingers probed at his entrance, insistent and rough. Lugh rolled his hips, arching into the intrusion in invitation. The fingers withdrew, replaced by the head of Zack's erection. Lugh braced, waiting for the pain, craving it.

Zack stilled, doubt shadowing the hunger in his eyes. "Lugh?"

"Yes...now." Lugh reached down to clamp his fingers on Zack's hips. He lay beneath his sergeant, panting, a distant part of him frightened he had lost control and ceded control all at once. "Please..."

On a heavy grunt, Zack thrust in, his moan mixing with Lugh's cry as the sharp pain lanced through him. He snapped his hips up, meeting Zack's ferocious assault, welcoming the burn, lacing his fingers with

Zack's free hand as they pounded at each other. Zack's mouth returned to his, his kiss hungry but oddly tender in counterpoint to his wild thrusts. Lugh fisted his cock, hurtling to completion faster than any time in his long life.

"My braveheart...faster," he gasped out against Zack's lips.

Zack complied with a strangled cry, his head flung back and eyes squeezed shut. Pain melted into sharp pleasure as Lugh increased the pressure on his shaft, pumping in hard frenetic strokes. The white heat of orgasm gathered at the base of his spine and rushed in on him before he was ready, pulling a sobbing gasp from him.

A few more hard thrusts that banged Lugh's skull against the headboard, and Zack bellowed his release, hips snapping in fierce, short strokes, his cries echoing off the walls. Zack collapsed on top of him, trembling. His breaths came in shivering gulps and Lugh wrapped him in a strong embrace.

"Are you all right?" Zack finally whispered.

"Quite well. That was glorious, love."

"Did I hurt you?" Zack's voice shook so badly, Lugh tightened his arms. He wouldn't mind at all if his love wept on his chest, but he knew it would embarrass Zack.

"Only as much as I wished to be." Lugh turned to kiss the blond head on his shoulder. "Are *we* all right? You and I?"

"Yeah. I think. Maybe. You gonna listen to me?"

"I'm here, love. I'm listening." He stroked Zack's hair, gratified when the trembling eased and Zack relaxed with a sigh.

"Look, I'm not saying don't go. I'm saying we have Carol make some calls in the morning. Have them delay the hearings until you can get there with a security detail and maybe some company. Faolchú and maybe even your grandmother. You know, some backup?"

"Grandmother has the island shielded. She cannot leave or the shield falls."

"Someone else then. You know what I'm saying."

"I do." He did. He knew that to take anyone else with him was to endanger them. They would appear to Diego as a threat and there would be violence. Innocents might be injured in the fray.

He shifted Zack to let his sergeant curl up against his side, deeply regretting what he had to do. There was no other choice. With a kiss to Zack's forehead, he gathered a bit of magic to him and sent the compulsion out with his words, "Sleep, my dear Zachary. Sleep deeply. Know that I love you."

* * * *

Sunbeams were well across the room when Zack woke, groggy and irritable. He ran a hand over his face before he realized two things. The damn clock said it was going on eleven a.m. and Lugh's side of the bed was empty.

"Shit!"

He rolled out of bed, scrambling to get his jeans on. Barefoot and shirtless, he barreled down the stairs, nearly slamming into Eithne at the bottom. He took her by the shoulders, managing to stop short of shaking her.

"How long has he been gone? Your son?"

Cat ears twitched before she answered him. "No one knows. Finn knocked on your door this morning and no one answered. He looked inside and you were alone. We were unable to wake you. I was bringing an elixir." She held up the bottle in her clawed hand.

He closed his eyes, fighting back the anguish. Everything he'd said the night before, everything they'd done. "Where is he now?"

"In Washington. Zack, something is...amiss. Come see. We have it on the television to play again for you."

She took his hand and led him to the den where worried fae had gathered. Angus nodded to them and hit the remote to play whatever they had recorded on the DVR.

"We saw him arrive on the news, apparently ready to speak against this registration act. Then the news people said he was in meetings with officials. An hour later, we saw this."

Zack let her pull him down to sit beside her on the sofa, a hard knot in his stomach as the recording of a press conference started. Lugh strode out to the podium in his regal best, dress uniform pressed and polished. Diego walked beside him.

Oh, damn. This can't be good.

The prince hesitated until Diego whispered in his ear. Then he leaned toward the microphones and began. "Ladies and gentlemen, I have a short prepared statement. I will not be taking questions at this time."

A buzz went up from the reporters but Lugh kept talking, as if he couldn't hear them.

A chill shot through Zack. *Or maybe he can't stop.*

"The Fae Collective would like to take this opportunity to thank Mr. Sandoval for his quick action during the current crisis. I have been instructed to inform Mr. Sandoval that he has our full support, mine and the governing bodies of the Collective, regarding the proposal he wishes to present to Congress this morning. It is imperative that Congress take action on the Defense of…"

Lugh stopped, jaw tight, his fists clenched on the podium. His eyes appeared to search for something until Diego leaned in and whispered in his ear again. Zack was watching for it and still almost missed it, the moment when Lugh's eyes went blank again, his expression a mask of stone.

"The Defense of Magical Beings Act as quickly as possible. For the safety and security of your nation as well as all the nations of the world and the Otherworld. We stand united in this and hope that your Congress will as well. Thank you."

With a twitch of his shoulders, Lugh stepped back and walked out of sight of the cameras.

"What the hell was that?" Zack asked the room in general, though he had a terrible feeling he already knew. "That wasn't Lugh. Was it someone he made look like him?"

Angus shook his head. "That was our prince. Physically."

Zack ran a hand back through his hair, trying to quell his frustration in the face of everything that needed to be done. "All right. Okay. He's under some kind of magical duress. Even I could see that. So first priority is getting down there and rescuing him and then—"

Every fae in the room regarded him with sorrow and concern.

"What? What now?"

"Faolchú went to look for him. He is no longer in Washington."

Chapter Seventeen

The Captured Prince

For the world's more full of weeping than you can understand.
—William Butler Yeats, *The Stolen Child*

"Look, we can't confront him while he's in Congressional hearings. He's always surrounded by diplomats and senators." Zack paced the dining room turned war council room. "And since Faolchú wasn't able to pick up a scent after Lugh disappeared outside Diego's hotel, we can be pretty damn sure he's not in Washington anymore."

The TV, appropriated from the den, looped through all the footage they had been able to find of Lugh in Washington, walking up the Capitol steps, standing with Diego prior to that last, bizarre press conference, getting into Diego's limo.

"Hold up. Pause it there, Angus." Zack stared at the image. "Finn, you recognize that guy? The one playing driver?"

The young man had his hair pulled back in a neat tail, but the pale skin, the hooked nose...

"I do, yes," Finn answered from where he slumped dejectedly in his chair. "That would be Diego's vampire acquisition from Los Angeles."

The vamp kid smiled and laughed at something Diego said before he shut the limo door. *Definitely does not look like that one's under coercion.* "Damn. This just gets worse and worse." He stared hard at the screen. Something seemed off. "Hold up. It's sunny in DC today. Why's that kid not curled up screaming or bursting into flames or something?"

Morrigan snorted. "Human myths. Sunlight does not kill vampires."

"It is not *healthy* for them," Sionnach broke in with a glare at her. "It weakens them, Zack. Makes them ill if they are exposed too long. But this one is fully covered and soon retreats into the vehicle. He would not suffer overmuch."

"Got it. Didn't take long for that conversion, did it?"

"The right promises win loyalty quickly," Danu said from her place at the head of the table. She had been unusually quiet, her dark eyes dull and wandering.

She's exhausted. Zack considered asking her if anyone was helping her with the damn shielding but decided he'd better not call her out in front of everyone.

"Right." He rubbed over his right temple where a headache was threatening. "So here's how I see it. Jump in, anybody, if you think I'm way off base here. Diego's in and out of Washington for the Congressional hearings, but since he can make a door anywhere, he doesn't have to stay there. He's got the magic users he's gathered stashed away somewhere, either locked up or working for him now, but not in Washington, or Lugh would be there, too. He can't spread himself too thin."

"So far, we have no disagreement," Morrigan said in her grating rasp, her black claws clicking on the table.

"Great. Now Diego's going to need to keep things stirred up, right? Make sure Congress realizes how fucked up the situation is so they jump on his proposal. Which means he needs more riots. He can easily cause a riot, snatch up anybody he wants from that city and make it back to Washington before the lunch recess ends." He waited a moment but the fae and his security staff all watched him expectantly. "I still think he's hitting Memphis."

A soft rustling pulled his attention to Finn shifting restlessly in his chair.

"Finn, bud, something on your mind?"

The pooka cleared his throat, eyes darting around the table. "Ah, well…as I understand it, this council…er, Congress, needs to have a fire under their collective feet in order to act swiftly. Diego would wish to be certain he has a large enough fire."

"Go on. Don't stop there," Zack urged softly.

"There will be more than one riot in a single day. Perhaps within a single hour. Several, unless I miss my guess."

"You have foreseen this, Fionnachd?" Morrigan snapped. "You with your prodigious skill in foretelling?"

Eithne waved a hand at her. "Hush, Morri, it's only sense. If they move too slowly, he must create a greater crisis."

Finn sat up a little straighter, obviously encouraged by the support. "So we must puzzle out which cities he will choose. And our Zack believes he is using Talking Heads' songs as a puzzle for us."

"Sionnach?" Zack unfolded the map he had brought in and thumb tacked it to the wall. "How many more are there? We've got Houston, Detroit and Pittsburgh, all already hit. Los Angeles, he just wanted to go after that vamp kid, so we'll throw that one out as an outsider."

"Outlier, Sarge," Marcus corrected under his breath.

"Whatever. What else is there, beautiful?"

Sionnach closed his eyes, petting his tail as he concentrated. "Memphis…that's from the *Cities* song, and El Paso…"

Zack marked the cities he'd mentioned with colored pins and added Sionnach's.

"Baltimore…New York…" The little fox Fomorian opened his eyes. "That's all I recall."

"Which probably means that's all there is. Okay. Four new ones. Are we thinking he'll hit them all in the same day?"

"It's a possibility we have to consider," Angus said as he caught Sionnach's nervous hands in his.

"Separate strike teams, Sarge?" Kevin asked from where he leaned against the wall.

I think we should split up. God, this is sounding like a bad horror movie. "Yeah. Much as I'd like to have a no-fail squad, we've gotta make sure we have each possible target covered."

"Field expediency." Kevin shot him a grin. "What Marines do best, right?"

Zack managed something that was half laugh, half-frustrated grunt. "But he has to have been there to make the doorway work, right? Anyone know if he's ever been to El Paso?"

"Not that he had mentioned," Finn said slowly. "New York, of course. We visited Baltimore several times. They have lovely art museums he wanted me to see. Memphis, also yes. He had a writer friend there, since passed on."

"Good enough. I want a mix of fighting and magical strength in each squad, so Morrigan, if you could lead the Baltimore team, Finn, you take New York—"

"Me?" Finn squeaked out, pale as tapioca pudding. "But I'm not...any of those things."

"Yes, you. It's the city you know best and damn it, you're one of the most inventive magic folks I know. Don't sell yourself short. You take Kevin and Marcus with you and you've got all the firepower you need. Princess Eithne, I guess you want to go with Morrigan?"

"It would be best." Eithne shot her lover a quelling look when the battle raven looked ready to argue.

"Good. Take a couple of the boys with you, too. Angus and Sionnach, you're with me heading to Memphis. Nathair, I'd suggest you join your wolf in DC. I want to keep eyes and ears there, just in case."

"Understood." Nathair shifted in his chair, obviously hesitating on a thought. "Zack, your teams should take the human children, as well."

The suggestion ground his spinning brain gears to a screeching halt. "Um...why?"

"If, perhaps, someone manages to detain Diego, how long would you be able to hold him? Truly? How long could any of us hope to?"

"Yeah, okay, but—"

"Zack, if you had the boy who caused the change with you, perhaps he could undo it. A few words spoken would be all that is necessary, from what I understand. It may be our best hope."

The headache blossomed behind Zack's right eye. He rubbed at his temples to ease the tightness. "He's only one kid and he can't be everywhere."

"No. But if he remains here, he has no chance at all of reversing the damage."

"Lugh didn't want the kids in danger." *And damn him, why in the hell do I still care what he thinks? Damn him for being a stubborn, bullheaded, manipulative...*

"Then they must go with you," Eithne said gently. "Who better to protect them?"

"Minky goes with me," Finn blurted out, then snapped his mouth shut.

Now what? "I'm almost afraid to ask, but why?"

"She's my...granddaughter."

Silence greeted this announcement, most faces around the table registering some level of disbelief or shock, though Eithne only nodded.

Marcus finally broke the silence. "How's that even physically possible?"

"Several times removed." Finn waved a hand as if he could dismiss further questions. "Not my literal granddaughter. It would simply take too long to puzzle out how many 'greats' should be added. But I...I wish to have her with me."

"Wow." Zack leaned back against the wall, wondering how much more his tired, unhappy brain could process in one day. "So does that mean she can shift? Like you?"

"Not that we've discovered yet."

"Um...okay. Since she's family, guess she better go with you." Zack rubbed his hands over his face. "You take the girls, Finn. I'll take the boys with me. Best we can do, I guess. Those of you who can pop in and out of places, please wait for your human and Fomorian squad mates. Carol, if you could get flights together? Thanks, everyone. Let's get moving. Faster we get there, better chance we have of finally getting ahead of him."

When the room had emptied, Zack took a moment to lean his forehead against the cool wall, concentrating on breathing slowly. Lugh should have been with them. After their bout of rough sex, Zack had promised himself that he would apologize for his loss of control. The damn prince hadn't given him the chance. No, the damn *prince* had used Zack's anger, let him get riled up and distracted instead of extracting the promises he should have been. Oh, he knew Lugh hadn't *lied* to him, and that was the problem. He'd let Zack fuck the hell out of him, then had spelled him to sleep while he'd been too sleepy-stupid from sex to think clearly.

"Sneaky bastard," Zack muttered to the map pinned to the wall.

A black-furred head peeked around the doorway, triangle ears swiveling. "You are angry with him. Even now."

He let go a painful breath, swallowing against the lump in his throat. "Yeah. I'm pissed as hell. If he'd really listened to me instead of pretending to, he wouldn't be missing now." Eithne laid a gentle hand on his shoulder and he fought against the sting in his eyes. "Yeah, I'm mad. But I'm damn worried, too. How is it that he hasn't gotten away? What's he going through that he can't just pop right back to us?"

"Zack..." Her soft hands guided his head to her shoulder and the urge to sob almost took him out at the knees. "I am sorry I raised such a stubborn child.

Though he has enough honor to know he wronged you. I am sure he regrets it now."

"Yeah, well, fat lot of good it does us if we can't find him."

* * * *

Lugh opened aching eyes and stifled a moan. *Still here. Great Mother help me...*

Wherever here was, of course. His knowledge of the world had narrowed to a windowless, cinder-block room and the agony circling his throat and wrists. Even padded with cotton, the iron burned, keeping him from reaching for his magic and leaving him weak and nauseous. Hours might have passed, or years, he couldn't say — his existence reduced to mind-numbing misery. When he had woken the first time, he had tried to pull the chains from the wall. Without the iron, he would have managed easily. Now he could barely lift his head.

The pain and weakness was still better by far than the nightmare of losing control over his body, unable to move as he wished, hearing his voice spout someone else's words, watching helplessly as if he were separated from his own body by a heavy glass shield. He had nearly fought free at the podium, swimming up through the spell to grasp a shred of control, but Diego had been right there in his ear again and he had been sucked back under in a dizzying rush. Just a few words, whispered in that Voice, the one that drove the compulsion spell. Diego had learned it from the boy who had changed his nature, but he had perfected it, the ease and control he exhibited terrifying.

Zachary had been right. Beloved Zack, who, once again, would believe that his prince had betrayed him. Lugh squeezed his eyes shut, fighting for a whole breath. The thought caused him more agony than the iron. He should have listened, should have stayed to let Zack make whatever arrangements he felt best instead of rushing off to soothe his own injured pride and feed his overinflated sense of honor. What good was either, now that he was trapped and caged, used by the very man he sought to stand against? *Have I always been such a fool?*

A metallic snick echoed through the room. A thin bar of light bisected the floor, growing wider. *Door. Yes, there would be a door.*

"Go rest, Theo." Diego's voice drifted in from the hallway.

"I'm all right, *jefe*," the younger voice answering was soft and respectful. "I'd rather stay."

I know that voice…ah. Diego's vampire.

"Thank you for worrying, *mijo*, but the prince is an old friend. I'm in no danger. Take a hint and relax for a bit. At least go grab…a bite."

Theo chuckled and, with a soft "*Sí, jefe*," apparently moved off, though Lugh heard no footsteps, just felt his decreasing *presence*. The bar of light widened and Diego stepped in, holding a lit hurricane lamp. He closed the door behind him and leaned back against it with a sigh.

"I *am* sorry about all this," he said as he stared at the ceiling. "Once you showed up in an official capacity, though, I had no choice."

"Diego?" Lugh winced at the thready, quavering sound of his own voice. "You know this will kill me."

"Oh, yes." The man who had been his dear friend sat cross-legged on the cement floor and placed the lamp and the bundle he carried beside him. "Eventually. But this is temporary. I don't intend to keep you here for months. Just until those idiots in Washington can get their heads out of their asses. I may need to trot you out again in the next couple of days if they ask for you, but I can't see this going on more than a week."

A week of endless torment sounded like an eternity. "And then?"

Diego shrugged and leaned back against the wall. "Then I hope my husband and my friends will begin to understand. When I am named head of the new Department of Magical Security, when you all see that the new legislation will help thousands of people..." He stopped and rubbed his hands over his face. "If you go peacefully, I'll let you go home."

"Zachary will be looking for me."

"No doubt. Of course he will. You're screwing him now, aren't you?"

From Diego, such bluntness was shocking and scattered Lugh's thoughts. "Yes. We have been lovers."

"Good...good." Diego nodded absently, finally turning his head to face Lugh. "I always knew you belonged together. Congratulations."

"Thank you." The bland, normal tone of the conversation bordered on the surreal, but Lugh desperately wanted to keep him talking to learn what he could and to distract himself from the pain.

"He's a good man. The best. Wish I had him here with me for security."

"Instead you have a vampire you plucked from an alley."

"Theo?" Diego's forehead crinkled, as if puzzling through a thought. "Theo's a good boy. He's just not terribly experienced with security."

"He is, from what I understand, a murderer."

Diego's smile held an autumn chill. "Justifiable homicide. Don't judge, my dear prince, until you know all the facts. He grew up in a bad neighborhood, but he was a good student, devoted to his family. The vampire mutation in his *kelan* seems to have occurred shortly after we reopened the door between the worlds. Some powerful magical echo or residual effect... I'm not sure how it works yet. It warped his *kelan* pattern. Apparently used to happen to a certain percentage of humans before the Veil was closed. But his family didn't understand. Even though they tossed him out, he still watched over them. When he found the pack of scum gang-raping his sister, he killed them."

"He told you this story?"

"I have verified enough independently to know it's true, leaving out some of the exaggerations of a wounded young man's personal filter on events. But if Theo had been able to find help when he changed, if there had been some official agency he could have gone to, he might not have turned vigilante. These are the people I'm trying to help, my friend, the ones who are lost and alone. The ones who risk persecution because no one speaks for them."

"But to insist that they all must be registered? Controlled?"

"Humans are infants when it comes to magic. They don't know how to deal with it anymore and I can't help them if I can't find them."

"As you did with Theo."

"Yes. Exactly." Diego beamed at him as if he had passed some test.

You set them up for the same persecution you claim you wish to prevent. Lugh kept this to himself, though, knowing that in his current state, Diego was incapable of listening. "You look tired."

"A bit. So much to do and Theo can't guard me all the time."

"You've no one else to trust?"

The smile slipped, distraction clouding Diego's dark eyes for a moment. "The others are...new. They've all sworn allegiance to me, but one needs to be cautious."

"Others?"

"Oh, yes. I've had quite a harvest. Twelve young people with twisted, dark *kelan* of various sorts."

Perhaps they were all self-appointed knight-errants like Theo, but he wouldn't lay odds. Lugh shivered, envisioning them turning on Diego and ripping him to pieces.

Diego shook his head. "You're cold. Of course you are with the iron so close. I brought you some things." He shook out the bundle to reveal heavy blankets and a pillow. "I have to keep you subdued for now, but no need to be barbaric about it."

He spread the blankets over Lugh's aching body and tucked the pillow under his head. "*Bien.* That's better. It won't be forever, I promise, then you can go home to have Zack fuss over you. There's a nice thought, eh?" He stood and retrieved his lamp. "I have things to do, but I'll have the young folks check in on you."

"Diego?"

Dark eyes that once would have held such compassion turned back to him, reptile cold. "Hmm?"

"You court disaster. Now and in the future. You cannot keep control of this."

Diego snorted. "Says the *sidhe* prince from his iron prison. I'll do whatever I have to do. Remember that."

With that, he walked out and closed the door, taking the light with him. Lugh lay shivering in the dark, trying once again to force his exhausted mind past the barrier of cold iron to call out to Zack. *"I'm here, my love. I'm alive and I'm so very sorry."*

Chapter Eighteen

Nate's Vamp

To expect the unexpected shows a thoroughly modern intellect.
—Oscar Wilde, *An Ideal Husband*

Another airport, another agonized wait watching the flight boards. It wouldn't have been too bad with some cheerful company, but all Zack had were an unhappy pair of fae and three very uncomfortable, edgy college kids.

Will wasn't too bad, though he was painfully shy and anxious. Nate would probably warm up with a little time...time they didn't have. But Brandon...that kid was an oversized mound of guilt and resentment, not a good combination when you paired it with a healthy ego. Either he needed to adjust his attitude, or he'd have to be watched carefully—also not good since the kid was apparently the key to the whole mess. The thought already made Zack tired.

"I'm so sorry about all this, Sergeant," Will said, his leg bouncing in an agitated rhythm.

"How many times are you gonna apologize, babe?" Brandon muttered.

Will turned on his boyfriend, his voice unusually sharp, "Don't be a dick, Bran! It's *his* lover that's disappeared. How would you feel if *I* got snatched up and no one could find me? Or would you even care?"

Brandon stared, open-mouthed, and slumped in his seat, arms crossed tight over his chest. "I'd care, damn it."

"Settle, guys," Zack said as calmly as he could. "Will, I know you're sorry. Brandon, we need you focused. We don't need extra—"

"Sarge." Nate actually tugged on his sleeve like a little kid.

"What?" He hadn't meant to snap, but the beast inside him seemed to make his temper harder and harder to keep a lid on.

Nate's eyebrows crept up but he didn't cringe away. "Thought you should see this." He handed over his phone that currently showed a newsfeed, the new, not-improved Diego Sandoval front and center.

"Good call."

One of the senators was in the middle of a question, "...the rights of magical citizens and foreign nationals? Is this in any way a concern in your rather high-handed proposal?"

The tone was confrontational and condescending. Their old Diego would have been flustered and irritated, hesitating as he thought carefully about how to respond. This Diego? His expression of reasonable concern never faltered. It never even flickered.

"Senator, I understand your apprehensions. As to foreign nationals, though, the fae community has already voiced its unconditional support. As for our own citizens, the registration process would no more infringe upon rights than registering for a particular party would during voter registration."

Zack sighed. "Yeah, if he wasn't so scary smart and didn't have such a good reputation with the politicos, this wouldn't be so easy for him. Why am I watching this?"

"Sarge..." Nate poked at the screen. "This is a live feed."

Zack stared at it a moment longer, then the light dawned. He managed something close to a grin. "Live. So they've got him tied up in session. So we've got some time to get where we need to go."

"Half a step ahead." Sionnach had leaned forward to watch the screen as well. "It's all we need."

"God, I hope so."

"Yeah? Even if we get there ahead of him and even if we do manage to somehow, hell knows how, pin him down, what the hell does everyone expect me to do?" Brandon snarled. "Tell him to be nice?"

Now we get down to it. That's what's bothering the kid. "Do you remember exactly what you said to him in the first place? With your Voice?" Zack asked softly, without accusation.

"Mostly." Brandon slumped down further. He looked so defeated, Zack felt sorry for him, but it wasn't the time to coddle him.

"Mostly? You need to be able to reverse what you said. Say the opposite. Give him back what you took away. You need to remember, damn it. Word for word."

"I remember, Bran. Will probably does, too. You know how he is about remembering conversations verbatim," Nate said with an elbow nudge to his friend's ribs.

Brandon's laugh wasn't a happy one, but at least he'd stopped trying to break his own teeth.

"Throws your words back in your face, does he?" Angus said with a rueful smile. "My sympathies. A certain fox does the same to me."

"Never," Sionnach breathed out, his eyes wide in pretended shock. "I would never dare to engage in word battles with the great Angus Farseer."

Even Brandon managed a real chuckle at that, since they all knew it was a huge honking fib. Tension broken, the flight beginning to board, Zack suddenly felt a little more optimistic. Maybe they could do this after all.

* * * *

Minky broke into a run as they hurried out to the car, trying to keep her great-whatever-granddad's pace.

"Hey, daddy longlegs!" Kara shouted after him. "Slow down!"

One of the security guys—she thought it was Marcus—caught up to Finn first and hooked an arm through his, forcing him to slow or be yanked off balance.

"We won't let him get away, ladies, don't worry," the bigger guy said in his gruff bear voice. "Besides, he can't drive."

They caught up at the end of the garage where the embassy's SUV, van and town car crouched, and where Finn had to wait for a human to open the car door.

Marcus did an odd thing first, shaking out a length of black cloth from his pack and handing it to the pooka, who wrapped himself in it before climbing gingerly into the back seat.

Silk. To protect him from the steel.

"Shouldn't he sit in the front?" Kara asked. "Instead of being folded in half?"

Gruff-bear guy, Kevin, shook his head. "Put him between you. Give him a little distance from some of the frame, at least. And hope he doesn't get sick. The town car's silk-lined, but probably not a good idea to take the prince's diplomatic vehicle into...whatever we're heading into."

Hunched in the too-small back seat with the silk pulled up over his head, Finn looked so ominous that Minky hesitated on a superstitious shiver. The helicopter ride and the rush down from the roof had frazzled her enough. *Now they want me to sit next to Death on one of his grumpy days...*

"Pile in, girls. We've gotta move," Marcus said as he slid behind the wheel, then turned to address Finn. "Where to, boss?"

"Brooklyn," Finn said, his voice faint and unhappy.

Minky slid in beside him, shocked at herself when she patted Finn's arm to comfort him.

"You sure he won't try Manhattan?" Kevin checked and re-holstered an oddly shaped pistol. He'd assured them that it was armed with tranq darts instead of bullets. "Make a bigger news splash here, I bet."

"No, he will return to the old neighborhood."

"How do you know?" Kara asked as they eased up the ramp.

"I..." Finn swallowed hard. "I know the workings of his mind."

"Okay, he's like your eternal love and stuff. We get that. But that was Good Diego, not Evil Bizarro Diego."

A low, rattling sound came from the depths of the silk shelter. *He's growling. I wonder if I can growl.*

"He's not evil," Finn spat out.

"Yeah? How do you figure that?"

"He is still the same, simply with a piece removed." Finn shifted and dug an elbow into Minky's side. "Your pardon. I had always found the human notion of 'morality' puzzling until I lived with Diego. His sense of right and wrong is as clear to him as a mountain lake. His sense that he must always be *right* is perhaps what has caused him the most difficulty over the years. This has not changed. He sees a way through to what he believes is right, what he feels *must* be done for everyone's safety, and he will not be moved from it. It is not so different from his insistence on certain things when we fought to rejoin the worlds. The difference now is that he engages in morality with compassion removed. *Any* action that furthers his goal is right and good in his eyes at the moment."

Kevin turned to lean over the bench seat. "The end justifies the means, right? Like that guy said, starts with an 'M' or something…"

"Machiavelli," Finn said softly. "Yes. So he did."

"What do you know about Machiavelli?" Marcus asked, a smile in his voice.

"I knew him."

"Right. I call pooka bullshit on that one."

"Well and fine. Perhaps it was a mite exaggerated. I did know someone who met him once."

"Okay, I'll buy that. But how's all that not evil?"

Finn was silent a moment, his fingers twisting under the silk. "It seems to me that this, what Diego does now, is wanting to arrive at the right thing but justifying whatever is necessary to get there as needful to the cause. A sort of...fanaticism, in a way. While evil...that would be knowing the difference between right and wrong and not caring, as long as one's own selfish needs are met? Yes?"

Marcus let out a heavy exhale. "Yeah, I think you got it. Probably better than some humans." He took a sharp corner, quiet while he concentrated on the road. Then his eyes searched out Finn in the rearview. "We're gonna get him back. Stop worrying so much."

"Why does everyone tell me this?" Finn muttered. "I will worry. It can't be helped."

Minky took his hand through the silk. For some reason, his fingers closing over hers felt normal and didn't make her skin crawl. "It's okay. We can be worried together," she whispered. She...liked him, no matter what Will and Bran said. So he had ferocious moments, but fierce and aggressive were obviously *not* a normal day for him.

"Thank you."

They rode in silence until halfway across the Brooklyn Bridge.

"Finn? Should we go see her?" Marcus asked. "That where we're headed?"

"Yes, please." Finn's head picked up as if he looked ahead to familiar sights. "To warn her if nothing else."

They pulled up near an apartment building, one of those old brick ones with the fire escape on the outside. It looked neat and well kept, but not like anything special.

"So what's here?" Kara asked, her expression the skeptical one Minky knew was just short of an epic eye roll.

Finn climbed out after her, leaving the silk on the seat. "I used to live here. With Diego," he said softly.

That shut even Kara up, though it didn't really answer the question. Finn bounded up the front steps without waiting to see if they followed. By the time Minky had scurried after everyone else, Finn had vanished. One flight of steps inside led down to the ground level, but Finn's boots clattered on the steps above. She reached the eighth floor out of breath, wondering why no one ever installed elevators in these old apartment buildings.

"Dear lady!" Finn pounded on the right-hand door. "Please say you're home for me? It's Fionnachd."

"*Dios*, Finn." The door opened and a little, white-haired lady peered out. "No need to make so much noise, *caro*. Come in, come in, and tell me why you are so out of breath."

The grandmotherly woman looked so sweet, but power radiated from her in muted waves, like a five-hundred-watt bulb with a red cloth tossed over it. An angry wasp buzz vibrated against Minky's mind, a feeling she could only describe as a magic shield thrown up against her. Minky shrank back to the wall by the stairs, suddenly too frightened to take another step.

"Do you know what you bring to me, Finn?" the woman asked softly.

"Oh, yes, your pardon." Finn held out a hand toward them. "You know Kevin and Marcus, and this is Miss Kara. She is, from what I gather, a finder."

"And the other, *querido*? I have never…"

"I know. She's faded again. It's all right, *Tia* Carmen. She's still there. This is my great-great-something-or-other granddaughter, Minky."

"Your…oh, I see. Yours? Well, that explains things." The shield abruptly vanished, the old woman's power subsiding as if she had it on a switch. She nodded and beckoned with her hands. "Come in, come in. I am sorry I frightened you, *pequeña*. I was not sure…you are so different."

Still she couldn't move. The casual display, from someone who could hold a conversation and maintain her appearance as a sweet old lady while the power crackled and sang around her, terrified her.

Finn faltered, one foot over the threshold. "Minky? Have you meant to do that?"

"Do what?" she said, her voice a bare squeak.

"You've disappeared entirely." Finn reached a hand out to her, obviously aware of exactly where she was no matter how invisible. "That's well done indeed."

"Oh…um." She managed to unfade a bit as she took his hand, whispering, "I didn't know she'd be so scary."

"*Tia* Carmen?" He gazed down at her, forehead creased in a puzzled way. "Ah. I think you mistake power for threat, little one. Perhaps because you only feel the edges still."

She looked up at him, meeting his eyes as she seldom did with anyone. "So I'm supposed to be able to tell if she's a good witch or a bad witch?"

His laugh, sudden and delighted, made her face heat with embarrassment and yet somehow calmed her. "Yes. Just so." His long arm slung around her shoulders, his familiarity more comfortable now so she didn't resist being herded into the apartment. Finn's voice held a hard edge when he spoke to the old lady again. "We are here to stand against him. He will come, to do as he has other places. I came to warn you, but I think you know."

Tia Carmen wiped at her kitchen counter, her eyes glistening. "Our poor Santiago. When you called the first time, *caro*, I hoped that it was a fever dream, or somehow you had made a mistake."

"I have wished the same, fervently. Or that I might awake and laugh with him over my terrible dream." Finn folded her in his arms. "I have not woken."

"You've come to ask me to help you?"

He kissed the old lady's forehead gently. "No. I only ask that you protect what is yours. If he comes here...simply don't allow it. He will try. But you mustn't allow it."

"You worry, *mi cuervo*, that I will be sentimental and wish to help him."

"I worry that he will charm his way to you and carry you off as he did Lugh."

"*El principe* is too honorable and too trusting. Old ladies are more devious. Finn, go. I will hold here. Go do what you must."

Just like that, they were done. The conversation hadn't made any damn sense to Minky and left more questions than they answered. Finn herded them back out without explanation, moving them down the street on foot. He seemed in a desperate hurry now, looking over his shoulder every few steps as they raced down Twenty-Third Street.

"Shannon!" Kevin barked out. "Where the hell are you headed?"

"Fifth Avenue. All the shops!" Finn shouted back. "He's coming. Gods of pool and spring... I feel him..."

He stopped so suddenly, Kara ran into him, but he merely steadied her as he stared at the top of Tia

Carmen's building. A strange, isolated wind blew across that roof, leaves and bits of paper whirled about in ever-increasing frenzy.

"He seeks to come through there. The place most familiar to him. To win Tia Carmen to his side if he can."

The leaves danced and shifted in confusion as a second whirlwind arose in opposition to the first, an unnatural, ominous cloud gathering over that one isolated rooftop.

"She bars the way. She will not let him come through there. Not on her block. He will grow frustrated and angry when he cannot overpower her, then he will target the street where all the merchants have their wares."

They stood transfixed for another moment, as the second whirlwind held back the first.

"You shall not pass," Minky whispered, though she hoped to God that Diego hadn't found a balrog somewhere.

"Come! Now!" Finn's shout got them moving again, this time at a dead run toward one of Brooklyn's most commercial streets. A shriek sounded behind them, most likely a displacement of air, but it sounded too much like a scream of frustrated rage for comfort.

They turned the corner at Fifth Avenue just in time for Finn to spot the beginnings of another magical doorway on a rooftop two blocks south of where the White Eagle Tavern had once been. He pointed, eyes wild with anxiety. "Kevin!"

"I see it, bud. Let us take point but stay close."

The run turned into a sprint with Minky falling further behind with each yard. Running was never something she enjoyed doing, and trying to keep up with three adrenaline-charged males twice her size just wasn't in her small bag of talents.

A young man suddenly strode out into the middle of the street near the rooftop doorway. Tires screeched. Horn blares and obscenities followed his passage. He ignored the angry motorists, lifted a hand, and fire blossomed from an empanada vendor across the street. The lady manning the cart shrieked, backpedaling from the sudden mini-inferno.

Half a block closer, a lamppost twisted in a screech of tortured metal and crashed to the pavement. That seemed to be the signal for all hell to break loose. Shoppers screamed and snatched up children, people ran away from the escalating violence and some, inexplicably, toward it. A parked car tipped on its side. The sharp shatter of glass echoed and repeated along the street. Hard to tell after five minutes who Diego had sent to start the riot and who were the local magic users acting out of panic.

Kevin had reached ground zero, where the riot had begun, and took aim with his tranq pistol at the young pyromancer who had retreated to their side of the street. Marcus had raced to the other side, in hot pursuit of the skinny girl who appeared to be doing most of the window breaking with her magic.

They said to stay close. How can we stay close if they split up? Minky's thought was a frantic wail in her own head.

As she tried to decide which way to run, a black and gray blur shot out of the alley beside her and, with an inhuman howl, knocked Kevin flat. A few yards in front of her, Finn snarled and leaped at the girl who was now punching Kevin in the head. *Werewolf. No, no, no, Finn can't take on a werewolf!*

She knew she had faded into invisibility and didn't care. Werewolf girl turned at Finn's snarl and backhanded him hard enough to send him flying. He landed on his back on the sidewalk, apparently stunned.

Glass-shatter girl had evaded Marcus when Pyro-boy had set a florist's display ablaze right next to him. The girl watched Finn from across the street with narrowed eyes, turned her attention to the burning empanada cart and clenched her fists at her sides.

The heavy pull of magic itched at Minky's skin, wild power that yanked in bits from everything around her. The cart wobbled and lifted six feet off the ground. It hovered there for an instant, a bizarre parody of the sun's burning chariot. Then the girl let out a high-pitched cry and the cart flew toward them as if a giant hand had pitched it right at Finn.

Finn...no! Minky's panic rushed through her, filling her body, numbing her mind. Unable to think, she acted on instinct alone, racing the few steps to Finn. The tingling rush coalesced, surging up her arms, and shooting from her outstretched hands. A wall of air smacked into the cart mid-street, powerful enough to stop its forward momentum and knock it to the pavement.

The crew Diego had obviously sent had vanished by the time she looked around again, her heart pounding in shock. The gathered power on the rooftop had winked out, so he must have retrieved them and snapped the doorway shut. They'd done their job, though. The street was in chaos and she had to grab Finn under the arms and haul him back into a doorway to save him from being trampled. Kara had a dazed Kevin sitting against a shop wall nearby and Marcus was fighting through the panicked crowd to get back to them.

"I think..." Finn began in a faint voice, shaking his head as if he needed to clear water from his ears. "That we've seen one way to unblock your channels."

"What?" she said in a distracted fashion as she helped him stand.

"Sheer, unmitigated terror."

* * * *

Zack lounged against the window partition under the Tater Red's Lucky Mojos sign, right between the 'Red's' and the 'Lucky'. If he really had been a tourist, it would have been one of his first choices to visit, if only to browse through the T-shirts and oils. Too bad. Maybe when things were finished, he could bring Lugh and...

If Lugh's all right. If I ever see him again, the big jerk.

He clamped down on the mess of anger and anguish in his chest. This wasn't the time to get distracted.

Before they'd left the island, he'd asked one of his security men, a native Memphian, where the busiest tourist area would be.

"You think Graceland, Bobby?"

"Naw, Sarge. Sure, it's busy there, but he'd want the most bang for his buck, right? Draw out the magic users, get as much chaos goin' as he can."

"So? Where?"

"Beale Street, Sarge. That's where you wanna be."

As far as he could tell, Bobby had hit it dead on. The street was packed with visitors and natives alike visiting the shops, clubs and restaurants, and Zack had picked up on the psychic scent of no less than twelve magic users just from the folks wandering in and out of the voodoo store.

He'd sent Angus up the street with Nate, and Sionnach down toward the river with Will and Brandon. The big kid seemed to like Sionnach and responded to him with the least resentment, so it seemed the best solution. Zack was on his own, with the reasoning that if he could get his hands on Diego, he was the only one who had a chance of holding their errant consul alone until the others could reach him.

His phone vibrated inside his leather jacket. "Morrison."

"Look sharp, Sarge," Marcus yelled over the tumult in the background. "He's just done with Brooklyn. Might be headed your way."

"Everyone all right? No sighting?"

"Finn and Kev are a little banged up, but we're okay. We *saw* him, Sarge, but couldn't get to him. No joy here."

"Define 'a little banged up'?"

Marcus let out a short, mirthless laugh. "They both got punched in the head by a girl."

"The same girl?"

"Werewolf, Sarge. You watch yourself."

"Always. Get 'em home, Marcus, and to the healers. Nothing more you can do there."

God. Diego had a vampire and at least one werewolf now, and hell knew what else. This was too damn dangerous for the kids to be separated from him. He was about to call his troops in to regroup when a familiar yank on the world's magic hit him. No time. Diego was opening the doorway now.

A woman in a Ramones T-shirt came running out of the shop, her eyes huge in fear. "What the hell is that?"

"Trouble, ma'am." One sniff of her and Zack scented her magic. She was powerful, but probably not powerful enough. Diego would want to snap her up. "Get to cover. Something bad's coming and you don't wanna be out here."

Her dark eyes regarded him with cool skepticism. "Who's going to protect us, wolf? You?"

"No guarantees, ma'am. Here to do the best I can."

Something flickered in her eyes, maybe recognition. He had been on the news a lot, after all. "Be careful then." She gave him a curt nod and hurried back inside.

His earpiece beeped, Sionnach's voice as clear as if he stood beside him. "He's coming through, Zack. Close to you."

"I know, bud. But I think he's inside a building somewhere. Can't see him."

"We're on our way back to you."

"Zack!" Angus beeped in on the channel, his voice tight and clipped.

"I heard. Regroup on my location. Time to roll."

Before his change, Zack would have been oblivious. Now the magic sang across his skin, making the hair on his arms stand up. Diego was opening a door—he was damn sure in one of the buildings across the street. He just didn't know exactly where. After a couple of minutes, it didn't matter, though. The man himself strode out of an alley, followed by four young people. The dark glasses and broad-brimmed hat didn't help to disguise him one bit. Zack would've known him if he'd been wearing a Ronald Reagan mask. Diego said a few words and the youngsters scattered fast, heading both up and down the street.

Sionnach reached him first, Brandon and Will trailing a full two blocks behind him. "Zack, he's…"

"I see him. He's got freaking minions, damn it. The dark-haired girl in the black tank top, see her? And the tall kid with her. Go after them. Cut it short, whatever he's ordered them to do."

Angus had joined them at this point, towing Nate by the hand so he would keep up.

"Angus, you guys follow those two, the redhead and the little blonde. Be careful. We don't know what these kids can do."

"And you, Zachary?"

"I'm going after Sandoval," he growled as he pushed off the storefront. "I'll hold him until Brandon can get to me. Go!"

His own companions scattered, mirroring Diego's. Before he could draw another breath and possibly regret what he was about to do, Zack *moved* with all the unnatural speed gifted him by his werewolf mauling. This time he didn't call out and give warning. This time he simply struck, before even Diego could turn, become aware of him and react. He snatched up Diego's slender wrists in one hand and slammed them into the wall above his head. With his free hand, he seized Diego's throat, partially cutting off his airway so the Voice wouldn't be an option.

The shock lasted only a heartbeat. Then Diego smiled at him. "Hey, Zack."

"Where is he?" Zack snarled, the beast barely below the surface. He knew he held too tight, knew his grip must hurt. He was having trouble caring. "Where's Lugh?"

"He's safe," Diego said softly, in a voice obviously meant to soothe him. "I can't tell you where, Zack, you know that. He's secure, but safe."

"Why can't I hear him? Damn it, Diego!"

"I will admit, there's some iron involved —"

"Fuck! How is that *safe*?"

" —but he won't take any permanent harm." Diego's dark eyes seemed disturbingly sane as they bored into his. "You could come see him, you know. Come with me. I'd take you to him. All you have to do is swear to the cause."

He hesitated, torn. To be able to see Lugh, to go with Diego, find out where he had set up his safe house, work on taking down his new organization from the inside...but they both knew he didn't lie well. Diego would know the instant he did. They'd been through too much together for that.

"I can't, Mr. S. You know I can't." He licked dry lips, trying to ease the growling in his voice. "Come home with me instead. Come home where people love you...where we can help you..."

"You know I can't. I don't want to hurt you, Zack. I don't want to hurt the people I love. You're going to have to come with me, or let me go."

"You are hurting them! You've already hurt Finn!"

"I know he's worried, but he's safe —"

"He was in Brooklyn, Mr. S.! Damn it, don't you see what you're doing? Your little werewolf clobbered him senseless and you didn't even know he was there?"

"In... He should have been safe at home. Zack...why was he in Brooklyn?" The first hint of uncertainty crept into Diego's eyes. It gave Zack hope.

"He's so damn worried about you. He wants you home. It's tearing him apart." Zack heard footsteps running toward him even as the shrieks and crashes began up and down the street from the blossoming magical riot. He had to stall. Just a few seconds more.

The war raged on Diego's face for a few seconds longer, then those dark eyes narrowed. "I will retrieve him when it's time. When it's safe. Tell him that. I counted on you to keep him safe!"

"It's not me who put him in danger."

Diego let out a frustrated, wounded bellow and Zack felt the magic gather under his fingers a moment too late. *Oh, shit...*

The electric discharge surged through him, whiting out his vision. His feet no longer touched ground, he knew that, but he wasn't aware of much else until he hit sidewalk again shoulder first. A lot of yelling went on over his head, familiar voices close by, unfamiliar ones farther down the street. Arms wrapped around him and dragged him a few feet. He thought he saw Sionnach's face hovering above him.

"Zack?" The little fox fae patted his cheek gently. "Can you hear me?"

"Yeah," he answered in a hoarse croak. "I'm... Yeah."

Sionnach turned his face up to speak to someone. "I think he will be well. He seems whole." Then the pretty face returned to look in to his. "I'm sorry, Zack. He is gone again. We have kept the damage to a small amount here. His henchmen fled with him."

He struggled to sit up, only managing with Sionnach's help. Brandon and Will both crouched beside him.

"Sorry, Sarge." Brandon's gruff, taut voice held more apology than his words could. "Didn't get to you in time. Fuck. Just a few more seconds."

"Hey. S'okay. Did your best." Zack pulled in a slow breath, trying to get the ground to steady. Magical lightning shock was definitely not fun. "Everyone all right? All here?"

"Angus and Nate are coming. I see them just down the..." Sionnach trailed off, surprised or puzzled by what he saw.

"What?" Zack blinked hard, trying to focus his fuzzy vision. That was Angus closing in on them, yep, Nate beside him, but Nate was carrying something...someone... "What the hell?"

"Um, okay, so I guess we didn't get him, huh?" Nate said as they came within earshot. The person cradled in his arms was the redhead who had come through with Diego, a shockingly pale waif of a boy with a mop of dark red hair that looked like dried blood against his pale skin. "Got one of his vamps, though."

"You got..." The strange urge to tell Nate to put it back gripped Zack and he shook his head. "How did... What happened?"

"Well, fine, I didn't do it. But there was this guy who lives here who got all ticked off or scared or something that someone was messing with his neighborhood. He pulled a wall down with his mind and it landed on the vamp."

"What, his mind?"

"No, Sarge. The wall." Nate beamed at him. "I figure we'd take him with us."

"Nate, he's dangerous. We can't do that."

Nate's smile faded. "He's hurt pretty bad. I think things are broken besides his arm. We can't just leave him for some hospital to find out what he is. And I figured it would be good to have a, you know, prisoner. To question and stuff."

Zack rubbed both hands over his face. "Nate. He's a vampire."

"And you're a werewolf."

"How would you even feed him?"

"There's gotta be blood in medical supplies on the island, right?" The impish grin returned. "Please, Dad, can we keep him? I promise I'll clean up after him and everything."

"It's probably the after-shock-treatment headache talking, but fine. Let's get going. And we're taking the damn vamp with us."

Chapter Nineteen

A Finding

"What's the most dangerous sort of adversary for you?"
"A wounded one."
"Ah. Because he'll turn at bay and be twice as vicious?"
"Nay. Because a sorely wounded foe can pierce my heart deeper and more swiftly than any spear."
—Interview with Faolchú Earthshaker on *Good Morning America*

"Finn's in the den, sulking," Minky told Zack when he got back. That was about the only accurate word for his having retired with an ice pack for his head to slump on the sofa, watch *My Little Pony* and refuse to speak to anyone.

Zack stood in the doorway a moment, sipping his water, blinking at the ultra-cute cartoon characters. Watching ponies, with his long body curled into a tight ball in one corner of the sofa, Finn somehow managed to project the image of someone who was six rather than several thousand years old.

"Hey, bud. Why isn't C-Span on?"

"I no longer wish to watch it. I wish to see if Applejack will return to Ponyville."

"Hmm. Yeah. I get the whole checking out from reality for a bit thing, especially when you're not feeling gr—"

"I was completely useless. Again. And did not even see him this time."

"Not how everyone else is telling it, bud. The useless part. But if you've decided you wanna give up so you can feel sorry for yourself, I guess th—"

"I'm exhausted and in pain!" Finn snapped. "If you have only come to scold me like everyone else, you should go away."

"Actually, if you'd let me finish a whole sentence, I came to tell you we have one of his vampires."

Finn sat up slowly and placed the icepack on the table with exaggerated care. "Have? Captured?"

"Well, see, 'captured' isn't really accurate here. He was injured and out cold and Nate picked him up off the street."

"He is *here* somewhere? Danu and Balor have *allowed* this?"

"There was some hard negotiating, but yeah. He's down in the cavern the boys were getting ready for my next change." Zack waited until Finn switched off the cartoon. "Silver alloy manacles and everything in there. Works out pretty good for vamps too, I'm told. And this kid...broken arm, broken ribs, cracked collarbone—he's not exactly a big threat right now."

"You have questioned him?"

"Not yet, bud. He wasn't awake. And I thought you should be there."

Finn stared at his hands. "Why must they all be children?"

"Something about unsettled *kelan* patterns, Lord Hssetassk said. I don't understand it, but the kids are more...susceptible to magic disease and twisted *kelan* latching on."

Finn's headshake seemed to indicate that Zack hadn't grasped his meaning, but he didn't contradict or explain. Pookas and kids...as he understood it, there was an old relationship there. A pooka might mess with human grown-ups, but he'd never hurt a child. *God, how much harder can this get for him?*

Not that any of the young people involved were really children, but the fae still saw them that way. Finn levered himself up from the sofa, wincing. He did have a multi-hued bruise spreading from right cheek to temple. Werewolf girl knew how to hit.

"Caverns?"

"Yep." Zack watched in concern as Finn continued to move slowly. "Need help?"

"A mite stiff. I'll manage." They made their way down the stairs to the fae caverns, through the hidden door pretending to be nothing but rock wall. It wasn't too long ago that the sight of his friend disappearing through solid granite would have left him flatfooted and staring open-mouthed. Now? Just a part of normal, everyday life at the embassy. *Normal, everyday life that should have Lugh in it...damn it.*

A heavy, silver alloy door had been fitted to the opening of one of the sleeping chambers with brass hinges. Moss-stuffed sacks lined the walls and floor, in anticipation of a trapped, raging were-beast, to keep him from injuring himself too badly.

The fae healers had made a moss and grass bed for their captive patient as well, and had set the broken bones using wrappings of their own manufacture rather than casts. The kid's unbroken wrist and one of his ankles were manacled to the wall but the chains were long enough so he could lie comfortably. Not a bad prison, as these things went.

From his spot next to the head of the mattress, Nate looked up when the door opened, chewing on his bottom lip. "Hey, Sarge."

"How's he doing?"

"He's all right, I guess. Mostly awake. Whimpers sometimes." He moved an inch closer to the vamp. "You won't hurt him, will you? You won't use CIA interrogation tactics or anything? Geneva Conventions and all that?"

Zack settled on the floor with a sigh. "Tell me you do something with your time besides watch bad movies?"

"There's another kind?"

"Right." Zack recognized Nate's need to make jokes as stress-induced. "You don't have to stay if you don't want to."

"I'm staying. You need an observer for these things. The UN says so."

"Funny guy." He reached out and patted the vamp's ankle. "Hey, there. You know where you are?"

The mop of red hair had fallen across the kid's forehead, giving him a feral look as blue eyes stared back out from beneath the curtain of hair with wary bravado. "Not in Kansas anymore."

"Great. Stuck with a bunch of comedians. What's your name, kid?"

Odd that the kid glanced up at Nate first before answering. Nate gave him a little nod, one Zack might have missed if he wasn't looking for it, and the kid answered, "Jasper."

"Thanks. I didn't really want to keep calling you 'the vamp kid in the basement'. I'm gonna ask again, just for medical reasons, since you did have a wall land on you. Know where you are?"

"Yeah." Jasper's voice shook. For a prince of the night, he wasn't doing too well with the menacing part. "At the Fae Embassy."

"You got it. Look, no one here wants to hurt you. I want that clear. You got clobbered, your friends panicked and left you behind. Nate picked you up 'cause he didn't think it was nice to just leave you in the middle of the street."

"He did?" Jasper's gaze wandered back to Nate again.

Way to focus, kid. "He did. How're you feeling?"

"Kinda crappy. The kitty doc said things are broken. The silver hurts like hell." Jasper swallowed hard. "And I think...um, I think I need food."

"We have some bags of blood in the med supplies. But first we need—"

"No." Jasper shook his head frantically. "I can't have bag stuff. Tried that. Makes me puke."

"Can you..." Zack wasn't sure how to ask the question. "Can you feed without, ah, hurting your food?"

"I can. I do. I mean I don't!" The soft voice trembled with emotions besides fear now. "I've never hurt anyone feeding. Never."

"All right. We'll see what we can do. But first you need to answer some questions, all right?"

"Sarge! You can't do that!" Nate sputtered, obviously horrified.

Zack fought not to roll his eyes. "I'm not threatening starvation. I just want a few answers before we make arrangements. Acceptable, Mr. Observer?"

"I guess."

Finn had stationed himself near the door, silent and watchful. His knees pulled up and his arms wrapped around them, he rocked fitfully. Now he decided to speak up, "Where is he, Jasper?"

Jasper tried to lift his head to see who spoke, gave up with a gasp, and, yeah, he really did whimper. "Who?"

"My husband. Where does he take all the children?"

"Nate? Help me out here, man. Not getting it."

"That's Finn over there by the door. Mr. Sandoval's Finn, that is." Nate actually put a hand on Jasper's shoulder. "And I think he calls anyone under, like, twenty-five 'children'. That clear things?"

"Yeah. Kinda." Jasper started to heave a sigh, aborted by his broken ribs. "If all y'all wanna torture me, whatever. Not like I can tell you much of anything. One day I'm at work, the next I'm at the hospital being declared dead. Only I'm not dead and I wake up in the morgue, hungry as all get out. So crazy hungry I bite the woman who comes to check out the noise. Thought I was a goddamn zombie. Didn't want the flesh, though. Just the blood. Got so freaked I didn't take more than a couple mouthfuls."

"I understand the freaked part. Hell, yeah," Zack said gently. "How long ago was this?"

"Couple months. I…did what I had to. Couldn't go home to my parents. Not like this. Mr. Sandoval, he found me living in an old warehouse. Said he was there to help. That he was gonna make sure it would get better for people like me. It all sounded so good. I didn't fight him. I went with him on my own. Not like some of the others. But I didn't know we were aiming to cause riots and stuff."

"What did you think you'd be doing?"

"Saving the world."

Zack wanted to shake the information out of the kid, but he kept his voice patient and soft. "Where did he take you?"

"To his compound."

"Which is where?"

Jasper turned his head to look at Nate again, the hair falling back to fully reveal one brilliant blue eye. "Nate..."

"I told you. No one here's gonna hurt you." He smoothed the hair back from Jasper's forehead and Zack struggled not to gape.

"They will... When I can't tell them, they will."

"Just tell the truth. It'll be okay."

The husky-blue eyes shut tight and Jasper whispered, "I don't know where it is. He always made one of those cussed magic doors. It's this abandoned asylum in the middle of nowhere. I don't know where."

Damn it. Should've guessed he wouldn't tell his recruits. "You remember anything? A sign? A landmark? Something that might place it?"

Jasper shifted, tugging on the silver cuff. "I can't...think..." He broke off with a sound between a hiss and a growl. "Please. I have to eat. Or I'll go all psycho. Please don't do this."

"He's injured, Zack." Finn's voice was muffled where he'd buried his head against his knees. "The blood stalkers...the vampires, the drive to feed becomes desperation for them when they're badly hurt."

Zack patted Finn's shoulder. "Stay here with them, bud. I'll be right back."

A few whispered words in Eithne's ear and she brought two Fomorian stalwarts to the containment chamber, one who looked like a giant otter with hands and the other with a hawk's head and clawed feet.

"Murchú and Séighín have agreed to feed you, little blood stalker," Eithne told him in her firmest 'I'm the healer, so listen up' voice. "You take *just* what you need. Do you hear me?"

"Yes'm," Jasper agreed in a spare whisper. His blue eyes had darkened to an unhealthy shade of red but he still managed to sound embarrassed when he said, "I don't...I've never had people watching."

"Go, dear Zack." Eithne made shooing motions at him. "Take everyone else with you. We have things well in hand."

"I promised I wouldn't leave him." Nate put his back to the wall, jaw jutting in stubborn defiance.

"Christ almighty." Zack rubbed a hand over his forehead. The headache was constant now. He was almost used to it. "Fine. Nate stays. The little guy seems to trust him, so it might go better that way." He pointed a warning finger at the moss bed. "Jasper, you behave yourself, boy, you hear me? We'll take care of you so long's you stay polite."

"Yes, sir. Got it."

He took Finn by the arm to steer him out since the pooka no longer seemed entirely aware of his surroundings. The blank stare could have been deep thought, or sudden catatonia. At one of the common caverns, festooned with colorful groupings of floor cushions, he stopped, took Finn by the arms and gave him a little shake.

"You with me, hon? You all right?"

"Asylum. In the middle of nowhere." Finn shook his head hard and pulled Zack into a tight embrace, all his tension telegraphing through trembling muscles. "There is a memory dancing out of reach and I cannot run fast enough to catch it up."

"If it's in there, it'll come. Hey, hey, it'll be all right. We're closer than we were, right?"

"Jasper," Finn said on a strangled breath. "He had my Diego's scent on him."

"What're you saying? That Diego was, what? Screwing him?"

Finn reared back, almost toppling them both. "What? Great Mother, no. Not that sort of scent. Simply…Diego. Where a hand had touched. Where they had stood shoulder to shoulder. It was still hard to bear."

"Yeah. I guess I didn't notice. All I smelled was vamp." *Sure as hell didn't smell Lugh.*

The stricken expression faded and Finn leaned in to kiss his forehead.

"What was that for?"

"An apology. Your love is lost in this as well. I have been selfish, forgetting that your pain is as sharp as mine."

"S'okay. I'm built kinda tough." He pulled Finn down with him and let the pooka settle, sprawled on the cushions with his head in Zack's lap. A couple of years ago, the position would've felt beyond weird. Now, fae-acclimated as he was, it was just a nice thing to do for a friend while they waited.

* * * *

Minky channel surfed while Kara went to the kitchen to grab them some snacks. Her hands shook a little but she wasn't freaked out and that worried her. She should have been. Being in the middle of a riot, suddenly finding magic singing through her, knocking flaming vehicles from the air, yeah, she should have been a mess. Maybe this was one of those states of denial people went into, not dealing with things when stuff was really, really bad.

Brandon flopped down on the sofa next to her, his hand automatically held out for the remote. She glared at the imperious gesture and retained a firm grip while Will settled between them. Bran snorted and the hand went away.

"Where's Nate?"

"Downstairs. Aiding and abetting," Minky muttered, purposefully putting on *Iron Chef*, which Brandon hated.

Kara sailed back into the room with a plate of crackers and cheese. "Just because he wants to keep an eye on things. Nate's doing what Nate thinks he has to do."

"Sorry," Minky mumbled automatically.

"Yeah. A lot of good we've managed to do so far," Brandon growled. The deep blush as he said it, though, made it obvious he was angry with himself. No one was mean enough to point it out. He scarfed down a third of the crackers before he seemed calmer. "Heard you had some badass moves today, little bit."

She shrugged. "Finn was about to get squashed by a flying hot dog cart—"

"Empanada," Kara corrected.

"Whatever the thing was. I just kind of…did it."

Nate chose that moment to amble in and plop down on the recliner. Mortar dust caked his hair. Dark shadows lurked under his eyes. But he still flashed his crooked, charming smile. "Hey."

"So give," Kara snapped. "What's the shit-eating grin for?"

He gestured with a piece of Gouda. "Seems that Fomorian blood is like vampire crack or something. Got halfway through his meal and started babbling and giggling. At least it acted like a painkiller, too."

"Is he still feeding?" Will asked as he nibbled on a triangle of Swiss.

"Nah. All tucked in and sleeping like a baby, poor little guy."

Brandon nudged Nate's ankle with his boot. "So there's a point to telling us. Or there better be after the build-up."

Nate chuckled and slathered a cracker with goat cheese. "Yeah, yeah. Getting there. So Sergeant Morrison, he went down there to question Jasper, that's the vamp. All polite of course, 'cause it's who he is, but Jasper's in so much pain and all ADD from needing blood, so he couldn't think past telling the sergeant that Mr. Sandoval is holed up with his posse in an abandoned asylum."

"Nate, fuck's sake. Stop enjoying yourself so much," Brandon insisted.

"Fine. Ruin a guy's story. Jasper remembered when he was all relaxed and happy that he'd seen a sign on one of the walls. Heersford, the sign said. Now we just have to figure out where Heersford Asylum is. Cinch, right?"

Minky already had her phone out, searching. "So we're on a first name basis with the evil people now?" The sudden silence disturbed her. She glanced up to find everyone staring at her, Nate's smile fading to something slightly stricken. "What?"

"Legit question, Nate," Kara said softly.

"I don't think that's right..." Nate ran a hand back through his dusty hair. "I mean, Jasper doesn't seem evil. He's lost and scared, but I don't think he's much different from us."

"Werewolf girl and pyro boy sure didn't seem like poor, lost kids," Kara said with a snort. "Definitely having way too much fun with the whole destruction thing."

"Okay, Jasper did say that Lila, that's the werewolf chick, and Magnus—"

"Magnus? You're shitting me," Brandon said on a choked laugh.

"No, not making this up. That's what Jasper said pyro boy's name is. Anyway, he did admit those two are total jerks. Apparently, Theo keeps them in line most of the time." Nate waved one hand over the other, a signal he'd gotten off track. "Anyway, of course some of the people Mr. S. has picked up are gonna be bad. He's looking for power, not model citizens. But I'm willing to bet more are like Jasper. Like us."

"Like us, but not like us," Will said softly, contemplating the wheat cracker in his hand. "There's one big difference."

"What's that, babe?" Brandon leaned forward to take Will's free hand, the muscles in his forearm taut.

"All of them are solitary."

Nate shook his head. "Not following. They come in packs. It's not like they acted alone."

"A group, yes." Will spoke slowly as if chewing on his words. "But each on their own. Some of them tried to protect each other, true. But did anyone of us, at any time, feel them pull power together? Did they work any magic at all…together?"

He glanced from one to another until every head shook 'no'ⁱ

Minky put her phone down. She hadn't found a damn thing. "There's no Heersford listed anywhere." She fiddled with the edge of her sleeve a moment, gathering courage. "Will's saying they don't have…us. Like we have us. A coven."

"Oh, please." Brandon sat back again, setting his boots up on the coffee table with an angry clomp. "Fat lot of good that's done us."

Will got up to pace, his hands waving in short, precise gesticulations. "Because we haven't done anything about it yet. But the dragon lord talked about it. Think about it! Think about how we came together. How much better we all feel together than apart. How our magic started to manifest only when we were all *together*."

"Babe, it's just coincidence."

"I don't think there is coincidence with magic, Bran," Nate whispered, staring hard at the carpet.

"We are a coven!" Will insisted, his voice trembling with the force of his conviction. "Five of us, in the old sense. We fit!" He began to point at them in turn, Brandon, himself, Kara, Minky and Nate. "Voice, Sight, Strength, Head and Heart! We're more powerful than they are because they're all alone!"

"Um, I get why you're Sight, Will," Brandon began, hands spread. "But Minky as the Head? Seriously?"

For once Will didn't back down. "Seriously. Think, Bran. Who's always spoken for us? You. Who tries to protect us? Kara. Who is it that makes peace, who made us whole? Nate. And when we've needed an idea, when we've needed someone to think for us, it's always been Minky."

"Oh, come on!"

"No. Put the ego away. I love you, Bran, but sometimes you're full of yourself. It was Minky's idea to contact Mr. Sandoval in the first place. She's the one who always emailed him. Minky said to use the catnip. *Minky* got us all to move in together."

Minky's mouth fell open, but she managed a squeak of protest. "I did not! Everybody agreed!"

Nate lifted his head. "But you suggested it. Will, I think you've got it. And if we're going to find this place, and stop all this mess, I think we need to start...pooling our resources. Putting our magical heads together, so to speak."

Kara rolled her eyes. "How did you manage to make that sound dirty?"

"Natural talent." Even through the teasing, Nate remained uncharacteristically grim. "We grab Finn and the sergeant, and we figure out how to do this. How to find this place."

"Finding a place when you don't know where to start. Like dowsing for water," Minky said in a distracted murmur. "We need a map."

* * * *

The dragon crystal remained dark. Diego barely controlled the urge to fling the damned thing across the room. Without the distractions of sentiment, he should have developed a better leash on all his emotions, but the *anger* only grew inside him like an invasive weed.

Beyond the frustrations of dealing with politicians, of seeing his plans moving too slowly, he couldn't fathom where the terrible depths of fury originated. It smoldered under the surface all the time now, sparking and blazing forth with the slightest provocation.

Like scrying crystals that refuse to answer. He had still been learning to use it before his change, though he had reached the point where he could ask it to show him people he cared for. It wouldn't even show him Finn anymore and Finn was *his*.

"Damn dragons and their fucking superiority complex," he muttered to the crystal. Dragons...those would be barred from the human world under the new laws. He had to make sure of that. Too much wild power — he theorized their renewed contact with the human world might well have escalated the return of magical maladies in humans. *Why else would the world suddenly have vampires again?*

As if the thought conjured him, Theo's mental voice called to him. "Jefe? *Could you open the door?*"

With a shift in concentration and a spare flick of his fingers, Diego reopened the door to the Memphis location they had used earlier in the day. Theo hurried through and stood clear so the door could snap shut behind him.

The boy didn't look happy.

"*Jefe.*"

Diego failed to keep the snarl from his voice. "You didn't find him."

Theo shifted from foot to foot, gaze glued to the floor. "No. I'm sorry. I found the trail...then lost it again."

Not his fault. With a measured breath, Diego softened his voice. "You did what you could. I should have realized he wasn't with us when I opened the door." He rolled his shoulders, trying to ease the tightness. "If the authorities have him, we'll hear about it."

"And if not, *jefe*?" Theo's head came up, his expression troubled. "If *they* have him?"

Diego rolled the crystal in his fingers, his mind racing. "Our poor little Jasper will most likely say something he shouldn't. He isn't as...experienced as you, *mijo*, and some of the fae can extract information from an unguarded mind. We need to be prepared when it comes."

"For what?"

"The assault."

* * * *

"There you are!" Nate descended on them in a dusty whirlwind. "Come on, you guys, you have to come! We've got something going, we think and—"

"Slow down, kiddo. Haven't you even had a shower?" Zack scrambled up, hovering between alarm and amusement at Nate's wild-eyed eagerness.

"No time! Come on! Heersford Asylum, Jasper said. We're gonna try and find it."

Finn's head snapped up at the name. He seized Nate's hand and ran from the cavern without a word.

"Hey! Whoa!" Nate scrambled to keep up on the stairs. "What'd I say?"

"Heersford..." Finn muttered. At the top of the stairs he stopped short, suddenly perplexed. "Where are we going?"

Nate held up a hand as he caught his breath. "Den...set up in the den."

The direction sent Finn barreling forward again, and while Zack kept up easily enough, his friend's behavior had him a little concerned. *Either he's remembered something or the poor pooka's cracked under the strain.*

The kids had pushed the coffee table to the center of the floor and knelt around it. Diego's huge atlas lay open to a political map of the world.

"You won't need that." Finn flapped his hand at the map. "I know where it is."

"Aw, man. Just when we were getting ready to try our coven thing," Kara said on a huff. "Well, where is it?"

Finn settled on the carpet and stared bleakly at the atlas, muttering, "I hate maps. How can anyone make sense of these blasted things? Zack, would you point to New York, please?"

Trying to keep up with events, Zack shouldered in between Kara and Brandon and put a finger on New York.

"Ah. Good. And now where is New Brunswick? I suppose St. John's, specifically."

Will reached out and placed his index finger over the coastal city.

"There." Finn flashed a triumphant smile. "It is somewhere between New York and St. John's."

The youngsters all gaped at him with varied expressions of disbelief and confusion. Minky buried her face in her hands.

"Um, dude…" Brandon finally found his voice. "I thought you said you knew where it was. That's kind of, ah, vague."

Finn's smile vanished. "Well, at least you won't be looking in Australia," he said in a small voice.

"Maybe if you explain to us where this revelation came from, bud." Zack gripped Finn's shoulder and gave him a little shake. "It's better than Australia, but it's still a lot of ground to cover."

Angel Martinez

With a shaky breath, Finn finally seemed to settle enough for explanations. "Before Diego began to open magical doors helter-skelter, we would drive to New York for visits. He liked the drive, he said. It helped him think. He would tell me things on those drives...stories about towns we passed and the people who lived there. Somewhere on one of those drives, he talked about Heersford. He said it was built some hundred years ago, meant to be the best place for treatment of various madnesses."

"I'm not sure that's a word," Minky said softly. She had edged nearer to him, as if to encourage him, and Finn smiled down at her. Odd to see the bond growing between them, but Zack sure as hell wasn't going to interfere. It was good for Finn, to have someone else to think about.

"Perhaps. In any case, the place had problems with money and fell into disrepair. Eventually, its caretakers left it to molder in the countryside, its gardens gone wild, its halls abandoned. Diego said he had seen it once and that a strange, peaceful melancholy clung to it."

"But you don't remember where he said it was?" Will asked.

"Not...precisely. No."

"That's okay." Minky turned the atlas toward her and leafed through until she found a detail map of the North Atlantic. "You sure narrowed it down a lot."

"That's right. We'll just do what we were going to in the first place." Nate bounced to his feet and tugged on Finn's arm. "Come on, big guy. You gotta back up a little. You're in our circle. You too, Sarge."

Mystified, Zack sat in the armchair across the room to give them space with Finn perched hipshot on the chair arm. The kids obviously had something magical in mind and he'd take any effort on behalf of the cause right then. Kara drew a silver chain from around her neck from which dangled a bat pendant made of some shiny black stone. *Focal point, maybe?* God, the stuff he *didn't* know about magic still could've filled volumes.

Kara got up on her knees so she could dangle the bat over the map. "So do we have to, like, hold on to each other?"

Brandon shrugged. "Can't hurt, right?"

"I think this first time, yeah." Minky nudged one and the other of them to points significant to her around the table, then settled herself between Nate and Kara.

Five of them...five points... Zack poked at his tired brain to get a rise out of it and the abused gray matter managed to pull itself together to realize Minky had made them into a pentagram. Those with free hands joined them and Minky held on to Kara's right shoulder, since she held the bat necklace.

"Now what?" Kara muttered.

"Everyone concentrate on Kara," Minky suggested, though she cringed when she said it, as if certain she'd get an argument. "Reach for the magic like the dragon lord showed us and think about finding Heersford."

For a long, agonizing minute, nothing happened. Then Nate closed his eyes and shuddered. Trails of magic flowed to him from around the room, little trickles until Zack's newly developed magical sense picked up an odd glow around him.

From Nate, it flowed *through* Minky until Kara began to pull in pieces of magical energy as well, hers coming to her in bright, dancing layered ropes rather than trickling streamlets. *Strength. Yeah, the girl has that.*

Brandon let out a gasp as a huge surge of power rushed into him, so fierce it should have shot through the top of his head and punched a hole in the ceiling.

It didn't. Zack narrowed his eyes, leaning forward in the chair. Will pulled Brandon's hand to his chest and channeled that terrible, untamed power, acting as a goddamn magical transformer, stepping it down until he could send it on. Once shared around the circle, the power hummed and crackled around them, each young person adding and changing it subtly, each one an end and a beginning in the closed loop of increasing magical flows.

"Now, Kara," Will whispered. "Try now."

A tremor ran through the silver chain and the little bat began to sway gently from side to side. The pendulum motion became circular as Kara concentrated on the bat, eyes wide, bottom lip caught between her teeth. The circle described the entire map, at first, swinging in a wide ellipse from Philadelphia to the Atlantic Provinces. Kara's eyes narrowed. The bat began to tug at her hold, pulling toward the north. The circumference of the ellipse tightened until the bat quite insistently circled over Maine.

The taut edge to Kara's voice was urgent, almost desperate. "We need to zoom in...shit! I feel like it's trying to pull me into the map!"

"Hold on, hold on," Nate murmured. He pulled in a deep breath and let it out slowly. As he exhaled, the atlas's pages turned. Nate kept up a constant murmur as the states flipped by. "PA, Jersey, New York, Nutmeg Land...come on...come on..."

"Maine! Stop!" Kara cried out, panting.

The pages settled and the bat began its ever-decreasing circle again. A bead of sweat trickled down

Kara's cheek but she didn't take her hand from Will's or stop to use her sleeve to wipe off the drop. Brandon sat panting, head down, his large body trembling.

Mr. S. always made it look so easy. Magic is a hell of a lot harder than I thought.

"We need more zoom." Kara's voice cracked. "How the hell do we do that?"

Cautiously, afraid he would disturb the flows, Zack eased up to peer over her shoulder. The bat circled the coast between Bar Harbor and Grand Manan Island. "Hold tight. Give me just a sec."

He dove for the computer on the corner desk by the window. Always powered up, it sat ready for any curious fae to play with. With one hand, he flipped on the printer, with the other, pulled up an online map. Once he'd zoomed in far enough to read the names of the smaller towns, he printed it. "Finn! Slide it under the bat!"

For once, Finn acted without question. He snatched up the printout and leaned carefully over Nate's shoulder, his long body allowing him to avoid the flows as he gingerly slipped the new map between bat and atlas. Again the bat circled, all the youngsters' eyes glued to it movements as it zeroed in again.

"Northeast of Columbia Falls!" Kara cried out, her voice nearly a sob.

Zack zoomed in further, moving up on the map to the area in question. He stopped when he could read the street names for the odd, twisty roads. *Skunk Ridge? Really?* But he couldn't stop for curiosities. He printed and handed it off into Finn's waiting hand.

The cycle of circling repeated once again, little whimpers coming from someone in the group. Kara cried out as she was yanked down, the bat finally coming to rest at a point where no immediately visible roads led.

"Here," she said in a shaky whisper. "It's here."

"Mark that!" Zack barked out. He didn't mean to snap out orders, but the tension in the room had him in knots.

Minky pulled a pen out of her pocket and circled the still quivering bat where it lay on the paper. "Let it go, everyone. Will, I think Bran's going out."

Even though she had physically broken the circle, the connection didn't break between them until Kara closed her eyes and let hers go. Zack watched in amazement as Her Prickliness let Nate gather her into his arms. She clung to him, shaking and not quite sobbing. Brandon would have collapsed face first on the table if Will hadn't been ready and pulled him sideways, cradling his boyfriend's head and shoulders in his lap.

"Well, that was...painful," Nate said with a shaky grin.

"But it worked. We did it." Will's eyes shone as he stroked Brandon's hair.

"Gets better with practice, I'd bet." Zack made the rounds, making certain no one looked shocky and Brandon's vitals were steady. "You did the hard part, guys. We've got a location. Getting there might be tricky, but we'll work on that next." He glanced up at Finn. "Did Morrigan and Faolchú make it back yet?"

"I heard the wolf champion some time ago. Of Morrigan..." Finn shrugged. "I would be the last she would tell of her whereabouts."

"You two have got to get over that old grudge, whatever the hell it was," Zack said with a little sigh.

"But Eithne's here. Duh. So of course they're back." He paced to the door, already intent on their next moves.

"Zack?"

"Hmm? Oh. Sorry. Calling a war council. We need a better plan of action this time."

* * * *

The vampire stood in the doorway, regarding him with an unreadable expression. "Could you eat something? He mentioned you might eat oatmeal."

Lugh tried to shake his head and failed even in that small movement. "No," he whispered, uncertain if the young man heard him.

"No, you can't or no, you refuse? He doesn't want you to die, you know."

"Can't. Iron's too much. *Sidhe* are...sensitive."

"But you're not fully *sidhe*, they say. Half and half."

"Yes. Not dead yet."

The distant expression became a frown, perhaps even a concerned one. "I don't understand. He said Finn survived prolonged iron exposure for many days."

"Pookas...different."

"Must be." Theo ventured farther into the room. His hesitance didn't smell of fear, rather he seemed undecided.

Gods, please help me. You have family. You understand... "My mother...must be frantic."

Theo crouched down near his head. "At least she worries about you."

"Yours?"

"Thinks I'm a demon." Theo shrugged. "Thought I could be 'cured'. Even brought a priest to the house."

"Why?"

"Exorcism."

"Oh."

Theo gave him the barest hint of a smile. "Didn't work so great."

"She…worries."

The smile vanished. "*Sí, verdad.* But accepting…" A second shrug.

It was hard to be angry with this young man, so lost and alone in the world. A single difference in his life, something he had no control over and could do nothing to change and suddenly his family's love became conditional. This was not how things should be. *My mother has always been my staunchest ally.* How would it be suddenly to lose her unwavering support, even her love?

Another heavy wave of pain and nausea washed through him, leaving him shivering hard enough to rattle his teeth. "Theo…" he whispered. "I won't last. Not…like this."

Theo stared at him for a long moment, his face blank again. Then he got up and left without a word.

I suppose I will never be done mishandling human intentions. Great Mother help me, I think I'm nearly done.

If he could have faded into the Dreaming to heal, he would have been fine, but the iron prevented that. Even if someone would remove the blasted collar, he could last several more days. No. He had said something wrong again, offended the young man, and now he would die.

Zack, my beloved, forgive me. Please think well of me when you remember me…

He had sunk so far into the pain and the sorrow that his eyes flew open in shock when his cell door swung open again. Theo had returned, dangling a long, leather strap from his right hand. Lugh blinked at it, wondering what purpose it would possibly serve to beat him now. *Unless it's simple cruelty.*

Rather than swing the strap and strike him with it, though, Theo knelt beside him and placed the strap on the floor. Up close, he realized with its buckle it was more belt than a strap, but it was far too short.

"I will make certain with him, but I think *el jefe*, he misjudged this time." Theo swallowed hard as if it hurt him to admit such a thing. "Will you swear to stay still while I switch this out?"

"Yes." Lugh coughed out the word. "I do so swear."

"I won't take the cuffs off *su alteza*, I'm sorry. The leather collar has a steel buckle, but I think this will be better."

Theo reached behind his neck and undid the padlock on the steel collar. He tried to stay quiet, but when the steel band lifted from his throat the sob of relief still escaped. Theo's dark brows drew together as he traced a finger along Lugh's throat and for one joyous moment, Lugh thought he would relent and take both collars away.

After a pause, though, Theo wrapped the leather collar around Lugh's neck, his hands surprisingly gentle as he buckled it and clipped on the eyehook for the chain fastened to the wall.

"There." Theo patted his shoulder, though his frown remained firmly in place. "Your eyes are brighter. I'll come back later to see if you can eat."

Again, the odd young man left him, this time with a kernel of hope rather than crushing despair. It was better. He couldn't escape, but he could think again and perhaps, if he fought hard enough, he might even be able to reach for the smallest grains of magic.

* * * *

With an irritating feeling of *déjà vu*, Zack found himself pacing the dining room again.

"No. I'm not starting a goddamn war here. A good size strike force, but not the whole damn Otherworld."

Faolchú grunted, leaning back in his chair. "I suggested no such thing. But a true war band would go a long way to ensuring victory."

Zack rubbed at his burning eyes, fighting to keep his temper. How long was it before his next change? Would he start to feel the effects a whole week and a half out? God, he wanted Lugh, wanted the big, stubborn jerk beside him, at his back, wanted that huge hand on his shoulder to bleed off some of the tension.

"I hear you, I do." He held up a hand, asking for a moment. "But we have transport issues and when we get there, I don't want to give too much warning. We go in with an entire battalion's clusterfuck worth of fae, we'll tip him off too early. He'll just vanish again."

"How many, then, Oh, Hero of the Iron Caverns?" Faolchú's clawed fingers drummed the tabletop and Zack recalled belatedly he wasn't the only one in the room with a temper.

Damn it. Diego is supposed to be here to handle all us macho walking egos.

"You don't think I'd leave you out, do you?" Zack managed something close to a grin and got a strained laugh in return. "I'd say no more than twenty, total. Nathair can do some shielding, but probably not more than that, right?"

All eyes turned to little Nathair. "No more, Zack. I can only do so much. Particularly with shielding against sound. We would move silently but, and I mean no offense, the young humans would struggle to do so."

"The kids have to come, though. No way around that. So, six humans, eight if I take a couple of my guys. Nathair and the big guy, of course." He nodded to Faolchú. "Morrigan and Eithne—"

"No." Morrigan's voice cut him off, short and harsh.

"No?"

"We should not endanger so many healers. Eithne stays."

Zack quirked an eyebrow and turned to the beautiful cat Fomorian. "Princess? I'd think you have a say in this, since it's your son we're going after."

Eithne's ears flattened against her head. "Morri speaks the truth, though. I am no warrior, dear Zack, as much as I would wish to rescue my Lugh."

"Got it. Angus?"

"I will go. But not Sionnach."

"Oh? You speak *for* me now, Farseer?" Sionnach pulled his hand out of Angus' grip, his tail bristling and twitching.

Angus opened his mouth, closed it and finally grated out, "You…your strength has not fully returned."

"You mean I fall to pieces on the slightest breeze," Sionnach said softly. "That does not change how I fight."

"I worry for you!" Angus flung his arms wide, his voice choked.

"And I love you for it. But perhaps it's time to stop pretending I am made of rose petals, yes?"

Angus stared at his feet, clearly in anguish, but he nodded. Sionnach climbed into his lap to plant a scorching kiss on his lips, the two of them so lost in each other that Zack was afraid they might start going at it right there on one of the dining room chairs.

"Um. Right. Let's try to focus for a couple minutes, at least. With Finn, that's fourteen. Faolchú, bud, you pick whoever you think's best for the last six. Probably — "

"Jasper should come," Nate blurted out.

"What? Hell, no."

"Just listen, Sarge. He's been there. He's knows the layout. And he wants to help."

"You have any solid reason why we should trust him?"

"He..." Nate squirmed as his coven mates turned varied looks of concern and amusement his way. "I let him feed from me. He — "

"You *what*?" Brandon bellowed. "Cooper, did you lose your damn mind?"

Undaunted, Nate patted his large friend's arm. "He's very gentle, Bran. Very considerate." A dreamy smile spread across his face. "It was amazing."

Somehow, Zack had the feeling there had been an exchange of additional bodily fluids besides blood. "Great. Just great. But the kid had a broken arm, Nate. Broken ribs, collarbone. It's — "

"Vampire, Sarge. With enough food and some sleep, he's almost healed. Should be a hundred percent by morning."

Call me the world's biggest fool. "All right. If I talk to him in the morning and I'm convinced he's on the up and up *and* that he's physically ready, he goes." He took a slow breath, trying for calm. "Transport-wise, I think our best bet is to take a boat down the coast, then rent four by fours in M — "

"Sergeant, I think there's a better way."

Really? Can I finish just one fucking sentence? He dry-washed both hands over his face, determined not to yell. "Yes, Will? What would that be? You gonna tell me your father's stinking rich and has a fleet of Harrier jets?"

"No, sir." Will flushed crimson. "I mean, yes, my father's Robert Schoenberg, and we could borrow his yacht if we needed it, but that's not what I meant."

"Christ. As in Schoenberg Electronics?"

Will nodded miserably. "Yes. I don't... It's not important." He lifted his chin in a defiant gesture. "And we don't need my father."

"Okay. I'm listening. What's your thinking?"

"If Mr. Sandoval can make doorways, then we should be able to."

Faolchú snorted. "No one has ever been able to make Diego's doorways. Not since the Veil closed."

Will held his ground, though Zack didn't miss the tight grip he had on Brandon's hand. "But the fae we've spoken to have said it's human magic. Unique to humans. Someone taught him that he *could* make one."

Finn pointed a long finger across the table. "Morrigan did it."

"I did what I needed to!" Morrigan snapped her sharp teeth at him. "To save us all. Do *not* lay this morass at my feet, Fionnachd!"

"If you had not encouraged him so..."

"Knock it off, you two," Zack growled. "Are you saying you could build a door, Will? Get us there?"

"If Morrigan is willing to teach us, I think we could do it together. As a coven. You saw it today, Sergeant. We're stronger together."

"Yeah." *Maybe stronger than anyone but Diego.* "Let's try it. Morrigan, you've got yourself a batch of human students."

Chapter Twenty

The Asylum

"Let your plans be dark and impenetrable as night, and when you move, fall like a thunderbolt."
—Sun Tzu, *The Art of War*

The figure on the bench kept his head turned away. Zack screamed at it, stunned and ashamed at his own drama queen behavior, "Why do you have to be such an arrogant prick? You never listen! You're not listening now! Why the hell won't you talk to me?"

Slowly, with a strange creaking sound, the head moved, swiveling toward Zack. Instead of Lugh, he faced a grinning skull. It opened a mouth full of rotted teeth and whispered, "Zachary."

Zack bolted upright in bed, his inner scream still echoing in his head. *Shit.* Why did he have to have such fucked up dreams?

"Zachary..."

His heart hammered. That wasn't any dream voice. *"Lugh?"*

"*Zack, my love…thank the gods…*"

"*Where are you?*"

"*Chained in a cell. I know no more than that.*"

"*Oh, damn. Was hoping you'd gotten free or something. Why didn't you answer me before?*"

Lugh's mental voice sounded far off and weary, but damn, it was good to hear him and amazing that they could 'talk' successfully. It might have been how long Zack had lived with lycanthropy, or how much stronger his connection was with Lugh now, but he didn't have time to worry about why their mental bond worked better.

"*They had collared me in steel. I could not call to you. Theo took pity on me and changed the collar for leather. It is still difficult. Zack…I owe you a thousand apologies. You must be terribly angry with me.*"

"*Yeah, yeah, I'll yell at you when I've got you home, safe and sound. We don't have time for this right now. If you rest and I need to call to you again, do you think you'll be able to answer?*"

"*I may have a day or two, love, before I begin to fail again.*"

A growl rumbled in Zack's chest. He understood what Lugh wasn't saying. Until the vamp kid had taken the collar off, his prince had been dying. "*I'm sure as hell not leaving you there that long. We're coming. You stay strong and be ready to answer me if I call you, got it?*"

A bit of dry humor tinged Lugh's thoughts. "*I hear and obey, my brave sergeant.*"

Lugh was silent for a long moment, and Zack thought he had cut the connection. Then there came a hesitant, "*Zachary?*"

"*I'm here, babe.*"

"*I love you.*"

Zack blinked hard against the sudden sting in his eyes. "*I love you, too, you big idiot. Now get some rest.*"

He could picture Lugh's smile, the feeling from him far more content as their minds drifted apart again. Zack lay back down with his heart still hammering. Two freaking o'clock in the morning. To force himself to rest, he began to take mental inventory of the medical supply closet off the kitchen, shelf by shelf, item by item, until his pulse slowed and he drifted back into an uneasy doze.

* * * *

Minky woke with a little moan. Someone had stuffed cotton in her mouth and now played bongos in her head. She had the bad feeling this was how a hangover felt, but she hadn't had any of the fun associated with getting one.

Some of that glowy moss stuff the fae liked lit the containment cell, so she could see her still-sleeping companions but it was hard to say what time it was. Nate had insisted on sleeping in Jasper's room. Naturally, they'd all moved in with him.

Almost all sleeping. Brandon was sitting up on his pallet, head in his hands.

"Bran?"

He whispered without lifting his head, "Hey, little bit."

"You don't look so good."

"Don't feel so good."

Not a big shock. Morrigan had taught them to make magical doors, using their apartment in New York as the experimental point. Some of them managed with more success than others. They used their power together each time, of course, but one person actually had to *make* the door. Nate's had been unstable, snapping shut before he was ready. Kara's had never been larger than a softball. Brandon's had blown a hole through reality and shattered their living room lamp. Minky couldn't do it at all.

"Pooka blood," Morrigan had said dryly. "Never mind, little one. This magic is not for you."

But Will...Will's doors had been perfect and precise. He could control the size and shape and pinpoint it exactly, opening doors to their kitchen, Nate's bedroom and even one in the shower without damaging so much as a single tile.

They still had a lot to learn, though, and a huge way to go before it was easy for them. Too much magic in one day obviously wasn't good for the human body.

"Mink?" Brandon whispered.

"Yeah?"

"I'm sorry."

She sat up carefully, pillow clutched to her chest. "For what?"

"For...everything. For this whole mess. For being such a jerk sometimes. Especially to you. For dissing your ideas and stuff."

His voice was choked and stuffy, and, damn it, Bran didn't cry. This wasn't right. She sighed and tried to think of nice things to say, but she wasn't Nate, and what came out instead was, "You are a big jerk sometimes. And a complete dork about some things."

Brandon nodded on a huge, shuddering breath.

"But you're our Bran. We need you. Nothing would be the same without you," she went on, her stomach shaking from speaking so directly. "Yeah, you screwed up. You get over it and fix it, right? And we're here to help you. See, you might be a big jerk sometimes, but you're *our* big jerk."

He wiped a sleeve over his eyes and managed a dry laugh. "Thanks, I think."

Good. That's better, and now Will's waking up to distract him. This, by the sound of it, really wasn't something to celebrate. Will rolled over with a pitiful moan, then scrambled out of his blankets to grab the bucket in the corner and heaved his guts up.

It did pull Brandon out of his own misery, though, as he crawled over to comfort a now sobbing Will.

And we're supposed to go with the assault team tonight? Yeah. This'll work. Minky's gloomy thoughts scattered when Eithne came into the room, a rush basket balanced against her hip.

"Ah, poor kits. You pushed yourselves too hard." Her tail stroked Brandon's shoulder as she went by to put the basket down next to Jasper's bed. She stopped to lean over him first. "How do you fare, little blood stalker?"

"Hey, Doc." Jasper looked up at her with a smile so sweet Minky could understand why Nate had such a hard crush. "Not so bad. Tons better."

"Good. Your companions seem to be in dire need, though." She turned to Brandon, arms held out. "Let me have him, please."

Reluctantly, Brandon relinquished his hold on Will, letting the princess gather him close to her furred bosom. She rocked him, purring, stroking his hair, and soon Will's breaths evened out, his taut hold on her arms relaxed.

"There now. Better?"

Will sat up with a nod. "Can you help Bran, too, please?"

Princess Eithne took Brandon's face between her hands and kissed his eyelids. He closed his eyes on a long sigh, and the lines of pain around his eyes eased. She simply brushed noses with Minky and the pain and nausea drained away through the floor. Then she woke Nate and Kara and repeated the process with them.

Oh, yeah. The whole healing thing. We definitely need to look into that when this is over.

"Now, Jasper. Sergeant Morrison would like to speak with you."

"Um...okay?" Jasper tugged at his wrist cuff to pull himself into a sitting position.

Eithne gestured toward the wall and the silver cuffs unlocked, falling to the floor with musical clinks. "In the kitchen." She held a warning hand up when Nate got up, apparently to go with him. "Just you, little stalker."

"Well, I hope he doesn't want vamp for breakfast." Jasper's smile couldn't hide the shake in his voice. "Nathan? Kiss for luck, maybe?"

Nate tilted Jasper's head up with two fingers and locked lips in a way that implied a lot more than well wishing.

"Eww." Minky turned away with a shudder.

Jasper glared at her. "Someone have a problem with me?"

"No." Nate gave him one last peck and turned him to the door. "With kissing."

"Y'all are a weird bunch," Jasper declared, shaking his head as he left them.

When the door closed, Eithne set about opening the basket she'd brought and distributing breakfast. They ate fruit and bagels with chive-infused cream cheese in silence for a few moments.

Brandon finally spoke up. "Did we just get called weird by a freaking southern-fried *vampire*?"

Kara mumbled around a mouthful of grapes, "Pretty much. Yeah."

* * * *

"So they got it?" Zack watched the cream swirl patterns in his coffee as he stirred slowly.

"Some more than others." Morrigan sniffed disdainfully at the coffee and grabbed a bottle of water from the fridge. "But, yes. The pretty blond made a more than passable door."

"Guess I'm not really surprised."

"No?"

Zack shook his head. "Will reminds of Diego. The real Diego. Yeah, he's more emotional, less steady. But the same, I dunno, kind of aura?"

"Their connection to the world's magic is much the same. The young one will never be as powerful as Diego, thank the gods. But they mirror each other in how they use it." Morrigan clicked her long, black claws on the countertop, an unreadable glint in her eyes. "The pooka's child is…interesting."

"Leave her alone, Morri," Zack growled. "She's not Finn."

"And thank the gods for that, as well."

Zack was about to answer when a cold, sharp scent slapped him hard. The hairs on the back of his neck bristled as he whirled with a snarl to face the dangerous predator who dared to invade his territory.

The shock on Jasper's face somehow spoiled the whole predator thing, and sure as heck negated the dangerous part. "Sergeant?" He swallowed hard and backed up a step. "You wanted to…see me?"

"Yeah. Yeah, sorry, kid." Zack blew out a hard breath. "Just, you know, say something next time. Warn a guy. Vampire scent, territorial instincts, all that stuff, right?"

Morrigan drifted out and gave Jasper an unsubtle shove back into the kitchen.

"Sorry, Sarge." Jasper ducked his head and managed a rueful smile. "Werewolf scent isn't real comfy for me, either."

"Still getting used to the whole thing myself." Zack motioned to him, then held his hands out, palm up. "C'mere. Hands on top of mine."

Jasper complied, obviously puzzled.

"Push down. Hard as you can. Attaboy. No pain? No twinges? Good job. Arms over your head. Okay, down and twist from the waist. Perfect. Nothing?"

"Nope. Right as rain." Jasper smiled up at him, too damned sincere for words.

His instincts yelled at him that Nate was right. Jasper was a gentle, honest soul. Zack leaned back against the counter, arms crossed over his chest. "Okay, here's the deal. Our man Nate says you want to help. Great. Perfect. But first I need to know what you think we're doing here?"

"Um, stopping the bad guys?"

"Maybe a couple. But, no, we can't think of it that way. This is a rescue mission."

Jasper nodded enthusiastically. "To rescue your boyfr—Prince Lugh."

"Hell, yeah. But also to rescue Diego Sandoval and everyone with him. You need to understand that, or you stay the hell here."

"Yes, sir." The boy chewed a thumbnail. "I get it. I mean, Nate told me what happened to Mr. S. Damn shame, if you ask me. And Theo…"

"Yes? Theo?"

"Theo thinks he's Batman or some junk. But he's...he's...not *bad*."

"Exactly. You got it. Rescue and retrieval. That's what we're aiming for." Zack pointed a finger at Jasper's chest. "I'm counting on *you* to get us where we need to go once we're in and to give me some intel. And to stay out of the way if things get nasty. Still in?"

Jasper's blue eyes were wide enough to serve as fae bathing pools but he said softly, "You bet I am."

The vamp from Houston proceeded to tell him there were twelve people left at the asylum, thirteen if one counted Lugh, that the kids all had sleeping space set up in the old common room except for Theo and Lila, who needed to get away from other people sometimes. Diego had one of the old doctor's consultation offices up on the third floor as his room and headquarters. Jasper drew a crude map as he explained, apologizing for his lack of drafting ability. He'd been a waiter in his former life, studying to be a pastry chef, not a civil engineer.

"Any odd magical abilities we haven't seen yet?"

"Guess y'all have seen Magnus, huh?"

"Yeah. Him. And telekinetic girl."

"Tele — pardon?"

"Moves stuff with her mind. Big stuff."

"Oh, Emily."

Zack cringed. Bad enough his adversaries were so young, but now he had names for a good portion of them. *Rescue and retrieval, Morrison, just like you told the kid.* "Right. Besides those two."

Jasper lifted one shoulder in a half-shrug. "Mostly, it's stuff like that. Moving things. Breaking things.

Though Callie can only move water and Auden talks to plants."

"Talks. To plants." Zack's voice came out flat and dry in his confusion.

"Guess I should say they listen to him. Lots of folks *talk* to plants. But Auden gets them to do stuff."

"Huh. Definitely a new one." *Not one of the ones we have to worry about, though, since we'll be indoors.* Zack planted his fists on the table and pushed himself up. "Thanks, Jasper. Let me process all this while you go get some rest, and I do mean rest. Don't even think about tiring Nate out, either, hear me?"

"Yes, sir." Jasper ducked his head, pale skin gaining just a hint of pink.

"Like him, huh?"

Peeking up from under his fall of red hair, Jasper spoke softly, his tone hinting at too much experience mixed painfully with optimism. "Yeah. I...I know some of it's a rescuer thing. I'm not stupid. He stopped to dig me out of the rubble with his own hands, carried me out in his arms. Stayed by me to make sure I wasn't scared. So, sure. He's my hero." His head came up a fraction more. "But I like him 'cause he's Nate, too."

"Not judging, kiddo. Just be nice to each other, okay?"

The sweet smile came back full wattage. "Yes, sir."

When Jasper had wandered out, Zack sipped his coffee, staring out of the window at the garden's central fountain. *Nice kid. Too damn nice for all this. All those kids downstairs are.*

Most likely, some of Diego's other minions were good kids, too. What the hell were they going to do about all of them once it was over?

* * * *

"So and so." Finn bounced on the balls of his feet, a barely contained, tightly wrapped bundle of anxious energy. "Is Balor coming? Do we wait until full dark? Should we all be armed? How will they know where to make the door? They've never been there, how will they know?"

"Deep breaths, bud." Zack gave him a quick, one-armed squeeze and steered him out into the garden where everyone had begun to gather. "I can't answer a damn thing if you keep spouting a hundred questions. No, Balor stays here to help Danu shield the island. The last thing we want is to allow Diego easy access across the Veil right now. No, I don't think we need the dark. No, don't you even think about talking Marcus into lending you a gun. Hell, no. And last—I have an idea about that."

"Zack..."

"Yeah?"

"I think I'm about to be very sick."

He gave Finn a gentle shove toward thick evergreen shrubs. "Then go puke your heart out, hon. You'll feel better after."

The young coven huddled near the fountain, talking in low, urgent tones. Kara's frown threatened thunder and lightning. Will looked positively miserable.

"What's all this?"

Will opened his mouth to answer, then shook his head on a hard swallow. Brandon tucked him under one large arm and spoke for him. "Sorry, Sarge. Will's all upset."

"I can see that."

"We thought we could find a picture of Heersford if we looked hard enough. Something to focus on to get the door to open in the right spot. We were so sure we could find it since we knew the county and the location. Figured there had to be a shot somewhere online, some photographer who thought it was a cool pic."

"Nothing, huh?"

"Not one freaking thing." A muscle in Brandon's jaw twitched. "We can't do this, Sarge. Will can't do it. Not if he doesn't know where the hell we're aiming for."

"I think it'll be okay."

"How?" Will forced out in a tortured whisper.

"Look at me, kiddo. You, too, Minky. Do you think you can include me in your circle? Use what's happening in my mind to guide you?"

Minky blinked up at him, dark eyes owl-round, a habit he'd realized meant she was processing hard. "I think...maybe. But you've never been there either."

Zack shot her a grin. "No, I haven't. But I've got a man on the inside and a direct connection."

Nate grabbed his arm. "You talked to the prince? You *can* talk to him, mind to mind?"

"I can. It's something we had on a spotty, on and off basis before, but after my little life-changing encounter, it's been getting steadier and more reliable. He couldn't reach me before last night because of a steel collar. Apparently, Theo thought he wasn't looking so good and took it off."

"Not realizing the prince would call home," Kara said on a sharp laugh.

"How did he sound?" Nate asked, his brow furrowed.

"Honestly? Tired. Exhausted and sick. But still himself." Zack reeled his emotions back in fast. This wasn't the time to dwell on how bad off Lugh might be. "Will, if I contact him and you all are connected to me, do you think we can get there then? Lugh and I have done it, me guiding him to where I am."

"I...don't know. None of us have ever connected mind to mind before."

"Willing to try? 'Cause I have this weird intuition that if any of you can do it, Minky can."

"Me?"

"Pooka blood. All the fae keep saying it. It's one of the things Finn's best at, long-distance comm links."

Brandon shrugged. "Great. I mean, what the hell have we got to lose?"

That diminutive, pixie-like face turned up to scowl at her large friend. "Bran..."

"Not being a jerk." He held up both hands defensively. "Honest. They all say you're different, so it could work, right?"

Minky looked away first, still blinking. "I guess we should try it then, huh?"

"It's not so difficult," Finn whispered in her ear, certainly for her ears only but Zack couldn't help overhearing.

Finn put a hand on her shoulder. It shouldn't have been possible, but her eyes grew even wider. He turned her to face him and he winked at her when she giggled. "There, you see? Only slightly harder than swimming downstream."

"You heard him?" Zack asked. "In your head?"

She shot Finn a shy smile. "Yeah. I did."

"And what was so funny?"

Finn pursed his lips, positively prim. "That, my dear sergeant, is between my granddaughter and me."

"Pardon me, your pookaness. So you think it'll work?"

"I will guide Minky. She will bespeak William. Have a bit of faith in me."

Zack patted his shoulder, glad that Finn's nerves were settling down to business. "Ever since you rose from the dead, I've had nothing but faith in you."

"You were dead?" Minky asked in a hushed voice.

"Declared dead." Finn shrugged. "One of the many reasons I mistrust human doctors."

The back door to the embassy opened and Faolchú wandered out with his arm slung around Nathair's shoulders, looking altogether too pleased with himself. The breeze carried a definite hint of sex to Zack's oversensitive nose. *Guess everyone has their own way of dealing with nerves.*

With the troops beginning to gather, Zack went to Faolchú to consult while the coven decided on the best placement of all the principles needed for door construction. Jasper wandered out in dark glasses and a wide-brimmed hat someone must have found for him. Morrigan was suddenly just...there. Kevin and Marcus came around the side of the embassy, probably just off the ferry ride from their apartment on the mainland.

His suggestion that he take another pair of security staff since Kevin had been roughed up more than once during this little disaster had been met with grim stares.

'Don't you even think of cutting us out of this now, Morrison,' Kevin had growled. 'Or so help me, I'll kick your ass so hard, you'll need a GPS to find it again.'

He really should have known better.

With Angus and Sionnach's arrival, along with the rest of Faolchú's mix of Fomorian and *sidhe* warriors, it was time to get down to brass tacks.

Zack planted himself in front of the fountain, arms crossed over his chest, and pulled out his best sergeant voice. "All right, people, listen up!"

Gratified that all chatter died immediately, he let everyone gather closer before he went on. "We're going into a hot zone here, and one built like a rabbit warren, so not the easiest site to secure. Our point of entry is most likely on a lower level, possibly even a basement, so I anticipate our moment of greatest hazard will be when we're bottlenecked on the stairs. You all know your assignments and your squads. Stay the hell with your battle group and remember what our goal is at all times. Subdue and secure. Watch each other's backs and protect yourselves, but remember these are human youngsters. They can't fade into the Dreaming to heal and most of them aren't Vamps or Weres. They're fragile."

He stopped for a breath, letting them absorb his words. "That said, remember we've assembled an amazing pool of talent here. Some of the fiercest fae warriors from both courts, magic users with thousands of years of experience, humans warriors with expertise in non-magical weapons and tactics, and human magic users, hell, a human *coven*, which I'm told is a unique and powerful force. We're doing this to prevent tragedy, to head off disaster and to stop the world's sudden need to trample the rights of magic users. We can't screw this up. Too much is riding on it. Everyone still with me?"

A deafening roar of assent washed over him, human and *sidhe* voices mixed with the howls and shrieks of

Fomorian warriors. His werewolf hearing picked up the whisper when Faolchú leaned over to Finn to say, "Now that, Fionnachd, is how you bolster the troops before battle."

Finn's mournful response would have been funny at any other time. "I don't feel particularly bolstered. Not a whit."

"Are we ready, Sarge?" Nate asked, with a hand on Zack's sleeve. The kid was definitely a toucher. Probably tugged on adult sleeves to snag their attention when he was little.

"Yep. Where do you want me?"

"That'd be a loaded question for some people." Nate ducked the swat Kara aimed at him. "Right in the middle. Minky'll hold on to you."

"Where's Finn go?"

"Behind Minky, hands on her shoulders," Finn supplied. Then he wrinkled his nose. "But the vampire needs to move away." He pressed the back of his hand against his nose. "His scent..."

Jasper turned to Nate. "But I —"

"He's not saying you stink, Jazz. I think your scent is gonna make him sneeze. And that would be epically bad. Uncontrolled shifts that look like someone screwed with the film editing or something."

"Oh." Jasper dutifully scrambled out of the way.

"We'd tell Nate to back up, too, Jazz, but at least he finally showered," Kara called after him and Jasper snickered.

Jazz? We already have a nickname for our vamp foundling? Zack shook himself, trying to silence all the stray thoughts. He had to concentrate now, in a way that wasn't normal for him. The coven joined hands around him, though they left the physical circle open between Will and Kara, since Will would have to open the door.

Nate closed his eyes and started to pull magic to him. All the short hairs on Zack's body stood on end, his nerves quivering from being so close to an actual working. He followed Nate's example and shut his eyes, thinking hard of Lugh, reaching for him, throwing all his love and anxiety into his call.

"Lugh? Can you hear me?"

Nothing. Not even an impression of Lugh's mind.

"Lugh? C'mon, babe, you promised you'd answer me."

Still nothing.

Zack's anxiety boiled over. He'd always thought of mental screams as so much bull crap, but now he did just that, practically howling with desperation, *"Lugh! Damn it, this is no time to give up on me! Lugh, answer me!"*

A soft touch caressed his mind. At first, he thought his own need had manufactured it, but finally, the whispered answer came. *"Zachary? Love?"*

"I'm here. I hear you. You all right?"

"Tired. So...bloody tired..."

"Stay with me, babe. Just a couple minutes, okay? We're coming to you now, but we need you to be the guide. You gotta concentrate on where you are. Hard as you can for me."

"I don't..."

Zack's eyes stung. Lugh sounded so defeated and weary. He'd obviously overestimated how long it would take him to start failing again. *"You're giving me excuses now? Big, tough sidhe warrior?"*

He felt the equivalent of a mental sigh. *"I will do my best. For you, my brave sergeant."*

An image developed in his mind, one viewed at an odd angle until he realized Lugh was lying on the floor. Cinderblock walls surrounded him. A sturdy door with the hinges on the outside lay directly in front, maybe ten or twelve feet, difficult to tell in the gloom.

"Finn, you got it?" Zack choked out.

"I have it," Finn murmured. "We have it." He bent his head to whisper to his granddaughter, "Now you send it on. Put it in a packet and hand it to William."

An odd sound came from Minky, half-whimper, half-growl, followed closely by a hard, shocked exhale from William.

"I have it," he whispered. "Oh, my, God. It's so clear."

"Don't lose it, Will," Kara snapped. "Do it now. While you've got it."

"It's so different from what we've done before," Will said, his eyes unfocused and wandering. "I don't know if I can."

Without losing his connection with Nate, Brandon leaned in to kiss his cheek, his deep voice soft and tender, "Take what you need from us. Everything you need. I believe in you, love. You can do this."

Will pulled in a shuddering breath and lifted his free hand, palm up. He stared at it with such intensity, Zack wondered if he was trying to start a fire with his eyes. Suddenly, he felt it, a dizzying shift in air pressure, a coalescing of magic so powerful, it could have ripped an M1 Abrams apart. A tiny, crackling band of lightning hovered over Will's palm. He whispered over his miniature storm, bounced it in his palm until it gained height then blew a hard breath at it, cheeks puffed out, face crimson.

That's sure as hell not how Diego does it. Zack's eyes stayed glued to the lightning torus as it appeared to *burrow* its way through reality. A tiny hole appeared in the air, a darker space amidst the bright afternoon sunlight. As Will continued to whisper, the hole grew to fist sized, then to the size of a watermelon. As it expanded, it revealed a dark room with a blanket-covered body stretched out on the floor.

Sweat ran down Will's face in little runnels, but he kept the door expanding, kept it steady. As soon as it was passable, Zack motioned to the nearest warrior, the one with the otter head. "Go, go! Everyone move! Step through and get clear of the doorway!"

One by one, the assault team stepped over the threshold, with an amazing lack of jostling for position. Finally, they were all through except for the group around the coven.

"Finn, go."

"I should—"

"Move your ass, Shannon, or I'll toss you through."

Finn raised a dark brow at him, but he moved.

Zack hesitated. "How do we get you guys through when you're holding the door?"

"We've got this, Sarge," Minky told him, though her eyes were on Will. "Go on. Right behind you."

Zack stepped through the hole in reality and watched in astonishment as the kids seemed to fold their magic closer to their bodies and threaded themselves through the door in what was obviously some prearranged order of precedence. Kara went first, anchoring their circle in the new location, with Nathan hard on her heels. Minky eased past Will more slowly, bringing the knotted middle of their magic web with her. Brandon put one foot through right after her, wrapped his arms around Will's waist and yanked them both through before the door snapped shut.

Zack fought the growl in his voice as he glared at Brandon sprawled on the floor with Will held tight to his chest. "Did you know that would work?"

"We, ah, had it figured out beforehand, Sarge."

"You guessed." Zack shook his head as he turned toward the most important point in the room, the blanket-wrapped bundle. "You kids are certifiable."

Kneeling on the concrete floor, Nathair peeled the blanket back to reveal Lugh's head and shoulders. He shivered violently, his eyes squeezed shut. Even in the dim light, Zack could make out his unhealthy gray pallor. He hurried the last few feet and flung himself to his knees beside his prince.

"Babe…oh, damn," he whispered as he reached over with shaking hands to undo the collar from Lugh's throat. He pulled the blanket off further, a growl rumbling in his chest at the sight of Lugh's raw, abraded wrists. "Somebody get those damn cuffs off. I don't care what you have to do."

"I got it, Sarge," Nate's soft voice shook, his expression grim as he joined them. He pulled out a penlight to make his way over to them, and put his free hand on the cuffs, humming to them. A warm golden glow of magic washed over the steel and the locks clicked open.

"Lugh?" Zack gathered him close, stroking his tangled, matted hair. "You need to go. Can you do it now?"

For a moment, Lugh simply shivered in his arms and Zack worried he might be too far gone. Then he nuzzled at Zack's chest, whispering, "You've only just arrived."

"I know. I'm sorry. But you're not looking so good."

"I've missed you."

Zack kissed his forehead. "Forgot already how mad I am at you? Don't be so damn stubborn."

Lugh managed a disturbingly weak squeeze of his arm before he nodded and heaved a shuddering sigh. Slowly, as if he were an afterimage disappearing from an old television, he faded from sight.

"Oh, my God." Jasper's stricken whisper cut through the silence. "Were we too late?"

"No, kiddo." Zack wiped impatiently at his eyes and tried not to think about how achingly empty his arms felt. "He's gone into the Dreaming to heal. He's safe now." *Thank God... Oh, thank God, he's safe.*

At least now he might be able to concentrate on what had to be done. He rolled his shoulders as he got back to his feet. "Will, you all right? Everyone set?"

"I'm fine, Sergeant. Should Nate get the door?"

"Nah. I got it. Don't think we need to be subtle." If Diego hadn't felt the magic door opening, he was either asleep or seriously distracted. Somehow, Zack found it hard to believe that they were unexpected, anyway. He gripped the knob in his right hand and one of the metal bars on the little viewing window in his left and heaved. The door squealed and the lock gave up the fight with a sad clunk. Super-werewolf strength was great up to a point, but time and neglect had made forcing the door easy.

"Faolchú, bud, you're on point. Let's get up those damn stairs as fast as we can. Nathair, now would be the time for a little stealth shielding."

If there had been any other way up, he would have split his battle group into squads immediately. But it was the single set of stairs or an old elevator shaft and he didn't trust anyone's lives to *that* in a crumbling building. Nathair's soft, green magic surrounded them as they moved forward. The individuals nearest Zack — Jasper, Kevin, Will — all looked normal, but anyone further up or back in the column became fuzzy around the edges, hard to pick out, their footsteps muffled. He hoped the effect was even more profound outside Nathair's shielding.

They headed left and down the dark hallway. Only a single, low-wattage bulb shone at the turn by the stairs, forcing the normal-sighted humans in their group to hold on to a magically afflicted human or non-human. Kevin kept his hand on Zack's shoulder. Farther back in the column, Marcus had Finn's sleeve. Not surprisingly, Jasper took Nate's hand. Zack wondered, for the forty-seventh time since they'd rescued the little vamp, if he should be discouraging their little liaison.

For such a huge fae, Faolchú moved with incredible grace, placing his padded feet so his claws didn't click on the concrete floor. When he reached the foot of the stairs, he went ahead of Nathair a few paces and tipped his head sideways, lupine ears swiveling. After moment, he waved them on, every member of their party endeavoring to be as silent as possible. Will seemed to be holding his breath.

Halfway down the column as they snaked up the stairs from the basement level, Zack motioned his team back when the vanguard came to a sudden halt. He lifted his head, instinctively testing the air.

"Someone's up there," he whispered in Kevin's ear. "See if you can't get up front for a clear shot."

Kevin nodded, easing his tranq pistol from its holster. He turned to squeeze past, placing his feet carefully on the stair treads.

"Who's down there?" a girl called out, presumably from the top of the stairs, her voice tremulous and angry. "Damn it, Theo! I'm not in the mood for ambush training. You're gonna be sorry if it's you."

Kevin ducked, swearing softly as a chair smashed into the wall where his head had been. He leaped up the next flight of stairs as Zack motioned everyone down. Just in time, since an old wooden desk flew by overhead half a second later.

"Shit! Who the hell are you?"

A sharp pop followed the girl's cry of dismay, then a thud. Zack leaped over those still ducked down in front of him, tamping down hard on the growl gathering in his chest. When he reached the top of the stairs, Kevin was down on one knee, securing the girl's wrists behind her with one of the plastic zip ties they all carried.

"That's one, Sarge," he whispered with a wry grin as he reached into his pack for one of the lead-lined aprons they'd bought from a dental supply company for this raid. Not much interfered with human magic, but lead sure as hell did.

"She okay?" At Kevin's nod, Zack waved everyone else up the stairs. "Jasper, which one is this?"

"That's Em." Jasper chewed on his bottom lip. "Emily."

All right. Good. Girl who throws empanada carts is out of commission.

"Stay sharp. Still ten left," Zack whispered. He pointed Faolchú toward the west wing where Jasper said the kids had set up their sleeping quarters and Angus toward the east, where Theo and Lila's private rooms would be. Bright afternoon sun still streamed through the quarter-sphere of the huge atrium dome in the lobby, so there was a chance that Theo might be sleeping.

Zack had chosen the most dangerous path for himself, up the grand staircase to the third floor to go after Diego. Finn, Marcus, the coven and Jasper went with him, all representing strengths of different sorts, with their ultimate goal to get Brandon where he needed to be to reverse his original spell.

Silence accompanied their soft, hurried footsteps up the stairs, the eerie calm broken only by the intermittent clicks and creaks of an old building complaining that its bones hurt. When they reached the second-floor landing, a whispering rustle pulled Zack's gaze up, just in time to spot the figure in black at the top of the stairs. *Theo.*

Both hands on the railing, Theo vaulted the banister, his black duster billowing behind him like the wings of a fallen angel. He landed in an effortless crouch on the landing, blocking their way up.

"You've come for him," he said, his melodic voice so soft and reasonable he could have been offering greetings or condolences. "I won't let you hurt him."

"We don't want to hurt him," Zack countered, hands held wide.

"So you come in force. Armed." Theo nodded at Jasper. "With turncoats."

Jasper stepped forward, though Nate tried to hold him back. "It's not like that, Theo. Y'all abandoned me."

Faced away from the atrium, Theo's face remained shadowed, his intentions hidden. "I came back for you. You were gone."

Zack tried to signal with a look for Jasper to stay back. "Theo, you know who we are. His husband, his friends. He's not well. Please, let—"

A snarling human missile slammed into his side. Hurled to the floor, winded, Zack fought desperately to keep snapping teeth from his throat. *Déjà vu all over again...*

The werewolf girl, Lila, had him pinned at an awkward angle, half on his side with his left arm trapped. His ribs hurt like hell where he'd connected with the floor, but he twisted hard to flip onto his back. She hurled punches at his head, though he blocked most of her wild blows with his forearm. The eyes...her eyes were the worst, yellow and half-mad, as if she were already sinking into the first stages of her change, though the moon wouldn't be full for over a week.

The hairs on the back of his neck prickled. Rumbling growls he couldn't control vibrated in his chest. With a roar, he surged up and seized her wrists, flipping them both to trap her underneath. She still struggled, snarling and bucking, and he had the terrible urge to sink his teeth into her throat. *My pack...* his blood sang, *you won't hurt my pack...*

Dear, God, what the hell is wrong with me?

Sudden movement tugged at the corner of his vision. Something wriggled at the bend in the hall where the main corridor met the west wing. The mass of *something* appeared to hesitate, then surged forward in a rush of green, resolving into curling vines reaching for him with strange, alien intent. *Conservatory...that's where Jasper said the conservatory was. Shit. Auden and his damn plant whispering.*

A bright blur streaked between him and the oncoming vegetative assault as Jasper hurled himself at the vines.

"Damn it, Auden! Knock it off!" he shouted, presumably at Auden, out of sight around the corner. The vines curled around his ankles, yanking Jasper off his feet and pulling him down the hall.

A distant part of Zack's brain realized he had completely lost control of the situation. Minky was no longer visible—no shock there—but Brandon was missing as well. Just as that realization hit, Finn shifted into a bear and charged the vampire vigilante on the stairs.

"Finn! No!" Zack bellowed in a voice too rough and guttural to be his own.

While the pooka was fast and dodged the first counterstrike, Theo moved at the speed of thought. Rather than retreat, he ghosted in under Finn's upraised paw and grabbed him by the throat, holding him off and squeezing the pooka-bear's windpipe.

Finn scrabbled at the arms holding him and wheezed out, "Oh, you really, really don't want to do this."

"I won't hurt you," Theo said calmly. "Just pass out for me, please, and I'll take you to him. He misses you."

Finn snuffled, his nose crinkling. "No, young sir, you misunderstand..." He pulled in a stuttering breath. "You really...don't...want to...stand there..."

Uh-oh.

The first sneeze to erupt echoed through the atrium. Theo's eyes widened as he found himself holding the long neck of a black goose. He lifted the goose higher, backing up a step as if he couldn't decide whether to take his prize right to Diego or to continue to face the rest of them. The second sneeze turned Finn into a porcupine. Theo cried out and nearly dropped him, but now the sneezes came rapid-fire. Finn shifted through hare, Pomeranian, bat, iguana, stork and python, and while Theo was clearly flummoxed and distressed, he hung on doggedly through them all.

Lila took advantage of Zack's distraction to twist out of his grip. She took one last swipe at him and ran, yellowed eyes darting back toward the strange scene on the steps. Marcus took a shot at her retreating back, but if he hit, the tranquilizer had no immediate effect. The pounding of her booted feet faded down the stairs.

Jasper, with Nate's help, managed to disentangle himself from the now-retreating vines. Will and Kara had picked up bits of broken furniture as improvised clubs, both wild-eyed and hesitating over which way to turn.

Just when Zack thought Finn might be finished with his uncontrolled changes, he gave a last, thunderous sneeze and shifted once more. With a splintering crack, dragon-Finn sprawled on the steps, taking up most of the grand staircase from third-floor to second-floor landing, his wings spread out over the balustrades on either side. Theo's right hand protruded from under the dragon's belly, evidence that he lay trapped beneath that huge body.

Finn twisted his long sinuous neck to poke his nose at that hand. "I did try to warn him," he said in a voice much too small to belong to a dragon.

"Brandon?" Zack snarled. Damn. Why couldn't he get his voice under control?

"I'm here, Sarge, don't worry," whispered Brandon's disembodied voice somewhere to his left.

"Shit. Where?"

"Mink's got me behind her...whatever it is she does. She thought it would be better."

"Ah." He couldn't say anything to that, since it was a brilliant idea to hide Brandon. A hard shiver ran through him as he got up, one arm wrapped around his ribs.

"You okay, Sarge?" Marcus asked as he covered the stairs, watching for any more surprises.

"Yeah. Mostly. Yeah." He heaved a hitching sigh and took the three steps to Finn. "Come on, bud. You gotta get up."

"But what if I've...squashed him?"

"No helping it now, I'm afraid. Let's see the damage."

Slowly, gingerly, Finn got his forelegs under him, then his hind legs, rearing up so he wouldn't drag his body over his fallen foe before he shifted back to just Finn. "I'm sorry," he whispered. "I didn't wish to harm him."

"Deep breath." Zack patted his now-naked shoulder. "Let me look first."

It didn't look good, and if Theo had been merely human, Zack would have called off the raid right then to improvise a backboard and call in a medical evac. The long, lean body lay twisted at unnatural angles. Zack was certain his back was broken and his right arm shattered. He put an ear to Theo's chest and while he didn't pick up a normal human pulse, he did hear the once-every-few-seconds thud-thump of a vampire's heartbeat.

"Jasper, stay with him. Don't let anyone move him. I think he'll be all right if he doesn't take any more damage." Zack took off his leather jacket and draped it over Theo, the only blanket he had. "Sooner we get this done, sooner he gets proper treatment."

Gaze ricocheting between him and Nate, Jasper tried to protest. "But —"

"No. Better you than, say, Marcus. Someone he knows. And while you're here, you might be able to talk your friend Auden out peacefully. Let him know what's really happening."

Realization dawned in Jasper's eyes. He nodded and settled beside Theo, his expression a mix of resolve and anxiety.

"Good. Minky…" He searched the landing but couldn't pick up a whiff of her or Brandon's scent or even a hint of magic. "Wherever the heck you are, take Nate under your shield, too, please."

"Why Nate?" Minky whispered, so close that Zack jumped.

"Damn it! Please, don't do that. Because he's where your magic starts for all of you. If you all start pulling power for something, we need a couple seconds where Diego won't know it. Hide Brandon until the last second, yeah, but hide Nate, too. Every advantage we can get."

"Why not Will?" Brandon asked softly.

"Because he finds Will interesting, I think as a possible protégé."

"I'm a distraction," Will said on a slow exhale.

"One of a couple, yeah. We can hope."

A small, disembodied hand appeared in the air near Nate and took hold of his elbow. He gave a cheeky wave as he faded from sight, joining Minky behind her wall of obfuscation.

"She's rather good at that." The corner of Finn's mouth twitched up.

"You don't have to look so damn smug."

Finn pulled his jeans back on, the one piece of clothing to have survived his shift-storm since they had fallen off the pooka-goose first thing. "I understand one is supposed to be proud of one's offspring."

"True, but how about later, okay? Let's move."

Up the stairs again and to the left, as Jasper had described, they hurried toward the corner room Diego had claimed as his. Roars and ominous crashes echoed from the floors below, a rumbling as of a small earthquake momentarily blocking the other sounds. Zack hoped to hell the rest of his team was having better luck securing the kids without damage.

The third floor only covered the center of the main building, a squat tower brooding over its domain. Here the four doctors who had run the asylum apparently had decided would be the least distracting place for offices doubling as consultation rooms.

The door was ajar, a soft glow sending fingers out into the hall. Zack had the oddest urge to knock first, but he was saved from such bizarre impulses by Diego calling out, "Come in! Please, come in! I was wondering what was taking you so long."

Cautiously, Zack pushed the door fully open. The glow emanated from Diego, who sat cross-legged on top of a worn metal desk near the far wall. Most of the office had been gutted, books and light fixtures long gone, drapes and carpet removed. All that remained was the huge desk. Diego had obviously added the mattress in the corner, and a few bits of detritus— sandwich wrappers, a towel, a razor—things that indicated a brief, temporary residence.

Bright motes of magic whirled around Diego in a white-gold sphere. Even in such dilapidated surroundings, he looked more god than man, a comparison that scared the hell out of Zack. He suspected the sphere was as much shield as it was show, and he set aside his initial plan of taking Diego down in a sudden rush.

"Hey, Mr. S. You doing all right?"

"Oh, yes, quite well. Especially now that you've come and brought my Finn and William both. Miss Kara,

Marcus, nice to see you." Diego's smile seemed truly pleased, only adding to the surreal atmosphere. "But where's Theo?"

Finn leaned against the doorway, unconsciously sexy in nothing but his black jeans, or maybe the pose was completely purposeful. "We had a small mishap. He made me sneeze into dragon."

"Is he…" Diego hesitated. "Did he survive, *mi vida*?"

"Oh, yes. Dragon-squashing doesn't seem to kill vampires. But Zack says he needs medical attention."

"That I can do." Diego's smile returned. He twirled a miniature tornado on his index finger. "Even my healing ability is stronger now."

Zack shifted to the side of the doorway to give the others room to come in. "All right, Mr. S. I think we've been through too much together for games. You had to know we were coming, if not tonight, then soon. You had to have heard us on the stairs. But you're still here and you haven't called in any troops. Like you've been waiting for us. What gives?"

"Right to the point, Sergeant." Diego's tone was almost wistful. "I've missed you almost as much as Finn, do you know that? Solid, reliable Zack, the best man to have at your back and never one to stand for bull crap."

"Thanks. But that doesn't answer the question."

Diego laced his fingers together and stretched, cracking his knuckles. The spinning golden lights jerked and crackled before settling into their previous orbits.

Zack glanced at Will and Kara out of the corner of his eye. *Are you watching, kids? It's not solid and it's dependent on his movements, his concentration.*

"Things will happen soon, Zack. I have a conference scheduled with UN officials. Two U.S. senators have agreed to draft a bill from my proposals. Congress wants to push through a vote in light of the current crisis. Governments all over the world have begun to debate the issue."

Diego glanced out of the office window where the sun had begun a painting project on the gathering evening clouds. He looked so tired, something that would normally have concerned Zack. Right then, he'd take any advantage he could get.

"We've watched the television, love," Finn said in a soothing tone. "You've been rather busy."

"Yes. Busy." Diego shook his head, as if to clear stray thoughts. "In any case, I need the people I trust with me now. I need you by my side through this. It's been difficult, I know, to understand my methods. But with you here, I can show you why all this is so important. Especially for you, Zack."

"For me."

"Yes. You're a monster now, an abomination."

"Insulting me's not really helping your case, Mr. S."

"I'm only saying what's true. You can't control the beast inside you. Someday, you'll get away from your keepers and you'll harm someone you love, perhaps even slaughter countless lesser fae before the royal families take you down. Is that how you want to be remembered? Is that how you want to live your life, in constant fear of the inevitable?"

"Not much I can do except make sure I'm caged well enough. You know that."

Diego's smile returned, charming and rakish and so not Diego. "Ah, but there you're wrong. I can control it. I can teach you to control it, to some extent, as Lila does.

She'll never be safe to let loose in the world since she doesn't *want* to inhibit the beast. The violence is too addictive for her. But I can set limits on her beast, on her madness."

"You're not making sense," Zack growled. "The only time the beast comes out is during the full moon. So long as I'm locked up then, there's no danger."

"I wish that were true, Zack, I really do. Think about it, though. In adrenaline-charged moments, in moments of extreme temper, or when faced with someone else's beast, hasn't yours struggled to break through? Haven't you acted faster than you should have, more aggressively, more...instinctively?"

"No." It was the first time since he'd known Diego that Zack had flat-out lied to him.

Diego nodded, hand raised as if to stave off future protest. "I understand. *Por supuesto*, it's a very personal thing, like asking how you're performing in bed these days. Not something I'd expect you to admit to." He leveled his right hand at Zack and the bright motes of magic circling him sped, whizzing around his sphere in frenetic, swooping trajectories. "But here's the problem. You *can't* control it. The madness will only grow worse, as it has with Lila. Soon, anyone powerful enough will be able to use you, because once you know how, the beast *can* be controlled."

Heat prickles ran up either side of Zack's spine, his only warning before pain tore through his gut. He doubled over, arm wrapped around his stomach, his free hand clutching the doorframe in a desperate attempt to keep his feet. *Shit, oh, holy shit...*

"I can drag the beast out," Diego said, his voice soft and regretful. "There will come a point where I'm not the only one, Zack."

"Stop it!" Kara yelled, fists balled tight. "You're hurting him! Knock it the hell off!"

"It's a necessary demonstration, Ms. Kara," Diego said in that same soothing tone. "Zack's stubborn but he's a smart man. He'll understand after this."

"What in God's name..." Zack gasped out, his voice dropping back to a guttural snarl again. The room spun. He dropped to his knees. "...am I supposed to learn...except...that you've...gone psycho?"

"No, my dear friend. I need you to understand how important registration and control of magical beings will become over the next few years. If you can't stay in control, if the beast can leap out when it pleases or when someone with nasty intentions wants to use it, how is anyone safe from people like you? If we don't have proper safeguards, proper tracking, proper education in place, how will the human race survive this ever-widening plague of magical disasters?"

"Some of which you engineered, love." Finn cocked his head to one side, incredibly calm and outwardly unconcerned under the circumstances. "Is your intent self-fulfilling prophecies now?"

"Giving the slow wheels of bureaucracy a push is hardly that, *mi amor*."

Zack lurched forward as a heavy wave of agony slammed into him. Spears of fire shot outward from his core. Tendons creaked, muscles spasming as they realigned. He cried out as his fingers stretched, nails pulling painfully into the beginnings of claws.

"Diego..." Finn took a step further into the room. "I came to stay with you this time. I won't be sent away again. All the politics and the human laws, you know they simply confuse me. My only concern is you, and keeping you safe. Please stop torturing Zack. We'll help him grasp whatever it is you need him to. But this seems a mite much, don't you think?"

"No, he needs to understand how dangerous his illness is. How dangerous *he* is. Who else can teach him how to control this? And if he can't learn how, then who else can offer him the control he needs?"

All the late-night talks when Diego couldn't sleep came back to Zack. All the support he'd given the anxious new consul, all the trust and all the confidences between them. *How can he do this to me? We're friends...good friends. The kind who have each other's backs. Fuck!* A magma pit of rage opened up in Zack's chest, boiling under red-zone pressure. A tower of blood-red fury would soon erupt from the top of his skull. Flesh. Gnawing hunger. He would rip the consul's throat out, drink from his partially severed neck, smash through his ribs and tear his heart from his chest. He would —

"Zachary. Beloved, listen to me."

The sudden, intruding voice spoke in his mind and in his ear. His beast paused in confusion. It stirred things, that deep, familiar bass, things the beast well understood and others that only deepened its confusion.

A large hand rested on his shoulder, warmth against his back that he had known in moments of ecstasy. "Lugh?" It hurt to rasp out the word, his voice barely human.

"I'm here." The whisper shook in his ear, echoed by the trembling in the arms that encircled him. "You were in dire need. I came. Stay with me, Zachary. Yours is the strongest heart I know, stronger than this affliction. Stronger than any compulsion laid upon you."

Zack whimpered, turning his face into that broad chest even with his teeth still bared. The rest of the room existed in a dim, distant way, but the sounds became muted behind Lugh's heartbeat, the scents faded under his heady musk.

"Who the hell let the prince out?" Diego bellowed. "Magnus!"

Heavy footsteps pounded down the hall. The boy who threw fire careened around the corner, probably from some pre-arranged hiding place in case Diego needed backup. "Shit! He supposed to be here?"

"Didn't I leave instructions to keep him safe?" Diego pointed Zack's way. It took a moment for his beast-fogged brain to understand he meant Lugh. "Take him back to his room."

The boy's eyes narrowed, anger in the set of his jaw. "Yes, sir. I mean...but not with that fucking animal wrapped around him. No way."

Both halves of Zack's brain, beast and human, didn't want the brown-haired boy coming any closer or laying a single stinking finger on Lugh. *Mine!* He wrapped an arm around Lugh and roared at the boy in the doorway.

"Shit. Lemme kill it, sir. That thing's worse than Lila."

Finn had turned to face Magnus, his eyes glittering with some fey emotion, hair whipping about in his own magic wind. "It's clobbering time, as they say." He threw a hand up and hurled a wall of air to knock the boy back to the other side of the hall.

Either the blow wasn't straight-on or the boy had his own defenses. Immediately, a fireball barreled through the doorway in answer. Finn crouched low, hand raised to deflect it. Trajectory ruined, it raked down Finn's side rather than striking him in the face and fizzled out in the center of the room, but it still left the pooka curled up over his knees, whimpering in pain.

"*Finn!*" Diego's scream held such raw fury and anguish, Zack almost expected him to turn were-beast as well. His handsome face contorted in rage, he flung a wind spell of such force it knocked holes in either side of the doorframe and flung Magnus hard into the opposite wall.

"Watch, my brave sergeant," Lugh whispered to him. "Watch and be ready. Stay with me. Remember who you are..."

Diego's distraction had slowed the rotation of his shielding and Zack wasn't the only one watching. Kara and Will nodded to each other, magic suddenly glowing around them, presumably handed to them from behind Minky's wall. They each tossed what appeared to Zack to be grappling hooks made of light. The hooks fastened onto Diego's sphere and began to pull in opposite directions, opening a rapidly widening hole.

"You are Zachary Morrison," Lugh whispered in his ear. "Not a beast, not a monster. Know that I love you. Go do what you must, my braveheart."

The words anchored his human half, allowing him to drag himself partway from the quagmire of the beast's all-consuming rage and hunger. He flexed his claws, waiting for the hole to grow big enough while Diego's attention remained on settling a cool blanket of healing over Finn.

Rabbit-sized. Dog-sized. Sheep-sized. Zack untangled himself from Lugh and gathered into a crouch, taut as a leaf spring. As soon as the hole reached a passable diameter, he pounced, leaping through that opening to seize Diego. He yanked one of Diego's arms behind his back, keeping a clawed hand around his throat.

Diego swallowed against his hand, his voice a strangled whisper as he said, "Zack, think. This didn't work out so well last time, remember?"

"Stay still." Zack yanked the arm up harder, making Diego cry out in pain. He still couldn't manage a human voice, and the rasping snarl sent shivers up his spine. "Don't tempt the beast. He's still here."

The side of the shield ripped open wide and suddenly, the two of them weren't alone inside the sphere. Brandon stood directly in front of Diego, the rainbow effect of his coven's magic surrounding him. He took Diego's head between his hands, their faces so close they might have kissed.

"You…" Diego spat out, obviously fighting to pull his magic in for some massive strike.

When Brandon spoke, his deep voice was soft and gentle, but the words seemed a hundred feet high, colored in the brilliant hues of sunset. "Take back your compassion, your kindness, your concern. Be the Santiago Sandoval your parents knew. That Finn fell in love with. That everyone trusts. Take back what I stole from you. Be whole again."

Diego jerked back as if struck. His mouth worked, but no sound emerged, his eyes searching the room in wild, twitching sweeps. Zack eased his hold and Diego lurched off the desk, stumbling three steps before he crashed to his knees with his hands clutched to his chest.

"Oh, God…" he whispered. "Someone help me…"

"My heart, my own." Finn crawled to him, reaching out a hesitant hand to brush a curl from Diego's forehead. "Are you ill?"

Diego raised his head, his eyes so full of anguish Zack wondered why the building didn't crumble around them. "Finn? I...oh, *Finn*..."

"The lightning sparks in your head, love," Finn told him gently. "Come lie down. You truly must lie down."

With careful nudges, Finn got Diego down on the mattress just before his eyes rolled back and he seized. As his limbs twitched and jerked through one of the worst seizures Zack had ever seen, every magic user in the room let go of the flows with a collective sigh.

Zack sat on his haunches, panting, staring at his hands. He wanted human hands to hold Lugh. He wanted them more than anything. The claws didn't belong. He didn't want claws. It hurt like hell, but he concentrated on those damn claws and forced them back, bit by bit, forced his hands to take back their human shape.

"You think it worked?" Nate was saying.

Finn nodded, tears streaming down his face. "Yes. He let me in again. I heard his thoughts. Heard him cry out in despair over what he had done. He is himself again. Oh, goddesses help him, but he is."

"At least we got him back," Marcus said on a hard breath. "Not sure what we're gonna do here, though. What a cluster fuck. Prince Lugh's out cold. Brandon's keeled over. Mr. S. is gonna have to be carried out. We've got a broken kid on the stairs. And Morrison doesn't look so good."

"I'm fine," Zack growled, relieved he only sounded irritated instead of bestial. "I've got the prince. Finn, you all right, bud? You think you can carry Diego?"

"For as long as he needs. I promised him once that I would."

"Good enough. Marcus, status check from the other teams. If it's possible, I want us to rendezvous on the second-floor landing so we won't have to move Theo too far. You guys need Brandon for the door?"

The conscious kids all looked at Minky, who was finally visible. "We... I think so. He's not usually out long. We'll manage somehow."

Zack hurt like hell and he wasn't sure he was entirely human yet, but he didn't much care. Time to wrap up the mission and head the hell home. With a grunt, he got Lugh up on his shoulders, the weight a welcome burden. The big lug should have stayed in the Dreaming longer, but Zack wasn't going to yell at him for that. He'd pretty well saved them all when it came right down to it.

"Sarge, Kevin says they're all accounted for. All secured."

"Casualties?"

Marcus pressed the earpiece, listening. "Yeah. One."

"Damn. Who?"

"The werewolf girl. Lila."

Zack squeezed his eyes shut. *Damn it, the girl was like me. I could've helped her. We could've...* "Where's Magnus?"

"Looks like he's run. I'll alert the team leads to watch for him."

Back down on the stairs, Jasper still sat patiently with Theo, though another young man, a skinny blond with delicate, elfin features, had joined him.

Jasper turned to him to speak, signing a few words to go with the spoken ones. "It's okay, Auden. That's the sergeant there." He tipped his head up to speak to Zack. "Auden's deaf, so you have to make sure you look at him when you talk."

Zack paused to ease Lugh down on the landing first, then turned to them. "Hey. I hear you like plants. I know a certain fae who'd probably love to talk to you."

Auden blinked at him before he nodded to Finn, coming down the stairs with Diego cradled in his arms. He voice shook when he asked, "Did you...kill him?"

"No. He'll be all right. He's had a seizure disorder for a long time. Just might be a while before he wakes up."

Auden nodded, but still seemed unconvinced.

"That's Finn with him. His husband. No one can take better care of him. And no one loves him more."

That seemed to get through. The kid didn't seem exactly relaxed after that, but he did seem more interested than terrified. The rest of the teams made their way up the steps in small groups, some of them leading unwilling captives, some leading frightened young folk by the hand. Faolchú came last, his steps slow and deliberate. He held the were-girl cradled in his arms.

Zack rose to meet him, fighting back the beast again in the presence of another large predator. "How'd it happen?"

Faolchú's ears drooped. "It wasn't something I intended. There was a pocket of resistance outside the kitchen. I made a small earthquake to scatter them. Only a small one. But instead of running away, the girl...this fierce girl...she ran toward me."

Nathair took up the narrative when Faolchú faltered. "The building is old. We are unused to thinking of such things. Some of the ceiling collapsed in the earthquake and she was caught beneath the falling debris."

"Zack, I am so sorry."

"I know, big guy. I know." Zack rubbed a hand over the back of Faolchú's neck. "Just...damn."

Angus removed a desktop from one of the offices and with the help of many hands, lifted Theo onto the improvised backboard. Will managed to revive a groggy Brandon far enough to include him in their circle, and the coven went about constructing the door back to the island.

When the door stood open, showing them the peaceful view of the garden fountain sparkling in the last rays of the setting sun, Zack took his prince up on his shoulders again.

"Let's head through, folks. Time to go home."

Chapter Twenty-One

A New Innocence

"Courage? No, see, real courage is getting up to go to a hard job every morning at oh-dark-thirty 'cause you have to take care of the kids. Fighting against something you know's wrong. Those things take courage."

"So you don't see yourself as a hero?"

"Different question. A hero's someone in the wrong place at the wrong time who had enough momentum and enough crazy to do something stupid that worked out better than it should. Courage is perseverance...persistence. Heroism is just an adrenaline-charged temporary loss of sanity."

—Zachary Morrison, interview on CBC News

"Beloved, stop, please!" Finn seized his husband by the shoulders and gave him a little shake, trying to halt the steady thud of Diego's head against the wall as he rocked in agony.

For a moment, Diego only stared at him without recognition, muscles trembling under Finn's hands. "I killed her."

Finn held his chin in a hard grip. "Did you make the roof fall, bucko?"

A hard shudder and a shake of Diego's head preceded his renewed struggles to wrench himself away. "No," he whispered. "I didn't need to. I'd already killed her. By bringing her there. By creating such chaos."

"It wasn't you! Do you hear me!" Finn tried to wrap him in a tight embrace even though Diego stiffened and fought harder to get away. "You cannot say it was you when you were not whole, only half of what you should be."

Diego abruptly stopped struggling and looked up, his eyes full of such terrible desolation that Finn whimpered. "They told us the darkness was coming. I was naïve and arrogant enough to think I could prevent it. I couldn't, Finn. I couldn't. Because I *was* the darkness."

"My love, my hero, my own…" Finn traced a gentle finger over Diego's jaw and down his throat, over the rope burn from Diego's failed attempt to hang himself the night before.

"I caused such destruction, *caro*. I *enjoyed* it while I was…like that." Diego lifted trembling fingers to touch Finn's cheek. "I hurt you. Again. I hurt you. I'm too dangerous to let live."

"No," Finn got out in a fierce whisper, dragging Diego into his arms to let him sob against his chest. "Don't say such things." *Don't leave me. By all that's holy, my light, don't leave me.*

* * * *

A shuddering cry woke Lugh. After a moment's anxious confusion, he realized it was his own.

"Hey, everything's okay." A warm hand stroking his stomach accompanied the soft words. "Home in bed. Welcome back, Rip van Winkle."

Zack lay beside him, leaning on one elbow, a tender smile on his face.

"Who is that?"

"Oh, sorry. This guy in a story who slept for a whole bunch of years, maybe fifty or something like that."

Shocked, Lugh gaped at him. "I have slept for...years?"

"Crap. I didn't mean to get you all worried." Zack pressed a kiss to his forehead. "No, babe. Didn't mean it literally. You've been asleep for three days. Your mom said to just let you sleep."

Lugh lifted an arm, his forehead wrinkling at the sight of burgundy flannel. "I seem to be wearing...pajamas."

"Yeah, we were having trouble keeping you warm. Biggest damn pair Carol could find and we still couldn't button the shirt. How're you feeling?"

"Parched. Weak as a newborn rabbit kit." He hated how badly his hand shook, but he still reached out to cup the worried face hovering over him, the most beautiful sight in both worlds. "Overjoyed to see you."

"It's good to see you, too. You don't even know." Moisture glinted in Zack's eyes, but he cleared his throat and seemed to catch himself as he took Lugh's hand in a steady grip. "Really thought...never mind. It doesn't matter now."

"My deepest regrets for causing you such worry." The hand around his felt like sunlight, like spring rain. *I have him back. Sweet Mother I don't deserve it, but I have*

347

him back. "Is everyone safe? Diego? Finn? All the human children?"

Zack turned his gaze out of the window. "Mostly. Almost all."

"Who?" Dread gathered around his heart. "Whom have we lost?"

"The werewolf girl, Lila. Faolchú brought the ceiling down. Not something he wanted to do, but she was caught in it." Zack hesitated, his eyes searching the garden. "We tried to find family. Someone to tell. To turn the body over to, at least. But she didn't have anyone. Faolchú took her across and buried her himself. He...it was by the Alainn, where he said he'd want to rest if it was him. Big guy took it hard. Sits by her grave and howls at night."

"It is hard for us, any of us, to have a hand in harming a human child."

Zack turned back to him, teeth worrying at his bottom lip. "Even an abomination?"

"Even so, though that is a word we should discourage." A fit of coughing cut him off and Zack reached over to snatch a bottle of water from the table, an arm behind his back to lift him so he could drink. When he'd finally caught his breath, he leaned gratefully against his sergeant, unable even to lift his head. "Who else?"

"Magnus is kind of a puzzle. He ran out of the asylum, we know that. Trackers followed his trail to a steep gulley. They think he fell down the side in the dark but they couldn't find him. Sionnach said he 'smelled death' down there but no one knows for sure."

"So the authorities have been notified? About the deaths?"

"Hmm. About that. We made discreet inquiries about any connections, but we know if we reported it to the police, the whole incident would have every alphabet agency from Langley to Los Angeles crawling all over this. We can't do that to those kids."

"And Diego?" That Zack had avoided the subject worried Lugh more than anything else did.

"Um, yeah. Diego. He's..." Zack cleared his throat again and shifted to wrap both arms around Lugh, letting him rest fully against his chest. "He's home and safe. He's *our* Diego again, no doubt about that."

"But there is guilt."

"There're huge freaking mounds of it. He just can't seem to dig himself out. The first day, he was just sick and listless. The seizure was really bad. But after that..." A shuddering breath ran through Zack. "It's serious clinical depression. Says he doesn't know how to live with what he did. He's...tried to kill himself twice."

"The things that were done, though, they weren't done by *him*. Surely, he understands that."

"Yes and no. He knows he was under a compulsion but he still blames himself. Even Danu's come to tell him that none of us hold him responsible, but it doesn't seem to help."

A shiver raced through Lugh and Zack hugged him close.

"Tell me he is never alone."

"Never. Not anymore. We make sure poor Finn gets a break sometimes, but there's always someone in the room with him who understands him and loves him. Maybe with enough time..." Zack's arms lifted and fell as he shrugged. "I just don't know."

"When I'm stronger, I will speak with him."

"I love you and all, but I don't know why you'd make a difference when Finn doesn't."

"Still, I will do my best. We all must, I think, and perhaps he needs someone's forgiveness."

"Hadn't thought of that. Yeah, maybe."

He had thought perhaps that they might need to shield Diego from some of the consequences of his actions, that he would need to be removed from the public eye for a time in order to combat some of the things his other self had set in motion. The thought had never occurred to him that they would need to protect Diego from himself. *How Finn must be grieving. How terrible must be the burden he carries. There must be something. When I'm not so blasted tired and can think again.*

"Are the other children here still?"

"Some of them. Our coven's still here, of course, and Jasper...did you meet Jasper?"

"I don't believe so."

"Nice little vampire we picked up in Memphis. Kinda attached himself to Nate. Anyway, Jasper stayed and his friend, Auden, too. But most of the other kids just wanted to go home."

"Theo? Is Theo well?"

"Why him specifically? 'Cause he took the steel collar off?"

"He was kind to me when he had no reason to be."

"Got it. He wasn't in the best shape when we brought him in, but he's recovering. We have him in the containment room downstairs for now. Hard to say how he'll react when he's good to go again. Doesn't say much. He asked about Diego once, but other than that and to tell us when he needs to feed, he won't talk to anyone."

A hundred and three things needed doing. Too many sticky problems needed solutions. Grains of ideas whirled in his brain in little sandstorms, refusing to settle and coalesce into anything useful. It was no time to lie abed. He tried to lift his head again and got no further than three inches from Zack's chest before it clunked back down. *Perhaps not yet.*

Zack's hand resumed its soothing stroking of his stomach, the warmth seeping down into his bones. He nuzzled the top of Lugh's head and declared, "I'm still really pissed at you, you know."

"Are you? Odd way to show it, love. Not that I will complain."

"This would be a good time to take this seriously. Just so you know."

Lugh turned his head so he could see Zack's face. He swallowed hard at what he saw there. "I do most humbly apologize for ignoring your sound advice, for running roughshod over your sensible protests, and for stealing off into the night."

"Okay. That's a good start."

"Must I beg forgiveness, then?"

Blond eyebrows rose, Zack's expression a mix of disbelief and stern censure. "You know what I need, Highness. I've hung out with you *sidhe* boys long enough to know how this works. You need to give me your oath and you better not be thinking of loopholes when you choose your words. This is never, ever happening again, hear me?"

"I... Oh." Even as he began to construct his promise, he found himself thinking of ways to circumvent it. The automatic response shamed him and in his mind, he began again. Finally, he had the oath he needed. "Zachary Morrison, my beloved, my heart, I will never again pretend to heed your advice with the thought of disregarding it. Never again will I use any spell of hindrance or compulsion on you, and in disagreement I will speak my mind in honest discourse rather than hiding my true intentions. Will this serve?"

"Yeah. Think that covers it."

"Then on the earth which sustains me, I do so swear." The stern expression softened into something tender and Lugh ventured, "Am I forgiven?"

Zack leaned over to place a lingering kiss on his parched lips. "I think you've suffered enough. I forgive you. Now, can I get you anything? You hungry?"

"Not yet. Perhaps later." He nestled his face against the crook of Zack's neck, drinking in his scent. "Lie down beside me. Stay with me. Don't go."

"Not going anywhere, babe," Zack whispered against his hair. "I'm right here."

* * * *

Early the next morning, Zack wandered down to the kitchen for coffee to clear the fuzz from his brain. He stopped in the doorway to take in the odd scene at the table.

"You can't move there. You're not jumping." Minky tapped a square on the board.

"But it's an open space. I can move into an open space," Finn protested, the offending checker still held in two long fingers.

"Right, but you have to go in straight lines when you're moving. The whole across the stick sides instead of over the pointy parts, remember?"

"Oh, bother. Yes, yes. I beg your pardon." Finn amended his illegal checkers move and glanced up. "Good morning."

"Morning, you two. Should I ask?"

Finn shrugged, leaning back so his great-granddaughter could contemplate her next move. "Eithne needed to rewrap Diego's wrists and she wished to speak to him. She rather unceremoniously tossed me out the door."

"She asked you nicely," Minky muttered as she jumped two of Finn's pieces.

"And I had nothing to do but fret, so Minky thought I should learn this blasted game."

"There's no numbers or words. You're getting it."

Zack poured himself a mug and took in one of the empty chairs. "Perfect. You don't seem to be losing too bad, bud." He watched a few more moves, oddly pleased when Finn jumped a piece legally. "You kids decide what you want to do? Just so you know, their majesties have said any magically inclined humans will be allowed Otherworld visas if they have fae sponsors. And you guys have lots of offers."

Minky blinked her dark owl eyes at him. "We do? Really?"

"Really. Finn's offered to sponsor you, of course..."

Finn ducked his head and waggled his fingers at her in acknowledgment.

"But the dragon lord spoke up for you, too. Kara and Will have about half a dozen offers each. Nate twice as many."

"Oh." Minky pushed her captured pieces into ever changing shapes, her pale skin turning scarlet. "And Bran?"

"Sionnach's offered for him. The little guy says he understands better than most how a big mouth can get you in trouble."

Minky nodded, her eyes still glued to the checkers. "It's for visas, though, right? I mean, we could visit. Go back and forth and stuff?"

"That's the idea."

She heaved a tiny sigh. "Well…good. It'd be great to stay. I mean, for me. But there's, you know, family and stuff. And the rest of them want to finish school. And Nate wants to apply to that new graduate program in Magical Studies at Berkeley…"

"We get it. It's okay. But the visas are there for when you need to come to the island. So you're not cut off from your teachers." Zack took a long gulp from his cooling coffee. "Jasper going with you?"

Minky's button nose wrinkled. "Yeah."

"Don't like him?"

"What? Oh…no. Jazz is nice and all. Just wish him and Nate would, um, keep it in private more."

Zack sputtered on a laugh and had to put his coffee down or risk spilling it. "It's new for them still. They'll calm down." He tapped a finger on his mug, his thoughts insisting on more serious territory. "Auden's decided to stay."

"Nathair seems quite fond of him," Finn offered after another triumphant jump. "They speak…without speaking."

"Yeah, it's kinda nice and kinda creepy all at the same time. He's another one we couldn't find family for, and Nathair could use help in the garden."

"And Theo?" Finn inquired softly.

"Everyone keeps asking about him. You'd think the fae wouldn't care about us abominations so much."

"Some perhaps would not." Finn cleared his throat. "But I squashed him."

"I have to give you the same answer I've given everyone else, bud. I don't know. Kid's shown he's dangerous. He's a killer, after all. I just don't know."

"Zack?" Angus stood in the doorway, shifting from foot to foot as he did when he was uncomfortable. "Their majesties wish to see you."

"Ah." Zack got up from the table and planted a kiss on top of Finn's head. "I'll come check on you later. Duty calls. Where are they, Angus?"

"In the den."

That caught him off guard. Danu and Balor in the fae realm were intimidating enough. In the den, together, they would take up the whole room. *I'm taking my coffee with me, damn it.*

Regal and reserved, Danu sat in the big armchair by the window, her green hair tumbling over the damask. Balor stood in the corner by the TV, arms crossed over his chest, as far away from her as he could get in the relatively small space. Zack's eyebrows shot up when he spotted the room's third occupant, though. Lugh reclined on the sofa, blanket tucked in around him, nibbling on a plate of sliced apples.

At least he's eating, but I think I smell an ambush.

"Zachary, sit. Please." Danu's voice was at its most soothing, which only made Zack's internal alarms scream louder.

He settled on the end of the sofa with Lugh's hooves in his lap. "Yes, ma'am. What can I do for you?"

"Much has changed since we first met, boy," Balor growled.

"Yes, sir. Can't argue that." *Not liking where this is going...*

"You are not the same." Danu picked up the thread. "Our worlds are not the same."

Liking it less and less by the second...

"We've argued and discussed until even the owls nodded off to sleep," she went on. "But we feel that you are no longer the best choice to lead Prince Lugh's security force."

"You're...firing me?" *Of course they are.* He held up a hand to halt any further explanations. "I get it, Majesties. I do. I couldn't keep your grandson safe. Failed him miserably. And I'm a werewolf now, which makes me a security risk all on my own. I understand..." His throat closed up and all the sensible things he wanted to say were trapped behind the hurt and misery. *What the hell will I do? Maybe they'll let me stay on as a medic for the security team?*

Lugh put a hand on his arm. "Beloved, you need to hear the rest."

"The rest? About how I'm an abomination who shouldn't be seeing their grandson?"

A low rumble vibrated through the floor as Balor spat out, "Damn the she-bear for putting such thoughts in your head."

"I do not recall you saying anything to un-put them, Heart of the Earth," Danu said with a bitter smile. "Zachary, be still and listen. Diego is terribly ill. We do not feel he will be able to resume his duties as our Human Consul at any point in the near future."

"Yeah, I'd say that's true."

"But we need a human to serve as our contact for the human world. Lugh serves well as Ambassador, but there are so many things Diego did and understood from a human point of view that Lugh cannot."

"I don't..." *Oh, no.*

"We wish to remove you as head of security so that you might become our acting Consul. Until such time, perhaps, that Diego might recover."

Some corner of Zack's brain registered he was doing a really good fish impersonation, but all he managed was a strangled croak. Finally, brain and mouth reconnected, "But…Majesty, I'm not educated, not like Diego. I got my LPN license through the military. Never even went to community college. I don't know a damn thing, begging your pardon, ma'am, about law or economics or…any of that!"

"We don't need a scholar right now, love." Lugh shook his arm gently. "We need a man who knows what is right, who knows when something is wrong at the core of his being, even if he lacks all the pretty words to say why."

"Your strength, your courage, Zachary Morrison," Danu said, her voice ringing clear, filling his head like cathedral bells. "You are whom we choose." Then she sighed and settled back again, her words returning to normal size. "We trust you. We love you. You are uniquely suited to this task."

"Diego didn't always know the answers." Lugh struggled free of his blanket and eased his hooves onto the floor. "When he needed help with money issues he called Miriam in New York. With law questions, he had a professor friend at one of the universities. Every consul must have advisors."

Zack rubbed at his temples with both hands. "Can I think about this?"

"Of course. If you do this, it must be willingly." Lugh leaned in to wrap him in a hard hug. "If you feel you cannot, we must look elsewhere. If only Nathan were older…"

"Stop. No emotional blackmail, please. I said I'd think about it." He rolled his head all the way around to crack his neck. "Not like Kevin couldn't take over the security command position. He's better qualified than I am."

"He would do well." Lugh put a hand on Zack's shoulder to lever himself up, swaying dangerously when he gained his feet. "Take what time you need to think things through, love. For now, I need your help with something."

Zack ducked under his arm to keep him from keeling over. "Help standing, for one. How the hell did you get down here?"

"Grandfather helped me." Lugh's voice dropped a few notes down the scale, rumbling through Zack's core and warming him through to his bones. "And now, as I have so often, I will rely on you."

"So where to?"

"Down to the containment room, please. I must speak with Theo."

There the boy was again. Like some pop star, his name on everyone's lips. "Yeah? What about?"

"That depends on him."

Halfway down the stairs, Zack was seriously considering carrying his prince. His powerful legs trembled more with each step, his breaths hissing with his efforts. But a *sidhe* prince's pride was a large and unwieldy burden, easily bruised, and this one's had been banged up an awful lot already that month. Zack simply tightened his grip around Lugh's waist and took as much of his weight as he could without actually hauling him down the stairs.

At the door of battle silver with its oversized handle and magic-reinforced locks, Lugh paused to catch his breath, leaning against the wall and pulling in huge, shuddering lungs full of air.

"Need me to run and get you some water first?"

Lugh shook his head, still gasping, and held up a hand for patience. "Perhaps...I should...have...waited."

"Yeah, well, closing the barn door when the horses have run off and all that. Slower breaths, babe. If you can't catch yourself, I'm throwing you over my shoulder and lugging you back to bed."

Lugh had the balls to grin at him. "Perhaps I would enjoy that."

"Not if I leave you there and tell you to go the hell to sleep."

"Ah." Lugh rubbed a hand over his chest, the black T-shirt not stretched as tight as it would have been a few weeks ago. "If you'll lend me an arm, Sergeant, I believe I'm ready."

Lugh called a little trickle of magic to unlock the door and let Zack push the heavy portal open. On the mattress that Jasper had so recently occupied, Theo lay under a pile of blankets. Only his ankle had been manacled, as a precaution, since he hadn't been able to move anything but his head with his back broken. His head, as it so often had been, was turned toward the wall.

"Theo? Doing all right, there?"

The head of tousled dark hair turned slowly, eyes widening a fraction. "*Su alteza?*"

"What's that?" Zack asked as he helped Lugh down to sit cross-legged beside the mattress.

"It means 'your highness'," Lugh answered softly, though all his attention was on Theo now. "How do you feel?"

Dark eyes, chill and emotionless as the vacuum of space, regarded him steadily. "I can move my arms again. Maybe even my toes. Why are you here, Prince Lugh? Have you come to pass sentence?"

"No. My place is not to judge a human boy, newly changed, who acted out of confusion and maddening hunger. Nor can I judge a young man who believed in the promises of a powerful mage who swore he would right all that was wrong with the world."

"Oh. What then?"

"I have only come to ask questions, ones to which I must have honest answers. You know you cannot lie to the *sidhe*."

"I've heard that, *alteza*. I don't lie, anyway."

"Good. What would you do if I sent you home to Los Angeles?"

Zack didn't think it was possible, but Theo's parchment skin paled even further. "I can't leave him. I swore to him, like knights used to do."

*Dear God...*the kid might have killed but there couldn't possibly have been anything more tragic in the universe than the grand, romantic naïveté of that statement.

"Let us, for the moment, keep this hypothetical, then. If he were to release you from your oaths and you returned home, what would you do?"

Theo's left hand, the one that hadn't been broken, twisted the blankets. "Go back to living on the rooftops, I guess. Watching the night."

"Playing vigilante, you mean," Zack broke in, and immediately regretted it when those cold-fire eyes turned to him. It was like looking into an abyss. There might have been something at the bottom, but he couldn't be sure what.

"Yes."

Lugh patted Zack's thigh, a small signal he took to mean he should probably shut up. "Just so. I would not have you foresworn either."

"Thank you, *alteza*."

"Diego cannot resume his work because he is so ill. Perhaps he may be for some time to come. But you do know that he works for the Collective, yes?"

A little crease formed on Theo's forehead. "Yes."

"We truly do aspire to the same things, he and I. The safety and welfare of magical creatures. Continued improvements in relations between the magical and non-magical. So to work for the Collective would still be to work for him. For his interests."

"If…if he says so, yes."

What are you doing, Lugh? Oh, holy hells…

"You must take my word that he would say so. Can you do that?"

Theo's eyes narrowed, his gaze boring into Lugh as if he could see into the deepest pockets of his heart. "Yes. I believe you are honest, *alteza*."

Lugh gave him a regal nod, all *sidhe* prince and then some. "Thank you. My Zachary will no longer be able to serve as head of my security—"

"You said I could think about it," Zack blurted out.

"I did and I do mean that." Lugh went on unperturbed, "But what lies between us has become too complex, too distracting. I cannot put you in that position any longer. Certainly, if you wish to still head the island's security, I cannot refuse you, but my own security? You are no longer objective."

"Oh. Yeah. There's that." Heat crept up his face. He should have thought of that himself, proof that he really wasn't thinking straight anymore where the prince was concerned.

"All that aside, Theo, this means there will be openings in my security team. Would this interest you?"

Theo was silent for a long moment. "Why would you even ask me?"

Lugh put his hand over the one twitching at the blankets. "In a dark moment of despair, in a moment when I was certain I would soon breathe my last, a young man came to me with soft, respectful words and gentle hands. His act of kindness is one for which I will be forever grateful."

The dark, expressionless eyes widened. "I couldn't let you die."

"Even so. You kept me safe then. Would you like to take that on as a profession? To keep me safe?"

Zack spoke up, despite his misgivings, "The pay's damn good. The hours aren't bad so long as you keep him out of the clubs and away from the catnip."

Lugh snorted but they both watched Theo, whose lips worked but apparently struggled to form words.

"I...would be honored, *alteza*."

Just like that—because Lugh was who he was, because he could use that majestic voice without any spell behind it and people still trusted him and wanted to fall at his feet—a vigilante, fledgling vampire was brought to heel and given a constructive outlet for his considerable energies.

"Good." Lugh leaned back and fished the cell phone out of his jeans pocket.

He turned it on and handed the phone to Theo, who stared at it with a puzzled frown.

"My first requirement as your new employer," Lugh said gently. "Call your mother."

Theo's mask slipped as his thumb flew over the touchpad. The hard glint of his eyes melted into confusion and pain. He suddenly looked vulnerable and oh, so damn young.

"*Mamá? Sí, es Theo.*" His voice was a spare, cracked whisper as he spoke into the phone. "No, not at the police station. I'm fine. I...got a job..."

* * * *

"Yes, Madame Flores. We deeply regret Mr. Sandoval's illness." Zack tugged at the stiff cuffs of his dress uniform jacket as he leaned forward to speak into the microphone. "But the Collective has asked me to take his place for now."

Lugh sat beside him, pride swelling his chest. This was not natural or comfortable for his Zachary, neither dealing with diplomats in an official capacity nor being the center of attention, but he faced it bravely, as he did most things.

The meeting with the UN General Assembly had been set and while Zack had asked in a small voice whether it couldn't be rescheduled, they both had known the answer.

Zack read the prepared statement about the recent magical crises in a clear, steady voice. He had such a beautiful voice, one that could be both commanding and gentle at the same time. But once he'd finished the plea for the nations of the world to recognize the need for a calm, compassionate response, he put the papers down.

"Secretary General, honored delegates, I know many of you have seen the recent footage from Washington regarding hearings on the magical crisis and the proposed Defense of Magical Beings Act. While the Collective is in large part supportive of the spirit of these proposals, the royal family has debated and discussed the particulars and has concluded that certain passages are dangerous to the magical community and to the world's human population."

Zack folded his hands on the table, the cameras focusing on his face and the sincerity pouring from those dove-gray eyes. "Registration of minorities is a dangerous business. History has too many examples where 'registration' for whatever reason has led to segregation, persecution, pogrom and even genocide. From a human rights—a sentient being rights perspective, we plead with the members of this assembly to take this warning back to your respective countries.

"Yes, we need magical education and funding for our young people. Yes, the world's nations need to decide how they will legislate magical issues. How to deal with magical assault, whether physical or in matters of compulsion. How to support and encourage the research and treatment of magical diseases. But mandatory registration will only further the stigma attached to wild human magic and its associated illnesses."

Zack took a deep breath and placed his hands flat on the table. Lugh was certain only he could see them trembling. "Prince Lugh mac Ethnenn has joined us here today so that he can share an offer the Fae Collective would like to make to the nations of the world."

With a little smile for his beloved, Lugh sat up, using his size to command attention. "Thank you, Sergeant Morrison. Ladies and gentlemen of the general assembly, while the Fae Collective cannot pretend expertise in human magic, we have a keen and vested interest in the health and welfare of human magic users. Your magic affects our magic and, for the denizens of the Otherworld, magic is life. With the current crisis, we fear that life is uncertain for us yet again.

"We feel that education and training of magic users is the only way to effectively combat spontaneous outbreaks of wild magic and the magical hysteria witnessed in the recent urban riots. The Collective has set aside funding, available to any country where we do not see human rights violations against magic users, for the founding of schools and university programs for the magically inclined. Proposals will be received at the Consulate on Tearmann Island, beginning immediately."

The Secretary General recognized one of the Eastern European delegates, who asked, "Your Highness, will the Collective consider any magical registration effort a violation of rights?"

"Yes. The language of the education fund specifically states that any country insisting upon registration of magic users will be automatically barred from receiving grant monies."

"Highness, is there a ceiling on grants?"

"Not at this time. All proposals will be dealt with on an individual needs basis. A school for elementary-age children in a small village, for instance, would require a good deal less than a new college of Magical Studies in one of the world's trade cities."

"Mr. Ambassador, do you claim this is not an attempt to influence how sovereign nations choose to deal with these unnatural aberrations?"

Zack shifted next to him, a sub-audible growl rumbling in his chest. Lugh gave his arm a reassuring pat and smiled at the speaker. "Mr. Aziz, magic is no more unnatural than gravity and we do not consider human magic users aberrations. We consider them gifted."

"And what of these…diseased ones? The ones that become monsters?"

Lugh fought the tightening of his jaw. To say such things with Zack sitting right there was bordering on an international incident. "We have encountered no monsters, sir. If you refer to certain afflictions of human *kelan* strands, the Collective would like to make clear that these are only monstrous in fable and in the minds of intolerant individuals."

The delegate sat back with a frown but refrained from saying more, ceding the floor to the delegate from Ireland.

"Will there be funding available for support and crisis centers?"

Lugh leaned closer to the microphone. "Yes, most definitely. Specifics for the recommended available services can be found in the fund's charter document."

The questions continued for some time, but Lugh answered them all with an ease he had never felt before in a human gathering. Nothing in his long life had ever been this easy before. Now, with his Zack beside him, with their hearts entwined and keeping the dark forever at bay, he could no longer imagine why such things had been so hard.

* * * *

"My heart, my own, it's time."

Diego only nodded, gaze locked on his feet as he rose, and that frightened the stuffing out of Finn.

He had exploded in a fit of rage when Danu had told him there would be a trial, in front of both courts, no less, but she had explained why this had to be. Step by step, Angus and Sionnach had told him what he needed to expect and eventually he'd seen a bit of wisdom in it. *Perhaps.*

It was all for Diego and, he hoped, another step toward recovery. At least they hadn't insisted he come in chains.

"Diego, love..." Finn twisted his hands together feeling helpless. "Should I carry you?"

Diego ran a shaking hand back through his hair. "No, I...I'll walk. Should I... Where are my shoes?"

Finn took his hand, pulling Diego close to tuck him under his arm. "We're going to the field. You don't need shoes."

"I should brush my hair."

"I did it, love. Just a few minutes ago."

"Oh."

How many times can a heart break before it shatters into too many pieces to retrieve again? Finn pulled the man he loved into an impulsive hug, wishing, oh wishing so hard for the thousandth time that Diego would come back to him, whole and strong.

There had been deluges of tears, the self-recriminations and the screaming nightmares. There had been the hopeless despair when Diego no longer wished to live. And now? Now there was this lost, hollow shell, this child-man who no longer remembered things from moment to moment, and who forgot to eat unless someone told him to.

Oh, this is cruel.

Perhaps he would simply take Diego away. Run off to Montana with him and hide. Forever. No one would find them and they could simply live a peaceful, quiet life…

Diego squirmed in his arms. "They're waiting for us."

Or perhaps not.

Down the stairs, through the doorway that Diego himself had helped build, the one permanent doorway between the human and fae worlds, and out under the brilliant blue sky of the Otherworld. Fae of all shapes and sizes packed the field, those attached to the courts and some who were not. A terrible stillness had settled over all those gathered, unnatural in races that were normally so restless and vocal.

It was not to be a trial as the humans had, not like the ones Finn had watched on television, those long, tedious tournaments of words between lawyers. This would be a trial in the *sidhe* sense of the word, accusation, declaration and sentencing.

Danu half reclined on the one great outcropping of rock that thrust up in the middle of the field, not an odd sight itself, with her court around her, but odd that Balor stood by her shoulder in silent accord. She lifted a hand and beckoned to Diego, who shook Finn off and placed himself on trembling legs in the empty spot in the grass before her.

"Santiago Sandoval y Romero, we accuse you. You have used your power to perpetrate violence without calling challenge, to create terror in the human world and to manipulate events to your own ends. You held a prince of our blood against his will, chained with cold iron, and your actions caused the death of one human child, possibly two. What say you to this?"

Finn knew it wasn't done, knew it was against all court protocols, but if he didn't speak, his heart would leap from his chest and run screaming into the wilderness. "He did nothing! He was under compulsion. You know this, Light of the World. It was not Diego but some shadow of him that did these terrible things!"

Danu's hair lifted in the magic wind she called, her voice sharp and terrible as she shouted him down. "Fionnachd, be still! You have no voice here! Sit down!"

Finn had no choice under the weight of her words. His legs crumpled and he sat hard. Diego, however, held his ground. For the first time in nearly two weeks, his head came up. His eyes shone clear and sharp.

His voice shook when he spoke, but he pitched it to carry. "*Majestad*, forgive my wounded husband. He grieves. He worries. I don't have enough apologies for the anguish I've caused him. But he's wrong. Yes, I labored under a spell of compulsion, my own native compassion removed, but the *rest* of me remained to do the terrible things I did. I didn't realize it before or maybe I refused to, but the arrogance of the Dark Mage was mine. The need to be proven right was mine. The certainty that *my* solutions were the only worthwhile solutions…was mine. Perhaps I wasn't whole when I committed these crimes, but I was still *me*. I have no defense. I am guilty."

The stillness grew heavier. Finn thought it might pound him down into the ground so far no one would ever be able to retrieve him.

Danu finally spoke again, her voice gentle and sad. "Listen then, to the shape of your punishment, our

Taliesin. You have caused harm in the human world and therefore will be banished for three years and three days. You may not have contact with any human during your banishment, nor may you speak with any member of the fae courts. Go and wander among the wild fae and perhaps you will find those things you lack to protect yourself and to protect others from you."

Diego swayed, visibly shaken. He had obviously expected something else. "Must I go alone, *majestad*?"

No! Finn screamed inside his head. *I am no court fae! They will not keep me from you, never, ever again! I will turn into a serpent and crawl after you through the grass if I must!*

"We are not so cruel to separate you from your husband again. If Fionnachd wishes, he shall journey with you."

"Thank you," Diego whispered as he dropped his head in his hands. His swaying grew alarming and he would have fallen if Finn hadn't lunged to catch him. "Finn?"

Finn held him tight. If he held him tight enough, he could squeeze all the darkness out and let the light filter back through into Diego's heart. "It will be like a vacation, a...what is that odd word? A *sabbatical*. Just you and I, beloved. We'll have a lovely time, won't we?"

Diego clung to him and wept, but it was a soft rain of tears this time rather than the howling thunderstorms that had come before. There was hope in that and Finn had always lived his life rock hopping from hope to hope. He would nurture that hope for them both, keep it safe as he would keep Diego safe, help it grow, and when it was big enough to stand on its own, hand it back to his love, and watch the light return to his eyes.

* * * *

They stood on the banks of the Alainn again, but this time everything was different. That other time felt like years ago instead of weeks, and all the beauty of the scenery had been sucked away in those weeks of frustration and fear.

"The end of innocence," Zack murmured.

"Just when a man thinks he has no more innocence to lose," Diego replied with a bemused shake of his head. "So much lost."

The canoe sat ready, tethered to the rushes at the bank. Diego's pack lay in the bottom, disconcertingly flat with the light packing. He wouldn't need much, of course, a couple of spare kilts, a toothbrush and razor, a gift for the dragons. Otherwise, the world around him would provide.

"Where will you go?" Zack hated the desolation in his voice, but he wasn't good at hiding things like that.

"Lord Hssetassk has asked us to guest with him for a bit," Diego managed on an uneven breath. "He...has things to teach me."

"That's good, right? He'll teach you to shield yourself better and stuff?"

Diego nodded, chewing on his bottom lip, going nonverbal again. For a man who had made his living with words, he seemed to have lost his power over them.

A bundle of blankets sailed over Zack's head to land unerringly in the canoe. Finn managed a tight smile and a bit of swagger despite the sorrow in his eyes. "Did you say a proper farewell to everyone, beloved?"

Again, the wordless nod, Diego staring at Finn with naked, helpless need. With a strangled sound, Finn crushed his husband close, holding Diego's head to his chest with a hand on the back of his neck. He whispered in Diego's ear, "A shoulder where Death comes to cry."

Diego whispered back, "Take this waltz, take this waltz."

They were reciting song lyrics to each other, or poetry, but it made Zack feel better despite the morbid words. This was a familiar thing, something Diego and Finn did with each other, a normal thing. A small, butterfly-sized shadow lifted from his heart. It helped.

He put a hand on Diego's shoulder and the other on Finn's. "Damn it, I'll miss you."

Diego got a hand free of Finn's long-limbed tangle and seized a handful of Zack's shirt. He yanked and wriggled around and ended up with his arms thrown around Zack's neck, shaking as if he might fly apart.

"Hey, shh. It's not forever. It'll be okay."

A muffled sob trembled against Zack's shoulder, Diego whispering, "I'm so sorry. I'm so damn sorry."

Zack turned his head to kiss Diego's temple. "Not gonna say it wasn't your fault, because I know you think it was. But you know what? I forgive you. I do. And so does Lugh."

Diego lifted his head. The pain in those dark eyes made Zack want to break down and cry. "He's not here."

"No, bud. He had to go to Washington. They're finishing up the hearings before Congress takes all the new magical law stuff into session to try to vote on it. He thinks the registration part won't pass now that his grandparents have put some cash value on *not* passing it."

"*Gracias a Dios,*" Diego murmured and rested his head back on Zack's shoulder. "I'll miss you terribly. I love you both. Even when…when all I felt inside was cold and hard, I still loved you, you and Finn and Lugh."

He took Diego's face between his hands, trying to convey the truth of what he said by sheer will. "I know that. So does he. When we were on that rooftop, you flattened me and you just held Finn still when you could've really hurt us. Even when you were forcing me through the change, you were trying to show me something. Teach me something. Even then, even though it was twisted, you were thinking of me."

Tears swam in Diego's eyes but he nodded. "So much to learn still, isn't there?" He turned his gaze downriver, where he and Finn would be headed. "Maybe it's not the end, then, but the beginning of a new innocence."

"Virgins all over again?" Zack managed what he hoped was a reassuring smile and his heart leaped when he actually got a little quirk of lips in return.

"I guess that's one way to look at it."

"Odd," Finn said as he bent to kiss Zack's cheek. "I don't believe I remember being a virgin in the first place."

That actually got a muted snicker from Diego and Zack felt that little seed of hope in his chest start to rock and shove out of its casing. He stayed on the bank while Finn helped Diego into the canoe, stayed while they paddled down the river into exile. When they turned, he raised an arm to wave, hoping he didn't look too forlorn. *I'm here. I'll be here. One faithful soldier waiting for your return.*

Epilogue

Catalyst

There are things you know about and things you don't...and in between are the doors.
—Ray Manzarak, *Newsweek*, 1967

Zack stared at the screen on Diego's desk. It was still Diego's desk, damn it, even though he'd occupied it for the last six months and still had two and a half years to go. Most of the time, it was fine. Making decisions on visa requests. Vetting proposals for the Fae Collective's Magical Education and Medical Fund. Seeing to the everyday running of the Consulate. He could do those things. It was the writing stuff that was tough for him.

He'd been trying to finish the article for *Mages Monthly* for the past three hours. Not that he had trouble with the subject matter. They'd asked for firsthand advice on lycanthropy and Zack had jumped at the chance to share what he knew. He'd talked about keeping an eye on the lunar calendar, about the importance of a safe room and getting to it in plenty of time at that time of the month. He discussed the mood shifts and how he dealt with them. There were detailed instructions on how to construct a safe room and what the beast would need to keep everyone safe.

But he couldn't just end it by saying, *And that's all I got, folks.*

An alert popped up onscreen, reminding him that he had two hours to get to his own safe room that evening. The reminder was followed immediately by an email reminder from Carol, which said the same thing in gentler tones.

"I know, boss lady, I know. I'm getting there," he grumbled at the message and flipped back to his article, typing at top speed. He'd thought of an ending.

The fae tell me that every thinking being has an animal nature. For them, it's easy to see. Many of them have a second form or aspects of their animal half as part of their bodies. Humans have tried to bury their animal natures for centuries. I think this might be why lycanthropy takes hold in the right set of circumstances and why it's so hard for us to deal with.

Something about not ending sentences in prepositions stopped him…but Zack didn't know how to fix it, so he forged on.

The were-beast, our transitional form, is us fighting against what lives inside us all the time. That fierce hunger, that terrible emptiness is part of being human and we don't want to accept it. As a Were, you're forced to accept it. You look it in the face and you acknowledge it every month. You make it part of you or you become one of those Weres who lose their sanity and their humanity.

Lycanthropy isn't evil. It's a disease process like any other, and like some diseases, there is no cure. Knowing how to live with the disease will save your life though, and make it livable again. I'm not a lycanthropy victim and I'm not a lycanthropy survivor. I'm a Were. With time, practice and the right support, I've found I can live with that.

There. That was the positive, hopeful message he wanted. If it helped even one person through the pain and the fear, he'd call it a success. He couldn't help a little chuckle. *I'm gonna be a published author. Diego would be proud.*

He sent it off and still had time to check through the emails Carol had forwarded to him. Most were day-to-day diplomatic business but one caught his eye. The 'from' line said *Silver Adepts*. He smiled and opened it.

Hi Zack —

Hope you and His Highness are doing okay. Caught the clips of you guys at the White House last week. Nate says to tell you that you rocked that tux.

Anyway, we'll be out there next week to meet with Princess Eithne and stuff and we have something we want to run by you, so Brandon said we better give you a heads up first.

Zack chuckled at that. If Brandon was getting bossy again, the kids were getting back to normal.

We had this idea. Maybe you'll think it's stupid but Bran and them think it's brilliant. Even Kara. So here goes. You know the plan's for Nate, Will and Kara to finish up grad school in a couple of years and then we'd thought about starting our own school, right? But we couldn't agree on what kind of school and things got icky.

So, I thought since we're kind of unique, maybe we should set up a special place, like a research institute. And since Nate will have his Masters in Magical Studies and Kara in Biotech, it should be about kelan studies and human magical genetics, right? Then Will said, "Where would it be?" and I know you'll think this is the crazy part, but we thought of Heersford. It's abandoned and stuff and it's a really cool building. Sure, it needs some work, but Bran and I can get started on that while those guys finish school. So think about it and tell us what you think when we come see you, okay?
  ~ Minky

"It's a freaking incredible idea, kiddo," Zack said to the screen. He made a note to call the lawyers after the full moon to see who owned the property.

The office phone rang, the double beep for an internal call, so Zack picked up.

"One hour, Sergeant," Carol said without even a hello.

"I'm on it. Is he back yet?"

"Just arrived. He's gone upstairs to change. Do I tell him you're on your way downstairs?"

"Yes, ma'am. I'm going. I'm going. Shutting down now."

"Just don't want you rushing and forgetting things."

He hung up, sent a quick reply to Minky and powered down. On his way to the stairs, he stopped in the kitchen to scarf down the sandwich Nathair had left on the table for him, a huge monstrosity of rare roast beef and cheese with the horseradish sauce he loved. A bottle of water washed it down, along with a multi-vitamin. They'd tried pain meds a couple of times, just to see if they might ease the transition, but the damn things just made him sick. Nothing sucked more than throwing up when you were in searing pain. But the vitamins helped in the aftermath, the wolf's body less depleted when he changed into lupine form.

The containment room door stood open, waiting for him, with Faolchú leaning against the wall beside the door. Just in case Lugh couldn't make it home in time, he had stand-in spotters—big, strong fae he'd trust his life to. Faolchú was one, King Balor the other.

"Is he coming?" Faolchú growled, a little snarl showing since he obviously already scented the beast.

"He's here. Carol says he's on his way down."

Faolchú let out a soft snort. "Thank the Mother for that. My bones thank you and my teeth thank you."

"Sorry," Zack mumbled as he went in and toed off his shoes. The one time Lugh hadn't made it home in time for the change, poor Faolchú had lost two teeth and had his wrist broken before the were-beast had changed to wolf. Of course, being fae, his teeth had grown back, but that didn't make Zack feel much better.

"No harm done, Zachary. Ah, I hear our bull trampling down the stairs now." Faolchú gave him a wave. "Luck to you both. I'll see you in the morning."

Lugh strode into the room then, the most beautiful sight Zack could hope for with his hair braided out of the way and nothing on but a black kilt. "Have you eaten?"

"Yeah. I didn't forget this time."

"Water?"

"That, too." Zack folded his shirt and jeans in a neat pile on top of his shoes and socks. "Door, babe. I'm starting to feel kinda flushed and woozy."

In an unhurried fashion, Lugh closed the door of heavy battle silver and set the magical locks. The calmer he was through all this, the easier it was for Zack to stay in control. He stripped out of his boxers and sat cross-legged on the mattress, slowing his breathing, willing himself to relax. No matter what he did, the beginning of the change always sucked, but they had gotten better at dealing with it since that first horrible time.

Lugh sat behind him and wrapped him in a gentle embrace. "My apologies for being so late. There are times when I sincerely wish I could simply tell human diplomats to, as the young humans say, 'shut the fuck up'."

"Ha! That'd be a milestone in fae diplomacy. One to tell the kids about." Zack grabbed onto one hard forearm and hung on tight as the first shot of pain lanced through him. "*Shit*."

"Breathe, love. Slow breaths, in…and out…"

He couldn't deny the beast, couldn't prevent it from emerging. It was part of him and part of the change. The ritual they had built over the past six months helped him stay in control, though. The beast got to come out and play, but Zack stayed behind the wheel.

"Ready?" His voice already rasped in the beast's inhuman timbre.

Lugh freed a hand and pulled off his kilt. "I am. Let it go, Zack. I have you."

He leaned back into Lugh's chest, the pain taking over in a red wave as his body creaked and snapped through changing forms. Every time, he tried to hold back the agonized howls. Every time, he failed, but having Lugh hold him tight and pet him through it helped a hell of a lot.

The claws forced their way through elongated fingers. His limbs distorted. His teeth grew sharp and long in thrust-out jaws. "Now!" he roared. "I need it now!"

Lugh flipped him onto his face, one hand on his neck holding his thrashing body down while his other, wonderfully large, warm hand cupped his balls from behind. All the beast's violent hunger immediately melted into searing sexual need. The beast was predictable and Zack was grateful for it.

He spread his arms, digging his claws into the mattress, pulling his knees up to present his ass. It wasn't subtle. It wasn't romantic. But Lugh responded to the raw, animal need as readily as he did more civilized courting. The prince lost no time getting lube on his fingers and two fingers shoved roughly inside Zack.

The moan he intended was more of a snarl as he shoved back against those invading digits. *Yes, fucking yes.* "Do it," he managed to get out through his unwieldy jaws. "Make it rough. Make it hurt."

"I won't cause you harm. I — "

"Now, damn it! Need you now!"

The mattress depressed around his knees as Lugh repositioned himself and spread Zack's newly furred thighs wide, kneading his cheeks. They went through this dance every time, Lugh still too careful, the beast still too impatient. Somehow, they got it to work.

Lugh grunted as he shoved the head of his huge cock through Zack's tight ring, far sooner than he would have in Zack's human form. Yes, it burned, it hurt, God, yes, but it was what the beast needed and it felt so damn good. Snarling, Zack shoved back, no longer capable of words, but Lugh still got it.

His hands gripped Zack's hips tight enough to bruise and Lugh thrust in hard, far enough to slam up against

Zack's overeager prostate. Two more hard nails on that same spot had him coming, clawing and howling, writhing on the thick erection impaling him.

Shudders wracked his body as each hard clench of orgasm rammed through him. He quieted for a moment, panting, until the dick up his ass made him hard again with only a few seconds pause. "More."

"Already?" Lugh sounded shocked.

"More!"

Lugh slammed back into him with such force that he flattened Zack on the mattress. He hammered at Zack until the next orgasm and the next, his stamina nothing short of miraculous.

After Zack had come six times in quick succession, Lugh's hips finally lost their steady rhythm and he bellowed out his release. Fae semen, hotter and thicker than a human's, satisfied something for the beast. The feel of it seeping out of him, running down his thighs, calmed him, filled some deep, empty place inside.

The fullness gave him enough peace, enough breathing room to force the last part of the change, much earlier than it would have happened on its own. Lugh gathered him up in his arms, holding him tight as the pain began again. Limbs shortened. Fur thickened. Ears changed shape. The tail grew from his spine.

The wolf looked up at Lugh and gave a tired lick to his cheek. He was never sure if his internal communication would work right away, but he had to try. *"Thank you. You're amazing."*

"So are you, my dear sergeant." Lugh smiled down at him, petting his fur. "That was much faster this time. Perhaps half as long as the last change."

"Practice, right? You okay, sweetheart? Did I hurt you?"

"No, love, you were a perfect gentleman. Not even a scratch."

"Good. I think we're getting the hang of this."

Lugh stood and opened the door for them. "Shall we go to the kitchen? Are you hungry again?"

"No, I'm good right now. Is it a nice night out?"

"A mite chill but the sky is cloudless and the wind relatively still."

Zack looked up at his half-*sidhe* lover, tongue lolling out in a canine grin. *"Wanna go for a run? Bull and wolf? Bet I can beat you to the end of the island and back."*

Lugh's brilliant smile lit the dim chamber. "Gentleman's wager. Winner picks something new to try in bed."

"You're on." With a flick of his tail, Zack took off down the hall and up the stairs, leaving Lugh scrambling in his wake to catch up. Sionnach happened to be in the kitchen and opened the back door for him as he barreled past. Moon shadows danced with bright pools of light in the garden, the scents of earth and wood and plants hitting him like a drug rush. Lugh clattered out of the kitchen behind him, shifting to bull as he cleared the door, and they ran, the joy of that simple motion, of his strength and speed coursing through him.

The world was bright and new, shining and stretched out beneath his pounding feet. The beginning of innocence, a new life to discover before him.

Want to see more from this author? Here's a taster for you to enjoy!

The Line
Angel Martinez

Excerpt

"Easy," Rafael whispered, stroking soothing circles on his meal's stomach. "Deep breaths."

The young man beneath him whimpered as Rafael scraped glistening fangs over his throat. With his hands bound tight to the headboard, the human had no way to fend him off and the tang of fear sent spears of delicious desire through Rafael's core.

The meal squirmed again and Rafael hissed in exasperation. "Hold still, Denny! Do you want a chunk ripped from your throat?" He thrust hard, pegging his dinner's prostate. Denny arched and yelped in delight.

"Rafael, beautiful Rafael, please take me. Take all of me. Take what you need."

Why, oh, why do they have to get so melodramatic? With a firm hand on Denny's forehead, Rafael licked his pulse line, preparing the skin. He snapped his hips with each thrust, pleased when Denny's legs wrapped around his waist. Precision was the key. Certainly, a vamp could just stab his fangs in and suck the life out of a meal, but where was the fun in that? Life was a buffet and it was so much better to be able to come back for seconds.

Pleasure building at the base of his spine and jaw, Rafael punctured through delicate skin, leaving two surgical-caliber entrance wounds. Hot blood hit his tongue as he fastened his mouth over the holes and sucked. He moaned and bucked, losing rhythm but not enthusiasm as the blood hit his system, sending wicked pleasure through his groin and head. Denny's wail as he came could have been unpleasant, but he was only aware of it in a distant, sensually drowned way.

Rafael let his body collapse atop his lovely meal, finally still and dazed, as he released the coagulant from his feeding gland. *Rule number five, always lick your plate clean and don't leave a mess behind.*

"That was transcendent," Denny whispered into his hair.

Transcendent? Really? What century is this again? "Glad you enjoyed it. You were very tasty." Rafael eased his cock out of Denny's wonderfully tight ass and reached up to undo his hands. "Stay right there and go to sleep. I'll see myself out, sweets."

"You're not staying?" The disappointment in those blue eyes could have been heartbreaking if Rafael had cared.

Rafael stopped halfway through buttoning his shirt and leaned over the bed to give Denny a soft kiss. "And when the hunters break down the door? What then? You'll fight them off for me? Poor little lamb. You couldn't fight off a pair of possessed bunny slippers. Go to sleep, Denny. I'll see you again soon."

Denny murmured something sleepy and regretful but curled up under the blankets like a good boy while Rafael finished dressing and let himself out. He breathed a sigh of relief when he closed the apartment door. That one would have to go on the maybe list of potential dinners. All those hints at possessive behavior set off his nuisance alarms. The prey relationship was less messy when they were happy-to-see-you-when-you-decided-to-show-up meals.

Sated, Rafael hummed as he trotted down the stairs. Long ago, in his human life, all the lies would have cost him sleep. No, there were no hunters in Olympia. No, he was not going to burst into flames if the sunlight hit him. Sunlight caused migraines and nasty sunburn, but neither of those things had ever proven deadly. Small details. Humans were food and he left them in puddles of melted ecstasy. Why should he feel guilty?

The city's riot of scents hit him as he stepped out onto the sidewalk. He breathed deeply, taking pleasure in how many odors he could sort and identify immediately.

"Good feeding?" The purring voice behind his left shoulder made him cringe.

He turned, barely controlling the urge to roll his eyes. "Priapus."

The pudgy vamp grinning up at him was annoying at the best of times, a territory-stealing thief at the worst. Bad enough he used the Greek god of male genitalia's name as his own, the height of pretentious bad taste, but he was an obsequious bastard, too.

"Nice tidbit in there?" Priapus nodded toward Denny's apartment building.

Rafael stabbed a finger at the other vamp's chest. "That one's mine. Hands, teeth and everything else off." Never mind that he had almost decided not to see Denny again. It was the principle of the thing. Actually, time with Denny would be much improved with a simple ball gag.

"Touchy! It was just a question. Polite small talk." Priapus leaned close, breathing in deeply. "Though he smells delicious. Lucky Raf. Don't you ever shower afterward?"

"Ew. No. Not until I'm home and in my own bathroom. If I so much as smell you in that building, our truce is off, hear me?"

Priapus held up both hands in surrender, grinning wickedly. "I'm not some macho idiot, Raf. Wouldn't stand a chance against you and I like it here." His smile slipped as he glanced down the street. "Watch your back all the same."

"Is that a threat?"

"No." Priapus looked up at him again, his gaze troubled. "Raf, something's here. In our city. I don't know what…yet. But it scares me."

Scared of his own shadow. "I'll keep an eye out."

Still, a shiver skittered through him as he watched Priapus walk away. The night and its scents suddenly crowded too close. Rafael turned on his heel and hurried home.

* * * *

The moonrise woke Rafael the next evening, acting as his alarm clock. While he had no need to feed for at least a week, he wanted to visit the new club on Fourth Avenue, gay-friendly and by all reports attracting the hottest boys.

Most humans—the barber, the owner of his favorite bookstore—would never know what he was. He could tease them about being a vamp if someone made a comment about commented on his pale skin and they would laugh, certain that he was simply anemic or that he needed more sun. He chose his dinners carefully, by scent, by attitude, by certain reactions. There were those who knew, both hunters and feeders, but the rest of the world would never believe them.

A brief hunt through his walk-in closet produced a pair of leather pants, black, and a skin-tight, sleeveless T-shirt, electric blue. With the window open to catch the night breeze, Rafael lay on the bed to shimmy and squirm until he could lace up his leathers. As he sat up to reach for his five-buckle boots, he froze. A scent drifted in, faint, tantalizing and strange. A hint of cinnamon overlay something earthier, more exotic. His heart raced. He opened his mouth to pull in as much of the scent as he could and a shudder slammed through him. Predator. Not another vamp, but something big had wandered into his territory.

Cougar? Grizzly? Neither felt right, though. He had encountered big cats when he lived in India and bears in the Smoky Mountains. Species variations would have some hint of familiarity. This scent was odd...alien.

It was probably just some new designer cologne, meant to contain pheromones or some similar nonsense. He shrugged off the feeling of dread and grabbed his leather jacket from the peg by the door, his mind already building scenarios of the upcoming evening at Clyde's. Several inches over six feet in his boots, his height and unnatural grace guaranteed both admittance and attention. As he walked down the block, he entertained lovely fantasies about grinding and gyrating in a frenzied sea of Adonises. Of all the vices from his misspent human youth — drinking, gambling, smoking opium — only dancing had survived as something he craved after the change.

Halfway down the next block, the hairs on his arms rose. The strange, threatening scent slammed into him with a shift of wind, putting every nerve in his body on high alert. A low-frequency growl vibrated in his chest, the first sign of territorial rage. *Damn it. Don't go all beast-of-the-night now. Have to keep a clear head.*

The scent pulled him on an invisible chain toward its source, dread pounding a counterpoint to his anger in his head. Whatever it was, it had no business in his hunting grounds. One of them would have to go and it was *not* going to be Rafael.

His walk became a full-out run as he raced down the street, weaving around the few frightened pedestrians in his way, unwilling to think about how crazed he probably appeared. Sounds carried to him over the pounding of his boots, an eerie snarling overshadowing a frightened wail. Not only was the invading predator in his territory, it had dared to corner prey.

He turned the corner into a dark, dead-end alley. His nocturnal eyes adapted quickly to the gloom. His quarry crouched atop a closed dumpster, something pinned to the lid. It was...

Holy hells, what is that thing?

Roughly man-shaped, it was difficult to discern details beyond long legs, since black-feathered wings spread out on either side of its body, mantling over its prey. When it raised its head to roar at him, blood glistening like dark marsh water against its pale lips, Rafael skidded to a halt, overcome with horror. Long white hair surrounded its head in a nimbus of matted snarls. Its ears came to sharp points and its eyes glowed with terrible, cold white fire. The color should have meant it was blind, but Rafael knew better. It had him in its crosshairs and those eyes turned his bones to quivering jelly.

Its victim struggled backward in a desperate bid to escape, and Rafael caught a hint of features as the terrified person turned his head.

"Priapus!"

"Raf, get away!" Priapus whispered hoarsely. "Run!"

His terror had expanded to most of his brain and he nearly did run. Every ounce of sense told him he should. Territorial imperatives surged up, though, and trampled down sense in short order. "Beast, this is my city. I did *not* give you permission to hunt here."

The thing snarled, climbing down from the dumpster lid to face him.

"Priapus…can you run?"

"I think so." Priapus dragged himself to the other side to put the dumpster between him and the monster. "Raf, you can't fight this thing. You can't."

"Worry about getting away, Pri. I'll handle this." Rafael cracked his knuckles. He was nearly a foot taller than Priapus, broader, stronger and more experienced in brawling. The stout little vamp had no chance against this thing. Rafael did.

Not that they were friends, nor did he owe the other vamp anything. Priapus lived in this city on his sufferance, but that also meant this was his territory, his fight, and they both knew it.

Rafael dropped into a crouch, weight shifted to the balls of his feet. The thing spread its wings. Maybe it had been human once. The soft, staccato snarls it made had never come from human or vampire throat, though. Hurried, limping footsteps registered in a distant way. Priapus had made his escape.

"You don't belong here," he told the monster. "I'm not sure you belong anywhere."

The thing roared and leaped at him, an impossible jump across half the length of the alleyway.

Wings. Not a fair advantage.

Rafael barely had time for the thought before the monster slammed into him. They whirled together in a horrid parody of dance. Rafael gripped the thing's wrists, preventing its claws from raking him. He set his shoulder against the wall on his right for balance and kicked out at where a rip in the jeans showed its kneecap.

Jeans? Monsters wear jeans and boots?

A satisfying crunch let him know he had connected with sufficient force, but instead of collapsing to one side or breaking off to howl in pain, the blow only enraged the monster. It yanked Rafael close, breath hot on his face, then swung them both around to slam him into the wall.

Dazed, certain something had dislocated, Rafael had a terrible moment of disorientation when his feet failed to find the ground. The monster held him a foot off the pavement, using its forearms to pin him, even though Rafael still held both its wrists. *Shouldn't be able to do that. I'm so screwed.*

It opened its mouth, baring sabre-tooth fangs smeared with blood.

"You really should brush between meals," Rafael said in as reasonable a tone as a shaking voice could manage. "Rude, you know, biting into your next snack with the remains of the last stuck between your teeth."

The thing hesitated, staring at him with its silver moon-disc eyes. It blinked and Rafael thought he caught a shift, from silver to a beautiful green. It had to be his terrified imagination since the silver was firmly in place again on his next panting breath. The monster roared and lunged forward, sinking its teeth into Rafael's throat.

He cried out in pain, sickening fear threatening to stop his heart. Then in the next moment, as if someone had slammed a floodgate, the fear vanished. Rafael floated on a warm lake of bliss, rocked by strong, gentle arms, caressed in soothing waves of pleasure. Was this how it felt for humans when he fed? No wonder so many of them wanted to offer their throats. It was heavenly, peaceful and so full of sensual delight…

I'm dying. The small part of his brain still concerned with self-preservation smacked him and told him he was an idiot. The monster would *not* stop in a moment and tell him he was delicious. It was draining him.

Rafael kicked out, suddenly desperate for some advantage. The thing grunted and released its teeth with a snarl. Rafael snapped his head around and sank his teeth deep into the muscle of the monster's forearm. It howled and dropped him, shrieking when Rafael still hung on and the muscle tore.

Oh, it doesn't like that. Not one bit.

The thing ripped its arm free and reeled back, apparently stunned that its prey would fight back so viciously. Rafael whirled and ran with all the unnatural speed his undead body could manage.

About the Author

The unlikely black sheep of an ivory tower intellectual family, Angel Martinez has managed to make her way through life reasonably unscathed. Despite a wildly misspent youth, she snagged a degree in English Lit, married once and did it right the first time, (same husband for almost twenty-four years) gave birth to one amazing son, (now in college) and realized at some point that she could get paid for writing.

Published since 2006, Angel's cynical heart cloaks a desperate romantic. You'll find drama and humor given equal weight in her writing and don't expect sad endings. Life is sad enough.

She currently lives in Delaware in a drinking town with a college problem and writes Science Fiction and Fantasy centered around gay heroes.

Angel loves to hear from readers. You can find her contact information, website details and author profile page at http://www.pride-publishing.com.